Unsaid (The Manhattanites)

Avery Aster

For fans who loved the snarky wit of *Will & Grace* and the epic love drama found in *Brokeback Mountain* comes Avery Aster's new full-length, standalone contemporary erotic M/M romance novel, *Unsaid*.

Chelsea's hottie Blake Morgan III has reemerged from a nasty breakup. His marriage was a frigid disaster beyond repair, and he vows to be single—forever. Bruised, but still hot in Prada, he creates his *Seven Desires* wish list, his sexiest imaginings. Blake soon realizes there's only one man he may trust to make these uninhibited intentions come to fruition: his best friend Miguel Santana.

Lower East Side multimedia artist extraordinaire Miguel Santana may be known as the cocky Latin stud in the city, but all he's wanted since college was Blake's hand in marriage. He was livid when Blake walked down the aisle with the wrong guy. Miguel has his own list titled the *Seven Needs,* which are quite contrary to Blake's dirty-boy deeds. They involve serious commitments, which may leave his new-to-the-singles-scene buddy sprinting for the door, destroying any hopes Miguel has for happiness.

Can these two hunks conquer their intimate fears and love one another as only best friends can? Join the star-

studded cast in *The Manhattanites* series and see for yourself!

Readers Advisory: Pent-up sexual tension between two best friends leads to water sports, BDSM, electricity, and fisting.

Reader Warning

Often while reading Avery Aster's books, readers have been known to experience hot flashes, orgasms, and laughter to the point of peeing in their pants.

It's suggested that you have a bucket of ice nearby, along with a chilled glass of champagne and your favorite sex toy—fully charged—before reading this story.

Please note that Avery's writing is not suitable for prudes, slut-shamers, or uptight readers who don't have a sense of humor about money, sex, or fame. Avery's books are not intended for anyone under the age of 18.

Have fun!

Swag and reader contests can be found on
Avery's blog at: **AveryAster.com**
Interact with Avery while reading *The Manhattanites* on Instagram and Twitter
@AveryAster using the hashtags
#TheManhattanites #EroticRomance

Praise For

Unscrupulous (The Manhattanites)

by Avery Aster

"This book blindsided me. The author's voice is fresh, witty, and completely hysterical… something not easily found in today's book market. "

—Same Book, Different Review

"I took a long cold shower after reading *Unscrupulous*."

—Books Are Love

"There's a new star in town. The name is Avery Aster. *Unscrupulous* is slick, juicy and narratively impressive."

—The Sleaze Factor

"*Unscrupulous* equates fun erotica. The humor runs toward the outrageous and raunchy but never tasteless. This is like Sex and City on steroids but younger and actually sexier."

—Ever After Romance Book Blog

"While classified as an erotic novel it is so much more than that. *Unscrupulous* is a love story between friends and more importantly is a story of a woman learning to truly love herself!"

—Tiffany Talks Books

"The Manhattanites is a throwback to Judith Krantz. It's filled with family drama, salacious back stories, rich people problems and the glitz and glamour of fame without turning into a saga of revenge and disappointment."

—Talk Supe Reviews

"I could relate to the main characters. The emotions they went through felt real to me. If you are open minded and looking for something…hot, then these books are for you. Avery Aster had me hooked, interested and connected to the characters."

—Bec's Books

"I learned so many new things while reading *Unscrupulous* like what DILF stood for, and about the Vajazzle. Avery's writing style is refreshing and so different from what's out there."

—Book Babes Unite

"*Unscrupulous* reminds me a lot of Jackie Collins' style of plot lines, intrigue and drama. The bitches are super-bitches and the heroine has a good heart underneath the tough exterior. When Taddy finally started to open up to Warner it actually made me tear up."

—I Love Romantic Fiction

"The female characters are all strong and that's a refreshing change from some of the heroines I've read lately in other books."

—Erotic Book Club

"I love the way Avery Aster wrote Taddy's character. You will love her even more when you peel back all of those layers. *Unscrupulous* is a deep and emotional book."

"*Unscrupulous* hooked me at page one. The crazy characters are positively perfect. Each holds their own and deserves their place. Aster's story is fast-paced, hot and had me laughing out loud! The Manhattanites live a ridiculously extravagant lifestyle and I so wanted to be a part of it."

"The shock value early in the book is high and is suited to the open-minded reader, not shy or afraid of sexually descriptive language and scenes. *Unscrupulous* is hot flash-inducing…trust me, I've suffered a few."

"*Unscrupulous* is a wild read filled with rich, dirty mouthed New Yorkers and it is just a lot of fun."

In Memory of Michael

Lover, friend, and angel. I miss you.

Special Dedication

To Brenda. I thank God, our Così salads, and the love we share for writing to have you in my life. You are the ultimate bestie. I double-heart you for that!

Unsaid

Avery Aster

Unsaid

New York, New York 10021
First edition: July 2015
www.AveryAster.com

Author's Note

Hello, Gorgeous Reader,

OMFG. I have a free ebook for you when you join my newsletter http://www.eepurl.com/CQ665

If you thought my other novels were over the top, wait 'til you get a load of *Unsaid*. It features two tops. *Wink!* Readers asked when *The Manhattanites* series gay hero Blake Morgan III would have his day in the sun. Slip your Chanel sunglasses on, pour the champers and break out the chocolate truffles…it's now!

In my two previous novels, *Undressed* (Lex & Massimo) and *Unscrupulous* (Taddy & Warner), you've witnessed Blake without love. Don't worry if you're new to the series, because you won't be lost. Each book may be devoured as a standalone and read in any order.

When I asked a group of guys and the men who lust after them what they fantasized about in their intimate relationships, they shared three things. One, they avowed true love. Two, safe sex, and the third was to remove the stigma within the homosexual community about being a power bottom. They desired a gay hero who owned up to enjoying *not* being a top or versatile. One who didn't feel it effeminizes himself but rather liberated sex in a positive way, to enjoy his body. Blake and Miguel's romance explores those three aspects—a bottom's fantasies, safe sex, and, of course, true love. After you've read *Unsaid*, be sure to join Jemma's erotic ménage romance in *Unconventional*.

Love,

Avery Aster

Cast of Characters

Major Players

Blake Morgan III (29): A gay anal virgin, he graduated from Columbia University with Miguel and works as Managing Partner at Brill, Inc. Coming off a divorce and a long bout of celibacy, he's keeping secrets and will do anything to put his past behind him.

Miguel Santana (29): Born into Mexican nobility, and raised on the Upper West Side, he's a relationship virgin. Touted in the press as the next Salvador Dalí, he's a prominent artist who's slightly closeted and trying to avoid casual sex.

Lex Easton (30): Owner of Easton Essentials, she's a fashionista who's marrying Prince Massimo Tittoni and having a hell of a time balancing motherhood, work and her magnificent Italian lover, Massimo's libido.

Massimo Tittoni (34): Prince to the royal House of Girasoli, he's engaged to Lex Easton, dad to their son Massimo Junior and adjusting to living on Park Avenue. He'll do anything to keep Lex barefoot and pregnant, especially if it means making love.

Taddy Brill (30): A diva millionaire who dates Warner Truman, and is Blake's lifelong friend and boss at

Brill, Inc. She has the largest accessory and hand rifle collection in the United States. Whatever Taddy says, goes!

Vive Farnworth (30): Met Lex, Taddy, and Blake in boarding school. Vive is the editor-in-chief of *Debauchery* magazine. As a party girl and heiress to Farnworth Firewater liquors, she's living her life large, one cocktail at a time.

Supporting Cast

Thor Edwards (31): As a socialite, trust-fund brat, he lunches, meddles and fundraises. He's Miguel and Blake's gay bestie and spends his days as an advocate for safe sex and a spokesperson for AIDS Life New York.

Diego Oalo (29): Blake's ex-husband. Due to his deadly sex games, he's wanted by the FBI for fifteen counts of attempted murder. He's taken all of Blake's money, is on the run and is counting on Blake to keep quiet.

Birdie Easton (52): An eighties glam-metal icon. Widow to Eddie Easton, she's Lex's mother who swung with Taddy Brill's mother, Countess Irma, back in the day. Her past is always a blur, and she wants nothing more than to see her daughter get married.

Jemma Fereti (34): Milan's most famous supermodel turned fashion designer and photographer. She works at Easton Essentials' Europe office and is dating Rocco and Luigi. Jemma's come to NYC to get Lex styled for her big day.

Part One

Blake's Seven Desires

THE MANHATTANITES

love, friendship, scandal, and drama to the hilt

"At eighteen, I fell in love with Blake Morgan. Eleven years later, I'm still in love with him. Does he know? Nope. I'd hoped after a while my feelings for him would stop or I'd be able to find someone else. They didn't and I haven't."—Miguel Santana, Lower East Side resident, Blake Morgan admirer.

Prologue

Miguel's Unwelcomed Invitation

Five Years Ago
Lower East Side

Miguel Santana collected his mail in the lobby of his apartment building.

Something fancy was caught between his invitations to gallery openings and his father's medical bills. It was an ecru-colored card stock envelope. Embossed in gold by Crane & Co. stationery, the letter was addressed in an eccentric Gothic-styled calligraphy.

The paper felt important in his hands. Who was it from? Mr. & Mrs. Morgan on Meadowcroft Lane in Greenwich, Connecticut. Blake's parents.

Blake, his best friend since college, had remained his secret crush even after all these years. But what did the Morgans send him? It was too soon for a Christmas card. The knot twisting in his stomach told him this was no holiday greeting.

Tearing the envelope open, he read his attendance was requested by Blake Morgan III as he wed Diego Oalo. *Fuck.* Diego was Blake's boyfriend, the asshole-turned-douchebag who their friends, Lex Easton, Taddy Brill and Vive Farnworth, secretly referred to as MLD—Missy

Limp Dick—for obvious reasons. Miguel had coined Diego with the nickname when they were freshmen in college. Five years later, it still stuck.

It appeared Blake was serious about marrying MLD. He'd questioned how he could let Blake get away from him. He'd assumed he'd have more time. Miguel never expected Blake to marry the first guy who'd come along. MLD was supposed to be his starter-boyfriend—to warm him up for the grand prize, himself. *Shit*!

His cell phone chimed, so he reached in his back pocket. The glowing screen read 'Thor Edwards'. "Wasup?" Miguel greeted.

"Eh mah gawd."

"Huh?"

"*O-M-G!*" Thor screamed.

"Thor, stop. What's wrong?" He didn't have the energy for his friend's drama that day. *Not now*.

"Did you get that *thing* in the mail?"

"*Sí,* I have *it* right here." Miguel paused before forcing, "Hats off to Blake for tying the knot. *Maravilloso* news, isn't it?" His eyes rolled even on his own sarcasm.

"You high?"

"Heavens no."

"Drunk?"

"No…"

"I'm coming over," Thor demanded.

"Stay put. I'm busy," he lied. His apartment was a mess. Last thing he needed was Thor Edwards, socialite amongst the foo-foo fabulous, poking fun at his bachelor-could-care-less-about-throw-pillows taste in decorating.

"Why didn't we learn about *this* sooner?"

"Blake knows we'd probably kill him." He also thought he didn't have anything to do with the wedding planning. *It must be Diego's idea.* The bastard was a gold-digging piece of shit who climbed his way to the top of Wall Street and Blake's bed.

"Whaddya say we head over to Macanudo's tonight and martini it up. We'll plan a way for Blake to get out of this."

"Not *up* for socializing."

"Taddy and Vive are going," Thor persisted.

"Did the girls get their invites?"

"Yup. Looks like Blake's mother wants us all to be part of the wedding party."

"*Mierda.*" Miguel couldn't imagine how Taddy and Vive would take this. They, of all their outspoken diva friends, were probably ready to tie Blake up to a tree in Central Park and hit him over the head with their Waterford crystal. Maybe the girls could knock some sense into him. "What good will happy hour do us tonight?"

"A few cocktails may lessen the blow." He pressed on. "*Cock* being the key word here. Come on, we'll make a night of it."

"Nothing's going to make me feel better."

"What're we gonna do?" Thor asked.

"You and I are going to put on our happy faces and support Blake's dream." God, he felt sick even saying that.

"Don't-cha mean our nightmare?"

"Same thing." Miguel stared at the invitation. The words on the card blurred into one spot.

"We are so not." He exaggerated the 'o' in 'so' and then paused for a second. "My strategy to prevent this from happening is when the officiant asks if anyone objects, you and I will raise our hands."

"No."

"Then let's kidnap Blake before the wedding. Send him to Jersey. Yeah, that's what we'll do. No one will find him over there."

"Thor..."

"Vive and I will drug Blake. Then throw his tight ass on one of those gay cruises, which go outta Bayonne. When the ship arrives in Barcelona a few days later, he'll have so much Latino cock rammed up his waspy hide, he'll never think twice about MLD." Thor spoke as if he had all the solutions.

The only Latin cock Miguel wanted going in Blake's ass was his own. Not Diego's, not anyone else's.

"We have to support this. It's what Blake wants." He would find a way to respect his friend's decision.

"You're gonna have to duct-tape me to the pew during their ceremony. I, for one, want no part in supporting this union. I can't stand MLD, and I know the girls can't either."

"That's nice, considering we're *not* the ones marrying Diego."

"Miguel?" His voice became serious.

"*Sí?*"

"I'm sorry. I know how much you loved Blake."

"Right." He noted Thor spoke about his love in the past tense, as if it was behind him and over with. It wasn't.

"I don't know what else to say..." His voice rose an octave.

The cell phone chimed as his screen read 'Lex Easton'.

"Another drama queen is calling in. I'll meet you at the club in a few, okay?"

"See you soon, buddy."

"*Adios.*" He clicked over. "*Hola.*"

"I don't...I won't...I can't...effin' believe this." Lex sounded as if she could barely speak, but she still, as always, managed to curse. "Did you get—?"

"*Sí,*" he replied, hearing the sadness in her voice. It appeared he wasn't the only one with selfish thoughts; others felt the same way he and Thor did. But it didn't really matter because the marriage was going to happen. "Thor and I are going to the club. Can you meet us and we'll talk about it?"

"Sure. I'll ring my driver and pick you up in, say, thirty minutes."

"*Bueno.*"

He hoped fresh air would calm his unease as he stepped outside. Could he risk not going to the wedding and stand his ground? Knowing Blake, if his friends didn't support the wedding, he'd most likely cut them off for good. Miguel's friendship to Blake was too important for that. Saying farewell to the hopes of making Blake his would be a lot harder than he thought.

Chapter One

Vive's Power Bottoms

Present Day
Upper East Side

Blake Morgan III often poked jokes at himself by saying, if CBS TV executives produced a spin-off show from Julianna Margulies's smash hit *The Good Wife* with a unique twist turning the iconic Alicia Florrick role into a gay male—they'd be sure to cast him.

He was always good—too good, in fact. At age ten, he'd given his Boy Scouts pledge to do his best, to do his duty to God and his country, and to obey Scout Law. At twelve, he'd attended Sunday services as an altar boy helping Reverend Robinson at St. Barnabas Episcopal Church in Greenwich, Connecticut, spreading word from the *Book of Common Prayer*.

At fourteen, he along with his friend, Thor Edwards, were the first boys admitted into the recently-converted-to-coed Avon Porter Academy in Cheshire, Connecticut. He'd blended right in with the other girls, and became fast friends with rock-n-roll royalty Lex Easton, European nobility Taddy Brill, and Scandinavian liquor heiress Vive Farnworth. The year he'd turned sixteen, he came out of the closet. His dream was to get married and be a dad one day. With no boyfriend in sight, he'd rallied his entire state into a mammoth fundraiser aiding to legalize gay marriage; an action Senator Taft coined The Land of Steady Habits Equality Movement.

Then he was accepted, with Senator Taft's recommendations, into the prestigious Ivy League Columbia University. He'd majored in marketing and met his good friends Miguel Santana and Diego Oalo. Diego and Blake had dated and at twenty-four, they'd married in an expensive wedding attended by New England's most elite.

Earlier in the year, his friend, Taddy, who he'd helped launch her eminent PR firm back in college, Brill, Inc., had promoted him from EVP to Managing Partner.

That day, all things *appeared* to be quite great in Blake's world. Except things weren't even good, and he wasn't either. At nearly thirty, Blake was divorced and eager to be bad, very, very bad. *Tonight, drinks and cock talk were in order.*

Blake felt the pale yellow liquid slide down his throat. His nostrils flared for relief from the burning sensation. Macallan's single malt scotch proved to be mother's milk for this Friday night.

"It's been six months since my ex-husband moved out. Time to put myself out there again." He sighed at his two friends, Thor and Vive, then sank his small fork into a mussel and ate it off the half-shell. The cilantro relieved his intoxicated palette.

Before cocktails, the three of them had shot off their steam at the Lipstick & Lead Rifle Range. Some people did Yoga or smoked pot to relax, but the Manhattanites preferred to shoot guns. He was getting better at hitting the bull's-eye.

"I'm not saying I want a relationship. Quite the opposite, actually." His fantasy of matrimony was over. The straights could keep the marriage thing as far as he was concerned. He'd thrown in the towel at trying to adopt kids, too.

"Gotcha, gorgeous. So, what do ya want then?" Vive inquired and leaned back in her chair. As founding editor-in-chief for *Debauchery* magazine, she tended to interview even her friends. Her knack for asking point-blank questions kept conversations moving at warp speed.

For a minute, he thought about what she'd asked, but nothing came to mind. Instead he glanced down at Hedda Hopper, Vive's Lhasa Apso, asleep on her lap. Though her days as Best in Show at Westminster Kennel Club had long passed, Hedda appeared brushed and in first place.

"I can tell you what Blake needs." Thor Edwards, the mouth of Manhattan, who often spoke on his behalf and everyone else's because he had nothing better to do, encouraged him to finally say it.

"What?" He didn't know what those two had in mind.

"Sex," Thor said.

"Mind-blowing, ass-ripping, butt-fucking sex," Vive added.

"No way!" He wasn't ready.

"Yes way." Thor argued. "Say it. Say it like you have to have it. Just fucking say it already. Say, 'I need sex'."

"I, ahhh...I would need a date in order to have sex. But I imagine sex would be nice." A true declaration. It felt good to say those words; he'd been holding out, holding back for far too long.

"What kind of sex, Blake?"

He hadn't thought about it much. "My new romantic life should be casual, but safe. Yes, nothing risky, just fun."

"Casual?" Flabbergasted, Thor's hazel eyes widened. "Now we're talking. I've never heard you be so cavalier before. It's about effin' time." Thor slid a piece of Bruschetta in his mouth, then licked the sauce off his manicured hand.

"Call it a date or sex, but either way, boys, it'll be here soon enough. Taddy bragged she hooked you up with a shit-load of dates. Tomorrow night starts with Nello Lamas."

The thought of going out with that Argentinean playboy made him nervous. "I won't know what to do with myself." Blake felt like a teenager all over again.

"Nello is *hawt!*" Thor took another bite, then said, "You were married to MLD for five years and he never gave your tight ass a hard pounding?"

"No." Thank the heavens.

"Not even once?"

"Thor, I said no, didn't I?" He shook his head, confirming his failure.

"I just can't fathom. I mean, really." Jerking his head back with great dramatics, Thor slammed down Scotland's finest. "It doesn't make any sense."

His ex-husband was incapable. Blake had made an effort over the years to let his partner take the lead, an interest, be a star. But Diego had come out on the bottom in every aspect. "I was in a relationship with a blowup doll."

A month into the marriage, Blake had realized they were headed for frigid ruin. Diego had refused to embrace real intimacy, let alone untamed intercourse, at least with him anyway. He couldn't speak for the others. Oh, and there had been several.

The marriage was history, the divorce papers freshly inked with their signatures. Blake Morgan III was unattached once again. *Look out, New York City*!

"You should've never gotten married to *him*. Even your parents said so."

Vive rubbed his face in it. She also never said Diego's name. She'd call him Blake's It, Needle Dick, and of course the group's pet name for him, MLD. Vive usually sang the acronym in a mock operative voice, even to Diego's face.

"I'm well aware of who my folks rooted for me to partner up with, thank you very much." His parents had urged him to marry their clique's Latin stud.

"M-I-G-U-E-L." Thor chanted the name as Vive toasted yet another drink, which woke up Hedda.

"*Caliente*." He loved mimicking Miguel's sexy Mexican accent when he wasn't around to flex his muscles, defending his Latino pride. "Speaking of the devil..." Blake glanced down at his cell phone. No text messages. "Where are Miguel and the girls?" he asked, worried he wouldn't show. Ever since Blake became single, it appeared Miguel avoided seeing him one-on-one. He couldn't figure out why. "He should be here by now."

Thor swigged and then commented, "Perhaps he's working on some painting or got inspired by something—"

"I bet his driver is stuck in traffic," Vive interrupted. "Christ, I don't get why anyone lives that far downtown. Below Forty-Second Street is uncivilized, let alone below Fourteenth Street. Isn't that right, Hedda?"

The dog never barked. Vive ran her long, sculpted fingernails through her pet's grizzle-colored coat. It fascinated Blake how Vive took Hedda with her into Manhattan's poshest restaurants and stores, and no one ever said a damn word. Maybe they were afraid Vive might slam their establishments with an editorial in *Debauchery*. Her ability to make or break a brand, eatery or business came from just two sets of words "loved it!" or "hated it!"

"The Lower East Side is unlivable." She crossed her arms, raised her taupe-painted brows, and asked, "Have we already forgotten Miss Sandy?"

Hurricane Sandy had taken Miguel's loft and the rest of lower Manhattan's power out for two months. He'd stayed with Lex and her fiancé, Massimo, on the Upper East Side. Lex had just given birth to Massimo Junior, and Miguel helped with the newborn responsibilities until his electricity came back.

"I love living in Chelsea," Blake commented. "But I agree about the Lower East Side. It must be published in some creative guide to being so bohemian that Miguel has to live down *there*."

"And where are Lex and Taddy? They should be here by now, too." Vive held up her cell phone showing no messages. "We're being stood up."

"They're probably still at that bridal photo shoot for the *Manhattanite Times*. You know how Lex can be about her hair and makeup now that she's going to be crowned Princess Tittoni." He didn't want to attend, let alone be in, a wedding the following week. The thought of cheering on matrimony when his own marriage had just crumbled, made his chest tight. Vive and Thor were trying to cheer him up, though. Lex had put them up to it. She'd been determined to make her royal wedding a celebration to remember.

"Well, if they're gonna be late, this'll give us a few minutes to discuss what you want for this new chapter in your life." Thor pulled out his tablet, made a few screen strokes, and held up the glowing flat monitor to Blake's view. It read 'Blake's Sex Wish List'.

"Yay! It's gay cock talk." Vive clapped her Chanel fashion-jeweled hands together.

Poor girl hadn't seen dick in months. She lived vicariously through everyone else's romps, especially her homosexual friends.

"Guys...no." It was one thing to talk about sex, but he couldn't carry out whatever they were thinking. In private, he'd vowed celibacy to himself, especially after Diego hadn't given him much of a choice. Blake regretted even bringing up the topic of sex, but from the looks on his friend's horny faces, there was no turning back. *Shit.*

"Blake—Yes." Amused with himself, Thor kept typing. "I attribute my fierce sex life to the fact that I exude positive affirmation to make men want me." He set his tablet down and reached for a crab cake. No one did seafood appetizers tastier than Club Macanudo. "You have to put these fantasies out into the universe. Then they'll happen."

"Sex is this effortless, huh?" Blake retorted. He'd try and humor them along for a good laugh, but that was where this would stop, joke only. Right? "From what I hear, Nello will be more than enough."

"Yup. You ever read *The Power of Now*?" Thor asked.

"No."

"Or *The Secret*?" Vive added.

Blake shook his head. "I don't believe in that hogwash."

"Your attitude explains why you're twenty-nine and have *yet* to bottom."

"Bottoming isn't everything." Blake forked at the crab cakes. In the last six months, he'd lost twenty pounds. He could afford the calories.

"Getting banged is, too. Submitting yourself to a man who wants to dominate your body is the most erotic form of expression on this planet." Thor said that almost lyrically. He lived and breathed through his asshole.

Vive leaned forward as Hedda's paws hung off her lap. "Amen to that, gorgeous."

"Take it from me, a power bottom. I know what I'm talking about. We need to find you a top, one who's hung and brutal." Thor bit down, making a loud crunch from the cracker. He continued with his mouth full. "I don't care what he looks like as long as he has a hard cock and knows how to use it."

"Why?" Blake asked, unsure he liked the sound of that.

"The better their body is, the worse the face appears. On the contrary, the better their cock is, the worse the body is. It's true." Thor pointed his finger in Blake's direction. "If only they could all be headless, it would go with their heartless ways and reinforce the only thing we really care about…dick."

"That's not true." Blake squirmed in his chair. Somewhere deep down inside, he sort of still believed in true love, again. Maybe.

"Let's hear it. Your wish list, please," Vive bossed. She got into anything relating to smut. It's what kept hers and Thor's friendship going. That, and the fact they both loved to gossip and were the offspring of two of America's richest families.

"Hmmm…" In hopes hydration might help him think, Blake reached for his water glass.

"Start with number one. What do you crave?"

I want—

His sexual fantasies were interrupted by the loud chime on Vive's cell phone.

She glanced at the screen. "Mother of pearl! Let the Lex Easton wedding drama begin."

"What?" Thor asked.

"It's a text from Taddy, look."

MELTDOWN ALERT: GOWN DOSEN'T FIT. HELP STAGE PUBLICITY PHOTOS!!! BRING CLOTHES PINS.

Meatpacking District

"Suck in."

"I am…" Lex Easton, bride-to-be, tried her hardest not to cry, but she sure as hell huffed. Her lifelong friend of twenty-nine years, Taddy Brill, was on the verge of crushing her body into what felt to be a gazillion pieces.

She squeezed on her…as hard as possible.

The dress *had* to fit.

Taddy zipped her up…as far as she could.

The dress didn't fit.

"Harder! Suck in harder!" Taddy shouted in her ear.

She'd arrived with Lex to the West Side Studios three hours before. They'd shared the same limo. After eighty minutes of coloring Lex's honey locks with guru extraordinaire Nackie, another sixty in makeup with dark-circle miracle worker Christopher, and the remainder of time spent getting every curve of her body stuffed into shapewear to make her shapeless, Lex should've been suited up by then…Lights. Camera. Action.

But no, the glam squad wasn't working to her advantage. It seemed impossible to try and get the right picture for *The Manhattanite Times*. At the rate they were going, there'd be no photos.

"Stop, you're hurting me." Lex empathized with every bride who had gone through this in the past. The whole process was really quiet silly when she thought about it. A non-virgin, twenty-nine-year-old woman, walking down the aisle to marry the man who'd already fathered her child. She questioned why she was even doing it. The notion of grabbing her fiancé, jumping in a cab, and going to the courthouse to get hitched seemed more practical to who she was.

The wedding wasn't for her, Massimo or their six-month-old son, but for her rock-n-roll iconic mother, Birdie Easton.

"Shut up, Lex," Taddy hissed, foaming at the mouth. Her Harry Winston chandelier earrings, the ones Lex had bought her for her birthday, swung and jingled with every exerted effort.

"Taddy. You're smashing my tits." Her breasts were like her waist, which was taking shape after her ass. No part of her wanted to fit into the gown she'd designed for her own wedding. Shit, even the pave-encrusted platform heels Stuart Weitzman had custom-made for her feet were suddenly too small.

"When did your boobs…get so Scarlett Johansson-ish?"

"They're full of milk." She thought she had pumped, but come to think of it, she hadn't. Her day had been booked with Easton Essentials showroom work, a newborn baby who required a diaper change more times than she cared to think about, and then there'd been the wedding preparations. Not just any wedding, but New York's celebrity-centric, 'posh to the max' extravaganza of the decade.

Crap. She needed a nanny, but Massimo, her fiancé, wouldn't hear of it.

"Hold it. Stop breathing. Let's try one more time."

"Ouch." The clasp caught a piece of her skin, the inch or two which refused to tuck in.

"I almost have…the zipper…up." Taddy seemed to forget the garment was attached to her. "Come on, you darn bodice. Work with me here." She talked directly to the champagne organza.

"It's too tight…" Lex stepped back. *Don't scream, don't cry.* "Let's call this quits. I don't think I can take any more."

"We need the photos. Not just for your personal memories, but for the marketing campaign. Hello," Taddy reminded, the wedding having been turned into a publicity event for Easton Essentials' new bridal collection.

The minute the wedding was announced, Lex went into entrepreneurial mode and launched a new line of bridal wear for Easton Essentials called Easton Weds. Not very original, but *Bridal* magazine had declared it the next Vera Wang.

With her runway-ready designs being a hit, the much-anticipated bridal debut focused on creamy whites, floral brocades, and flirty silhouettes. It was supposed to be timeless, thoughtful, and hugging her body just right. The forty-piece line was carried in over three thousand bridal boutiques across the country. Sales exceeded all projections, but the stores required more images of Lex for collateral support.

"We could hire body doubles. Or use other models. I'm getting sick of seeing your face in all the ads, anyways," Taddy joked.

Chubby as a child, Lex had shied away from the spotlight as an adult. Once Massimo fell in love with her, she'd experienced a level of self-confidence like never before. She learned to love her body and herself. Her face was on the label, the billboards in Times Square, and on every magazine cover from New York to Dubai. Their bestselling dress sizes were double digits. Consumers loved Lex's curves.

"Ha!" Lex felt an urge to kick her, but knew Taddy meant well. She always did. "It was your idea to put my face on this label. I wanted to stay behind the scenes, remember?" For the first two years of Easton Essentials' success, no one had ever met Lex. Massimo, who was her fabric supplier at the time, thought she was a man. He was pleasantly mistaken.

"Blah, blah, blah. Humanizing you was genius. The shoppers wanted to see the wizard behind the curtain at Oz and they have. You've made millions off the campaign. Correction, *we've* made millions." Taddy crossed her arms and eyed Lex up and down. "We'll leave the dress open in the back. Minus your 'cup runneth over' cleavage, no one will notice." She glanced at the clock on the wall. "Vive should be here by now with those clothes pins."

"Screw that. The Jaws of Life won't get me in, or out, of my gown. Nothing will help." Lex couldn't believe the dress was too small. She'd worked out for months, getting fit to look the part of a princess when she married her real life prince, Massimo Tittoni, royal heir to Isola di Girasoli and CEO of Girasoli Garment Company.

She'd adopted Taddy's cardio schedule of ninety minutes on the elliptical daily. She'd stuck to Vive's diet of twelve hundred calories a day—no more, maybe less. And she'd incorporated Blake's panache for weights—lift, lift, lift.

As a designer and owner of Easton Essentials, the world's fastest growing fashion brand, not fitting in her wedding dress was a rather big fuck-up.

"Let's tease your hair higher. Maybe do some extensions. A Dallas hair-do will make the rest of you appear smaller."

Taddy was always full of great ideas, but somehow that one hurt Lex's feelings.

"Fine."

She waved her hairstylist Nackie over, who brushed then sprayed. Lex closed her eyes and tried to breathe through her mouth, but caught the taste of what reminded her of rubbing alcohol.

"As soon as we leave here, I'll call Dr. Fassenbender." The sounds of Taddy rummaging through her Givenchy satchel became louder. "Come to think of it, I may have one in here."

"One what?" Lex asked, opening her eyes. There was no time for cosmetic surgery, not even lunchtime liposuction.

"Water pill. He has these kick-ass ones. Your bloat drops overnight." A little blue capsule appeared in her hand. "Tah-dah. Here, take it."

"No." There was one thing Lex learned from her parent's mistakes: don't take pills.

"Suit yourself." Taddy popped the dot onto her tongue. Closing her mouth, she smiled and swallowed.

"Dammit. This can't be happening." She shouldn't have designed a ball gown pattern to wear. What was she thinking?

Elaborate Swarovski crystals scattered throughout the bodice from front to back, and a richly textured layering of the full skirt gave her the fairytale she'd always envisioned. But she'd have to take the zipper out and make a corset back. God, she didn't want to do that.

"My darlings, forget the dress!" shouted the photographer, Jemma Fereti, as she moved Nackie back to the sidelines. Jemma had been flown in from Milan at Taddy's request to capture the pre-wedding photos of Lex and Massimo. "Taddy has a good idea. We'll focus on head shots of you wearing the crown of Tittoni and the veil. I want you *nuda*."

"Naked?" Lex gasped.

Known as Europe's top fashion model, turned co-designer at Girasoli and photographer, Jemma caught erotic femininity on film. She had wanted Lex in her birthday suit from the start of the shoot.

She stalked over to Lex and held out her hands. "I get that you're frustrated. But I'm not here to shoot fashion. I'm here to get on my camera those beautiful jewel-toned eyes, those full lips, and the look of happiness you have when you think of Prince Tittoni."

Such a smooth talker. "It's been six months since I had the baby, Jemma. The weight should be off by now." Her eyes stung with tears.

"No crying, Princess. Get out of the gown. We'll do some abstract photos, *sì*. I promise to capture your real beauty, my darling." Jemma stepped back and swapped out the camera she held for another with her assistant.

Yeah, lady...real means real fat. I don't want that. I wanna be glamorous. "I can't go nude," Lex pleaded as she appeared to have made up her mind already. "These photos are not only going to *The Times*, but over to *Vogue* and *Town & Country*. They have to make a statement of class and elegance."

"Sì, " she said agreeably.

"These are royal photos." Her face was going to be blasted on the Easton Weds hangtag labels and on every major media outlet in the world. Next to Kate Middleton, her wedding week was going to be the paparazzi's biggest swoon. Millions were projected to follow her, if not in person then on TV, as she made her way down the aisle.

"Lex, she's the best there is," Taddy interrupted then lowered her voice to add, "Jemma will get more photos later with other models, otherwise known as Photoshop."

There was one thing her BFF knew better than anyone else in the world and that was the importance of a good public image. If Taddy said yes, then she'd have to go with it. She trusted her; she always had.

"The pics won't be going anywhere if we don't have any. Now, get out of that gown and keep the headpiece on." The dominatrix was coming out in Jemma as she bossed her around. "Go get changed." She faced her assistant. "Dim the lights."

I can't go nude.

Chapter Two

Thor's Boy Pussy

Blake hesitated, sucking air through his teeth and taking in the Rachmaninoff-ish music playing in the background. The orchestra tunes set his anxious mind more at ease.

Vive had refused to head over to the photo shoot 'til he gave her an answer.

He never spoke about his sex life much because he never really had one. Odd, right? He'd come out about being gay at such a young age, and yet Blake never went balls-to-the wall for cock-n-balls. But Thor and Vive, they more than made up for him with their sexual activities, though he never judged them or anyone. Well, except maybe Diego.

Now, there they sat, waiting to hear what he desired for his new sex life. It should've been a defining moment, one to mark a new chapter as a Manhattanite. He didn't know what to say, and certainly not the truth as to why he abstained from sex, so he played along. This was all hypothetically speaking, of course. "I've never…"

"What the fudge-balls is it, Blake?" Vive demanded.

"Bottomed. I've never bottomed." He forced a fake grin. Maybe if he smiled enough he'd get into this.

"Before I turn thirty, I *should*...ya know...try it, at least once." Slightly embarrassed, he lowered his voice, leaned closer, and confessed, "I've always dreamed of a guy breaking me in. Topping me for a few days in a row 'til I was his...all his." Lord knows his ex-husband didn't touch him. He almost believed what he was saying to his friends. It felt close to natural to have those desires.

"That's sweet. You're such a romantic." Thor stuck his pointer finger toward his tonsils, motioning as if he was going to puke. Then he typed on his tablet computer.

She rolled her heavily shadowed eyes and encouraged, "Great, now keep going, gorgeous. How do you wanna be topped?"

"I've always been in control. Perhaps I should *surrender* as you said. Test the submissive waters." *Yeah, that's it*. His friends loved this.

"*Ooh*, you'll never go back to topping again. It's too much work," Thor confirmed from vast experience. "Topping is like Zumba, only worse, all that thrusting. I'd rather rest on my back, not on my laurels, and take it like a good bottom should."

"I'd love to be...tied up." If he gave into the fantasy, he might as well go all out. Bring on the dream. Right? "Have a man worship me. Dominate me. Whip me. Fuck me."

"*Meow*." Vive curled her gold, glittery nails and projected a feral kitten's paw in heat. Hedda started to lick her hand.

"Fabulous. What else?" Obviously, Thor's patience faded quickly.

"That's enough." Game over, Blake couldn't imagine anything else other than bottoming and being tied up. What the hell else was there?

"No, my little ingénue, it isn't," Thor disagreed.

Vive lowered her face down to Hedda's and kissed her behind the ears. She knew better than to pressure anyone to do anything, but when it came to sex, Blake noticed she was struggling to keep her mouth shut. What more was there?

"You should get face-fucked, pissed on, and fisted," Thor suggested.

"What?"

"Ahem," Vive added. "Let's not forget topped raw, and my favorite, gangbanged—"

"STOP." Except for the raw and fisting part, Blake appreciated most from the list. "I'd get face-fucked, sure. Have a man hold my head back and pillage my throat with his cock, shooting his cum on my tongue. Then I'd spit it out."

"Done." He typed. "Have you ever swallowed a guy?"

"*Swallowed?*"

"You know, taken his load in your mouth when sucking him off?" Vive was, for many years, the group's sex expert.

"Nope." To him, swallowing was right up there with raw sex, which he equated to HIV.

"Cum doesn't taste bad." Thor stuck his pinkie in the dipping sauce and licked it.

Vive smacked his hand from the condiments. "Cum doesn't taste good, either. Now, I can't accept you never swallowing."

"It's true." Blake didn't have much experience. Once he'd found out about Diego's sex parties, he swore celibacy during his marriage.

"Did you know one out of four women takes it in the mouth?"

"Gay men in this town are a little different." He smiled, trying to get comfortable with the unimaginable. "Anyways, I'd be willing to try a golden shower." No harm in a little pee.

"Now we're talking. Keep going," Thor ordered.

"A three-way. I'm the only *homo* in Manhattan who's never indulged in a ménage à trois." He only said it to appease them; there was no way in Hell he was going there.

"Two guys in one bed is too much work for me. You have to ride one while sucking the other. I don't have the rhythm, especially with all those cocks flying around at me." Vive laughed. "Isn't that right, my sweet jelly bean dog?" She raked her fingers up and down Hedda's back.

Blake never imagined anyone could love a pet as much as she did. Hedda was her everything. She'd lost her first love in high school and had given their baby up for adoption at sixteen. Vive had never recovered from her past. Taddy had made them swear for everyone's sanity when they moved to Manhattan never to speak about it—ever.

"It's always been this city or bust with us. I couldn't imagine living anywhere else." He smiled and thought about New York and how there were many more men out there to meet. Right? There had to be some guys in the city who didn't know him, Diego, or what happened in their past. *There must be.*

"What about raw sex on this list?" Thor asked.

"Not sure I could find the right top for that." Blake lifted the glass to his lips and slurped crushed ice. This was making him uncomfortable. Even with his two best friends, he knew the topic of being uninhibited in the gay world was…taboo. Did he fantasize about making love without a condom? Absolutely. He even hated to watch the pornos where the actors wore them. But it was what it was. And what it was…was smart.

"Say what?" Vive tilted her head and frowned. "Sweetie, I know condoms are a must. But what about after you've been with someone for a while? Don't-cha wanna take the gloves off?"

"Diego and I always used latex." The condom era of their relationship was way, way into double digits, way-way-way before they'd married. When they'd enjoyed sex, when Diego could and would have sex with him, seemed a lifetime ago.

"How innocent, b-o-r-i-n-g." Thor mocked him with a zzzzz sound.

He had no idea what went down with Blake's ex-husband. If he did, he would never respond like that. "If I found a guy I trusted, we tested together, and were both clean, I'd consider it." He didn't think it was ever possible, but a guy could hope. Couldn't he?

His jaw hung open. "You're making me hard." He air-jacked his right hand as if beating off. "I'll be spreading my pre-cum on our crab cakes as dill sauce in a few."

"You're *the* king of nasty. You know that, right?" Vive scolded as if forgetting she made a living out of trash-talking.

"Duh. Let's recap your wish list." He handled the tablet, acting as if he was James Madison who had just freshly penned America's Bill of Rights.

Blake read over the notes:

#1 Face Fucked & Load Swallowed

Maybe he could get into a brutal blow job, though he'd never swallow.

#2 Pissed On

It sure beat being shit on.

#3 Rimmed

He wasn't sure what that even was.

#4 Fisted

No way!

#5 Tied Up, Whipped, & Dominated

Yes, please.

#6 Ménage à Trois

Yawn, cliché. So Vive in college, but whatever.

#7 Topped Raw

No-no-no.

"For fuck's sake, I never said number three and four, rimmed and fisted?" The list was extreme. Blake couldn't. He *wouldn't*. But why was the talk of those sexual activities suddenly making his nipples sensitive? They poked, more or less, through his checkered, button-down shirt. Why was his cock stiffening in his gabardine slacks? Was there a man-whore lingering underneath his dandy exterior, waiting to bust loose?

"Thor added some for good merit to get you ready for Nello. Taddy has about ten more guys coming your way. I think number two is Gunter Khan."

"*Guns?* That's what the boys call him." He couldn't believe Taddy had pulled it off.

Rumors at Brill, Inc. offices ran rampant saying her assistant, Kiki, had made the calls and booked the dates. Gunter Khan came from Pakistan. The gays in town coined him 'Guns' for one good reason: his biceps were loaded. So huge in fact the Paul Stuart store on Fifth Avenue custom-made his shirtsleeves. His body resembled steel.

"Now, if you're gonna start being a good lil' bottom, you'll need to get warmed up." Vive nodded Blake on and said, "I know my asshole takes a little more foreplay than my vajayjay. Hell, my puss-puss is always on, ready to cream at a second's notice."

Her vagina monologues almost made him yak. "I don't know how good I'll be at casual sex. Anyways, how does rimming and fisting get one...warmed up?" Blake wasn't considering it by any means, but he was curious.

"The best way to take a guy is by first lettin' him eat your ass." Thor flashed his lustrous whites at Blake. "That's my favorite pastime."

"Rimming? *Really*?" Vive asked and then confessed, "I love sucking dick myself, but I'll never lick a man's crack. Men have asked, though."

His friend nodded. "When a guy's rimming me, I can come without touching myself. It's euphoric. It happens when I'm being topped, too. My body shoots off all by itself."

"Like Taddy's shotgun without the safety switch on." She pointed her fingers in Thor's direction then blew on the tips off her nails, mimicking a smoking gun. "Gunter is gonna expect your ass smooth and tight, honey."

"You're making up this handless orgasm thing," Blake snapped. It didn't exist. He'd never come without yanking his shaft twenty times over.

"I am *not*."

"And the fisting?" He clenched his hand and punched the air.

"Thor, I'm turning the mic over to you. I'm out all things non-penis for penetration. Hell, I can hardly take a dick up my ass let alone a fist."

Taking the conversational stage, he elaborated. "Sometimes when you're getting rimmed, you'll open up. That's when he slides his fist in." He demonstrated by taking his fist and pushing it through his other hand.

"As if my hole is gaping wide and set for a fist punch?" He thought his friend was full of shit.

"I never said 'fist-punching' your ass," Thor responded with air quotes. "You're *not* ready for a punch, you dumb twat, but fisting, yes."

Vive got all ladylike. "You know I've talked to you about saying that 'T' word when you're in my presence."

"What 'T' word? *Twaaaat?*"

"Boo, I'm gonna hurt you." She rolled her sleeves up and mocked a punch. "Now, what the hell is the difference between a fist punch and fisting?"

"There's a big difference between getting fisted and fist punching," Thor replied.

"Geez, Louise. Excuse me." Blake felt as if he required a manual with a vocabulary key.

"Interesting. That reminds me, if you're gonna do anal activity, we'll need to get your cookie sugared first thing tomorrow morning," he encouraged.

"*Cookie?*"

"Your asshole. Don't you have a nickname for yours? I call mine my Thor-cookie. Because it tastes sweet, like—"

"Shut up." He'd heard enough. The conversation was over. "I call my arse *my ass*," he added as Vive cackled next to him.

"Hmm." Thor frowned.

"And what the hell is *sugared*?"

"It's in *Details* magazine." Vive shot him her you-should-know-better look. "It's similar to waxing, but they use sugar and lemon water. It's gentle on the skin, more so than the traditional hot and cold wax. Sugaring goes back to the Cleopatra days."

"On my ass crack?" He winced at the painful thought.

"From shaft to tailbone."

"I am *not* doing that." *No way in Hell.*

"Yes, you are." Not taking any arguments, she clicked her fingernails together in Blake's face. "If Taddy, Lex, and I get Brazilians to keep the cock a-coming, so will you, gorgeous. Hell, even my little Hedda gets her muffin clipped."

He looked down at Hedda and wondered if she enjoyed her grooming services. "If a guy wants to fuck me, he'll have to take it as-is."

"No!" In his usual melodramatic way, Thor banged his drink on the table. "Have you ever seen a Boeing 757 land in the woods?"

"Can't say that I have…"

"It'd crash and burn," Vive reasoned.

His jaw dropped in reaction to the insult. "My crack is not some hairy forest."

"Ass cheeks have a little fuzz down there. It's natural. The sugaring will remove it all. You'll see, and you'll thank me later. You always do, boo." He smiled.

"Every last speck?" Blake didn't think his ass sprouted any hair. Though he admitted he never backed his butt up to a mirror to check, either.

"Your tushie will transform into white marble." Thor leaned close. "Or as I say, your *boy-pussy* will be skinned."

"Cookie, boy-pussy," he repeated. "Enough with the nicknames."

"I didn't call your ass a man-cunt or anything."

"Thor, stop it." He couldn't envision himself in bed with some top guy hovering over him and his legs hoisted over his shoulders while he yelled, *"Take my man-cunt."*

Blake wasn't convinced. "Tell me, why is sugaring crucial?"

"A sizeable, thick, veiny dick requires a landing strip—a smooth tarmac for touchdown."

"No turbulence?" he joked.

"Not even a ripple."

"You're nuts. Except, I guess you're right about your sex life preparations." He had heard about Taddy's Brazilians for years.

Thor grabbed the device from Blake. "I'm going to log on and book you an appointment for tomorrow morning." He typed away. "I'm also e-mailing you *this* list so you'll commit it to memory." Hitting one final stroke, he then threw the tablet into his messenger bag. "You're all set, babes. I want you to make the *Seven Desires* a priority. Gunter or Nello, I don't care which, but it's gonna happen." He chomped on another crab cake.

What was he getting into? No man on Earth would agree to do this for him. It was nice to dream, but this wasn't really his cup of tea. He'd been celibate, and for good reason.

Miguel Santana straightened his jacket while his driver pulled the black Mercedes-Benz up to the club's entrance. He'd planned to meet his friends for dinner. Lately, his days were spent working on his art, and at night, he'd often hook up. Although, in recent months, he hadn't been having sex; he'd rather spend time alone with his dog or watching a movie.

Feeling vibrations from his rear pocket, Miguel reached for his cell. His screen glowed with an e-mail from Thor sent to Blake and bcc'd to him. The subject heading read, *"Blake's Seven Desires."* Hot damn. The e-mail listed sexual acts fit for the most perverse.

Miguel's cock stiffened with excitement. He'd mastered one through six ages before. Number seven, raw sex, remained TBD in his life. He'd never had a boyfriend long enough to give being uninhibited a go and he didn't want to catch the *bug* trying.

He thanked his driver and stepped out from the car.

"Hmm." Uncertain if he was reading it correctly, he scrutinized the details. Yes, Blake Morgan's e-mail was the recipient, yet he couldn't see his frigid friend trying any of the items on the list. Blake was too much a goody-goody to even think such thoughts, let alone carry them out.

Or was he becoming a bad boy?

The e-mail also held an address to the Exhale Bliss Spa on Fifth Avenue. The message confirmed Blake's appointment for the following morning. This had his friend's crazy ways written all over it. Were Thor and Vive up to their old tricks, trying to get Blake and him together? It wasn't going to happen. *No, not this time.* He'd learned his lesson a long time ago. Blake was out of his league and off-limits, for good. *Adiós, amigo.*

He pushed the glass door open and stepped inside. Seated facing sideways, Thor's ash-blond hair made him easy to spot.

Next to Thor and Vive sat Blake. His chiseled face supported a perfect Hollywood grin. He had a Channing Tatum hot factor mixed with a Ryan Gosling cuteness, which made him simply irresistible.

Miguel's peripheral vision blurred. After all these years, he found the man gave him jittery feelings as if they were still eighteen, meeting for the first time.

Thor stepped forward and high-fived Miguel. "Hey, buddy." He sat back down and reached for his drink.

"We started without you." Vive blew him an air kiss, mocking Marilyn Monroe, then held up Hedda's paw for a wave and woofed in a dog voice, "Hi, Uncle Miggy."

He petted Hedda and gave Vive a kiss on the cheek as he turned his attention to Blake. "*Hola.*"

"Hi, Mig."

From the table's rear Blake stood and approached, a muscle quivering at his jaw. His mouth kissed Miguel's lip to lip for a nanosecond. He felt a mutual sensuousness between them and wondered if it was just his usual wishful thinking.

Releasing his smooch, Blake stood with only an inch distance between them. "I've missed you."

Te huelo muy bien. God, he smelled good. The best asset on Mr. Morgan and a unique feature for any gay Manhattanite was his unawareness and overt cluelessness to his own male beauty. He was fucking hot.

His fingers trembled with eagerness as he wrapped his arms over Blake's shoulders. They were close in height. His palms remained on his shoulders for a minute. He didn't want to let go.

Fuck, he felt good to his touch.

He'd been working out and lifting weights. Miguel heard from Massimo that the group had gone to Secrète de St. Barth together, a resort in the Caribbean which Taddy's boyfriend owned. There, Blake had enlisted in a post-divorce boot camp, Lex had attended the bridal fitness program to get ready for her wedding, Taddy PR'd the spa, and Vive…well, she'd spent her time doing her favorite pastime: boozing.

In his arms, Miguel felt confirmation under Blake's shirt that his back was broad, biceps hard, and chest firm. Tempting? Yes. Fuckable? Very.

"Sorry I'm late." He spoke as if time stood still. "Where are Lex and Taddy?"

"Stuck playing dress-up for a bridal spread," Blake griped.

He noted the lack of wedding cheer.

Excusing himself, Blake motioned to the bathroom, and Miguel instinctively followed him. He wanted to talk to him more.

"There's only one restroom here. Looks like I'll be a while." A long line filled with girls waiting to touch up their faces stood alongside the far wall. "Go sit. Catch up with Thor and Vive."

Miguel watched Blake walk off toward the line for the bathroom. Standing there a little longer than necessary, he admired his friend's cute ass. *Ay, qué chulo.* He took a chair next to Thor, glancing over his shoulder to ensure his friend wasn't within earshot. "What is with the e-mail you sent?"

"Yay. I'm so happy you received Blake's *Seven Desires.*" Vive's enthusiasm piqued, while Hedda didn't pay him any mind.

"Fierce, isn't it?" Assuming, as always, booze was in order, Thor poured Miguel scotch from their reserved bottle. He handed him the drink and said, "That's his wish list."

"*Sí.* But what do you want *me* to do with it?" Curiosity set in.

Both his friends blinked their eyes in a flirtatious encouragement. "You know—"

"No way, José. I'm not doing *this* for him." He'd topped enough guys in town to know it didn't work out the way he intended: a relationship.

"Come on, please with sugar on top?" Vive pleaded. She held up Hedda's cute face and pouted again in a doggie voice, "Please."

"Or should we say, with *you* on top?" Thor snorted loud enough for the onlookers seated one table over to catch the giggles.

"No." Miguel couldn't, *wouldn't*, get hurt again. No way!

Thor sat back in his chair. His stone eyes narrowed while he glanced intensely at Vive, possibly for back-up. What more could they say?

"You know Taddy has booked him with dates this week." She was pulling out the ammunition. "Fancy dinners, with hot men, leads to kinky sex. Or so I'm told."

"Good for Blake." He felt sick to his stomach, but what could he do? It wasn't any of his business. His father had always said, "You'll have friends for life if you mind your own business." But right then, Miguel wasn't so sure he wanted to listen to his father.

"Every guy in town wants to take him out," Thor added. "Blake's a rare find. He's rich, an anal virgin, smart, and has those blue eyes everyone loves."

"Who is he going out with?" Miguel didn't care for the sound of this. Names! He wanted names. He hadn't objectified Blake in the way Thor did when he'd just summed him up, but it was true. Blake Morgan III was a great catch.

"He and Nello Lamas are having dinner tomorrow."

"Is that so?" He couldn't believe it. Blake had only been single for a few hours and already the city's elite were lining up. Typical. He wouldn't get in line. But Nello Lamas? Really?

The thought of Nello, who hosted bare-backing parties, touching the all-American boy-next-door pissed him off. Loosey-goosey Lamas was a bottom-feeding whore. Miguel always thought Blake should've ended up with a dominant, sweet, yet, loving top, like himself.

"Meningitis is flying around town faster than the flu. How could Taddy be stupid enough to set him up with Nello?" Maybe she didn't know the dark side he led at night. Most straight people were clueless as to the goings-on in Manhattan's gay underground sex scene. Men who got sexually aroused on being beaten up then fucked. A new trend was negative guys who had unprotected sex with positive guys for the thrill. The list went on and on. "He's a bottom. Blake will get bored with that real quick." Miguel didn't buy those words as he said them, but he hoped they'd come true. *Please get bored, buddy.*

"For a top, Taddy booked him with Gunter Khan."

"Gunter? Are you joking?"

"Nope. The day after tomorrow. Too bad you can't intervene." Vive twirled a sapphire ring on her middle finger, probably from Cartier. Sighing, she crossed her long, skinny legs and murmured, "Oh, well…"

"Those guys aren't right for Blake."

The corners of Thor's mouth curled up. "Agreed."

"Not even for a rebound." Miguel hated to hear this.

"We know," Vive snapped.

Gunter was no better than Nello. He was a Dom, all right—the kind who was into fire play and had burned several of his subs, leaving them scarred. Blake's white skin seemed too perfect to be ruined by the likes of Gunter 'Guns' Khan.

"That's who Taddy is setting him up with, one top and one bottom." Thor raised his hands in the air and finished with, "Unless…you…step up."

Miguel knew Blake's self-esteem wasn't what it used to be, not since the divorce. He hoped his friend would be strong enough not to go too far with those guys. But he'd seen it on his friend's face when he'd walked in. Blake wasn't the same anymore. He hadn't been for quite some time. His body might be amazing but his eyes…oh, those beautiful blue eyes, which once radiated life were sad, and for the past few months cast hopelessness.

Shaking his head, he just couldn't do it. "No. I'm not having my heart ripped out again. It was too hard the last time. We didn't talk for almost a year after Blake and Diego were married." He couldn't bring himself to hang out with them as a couple. Diego had been on the fast track on Wall Street, and Blake'd been renovating their penthouse. Watching them play house made him sick. "He made it clear he didn't want me when he walked down the aisle with his loser husband."

"He made a mistake. They're divorced as of today." Vive stated the familiar facts privy to them all.

He'd also read the newspaper, which had a gossip section. It talked about Diego leaving, but it didn't say why. The guy bought a condo in Hell's Kitchen. He figured Blake must've purchased it for him because of his fall from grace during the recession. Diego had lost everything including his job when the market tanked.

"Blake's single and ready to move on." Thor spoke his language.

"*Bueno*, he *can* move on…with someone else."

"He doesn't want Nello or Gunter."

"Oh, no?" He was happy to hear it. Maybe Taddy could find him someone a little more caring and not as selfish. A man who respected him, treated him well, and loved him. Like he would, but he couldn't.

Annoyed, Thor crossed his arms and extended a high-maintenance, manipulative pout. "Blake wants you."

"¿Qué?" What in the hell were they talking about?

Chapter Three

Lex's Bridezilla Breakdown

Meatpacking District

I cannot effin' believe I'm doin' this. I'm gonna pose nude. Lex held onto Taddy's arm while she pulled on the fabric. "I don't get it. I have been dieting and exercising my ass off." Come to think of it, she did feel a little more bloated than usual. And she was still hungry, starving actually.

"Darling, I know you have. Jesus, Blake did it with you."

That man exuded six-pack fabulous. During his marriage, he'd gotten a little bearish—his words, not hers. But the minute Diego left, that weight flew off Blake's body so fast. No longer a bear, he'd become an otter. Again, Blake's words, not hers. She didn't even know what those animal nicknames meant until Vive had told her. Either way, she was jealous. She wanted to be an otter, too. Or was it a seal or a cub? She couldn't remember which.

"Why does Blake look amazing and I don't?" She wiped her forehead. "Bears, otters, men. Screw 'em all and their ability to drop weight so fast."

"Does Blake run the top fashion company in the world?" Taddy patronized her.

Lex didn't care. She needed to hear it.

"No. I do." She was proud of her accomplishments. Who wouldn't be after their father overdosed, leaving her mother and her bankrupt and homeless? Easton Essentials started with one garment and no money, only a pattern and some fabric.

"Did he spend eighteen hours in labor giving birth this year?"

"Nope. I did." Lex wouldn't trade her son in, even if it meant she could have her old body back. Other than having Massimo in her life, her baby, Massimo Junior, was the best thing that had ever happened to her.

"Does Blake have a lover who desires blow jobs in the middle of the night?"

Laughing, she shook her head. "That's my Masi." She enjoyed giving her fiancé head. Better yet, he was the best at eating her pussy. Massimo made her crawl the ceiling when he snarled between her legs like a Beast Kindred in an Evangeline Anderson novel. "Well then, there you have it."

"What?" She didn't understand.

"If I had Blake's life, I'd be fit, too."

Lex thought Taddy had just summed up Lex's mom-fiancée-entrepreneur cluster-fuck perfectly.

"I guess." It had been over a year since she'd let her hair down and had any fun.

She and Massimo met and merged companies while starting to date. They were only a few months into their relationship when she realized Massimo Junior was on the way. Fourteen months after the day they'd met, there she stood, and her life had been nothing short of a glittery whirlwind.

Her wedding week was supposed to be enjoyable. She thought ahead to the reception and imagined all of her friends dancing around them. "I feel bad for Blake. He really needs to cheer up. He looks good, and yet he's still miserable."

"He's depressed, has been since he kicked Diego out."

"There's no chance those two can work it out, not after what Diego did." Initially, Lex hoped they'd at least do a trial separation and counseling. Blake and Diego were together for so long, but some things seemed too unforgiveable.

"Nothing makes Blake happy anymore." Taddy lowered her voice and added, "He's been unbearable at work. You have no idea."

"Oh, I can imagine." Lex respected Taddy and Vive's diva ways, but when compared alongside Blake and Thor, they appeared humble.

Maybe asking Blake to be in her wedding was a mistake. Was she being selfish?

"With everything going on, does he even want to be a part of the bridal party?" She felt bad for asking, but her own happiness had to go on. If she waited for the perfect moment in everyone's life to get married, it might never happen. It was bad enough she'd put the wedding off as long as she did.

"Don't ask such silly questions. He wants to be in your wedding." Taddy rolled her green eyes dramatically. "We all do."

"I hope so. When I asked Blake if he wanted to walk me down the aisle and give me away, he didn't seem too inclined." Lex tried to look at the bright side. It was only the dress she was upset over, right? He would snap out of it during the week. He had to.

"Lex, hello? What happened in his life the week you asked him to be in the wedding?"

"The private investigator told us what was going on."

"Duh! Cut him some slack. Could you imagine if Masi had done that shit?"

"I don't wanna talk about *that*, or MLD. The mere thought of what went on makes me sick." She balled her hands into fists. She'd never been so tempted to cause physical harm to another human being in her entire life as when she'd learned what Diego was up to.

"His ex-husband makes more than just my stomach upset. Look, some of my hair has fallen out over this." Taddy flipped red locks back to show the thinness. She'd stressed on Blake's behalf, and then some. Only they knew about the private investigator's findings, no one else. "If I ever get my hands on that piece of shit, I'll blow his head off. I will."

Lex didn't doubt her. Out of all her friends, Taddy was the one who carried a handgun in her Fendi at all times. She had since college. But that was a whole other story.

"You shouldn't talk like that."

"It's true. I hope he gets locked up." She cursed as she pulled down on the hem. The garment was stuck. "Every morning I wake up and turn on the TV, hoping Diego will headline the news with an arrest."

"Shut up, Taddy. We're not supposed to talk about *it*." She forced a smile and thought about what she needed to do to fix her dress. There'd been no hope for Diego. "Jemma's boyfriends shipped a few more gowns from Milan. They should be here tomorrow."

"Love how you say 'boyfriends' and not 'boyfriend'. I didn't want to pry earlier when Jemma was trying to take your picture, but does she still have both Rocco and Luigi?" Taddy asked.

"Yup, the love triangle is going strong. Jemma loves Rocco and Luigi. Rocco loves Luigi and Jemma. Luigi loves Jemma and Rocco. They're staying at our place this week."

"All in the same bed?"

She nodded. Thank God it was a California King.

In shock, Taddy played with the beading on the gown for a minute. "We have the Poppy White TV show taping later in the week. She's doing a whole pre-wedding exposé."

"Right. We'll figure something out before Poppy. I have other dresses we can use." Lex knew they'd come up with a solution.

Her bestie wrapped her arms around her. "This week is going to be a dream. Jemma will take care of the dress. Vive and I will take care of Blake. All you have to do is take care of you. So, don't worry your soon-to-be-covered-in-royal-diamonds head. Okay, darling?"

"I'll try."

"Ready?" Taddy held her hand while she de-glued from the shapewear. The tight fabric felt like gauze and caused a loud suction noise when it released. How mortifying.

"This is just my effin' luck." Standing in ivory-jeweled stilettos, Lex ran her palms over the crease marks the shapewear had left on her skin. In a thong, she tried to buff the lines out. Her skin appeared to be the product of a bad wash and fold from Canal Street's Laundromat.

"Magnifico." Jemma came over, held out her hand and walked Lex back over to where the lights were set up.

The camera flashed and she tried to get into it. But how could she? She was practically naked.

"Get up on the box, give me your backside, and turn your face over your shoulder."

Lex did as instructed, but she didn't feel right. Something other than the heat from the lights of the set was making her sick.

The music came up from a stereo in the back. She could see her bestie shaking her shoulders, being goofy, trying to lighten the mood.

"Perfezione. Now, look happy."

From the corner, Taddy stepped forward. "Clear your mind. Count your blessings. Think of all the wonderful things you have in your life, right now. Okay?"

"Got it. Thanks, bestie." She wiped her forehead. *God, it's hot in here.*

"Shake your body, honey. You're getting married." She screamed then clapped her hands. "Jemma's pictures will reflect whatever you're feeling on the inside."

Oontz. Oontz. Oontz. The tempo sped up.

Wondering why Vive wasn't there yet, Lex licked her lips. Her mouth felt full of cotton as she forced a smile at Taddy who'd receded against the wall, next to Nackie. She thought about the gifts she'd been given over the year. Her mother was sober and doing well, health-wise. Massimo was spending more time with her and their son in Manhattan, and less time in his hometown of Milan. Massimo Junior, her eighteen-pound, twenty-five-week-old baby was almost sleeping through the night without waking her up—almost.

Everything in her life seemed princess-perfect.

Then why was she so blah? Almost anemic, exhausted.

POP. Flash! The flashbulbs went off.

"Meravigliosa," Jemma complimented.

The music's tempo spun faster.

Dizzy, she felt dizzy.

Clickety-click. POP. Flash!

"Think happy thoughts, as Jemma said," Taddy encouraged.

She closed her eyes and tried to focus.

Untz. Untz. Untz. The music's base became louder.

Clickety-click. POP. Flash!

Ill, she felt so very ill.

Lex's legs buckled. She smacked the floor, hard.

"Merda," Jemma cursed.

The room went black.

"Call 911!" Taddy screamed as she ran toward her.

She felt her breath on her as her friend shouted.

"Lex! Wake up…"

Eyes closed, she couldn't see her best friend anymore. But she could hear the panic in Taddy's voice as she was shaken.

The music turned off. Everything got quiet.

My son… Who would feed Massimo Junior later? Who would wash and put him to bed? That was all she could think about. *Let me see my baby boy.*

Taddy's grip on her shoulders tightened. Lex tried to sit up but couldn't, as if she wasn't in her own body anymore.

I can't… No matter how hard she tried, she couldn't wake up.

"LEX!" Taddy shouted, looking around for Vive. Why hadn't she shown up yet? "Please. Somebody. Help."

Upper East Side

Miguel's chest tightened. Had he heard Vive and Thor correctly? They'd said his best friend wanted him, right? The man he'd been in love with for over a decade had feelings for him? Adrenalin pumping, he bit his lower lip so hard he tasted blood.

"I said Blake wants you." Thor repeated. "Do the *Seven Desires* with him already, geez!"

No, he wouldn't be Blake's sex instructor, let alone rebound wingman. Although, the idea tempted him on so many occasions; usually at bedtime, in the shower, in the morning or at the gym. Okay, okay! The thoughts ran through his mind pretty much twenty-four-fucking-seven.

"Don't play dumb. You two are meant for one another."

Vive sat up in her chair, tucking her Swedish white bangs behind her ears then grabbing Miguel's hand. She may be a chatterbox, but there was one thing Viveca Farnworth was not: a liar.

Sure, he'd fantasized about fucking Blake over the years. In fact, he'd jacked off thinking about topping him two times a day for the last decade. Running the numbers in his head, seven thousand three hundred dreamy moments were spent fantasizing about Mr. Morgan.

"Hello! Blake called Diego *Miguel* a few times in the bedroom. By accident, mind you." Thor swiped Miguel's drink away from him.

"He did? He really called him by my name?" He didn't have any idea, never knew. Why was he suddenly getting turned on? This was wrong. They were friends.

Thor kept going. "Ah-huh. The 'Miguel/MLD wrong name on the mattress fiasco' occurred a few times before they were married." If anyone remembered every nuance about a friend, it was Thor. He could tell Miguel what shoes he'd worn the day they'd met. Leave it to him to know this small detail about Blake and Diego's relationship.

"I heard the same from Taddy. She told me, in confidence, that back when Blake and Diego were having sex, he shouted your name out a few times," Vive confessed. Okay, when Thor said it, he could perhaps dismiss it. He exaggerated, and sometimes flat-out fibbed. But to have Vive confirm it, had his cock about to hit the ceiling.

Amazement flew through him. Suddenly, he felt more alive. Unable to fathom, he studied their faces for a bluff. Thor's Fire Island sun-burned skin and boozy glow made it hard to decipher the truth. And Vive with her Botox overload and opaque makeup indeed made it impossible. "You're both full of it." He still didn't buy it.

Thor shook his head as he stuffed his mouth with appetizers. "Ya never noticed...how..." He chewed the rest then swallowed. "MLD despised you?" He reached for his cocktail and took a gulp as though it was tap water. His eyes appeared teary, possibly from the alcohol, for a second before he wiped them.

"*Sí*, I did." He was tempted to punch Diego out on a few occasions. God, he'd wanted to smash his face in when they got married, and again when they got divorced. "MLD and I were friends in high school. He was as close as a brother to me growing up. Then he ruined everything the night I told him I had feelings for Blake. That same night, Diego decided to make Blake his boyfriend once and for all."

Asshole!

Miguel looked around to see if Blake was returning from the bathroom. He wasn't. "Diego was resentful?"

"Yah," Thor confirmed as Vive nodded.

"There's a lot to be envious of," he joked and flexed his pectoral muscles through his sheer, red cotton T-shirt. Diego may have had the charm, but he always had the heart. "Besides, I'd only perform those items with someone I was in a relationship with—a committed one." He pulled out his phone and recited, "Pissing, raw sex... Are you two nuts?"

"Gorgeous, I've been cray-cray for years." Vive giggled.

"Me, too. At least, that's what my two-hundred-and-fifty-dollar-an-hour West Village shrink tells me." Thor scooted his high-back chair to the table's edge. His citrus cologne, as always, was synthetically strong. "Listen, you two start with number one. I bet by the time you get to number seven, you'll be together, as boyfriends, once and for all." Thor raised his cocktail to toast the notion. "I'll wage a thousand dollars on it."

"That's Boardwalk play money for a good 'ol game of Monopoly. Puh-lease, we're Manhattanites. I say we up it to ten thousand dollars if they are living together as boyfriends within the year. Yes, a grand for every year lost that they should've been together."

Ten thousand dollars and living with Blake Morgan III? This conversation was going at warp speed. "Guys, slow down."

"Slow-*smow*. It's now or never, Miguel." Vive confessed "You need to top him, go all Dom on him. We've been waitin' for over ten years. Get on with *it* already. You have nothin' holding ya back, but your own damn inhibitions."

"Well said. Thanks, Vive." Thor nodded.

Miguel wondered how many drinks she'd had before he'd shown up. But he could tell from the look on her face she was on a roll, especially with Thor at her side. They could have their own talk show like their friend Poppy White.

"I'd fuck Blake if I had a penis." She laughed. "But no matter how many times I pray to the Universe, I wake up in the morning with my beautiful blonde pussy. There are spider webs growing off my clit this year." Amused with her own vulgarity, she snorted and continued, "Hell, I'd be happy with having sex with a gay. You're one delicious posse."

Vive made a sad face. He forgot she'd been off the dating scene as she battled her prescription pill addictions. Those were her doctor's orders. Miguel was surprised she hadn't quit drinking yet.

A *real* boyfriend wasn't in the cards for him, though. Always the stud, he was the top most guys picked up first at the bar to fuck. Magnum condom and all. No one ever took for anything except his initial offer: a hard ride. No one invested the time to get to know him and his family, to learn what made his mind tick or his heart beat. He'd gained a reputation for being an asshole in town. In reality, he simply refused to chase a guy. His ego wouldn't allow it.

"Zip it. Here comes Blake," Miguel whispered.

"Promise us you'll meet him at the Exhale Bliss Spa tomorrow," Thor begged.

"We'll have Blake groomed for you. He's going to get the full service." Vive never forgot the small details.

Miguel's dream, his castle in the sky, was being served to him at the Exhale Bliss Spa. His yearning was Blake Morgan III. No matter how hard he tried, he never stopped thinking about him in that non-friendship way. He *must* go for this, one more time, if not for his own selfish reasons then to prevent Blake from hooking up with people who could do him harm. *Yes, that's it.*

"*Sí*, I'll be there." He owned it, taking charge with quiet assurance, and confirmed no one would touch Blake but him. Not Gunter or Nello. *Only* him.

Thor clanged his tumbler into Vive and Miguel's. "Bottoms up, buddy."

"*Bottoms up,*" Miguel echoed as he toasted an unfamiliar enthusiasm. He didn't think he'd ever have the chance to try again. Surely a decade of thinking was worth a few days of trying, right?

Vive chuckled, probably pleased she and Thor had gotten their way. They always did. Sitting down at the tail end of the conversation, Blake offered a questioning smile with a pause then asked, "Whose bottom are you three toasting?"

He was so innocent. So sweet.

"Why, yours, Blake, of course." Miguel basked in the new knowledge. *Who knew you wanted me as I've always wanted you.*

Simultaneously, they nodded as if they'd been in cahoots together. Vive focused on her cocktail while Thor sat on his hands rocking forward.

Blake's brows drew down in uncertainty. "Huh?"

Vive's cell phone chimed. "Taddy's calling. I should've been there by now. She's gonna kick my ass." She held out her phone and answered, "Brill, gorgeous, I'm on my way." Suddenly, her gray eyes widened into saucers and her face reddened. "*What?* Is Lex okay? Where's Massimo?" Panic filled her voice.

The room's mood hit the floor when Vive put Hedda in her bag. Frantically, she knocked her drink over.

Miguel stood when she did, waving everyone up.

"We're heading over right now! Bye," she said into the phone before hanging up.

"What?" His stomach twisted. "What's wrong?"

"Lex collapsed during the shoot." She almost started to cry.

He'd never seen her that shaken. She rarely showed emotion.

"Where is she?" Thor waved the waiter for the bill and handed him his Amex.

"She's been taken to Empire General. We gotta go."

"We have to call Lex's mother, Birdie." Blake reached for his phone.

"I'll get my driver." Sprinting into action, Miguel ran for the door.

All he could think about when his heart jumped into his throat was Lex's son. How Massimo Junior's life would be if something bad ever happened to his mother.

How *all* of their lives would be if Lex wasn't a part of their group.

Unbearable.

Chapter Four

Massimo Always Gets What He Wants

Lenox Hill

Blake sat with his friends. Neon lights glowed above them as they huddled together on two large sofas in the waiting room. He breathed through his mouth because the disinfectant smell of Empire General Hospital was too nauseating to inhale through his nose.

The worry amongst them felt palpable. He didn't know what to say or do to put everyone's mind at ease, especially since no one knew what was wrong with Lex. He'd seen her earlier that day. She'd stopped by the Brill, Inc. offices, wanting his opinion on fabric samples Easton Essentials was trying out for the following season's collection. Her son had been in her arms and she *did* seem stressed, but no more than usual.

Next to him sat Miguel, who hadn't spoken much. With Taddy, Vive, and Birdie, he could barely get a word in.

"What do you think the doctor will say?" he asked Lex's mom.

"To get off those diet pills Taddy keeps passing out like Skittles."

"Don't you dare blame me." Offended, Taddy inched to the edge of her chair.

"This is all your fault!" Dramatically, Birdie pointed a finger at her.

"Let's not get worked up." Vive stroked her arm.

Blake figured it was to calm her down. Lex's mother had been on the verge of hysteria since she'd arrived. Who could blame her? Her only child was sick. Empire General probably brought back too many painful memories. It was where her husband was taken right before he died.

"Her collapse is from stress. Not dieting," she defended in a staid voice.

"Taddy, stop it!" Blake shouted.

Miguel put his hand around the lower part of Blake's neck, signaling him to cool it, too. No one noticed him reach around him, but it sent an unexpected warmth all up and down his body.

"Is that so?" Birdie's eyes narrowed. "She went to Secrète de St. Barth and worked her ass off to get in shape. That boot camp nearly killed her."

"How dare you? I call bullshit." Taddy jolted to her feet then paced. Hands on both hips, her face looked as if her mind was racing. "This is from work. Easton Essentials is all-consuming."

The brand was becoming too much for all of them. Blake had let some of his other accounts go so he could spend more hours dedicated to building Easton Essentials with them.

"If that were true, then why did your PR firm launch her bridal line knowing it would be so demanding of her time?" Birdie wasn't easing up. "You're still to blame."

Blake looked at Miguel to do something. This was only getting worse.

"Easton Weds Bridal Couture wasn't my idea." Taddy turned on her heel and stalked off.

The flip of her wavy red hair over her shoulder signaled she was done with the conversation. After being friends with Taddy for close to fifteen years, he could read her pretty well.

"The new line extension was Lex's idea," he spoke in Birdie's direction, freeing his friend from the hot seat. "We thought Lex could handle it." He remembered how excited she was when Massimo proposed. Massimo's sister, Paloma, had designed the most exquisite engagement ring they'd ever seen. They'd only known one another for a few days. The chemistry between them was still intoxicating.

Miguel drew his mouth to Blake's ear. "Don't argue with Birdie."

He bit his tongue against the warning and the sensation of his friend's warm breath on his neck.

"Does it matter? The line is a hit."

Being the brand guru and PR maven Taddy was, Blake didn't anticipate her apologizing, even if her business strategy caused Lex's exhaustion. Easton Essentials had made Lex, Blake, and her millions.

"And you're one to talk, Birdie. This big wedding was all your doing."

"Well..." Defeated, she slouched back in her chair.

She'd admitted to him, on many occasions, that she'd dreamt of Lex wearing a white dress when she married, from the moment the engagement announcement was made. When Lex became pregnant, it was Birdie who suggested they push the wedding back by six months until after the baby was born, to make it a separate event.

At first, Blake thought she was nuts, but soon realized she'd never experienced her own big ceremony when she married Eddie. Therefore, it made sense why she insisted on the upcoming St. Patrick's Cathedral ceremony, followed by a formal dinner reception at The Plaza Hotel.

He recalled many instances growing up where he'd witnessed Birdie living vicariously through her daughter. At school dances, Lex was often overdressed, like a doll on display.

"We need to do more for her," Miguel finally said. "Blake and I will take turns watching the baby."

"Huh?" He had never babysat before. He wanted to, but the little bugger sort of scared him. Even more since the divorce because he'd let go of the idea of ever having kids. He didn't want to parent solo.

"*Sí.*" Miguel leaned forward, getting more into the conversation as Vive and Birdie listened. "Lex should go part-time at Easton." His reasoning: the brand was established, it was time for her to take a backseat and enjoy her family.

"No way." Taddy shook her head.

"Massimo has been begging Lex to cut back," Blake said.

Miguel had grown close to Massimo since she introduced her fiancé to the group. Blake liked that Miguel was a guy's guy. He himself was more of the girl's gay husband.

"At her *own* company?" Taddy huffed as if they'd stated the impossible.

Blake had watched the two women grow their businesses over the years. It took all the get-up-and-go they had to launch their enterprises, and twice as much energy to grow and maintain them.

"We'll do whatever she needs." Miguel's voice grew louder. "I know Massimo refuses to have outside help. He only wants the family and *us* around." He wasn't used to anyone in the group challenging him, not even Taddy.

Blake appreciated the respect everyone gave Miguel. It made him more attractive to him.

Birdie wiped her eyes. "I told them to get a nanny. I can't be there all the time."

The night's stress obviously overwhelmed her. She'd buried Eddie four years before and helped Lex with Easton as well, while climbing her way out of bankruptcy. And like Vive, she also struggled with her addictions. The year was supposed to go smoothly. No more drama.

Taddy came up and kneeled beside her. "Blake and I will help you with the responsibilities at Easton."

She played hardball, but Blake knew better. Deep down inside, she was a softy and would give her left arm for her best friend.

"Thank you." She patted her hand for understanding.

He watched Birdie argue with Taddy a lot over the years, especially since she owned a large portion of the Easton business, but in the end, they always seemed to work it out.

"We're getting ahead of ourselves," Vive blurted out loud. "You're all talking about Lex as if she's an invalid. She'll do whatever the hell she wants. She always has."

"Right, she's gonna be fine." He'd been telling himself that for a few hours now, but hoped by saying it out loud everyone would believe it. He'd never known her to even have the flu. At the Avon Porter Academy, it was Taddy who was always in the infirmary, maybe a cry for her parent's attention. But their fashionista was sorta of made out of steel. "Do you guys remember in the tenth grade when Lex fractured her arm?"

"I sure do. Our Bionic Girl played through the entire softball game, then turned to the coach and said, 'I think my arm is busted.'" Vive gave a little laugh. "She's such a sport."

Birdie smiled as tears fell down her cheeks. "My daughter sure is lucky to have you guys."

"Lex is lucky to have you, too." Taddy pulled her in tight as she sobbed. "We all are."

"*Principessa.*"

Lex heard Masi whisper in her ear. His warm hand grabbed at hers as she started to wake up and open her eyes.

Caressing her hands, he said, *"Ti amo."*

"I love you, too."

On the hospital bed, tucked under the covers, the mattress felt thinner to her than their bed at home. Shit, it felt as if she were on the hardwood floor. She estimated three hours or so must've passed. Earlier, blood was drawn. She must've dozed off as they waited on the results.

"You want him, *sì*?" Massimo held up their son.

Eyes wide, Massimo Junior smiled.

"Please." She sat up and reached for him. "He needs to be fed."

Her son felt heavier in her arms than she remembered. Massimo Junior, Massimo the second, or 'M2' as they'd nicknamed him, was growing up fast.

Lex uncovered her right breast from the cotton gown. "Hi, baby," she cooed as he took her nipple and began to suck. She winced and closed her eyes for a minute, trying to get comfortable with the sensation. "Where is the doctor?"

Massimo got to his feet and poked his head out the doorway. "Taddy and your mom appear to have stopped shouting at one another."

Her best friend had ridden with her in the ambulance. She'd demanded of the hospital administrator that Lex get the top private floor—a wing reserved for dignitaries and celebrities, which she would become very soon. And being the daughter to Eddie and Birdie Easton made her a celebrity, even though she never thought of herself as such. She hated to receive any special treatment.

"Who's still here?"

"Everyone but Thor. He took Jemma to get a bite to eat."

"Blake and Miguel?"

"*Sì*, with Vive, Taddy and your *madre*."

"Send them all home." She loved her friends and it was sweet that they'd come, but she felt fine and didn't want to make them worry.

"They aren't going to leave 'til the doctor tells us what's going on." Massimo had grown to love Lex's friends as much as she did.

"I'm fine. I'm tired is all." She let M2's head rest against her arm. Once his little belly filled with her milk, he'd doze off leaving his mouth open. It was the cutest thing.

"Lex, you're *not* fine. You can't keep going on like this."

Oh, God. "What's that supposed to mean?" She tried to keep calm and her voice low. Embracing M2 kept her from getting too worked up when Massimo started in on her.

"*Principessa*, you're doing too much."

"Then why do I feel as though…it's not enough?" There weren't enough hours in the day to get her punch lists done.

"You need to stay at home and be with our son."

Shit, there it was. *What every new mother who also has a career hates to hear.* "I don't want to be a stay-at-home mom. We've gone over this a zillion times. I run my company and co-manage yours." They'd merged Girasoli Garments, his company, with hers a while back. Together, they ranked as the second-largest apparel manufacturer in the world.

"M2 needs you."

"He has me. He comes to work with me. I'm at home with him as much as any other mother can be. Just because we have money doesn't mean I don't have to work."

"You don't *have* to work, Lex."

"Work is who I am." She hated when Massimo did this. He made her feel guilty for having a desire to have a career. "Don't be so Italian."

"Don't be so *American*." He never let her get away with sassy talk. She loved that about him. He'd kept her on her toes from the minute they'd met. He was also the greatest lover in bed. But right then, she wanted to punch him.

"We should've waited to start a family. But *no*, you insisted against birth control." She hadn't been sexually active much before she'd met Massimo. Hungry for his touch, she'd fallen passionately into their lovemaking without thinking clearly.

"We have a beautiful son."

"That we do."

Lex'd only wanted one child. Massimo had wanted a dozen. They'd agreed on three kids, and then her tubes would be tied. She didn't think she'd get pregnant after their first romantic weekend together.

"Miss Easton." Dr. Reed Cedar greeted them as he came in the room.

The doctor had been with the family for years. Ever since her father broke his back, Dr. Cedar had been a part of their life. Back in the late '90's at Madison Square Gardens, Eddie had jumped out into the audience, expecting the crowd to catch him.

They didn't.

Her father hadn't realized during his Eddie's Gone Mad World Tour, while his fans loved him, most were high. Too stoned on marijuana to realize the flying object coming at them was real, let alone in need of being caught. When he broke his back, he was taken to Empire General and cared for by Dr. Cedar.

"We have some of the test results back."

"What is it?" Lex covered herself, sat up, and took her son over her shoulder. M2's body warm against hers. Rubbing his lower back, she burped him.

"Congratulations, you're pregnant."

"Meraviglioso." Massimo clapped his hands together, making a loud noise in the room as if he'd won another round. "I knew it."

"No." So soon? She didn't think it was possible, but realized she hadn't gotten her period in God knew when.

Not again. Damn you, Masi.

"About eight weeks." Dr. Reed stepped closer to the edge of the bed. "Your blood pressure is high, but manageable, and your iron is low. Everything else checks out fine. I'll have the nurse get you started on the vitamins."

"Two years of my life is going to be spent knocked up? I don't believe this."

"Bella." Arms wide, her husband-to-be came at her for a hug.

"Get away from me."

His eyes glassed up as he grinned. "This is *incredible.*" Massimo kissed M2 on the forehead. "Our *bambino* will have a brother or sister."

"Good, then you can carry the baby the rest of the way. I quit."

He rolled his brown eyes and laughed.

"Lex, I see from the OBGYN notes your first pregnancy was difficult."

"Two days of labor with no effin' epidural is not *difficult.* It was Hell." She'd tried to go natural. The editors at *Marie Claire* and *Harper's* had persuaded her to. It was the right thing to do, they said. Wrong.

She didn't want to be judged as a new mother by the cliques on the Upper East Side. Labor was all those ladies could talk about. How they delivered, what method they used, who their doctor was. The delivery chatter was worse than keeping up with the Jones' pretentious fashion labels. But once the epidural window of opportunity had closed, she realized she'd made a mistake. A painful one.

"Lex, *mio amore.*"

"It's torture…I haven't recovered from the first delivery. I was actually contemplating having a surrogate carry the rest of our kids. Christ, I'm almost thirty. My body can't handle this."

"We don't have to do it like last time." Dr. Reed didn't seem fazed by her surrogacy confession. What was wrong with having someone else carry her baby? Over the years, if stars like Sarah Jessica Parker and Grace Hightower could pull it off without Manhattan's society getting all righteous, she could do it, too. Granted, she was a little younger than them, by a decade or two.

"I want you to knock me out and take the kid from my belly. Let's schedule a C-section for when the time comes."

"*Basta!*" Massimo glared at her.

She knew she was being ridiculous, but...

"Our staff will make your pregnancy a joyful one, for you and your family," Dr. Reed tried to reassure her.

"Joyful as in painless?"

The doctor deadpanned and eyed Massimo with a questionable look on his face.

"I'm serious." Lex inhaled the sweet smell of her son's nape as she hugged him close. Did she want another baby? Yes. Just not so soon. Unwed, she'd never gotten to be a wife, not yet. M2 had come so fast. And she couldn't forget her business. In its own right, Easton Essentials was similar to having another baby. A four-year-old business, which required constant care and looking after. Another baby was on the way. Could she do it all?

"Miss Easton, you may go home tonight. We'll set up your next appointment in a few weeks. You'll need bed rest tomorrow." Dr. Reed shook their hands, again congratulating them. He left the room, whistling one of her father's songs.

One day in bed isn't so bad. "Masi, will you please get my clothes."

"*Sì.*" He had that 'I'll take care of you' look in his eyes. The one he'd had for her throughout her first pregnancy. It was part adoration, pity and fear.

"Let's go."

Sitting up, she put her feet on the floor. She'd have to get the extra bedroom ready, the one Jemma, Rocco and Luigi were going to stay in that week, and block out her schedule six months down the line. They were going to have another child. But first, there was a little thing called a wedding they had to take care of.

Chapter Five

Dirty Birdie

Midtown

Nestled ten floors up from New York City's exclusive shopping strip was the Exhale Bliss Spa on Fifth Avenue. Voted by *Allure* magazine as the best urban retreat, Blake had no idea the sprawling space of tranquility was so exquisite. Sure, he'd heard about the place, who hadn't? But he didn't take time for pampering, not like this. As he talked about the previous night to Thor and Vive, he wished Lex was with them today. She'd probably enjoy this.

Of course, she was pregnant. They'd been foolish to think it was anything otherwise. He was excited for Massimo, M2, Birdie, and her. Their royal family was doubling. But why did her good news make him feel even more alone?

Lex would always be a part of his life. So would Massimo and their children; he knew that. Nevertheless, he couldn't help but wish *he* was the one starting a family. Instead, he was coming off a divorce, and at some spa getting a manscape makeover to prepare his body for some sexual fantasy he knew would never happen. But he enjoyed his time with Vive and Thor, and they were putting him in better spirits.

"Why am I anxious about getting sugared?" Blake asked Thor who sipped loudly on a mimosa next to him.

Vive had downed three, maybe four, champagne flutes already. Opting for no orange juice, she was also in a great mood. "You're nervous 'cause we're wearing bleached cotton." Her slipper flopped to the floor as she crossed her legs and rolled up one of the long sleeves on her robe. "Seriously, this shit itches. They need to call our Lex and have her design their spa wear in cashmere."

"We're gettin' naked in a few, Viveca. They could dress us in organic barbwire for all I care. Geez!" Robe open, Thor didn't bother covering up. He let everything hang out.

From the end of the hall came a hot Asian man. Standing at about five-ten, he had almond-shaped eyes, which spoke of seduction. His jacked body exuded sex.

"Mr. Edwards, ready for your pedicure?"

A southern accent. What an alluring combination.

"Why, hello there, Mr. Kim Lee. It's good to see you again." His friend stood.

"Close your robe," Blake sassed.

"Mind your business." Gingerly, Thor tied himself at the waist, but only after a lasso-style swing and spin, which gave everyone in the 'quiet room' a peep show. "Have fun, you two. I wanna see cum in your hair, Vive, or on your face, Blake, when I get back." He winked and was off down the hall following Mr. Kim Lee.

"Cum is good for the hair, thank you very much!" Vive shouted. She didn't miss a beat.

"Funny." Blake sat up. "So, that's the famous pedicurist you girls rave about. He's cute."

"Mr. Kim Lee is *hawt*. He does this razor action on the soles of my feet. I'm all ballerina-iffic when he's done. We love him." On the sofa, she scooted over, looping her right arm around his as she drank more champagne. "After sugaring, you'll feel like a shiny new penny." Her head rested against his shoulder.

"Love the sound of that." He inhaled her scent. Vive always smelled expensive.

"If I haven't told you lately, I'm proud of you."

"You are? Why?" He couldn't imagine.

"No one knows better than me what it's like to bury your past." She blinked. "See, you may never get over Diego. And that's okay, Blake. But you *will* move on. I promise. A step at a time, one day after the next, you'll carry forward."

She might be three sheets to the wind most of the time, but the girl had a big heart.

"How did you move on after San?" he asked, remembering Vive's first and only love, Sanderloo Konjik.

Sanderloo had attended the Connecticut Military Academy a few miles down the road from Avon Porter. He'd been accepted into West Point for college, when he was killed. Blake had blocked out of his mind the events which led up to his death. They were horrible. But he'd never forget Vive had always loved Sanderloo, enough to carry his baby to term and give the infant up for adoption.

"I drink. That's how I move on." She squeezed his arm, tight. She rarely spoke about him, but he could tell Sanderloo was *always* on her mind.

Two tall, masculine figures came from the hall.

"Here they are." Excitement rang in Vive's voice.

Hans and Franz-type hunks in tight T-shirts with fitted pants approached. The black-haired one, whose arms reminded Blake of Popeye, referenced the clipboard.

"Miss Farnworth?"

"That's me." She raised her hand and giggled, girlishly.

"You've booked the four-handed massage. I'm Dar and this is Weber. We're your massage therapists for today."

"Allow me." Weber extended his hand, helping Vive up as she thanked them flirtatiously.

"My assistant, Bari, a little blonde, annoying thing, raves about you two. Says you're orgasmic." She covered her mouth as if she'd let a secret slip. "I mean, Bari says you two are the best at working out muscle tension."

"Bari, the former Miss Mississippi?" Dar asked.

"That's her."

She turned back to Blake and whispered in his ear to relax and go with the flow. Like Thor moments before, Vive toddled off with a spring of sudden excitement in her step.

If Blake's spa tech looked half as exotic as Mr. Kim Lee, as muscular as Dar or as suave as Weber, he'd be in Heaven. Spa Heaven.

Resting his head against the sofa, he allowed his eyelids to become heavy. He must've dozed off as he heard his name being called.

"Huh?" Blake looked up to see a guy, early twenties, common face, no body, no muscles.

Dammit.

"Sugaring, right?"

"That's me."

"I'm Ernie. Follow me please."

Ernie? What the hell kind of name was Ernie? Why wasn't he given Dar or Weber?

Blake followed him down the dark hallway to a quiet room. White and posh, the area was about eight feet wide by ten feet in length. Blinds drawn, one window.

"Mr. Morgan?"

"Yes." Blake jumped a little. Though the room smelled of lavender, he was still jittery.

"Relax, make yourself comfortable. I'll step out while you get undressed."

"*Undressed?*"

Ernie nodded then pointed to a hook. "Hang your robe on the back of this door."

"Right, of course." He tried to act as though he did this every weekend. He didn't. "Umm, then what?" Clueless, he'd never had hair removal. Did he sit in some special chair? Or do a handstand?

"Is this your first time?"

"Ah-huh." Nervously, he laughed. "Sugaring is new for me."

"Okay, have you had a massage before?"

"No…not really. Only once—I was clothed. One of those chair massages at some Zen Buddha store over on Madison Avenue."

"I see." Ernie's face lit up a bit. He smiled with confidence, assuring Blake was in good hands. "Lay down on the bed, backside up. Put your head in the bolster."

"Sounds easy enough." Maybe he'd enjoy himself.

"Give me a holler when you're ready." He dimmed the lights and closed the door.

The robe hit the floor with a loud thump. Naked, Blake stood there. The AC vents blasted cold air upon him, causing his skin to goose bump. Other than his husband, he'd never been touched by another man before. Hell, he'd never been naked in front of anyone else but Diego.

What if he got hard? *Hmmm.*

Not to worry, Ernie didn't get his juices flowing. *Could be a good thing.*

Maybe it was for the best that Ernie wasn't like Vive's or Thor's therapists. He reminded himself why he was there: Nello. Their date was tonight. Then later in the week came Gunter.

Funny thing was they didn't appeal to him, either. Taddy professed the best way to attract a new guy was to date other guys, even if you didn't like them.

It all sounded exhausting, so he focused on the spa treatment at hand.

Upper East Side

"Morning, Mom." Lex sat up in bed, yanking down the comforter Massimo had bundled her in before he'd left. Her satin chemise clung to her body. She wanted to take a shower, but Massimo wouldn't let her. He'd threatened earlier he was going to handcuff her to the headboard with their kinky cuffs if she didn't stay still.

"I let myself in."

"You always do, Birdie," she said in amusement, remembering back to her childhood when her mother made her call her by her first name whenever they were out in public.

Her mom had a knack for getting in the elevator without having the doorman downstairs buzz ahead. She pulled a stack of shoe boxes behind her in the red grocery buggy her maid used for errands. The faded exteriors of L. A. Gear, Pony, and Doc Martens labels told her the '80's shoes were long gone.

"Honey, I have no idea what's in these but I'm sure it's every photo ever taken of you." Her jeweled hand swept over her forehead as she pushed her jet-black hair away from her tight face. She took the lid off a small box and plopped it onto the bed.

"Thank you for bringing them over." They were going to sort through the images. Each guest would be featured in a small, sterling silver frame at their assigned place setting as they sat enjoying their seven-course meal.

What was the purpose of all the extra hoopla? To put her friends first. Lex copied the tip from Blake's wedding and thought it was endearing.

"Where are my boys and Jemma?" Birdie poked her head around then went to the large window which faced west, out at Park Avenue, and opened the blinds.

White light spilled into the room. Lex noticed the film of dust covering the Mother's Day card on the nightstand from two weeks before. It reminded her to tidy up, but not right then. No, Massimo would shit if she was caught out of bed. If he didn't let her shower, what made her think she could dust?

"Masi took M2 out for a walk. Jemma didn't come home last night. She texted saying she and Thor had gotten invited over to Tom Ford's house for a party."

"Good for them, and how nice of Masi to take M2 out and about." Birdie rounded her shoulders as her face smiled with approval.

"It's become their Saturday morning ritual. He should be back in an hour or so."

She was grateful Massimo had developed a routine. Her fiancé, a morning person, bathed and dressed M2. Lex, the night owl, repeated the routine and put her son to bed. She wondered, for a second, how their schedules would change once the second baby came along.

Her mother sat on the mattress and pulled what appeared to be a family album out as well as a few stacks of envelopes. "I haven't gone through this stuff since—" Birdie started to choke up. "Before your father left."

She hated when her mother referred to her daddy as 'leaving'. He didn't leave—he killed himself. Murder was how she thought of suicide, and she'd never forgiven him for it.

"This will be good for you then." She wanted her mother to move on.

"Eddie isn't dead," Birdie hissed softly under her breath.

"Please." Every fiber in her pregnant body went cold. "Don't start in on that Charmain shit." Curses fell from her mouth as she glared at Birdie to stop with the nonsense.

"Don't *you* swear at *me*."

Two years before, Birdie had given a little over half a million dollars to a Caribbean psychic named Charmain Whitedove in exchange for her medium services to channel Eddie from the dead. Miss Whitedove's clairvoyant powers told her Eddie Easton, the world's most famous rock star (next to Elvis Presley), wasn't in Heaven or Hell. He was living it up in the US Virgin Islands. Therefore, Eddie was unchannelable. This, of course, drove Lex insane.

"Your father will be back, honey. One day, we'll see him again."

Birdie never got over her husband's suicide. Lex caught her mother talking to Eddie all the time as if he was in the room with her. It was the only way she could get through the day. At first, she thought her mother was on drugs, but since Eddie's heroin overdose, Birdie had avoided all illegal and prescription substances. The doctors said she'd been scared into sobriety. Hallucinogens aside, her mother was still bat-shit crazy.

"We'll see Dad in Heaven. He's with the angels." *Knock it off, Mom. You're freakin' me out.*

Birdie's head shook, pursing her mouth as if she was forming an argument, but she suddenly stopped and released a gasp of air. She forced an obvious tense smile in Lex's direction. The grin was painted across her made-up face, probably in the shade Melonlicious by Baden Cosmetics, a Brill Inc. client, and her favorite coral lip-gloss.

"Mom, you okay?"

She held her breath; Lex could tell by the way her chest came up against her pearl and diamond statement piece, which was around her neck.

Suddenly, she chewed her lower lip. Birdie grabbed onto another stack of photos. "It's a nice touch that you're doing the tables like this. I loved seeing the guest's reactions over them at Blake's wedding."

Thank you, Mom. "Me, too." She felt a sense of relief come over her as her mother changed the subject. Lex acknowledged to herself that it wasn't easy for her mom to let go. Birdie loved to argue and she usually won, even when she wasn't right. And she was rarely right.

"Blake had the best reception I'dve ever attended." Birdie placed a glossy picture flat on the bed and looked at it fondly.

"Is that so? Better than your gal Rachel's wedding to Rod Stewart?"

"Yes. Even more fabulous than when Heather married Richie Sambora in Paris." Birdie spoke of her celebrity friends in jest. After one platinum album, a Playboy Centerfold cover, a Grammy, and her own line of perfume called Dirty Birdie, the woman knew everyone.

"What did you like most about Blake's wedding?"

"How proud Blake II and Paulina were of him. Aside from when Elton John married David, it's the only gay wedding I'd been to. His parents, and everyone, were so happy for Blake, particularly me." At Avon Porter, Birdie was the first mother to get behind Blake when he came out. She encouraged Mrs. Morgan to join Parents, Families, & Friends for Lesbians and Gays (PFLAG) and spoke publicly for teens coming out.

"You were always good to him, Mom." Lex loved that about her mother. But back then, when they were teens, it did bother her. Birdie could be a better mom to other people's children, but when it came to her own, she'd failed miserably.

"Damn that ex of his for screwing up." Her mother made a tsk-tsk noise. "Such a shame."

"Indeed. I remember the toast they gave right before cutting the cake. That they'd adopt a baby within a year." She didn't like to see her friends fail, especially not in love. "Blake had so many hopes of having a family…"

"How's he managing since the divorce?"

Lex felt guilty. She wanted to do more for him, but hadn't found the time. Recently, their only moment together was at Secrète de St. Barth. They'd been so busy working out they didn't get to have much fun. Blake was angry, too upset to talk about what had gone down with his marriage. All he did was lift weights. "Taddy and Vive have been with him around the clock. He's getting better."

"What has he said about MLD?" Even Birdie refused to call him Diego.

"That he was tempted to hire some Staten Island hit man he'd seen on that reality show *Mob Wives* to take out MLD for good."

"I don't blame him."

"Taddy talked him out of it. Said he'd get caught and be an embarrassment to his family."

"MLD *should be* roughed up."

She joked, but Lex knew she was serious. Her mother was a bully in her heyday. She'd gone after many of Eddie's lovers. If she didn't beat them up, one of her 'fans' did it for her.

Birdie pulled out another folder and held it up for her to read the label, *Avon Porter.* "I remember when Blake enrolled at your school. You girls fought over him."

"Avon Porter had just gone coed, Mom. Blake and Thor were the first male students admitted."

"Blake was also the cutest boy you'd ever seen."

"Says who?"

"You, at fourteen. I was in London staying with David Bowie. I remember because you called me saying you'd met the nicest boy in class." She held up a photo of Blake being hugged by Taddy and kissed by Vive.

Lex remembered snapping it out in the courtyard between classes. Everything seemed easier then. "True, he was. Thor was cute, too. But Blake was, and still is, classically handsome. He gets better with age, like fine wine." She took the photo and put it off to the side of the bed to be framed. That one they'd put on Blake's table. "Vive won the battle of who would try and flip him."

"Alexandra Easton, my ears. Please don't talk like that." Birdie shushed her.

"Mommy, don't act like such a prude. After all, you were a swinger."

Her mother was a playgirl. But ever since her father died, Birdie carried on as a reborn virgin. Lex figured it was her Alcoholics Anonymous meetings. She'd given up pretty much everything but eating iceberg lettuce with French dressing and Coke Zero. Whatever worked to keep her mother sober, she'd go with it.

"Sex is overrated."

"Since when?" she asked, shocked to hear her mother say this. Birdie in her prime had been known to have slept with thousands. At least that's what her unauthorized biography stated.

"The scars of my life say so. I regret all that wasted effort I put into partying and having sex. It ruined me. Sucked the energy right out of me."

"I'm pretty sure that was the cocaine, Mother." Lex tilted her head, giving her mother a sidelong glance. Pride normally prevented her from arguing with her about most things, but Birdie's past mistakes weren't part of them.

"Cocaine, cock, it's all the same." Birdie held up another photo of Taddy and Lex as toddlers. In diapers, they were both covered in what appeared to be strawberry ice cream. "What matters are your friends. Don't forget that." Sadness rang in her mother's voice. "After your father *left,* I realized I didn't really have any girlfriends."

"Put that photo with Blake's. I'll use it for Taddy's table." Lex noticed her mother was hanging on to that thought about friends and wasn't paying attention. "Mom? Hello? You're zoning out."

Birdie nodded, "You girls will always have one another. No one can take that friendship away."

"I know. She's my bestie, Mom. Vive and Blake are, too."

"Taddy is special. Always has been. You've known her since the day you were born. That girl hasn't had the same luxuries as you."

Lex looked up to her. The Brillfords had dropped her off at boarding school and never picked her back up. Emancipated as a teenager, Taddy had turned herself into a self-made millionaire.

"I can't imagine my life without my BFF."

She reached up and pulled out an envelope labeled, *Eddie*. Whatever was inside that one, she knew it would send her mother off a cliff. Regardless, she wanted to fill the reception with images of her father; not a ton, but a few. It wasn't as if she was going to play a memorial video of her father like the wedding planner had suggested. That would've been too much. Instead, a few photos around the room to see his face while she danced were all she needed.

"Look." The first image she grabbed was of her mother, pregnant.

Birdie's eyes narrowed as she focused on the picture. "1983. My Lucifer's Mistress World Tour. That album went platinum. I was seven months preggers with you."

"I hate that song." The ballad peaked at Number One on Billboard Top 100. It was the first song written to address the art of female submission. At Avon Porter, boys had taunted Lex in class. They asked her if she was as easy to submit as her mother.

She wasn't.

"That ditty put me on the map, honey." She hummed the chorus, *"Take me now, take me tonight, I want you to take me any way you'll have me. T-a-k-e me."*

"Playboy made you famous. Your music just made you rich."

"I loved that tour. Back then, your father and I were so in love. We'd spend every free minute together. Then…I had you." Her smile soured.

She'd tried to hide it, but having Lex and becoming a stay-at-home mom had ruined her career. Over the years, she'd been told as much on many occasions, usually when Birdie drank.

"Yup, I'm the catalyst for your demise."

"Don't talk like that. When you were young, I was—"

"*Mean.*"

"A little."

"You took it out on *me*, Mom."

"Let's not go there again. We've been over this a million times. If I could have a do-over, I would."

Birdie's way of learning was by trial and error.

"Okay, what would you do differently?" She didn't blame her parents for everything. Finger pointing wouldn't get them anywhere. Her new approach, which Massimo had taught her, was to ask, listen, and try to learn from her mother's mistakes. There were hundreds of them to pick from.

"You don't want to hear it, Alexandra. Let's change the subject...now, what time are Rocco and Luigi getting in from Milan?"

"Let's *stay* on this topic. I wanna know, Mom. What would you have done differently?"

Birdie frowned.

You're not gettin' out of this one, Mother.

Chapter Six

Sugaring Blake's Cookie

Midtown

Spread out as if he were a bald eagle with a vast wingspan, Blake was flying high. He lay on the massage table, naked. Ass up in the air, his face hung low in the aromatic pillow.

Ten minutes and counting of sugar torture made his crack feel velvety smooth. He knew this because he kept touching his bum in disbelief. Thor had lied. Sugaring hurt as if a colony of fire ants were attacking a wounded grasshopper. Though, Blake was starting to enjoy the silkalicious titillation. *Maybe I am a masochist after all.*

"Mr. Morgan, we're almost done here. All that's left is trimming up your pubes and shaving your nuts. You'll be good to go."

"Are you serious?" At this rate, he'd be made into a prized Lhasa Apso, like Hedda, in no time.

"That's what Thor and Vive ordered for you when they made your appointment. Your friends are our best customers."

"That doesn't surprise me." *They give quaffed a new meaning.* "I heard Taddy made you list Vajazzle on your spa menu." He'd been the last of their group to join in the Exhale Bliss Spa fan club.

"Yes, and anal bleaching." Ernie laughed.

"Lord, really?"

"It's all the rage. Vive refers us a ton of clientele, too." He stroked the back of his neck. "Close your eyes and rest your face in the cradle."

His cheeks squished with his mouth as he did as instructed. "I must look like a blow fish." He tried to laugh and opened his eyes, but couldn't really see. The face cradle blocked out all light.

"I'm going to put some Paraffin wax on your skin."

"Why?" he asked, staring at the darkness.

"We infuse the paraffin with Azuline. It'll soothe your skin. First, I'm going to cover your hair line." Ernie placed a hot towel over the back of his head. Blake had been meaning to get a haircut; he just hadn't found the time. He wondered if the spa could cut his hair when they were through with his manscaping. They'd done pretty much everything else.

"I'll dip gauze strips in the paraffin then place them on your skin," Ernie said.

Blake felt it as the first one was applied, and instantly his back muscles relaxed. He wiggled his butt, getting more into it. "Amazing," he murmured as the final strip came over his shoulders.

"Rest. I'm going to step out and get some lotion. Be right back."

A few minutes passed and he heard Ernie return. Blake felt the sugaring guru's fingers glide over his ass cheeks with cream. They were affectionate, with intent. *Damn.*

He grew nervous. "About done back there?"

Ernie didn't say a word. But his breathing sounded louder, more irregular, different.

Sure, the sugaring therapist was okay, but not so cute that he'd want the service to go any further than what it was. But he'd go with it. He had to. Closing his eyes, Blake tried to take a few deep breaths to relax. He lowered his shoulders to the table, and then he felt...

Huh?

Fingers. It had to be. They traced around the edges of his asshole. With his face pressed into the pillow, he tried to think. *Lotion doesn't go in there...fingers don't, either.*

Except, they did.

Before he could ask Ernie to stop, two thick fingers slid in deeper. His body quivered. Every inch of him awoke. *Hello.*

Digits, thick and long, man-hands, slid back and forth as he was stretched out. Just as he let his mind wander and his ass opened, he clenched tight. This was too much. He couldn't. No way. He wasn't ready for this.

Maybe the therapist could tell his body needed to be touched. That's why he kept on massaging his ass. *Ahhh.*

To his surprise, Blake relaxed a little. He inhaled deeply and held his breath for a few seconds. *Relax.* Upon exhale, his fissure unglued as never before, taking the penetration of several...more...fingers. *I can't believe...I'm letting some stranger...do this.*

Blake's hard cock pressed into the table. Slightly closing his eyes as they crossed, he saw brilliant stars. The previous night's single malt scotch and Lex's pregnancy news became a distant memory.

Ernie reached under him and stroked his balls. They tightened as blood rushed through his cock. His head swelled. *You're just back there, playing with my butt. How can I turn around and face you?*

Ass-play remained new for him. He buried his head further in the pillow. He saw nothing, only black. His legs spread wider. Letting his guard down, he allowed himself to go there and pushed his back up, a little, in the air. He'd never aimed his ass for sex before, but somehow, someway, his instincts were guiding him along.

"Go. Deeper. Please." He had an urge to growl something animalistic.

Sandwiched between his trembling legs, friction fashioned a heat. Blake had craved the violation for some time. He couldn't remember how long.

Often, he masturbated to the fantasy of a guy playing with his ass. The top would worship him, tear him apart, and force entry. Maybe this was the power of positive thought Thor had referred to last night. He'd wished for it, and it had come. *Should I come now?*

He pressed his forehead further into the cotton, lavender aromatic pillow and drew air in through his dry mouth. *Do it.* He tried to make sense of this. Again, he arched his back for Ernie as electricity-like enthusiasm darted from his sphincter muscle. The stimulation ran in guilty excess over his groin, down his thighs, out his toes, up and down his cock, which, to his surprise, oozed pre-cum. *Whoa...*

Reaching down, Blake stroked his dick. Slick and wet, the moisture confirmed his arousal. Pre-cum seeped.

Fuck. Even my scalp tingles. This is exhilarating. I will never doubt Vive and Thor as long as I live again.

He didn't have a clue he'd be paying for sex, disguised as spa services, to get his *Seven Desires* done. But, he realized it right then. How could he have not figured this out sooner? He hadn't been with anyone except his ex-husband. He kept telling himself that nothing bad was going to happen.

Everything on his body was acutely sensitive. Nipples hard enough to cut glass, this was as close to natural ecstasy as he'd ever experienced. Why hadn't he played with himself like this before? Diego was the first excuse which came to mind. His masturbation rituals were jacking off, never massaging his prostate, ever. It sure did feel good, though.

Regrets from five years of his failed marriage consumed him. How could he have shared his life with someone who'd never enjoyed his body? Embarrassed, he worked through his despair and pushed the bad thoughts away. Warm tears washed over his face and collected on the cushion. He didn't care. To be touched like this...he couldn't remember the last time...it had been that long.

Fuck you, Diego. I am better than our pathetic excuse for a marriage. I deserved to be treated better. What you did was criminal. More tears flowed. He didn't wipe his eyes.

No longer slow, Ernie's fingers built up speed. Then they became fast and furious. Two fingers slid inside him from what seemed the other hand. Suddenly, different fingers, from what must've been the left, slid in and out. This guy, a stranger, was in tune with his needs. How did he know to touch him like that?

"Please—don't stop. You feel so good." He begged for the sensation to continue. It must. His body—and he realized, his mind—needed it. This was his prescription for happiness.

Blake forgot how non-hot the guy behind him was. *Who cares? Right?*

He started jacking himself off. *Come on.* The sound of his hand slapping his flesh was loud. *That's it.* Focused on how good this felt, he was going to come at any second.

Ernie sunk deeper into his ass.

"Yes."

There must've been at least four fingers in him, shattering his innocence apart.

"I'm going to come."

Ernie swatted Blake's hand away as he tugged, hard, on his cock.

Huh?

A gentle smack on his ass followed with a lick as if to say, *No, don't come. Not yet.*

"Keep going." He dropped his shoulders and held on to the table's edge, begging for more. His back pushed up higher, letting the tech go to town on his crack in a total ass-busting frenzy. *Cloud nine, here I come.*

From the fingering sensation, he felt a surging wetness and softness, which, to his best guess, came from a tongue.

Oh. My. God.

Rapture. He was being rimmed by a complete stranger.

"That's it. Right there. Uh-huh, yes. Yes. YES. Amazing." Blake stuttered as if having a form of Tourette's. "Get in there. Eat me." He'd never felt so sexy before. *This must be how Thor climaxed without touching himself.* It all made sense to him right then. Would he be able to come without stroking himself, too?

Quaked in arousal, he didn't care how hideous the spa tech was. He needed to see his face, buried in his hole. What a hot sight that would be.

Lifting his head from the bolster, Blake opened his moist eyes and glanced under his pelvis. Ernie's legs were all he could see. He tried to turn around.

Whap. Ernie smacked his ass—hard. He held him down by his backside, preventing him from examining the situation. His cock stood at rapid attention.

"Let me see you." The hot towel on the back of his head and neck fell as he turned.

With a grunt as if to say *no*, Ernie kept eating his ass and biting at his cheeks. The sugaring expert showed his masterful skills. He tapped him from behind, and Blake felt the lengthy tongue withdraw.

"Don't stop."

Wet licks to the inside left cheek blurred his ability to think clearly. Then came a long stroke to the right, followed by the tongue dancing clockwise around his pucker.

"Harder. Get your tongue in there."

A deep moan came from within, and then the tech plunged his tongue inside as if he was fucking him. Not that he'd know what getting fucked in the ass felt like, but he imagined the tongue thing was pretty darn close.

His hands held the edge of the table like he was taking off on some ride. He didn't know where to, but wherever they were headed was surely someplace new, and nowhere he'd ever been before.

Once the tongue plowed in, perhaps as far as it could humanly go, it turned and twisted and stimulated the nerve-endings in his body. He curled his toes. How cliché, right? But they, in fact, coiled tight as he arched his feet. *Don't get a Charley horse now. Please, no.*

The tongue stabbed him with determination. Then followed a spit, a lick to the left then to the right, and started all over again and again.

Blake cherished his newfound capitulation. The guy was a loud rimmer. *Oh, man, is this fucking hot.* He wanted to see the guy's face. Enough already.

He'd have to use his leg muscles to overturn himself and get free from Ernie's hold.

On three...*One. I can't believe I'm doing this.* He inhaled. *Two. I hope the guy won't be pissed. Three...*

He flipped over so fast the tech didn't have a chance in Hell to respond. Blake sat up in shock. "What the f..."

Upper East Side

Lex waited for a response. She needed to know what Birdie might've done differently as a parent, a question she imagined any new mom would ask. "You're sober now. I'm sure you've reflected over the past. Please, tell me." They'd never gone to counseling together, but she'd been tempted to make an appointment.

Birdie straightened a pillow on the bed, collecting her thoughts. "Like you...I wasn't married when I got pregnant. Eddie was already an established musician. He had a dozen albums out by then, had won countless Grammy's."

"And you?"

"Lucifer's Mistress was my first song to go big. Glam metal, which I largely invented, was a worldwide phenomenon. I was just getting started. I didn't want to be a one-hit wonder." Birdie pulled a string on the pillow. "Lex, honey, I fought so hard to get that spot. Then you came and everything...changed."

"Right, I ruined your life."

"No, you didn't." Her face reddened. "When a sex symbol has a baby, the fans' perceptions of her changes. People don't see you the same anymore."

"So—"

"I wasn't booked for parties. No more endorsement deals. As your mother, I should've evolved with my new role. Instead, I fought to hold on to the past, to the way I'd envisioned them." Her dark eyebrows drew up almost as one and she put her hand on her hip. "Sound familiar?"

Oh, brother. "I am not doing the same thing with Easton Essentials and my family as you did with your singing career and me. Nice reach, though."

Birdie's long, false eyelashes flittered as she cupped her hands under her chin and nodded. She didn't say anything. But in a way, she'd already said enough.

"You really believe I parent M2 the same…"

"What's the saying?" Birdie snapped her long fingers causing the diamond bangles to clang; the ones she never took off because they covered her track-mark scars from years past. "History repeats itself."

"I'm nothing like you."

"Really…is that so?"

"Mom, I don't do drugs."

"Thank the Lord & Taylor." Birdie rolled her eyes, matching her sarcastic tone.

"Massimo and I are monogamous, Mother. We don't swing or screw around like you and Daddy did."

"I get that, honey. But I'm talking about the time you spend with your family as a wife and mother. Not at work, being all fashion-designer-famous."

"Oh." Lex had worked so hard over the years to be nothing like her parents. She didn't factor in that while her folks partied their life away, they were indeed working. Or so they thought. She guessed it was no different than her hours spent in the showroom creating fashion. "Maybe I am…you…after all." She wasn't comfortable saying that.

"Honey, you don't have to be. Embrace being a mom. Learn from my mistakes so you don't repeat them."

"I do love being a mother to M2. I do."

"No, I mean be proud of it. Motherhood is the greatest gift you'll ever be given. More than designing a dress, getting some CFDA award, or having your line sold at Saks. There is nothing greater than being a mom."

She didn't know what to say. Sobriety had brought Birdie a sense of newfound wisdom.

"Promise me something, honey."

"Anything."

"That you will cut back on your schedule and play with your babies."

"I will."

"Have fun with your family."

Her cell phone chimed. The screen lit up, *Edwards*. She hit the speakerphone button and greeted, "Hi, Thor." She glanced at her mother who pulled out a stack of envelopes.

"Lex-love, I'm with Preston Bailey, your florist."

"And?" Awkwardly, she cleared her throat. Whenever Thor or Blake addressed her as 'Lex-love', she was in for an earful.

"We've got a *problemo*."

"What's wrong?" She flinched as her mother's hands went up in the air.

Flower fiascos could be any number of things. From hanging pomanders to the three hundred night-flowering cereus, which were scheduled to bloom during the cocktail hour. The room for errors was huge. The ballroom was one of the largest in the city.

"Our passionflower shipment, you know, the ones designed to go into the floating bowls at your red wine station, won't be here in time."

"How come?"

"Uruguay is having a drought, *girl*. Dried everything up."

"What have they offered as a backup?" She remembered the insurance they'd taken out from the florist, so Plan B was guaranteed.

"Cacti."

"Oh, dear." Birdie gasped as her expression grew serious.

"Can't beat Mother Nature, can we?" She tried to joke. A Santa Fe-style reception would certainly clash with the old-world luxuries of The Plaza.

"Let's go with the standard, white roses." Thor had suggested this from the start.

"Boring." She glanced up at her mother who encouraged her to agree. Earlier, Birdie also thought traditional flowers for The Plaza were best. Lex didn't see it their way. Or would she?

"Calla lilies?" Thor suggested.

"Too typical."

"*Miss Thang*, how about gardenias?" His voice became saucy.

"Yuk. I can't stand the sweet smell of them." As New York's most promising fashion designer, she didn't want any of the above. Style, décor, and uniqueness were her calling card. She couldn't have the usual. However, she was realizing why everyone always opted for the same.

They were easy to come by and reduced the onset of unnecessary headaches such as the one starting to dance at her temples.

"Honey," Birdie interrupted.

"Thor, one sec."

"Spend the day in bed sorting through the pictures. I'll get your driver to take me down to the florist. Thor and I will fix this. Don't worry."

A clanging noise came from out front in the foyer.

"*Bella*," Massimo whispered in his usual 'the baby is asleep' voice. "We...are...home."

"Thor, my mom is coming down to help. She'll see you in about twenty minutes." Lex said her pleasantries, thanked him, and then hung up.

"I'll be back in a few hours." Birdie reached for her purse then turned to look at the pile of boxes she left behind. "We need about five hundred more pictures."

"Noted." She had a long day ahead of her. Maybe one of the girls could come over and help.

"I'm glad we talked. I love you." She blew her a kiss.

"Love you, too, Mom."

Birdie walked toward the bedroom door as Massimo entered, and they hugged. He kissed her the European way, on both cheeks. Each of them talked softly for a minute. Lex couldn't hear what they were saying, but she could tell it was about her by the way they kept starting at her.

Massimo approached with his warm, perfect smile and black romantic eyes, which never failed to melt her heart.

He tucked the covers up over her. "M2 is asleep in the stroller. I'll take him out when he wakes up."

"Wheel M2 in here. I'll watch him." She tugged at the sheets to get up.

"No, *relassarti*." His big hand covered hers, tapping fingers as he told her to relax over and over again. "You need your rest." Massimo took her iPhone from her bed and slipped it into his front pocket. "No *distrazioni*. No stress."

"Masi..." She couldn't believe him. She wasn't sick.

"I'll make us lunch."

"I'm not hungry."

"*Sì*, you are eating and then resting."

He basked in the power he had over her. The glow on his face told her he enjoyed taking charge.

"Give me twenty minutes. I'll come with M2. We'll eat together."

"Yes, sir." She winked, knowing there was no arguing.

Lex admired his hot backside as he left. Not only was Massimo the sexiest man she'd ever met, he'd taken up cooking. It didn't get any better than Prince Tittoni. His efforts in the kitchen awarded him countless hours of lovemaking in the bedroom.

So much to do. She waited until she was certain he was in the kitchen. Her attention returned to the box labeled *Eddie.* She pulled out a stack of photos, along with an unfamiliar small, thin envelope in the folder addressed to her father. It was postmarked to their old penthouse at the San Remo on the Upper West Side. Dated a while back, Lex figured she'd been around thirteen when it was sent.

She opened the letter to read:
City DNA Labs
555 Park Avenue
New York, NY 10065

Alleged Father: Easton, Edward
Mother: Brillford, Irma
Child: Brillford, Tabitha
Alleged Father's Race: Caucasian
Mother's Race: Caucasian
Blood Rec'd: AF-05/02/96, M-05/02/96, C-5/02/96

Comments:
Mr. Eddie Easton is not excluded from being the father.

Probability of paternity remains uncertain due to a human error at our facility. The sample was contaminated and disposed. Please call to reschedule another test. We apologize for the inconvenience.

(Accredited for testing by the United Association of Blood Banks.)

An icy knot formed in Lex's stomach.

Was Taddy Brill, her best friend, also her sister?

"Daddy, what did you do?" she said aloud.

For a minute, she just sat there, floored, trying to make sense of the letter. It was dated the summer she and Taddy were sent off to boarding school. They'd left Manhattan, not returning until college.

Come to think of it, Taddy's parents had separated that very month. Birdie had overdosed, twice, shortly thereafter.

At that instant, her pulse soared. She needed answers.

Lex ignored what the doctors advised and got to her feet. One leg in front of the other, she ran down the long hallway toward the kitchen while clutching the paper in her hands.

"Masi." A faint thread of hysteria was heard in her own voice as she screamed, "Look at this!"

Chapter Seven

Miguel's Manscaping Talents

Midtown

"Mig!" *My best friend?* "It's you?"

Mixed emotions surged inside Blake. Bits of gauze and wax fell off his back as he tried to catch his breath. The air felt thin in the room, the walls coming closer. Miguel stood there, confident and somewhat calculated, as if this had been planned all along.

"*Papi*, it's me."

His friend wiped his swollen lips, his nose and cheeks reddened, probably from being buried in his ass. Eyes dilated, pupils eclipsed, a colossal bulge emerged from his jeans. Miguel's cock popped out from his denim waistline seemingly chanting, *Suck me. Suck me.*

"What the fuck, Miguel? Was it you the entire time?"

"*Sí.* I switched places with the tech when he went for your lotion." His confidence rocketed through the air. "Did you enjoy my rim job?"

Rim job? His question didn't quite register on Blake's dizzied senses. "Ummm, you sneaky fuck. Why are you doin' this?"

"I'm helping you complete your *Seven Desires*." Encouragement graced his handsome Latin face.

The thought tore through his insides. "You're kidding?" Blake was mortified, flat-out humiliated he'd read his wish list. "How did you get a copy of *that*?"

"Last night, Thor and Vive e-mailed it to me. I agreed with them that I'd be the one to help you."

The *Seven Desires* was a fantasy, a joke created to placate his friends to avoid the lecture about casual sex. He wasn't dumb or naïve; he knew his body needed it. But was his mind ready? Could he trust him? And if he *did* move forward with the list, should he tell him truth about why he divorced? He wasn't sure he could go there.

"You'd do my *Seven Desires* for me?"

"Would you rather have the guys Taddy was going to set you up with do it?" His face illustrated confidence.

"No." Blake didn't trust Nello or Gunter. He wasn't sure if he could trust Miguel, either. Hell, he thought he could trust Diego, and that didn't work out so well.

"That's what friends are for." He adjusted himself.

"Guess I should say thank you."

"Don't get all warm 'n' fuzzy. You're going to have to work for it."

"Huh? What do you mean?"

"I have my own list, too." His sexy smirk grew wide.

Blake held his breath for a second then asked, "You do?"

Ernie appeared at the door with an amused smirk. He handed Miguel a large bowl. Blake heard the water moving around inside as steam came up from the top. A disposable razor, shave cream, and a few small, Turkish hand towels were placed at their side. The electric clippers lay on a tray by the massage table.

"Lie back. Let me trim your pubes, and I'll tell you what mine are."

"You're going to shave my nuts?" Another wave of apprehension swept through him. Seconds before, Miguel's fingers, two, then what felt like four to be exact, were inside his ass. What would it hurt to have his nut sac in his grip?

"*Sí*. I do it for my fuck buddies. Don't worry, I know what I'm doing."

"Right." That's what Blake would become, number eight hundred or so in his numerous fuck buddy lineup. He detested the 'FB' term. It made sex a social club. He'd never been one for casual. Lord knew he topped every tight ass in Manhattan, Brooklyn, and Queens. His dominant top reputation made him notorious with all the subs. "Your *fuck buddies*. How could I have forgotten?"

"I hear contempt in your voice." He reached down and placed the shaver in the water. "Don't be so judgmental."

"Sorry." Blake resisted the urge to laugh. "But you know you're a man-whore." From the reaction in Miguel's eyes, he should've shut his mouth. Did his friend want something more for once in his life, other than a tight piece of ass?

"We can't all ride on our prudish and prejudiced morals. Or run off and marry the first and only guy we've ever banged."

Blake released the air stuck in his lungs in a loud gasp. No one really knew the half of it, except for Lex and Taddy.

Miguel grabbed the clippers from the tray and plugged them into an outlet under the massage bed. "I'm sorry. That was snarky of me."

"Accepted." Blake noted his remorse.

"Sorry your marriage didn't work out, too."

"Thank you." Unlike the Manhattanite gossipmongers, his real friends never asked what happened. They offered their condolences and kept him moving forward. Their concern was his happiness, not the semantics as to who did what to whom. Or who was right and who was wrong, which worked out well considering he hated to point the finger at his ex-husband.

"You wanted to make a home with Diego and live happily ever after."

"That I did. That I tried." His guard grew stronger and higher than before.

"Still judging me on my sex life after all these years, aren't you?"

"Nooo." Blake dragged the response in hopes it would show conviction. He was a horrible liar.

"I see it in your eyes. You don't know me very well."

Miguel pushed the switch, buzzing the clippers into motion. He held on to Blake's shaft, guiding the head down, and trimmed the pubic hair.

Fuck. He's touching me. It feels so good. "Of course I do," he tried to reply. He thought his friend was a pig—a sexy, hot pork bite. "We've been best friends for over a decade. You've probably smashed at least two thousand or so hearts by now."

"As I said, you don't know me very well. But you will…soon." He kept his dark eyes on Blake and groomed his pubes.

"What's that supposed to mean?" Christ, did Miguel have to stroke him so slowly? He'd never been as hard as he was right then.

Miguel shook his head. "I'll tell you later. Now, lie back and let me groom you."

"Whatever you desire." Blake chuckled and put his hands over his face. His mind raced with sexy thoughts. He imagined his dick inside him, but a warning siren went off in his head. *Don't get hurt, again. You don't have to do everything on the list. He might understand if you tell him.*

Fuck buddy. No harm. Sex only.

"You have a nice cock, Blake. I had no idea you'd be so thick."

Miguel's coarse hands from doing his artwork scraped the smooth skin of Blake's penis in an erotic way.

"Are you clipping my pubes or jacking me off?" *Please, dear God, jack me off already.*

"You aren't coming today, boy." He winked. "I'll make you earn your release." Trim completed, he turned the clippers off and covered Blake's crotch in a hot towel. "About your list—" The palm of his hands suddenly grabbed onto his cock hard and tight as if he owned it.

"Here we go."

"You should only do those activities with someone you care about and trust."

Was he scorning him? The Big Apple stud was preaching moral conduct? Impossible. But the grip he had on his cock told him otherwise.

"I appreciate your concern."

"Raw sex?" He didn't let it go.

I'm not bare backing. Blake rolled his eyes.

He reached for the shave cream, lacing Blake's nuts in white foam. The sensation brought his dick to the fullest attention.

His wet hands grabbed onto his shaft. "Look at what a grower you are. This cock is fat." Slowly, his fingers glided up then down. "Keep this erection. I'll shave your shaft." He cupped the scrotum in his left palm, gliding the razor with his right. "I don't want to cut you if your dick goes soft."

"Ahhh, it won't."

At contact, Blake's nuts cinched, pumping more excitement to his cock. His tender balls were cared for in Miguel's large, callused Latin hands.

"Mig…" He became more turned on. A part of him wanted to jump off the table. Another part of him wanted to orgasm.

"*Sí?*"

"Nothing." Blake bit the inside of his cheek and arched his feet. He refrained from squealing. Boy, he was so close.

Miguel took his time. "How's that feel?"

The blade glided slowly against his hard flesh.

Up. Down. Up. Down.

"I'll be hard for a month after this." Manscaping was erotic. No one had touched his cock in years. "And about the raw sex, I've never done *that*. Have you?" He wanted to, but with Diego he couldn't. Once a guy was infected, there was no taking it back. You were either positive or negative, no in-between.

"No." With the razor in his hand, Miguel swiped his shaft from bottom to top.

Blake eagle-eyed his best friend shaving his nuts; he'd never felt so stiff. The pressure of the scrape against his skin was intense. With each swipe and release showing freshly shaved skin, he felt, in a way, reborn. This was a new beginning, a fresh start.

"With your sexual conquests in the millions—" He heard his own exaggeration and laughed. He lowered his voice in all seriousness and continued, "I mean, with all the subs you've broken in, guys you've dated, slept with, group sex, and so on, you've never topped without protection?"

"Never. That's suicide," Miguel answered with staid calmness. Leaning closer, he went over his skin with great care.

His breath smacked Blake's cock. Did Miguel want to lick him clean?

"So, you haven't gone to any of those bare backing parties."

"What are you talking about?"

"Never mind." He didn't want to go into detail on the topic. He felt a bit of relief hearing he'd never gone, though. Diego made it sound as though everyone attended. "What are we going to do?"

"After we're done here, we'll get tested. You know, with the rapid-results swab at the walk-in clinic."

"Good idea." Blake's defenses began to subside. Knowing Miguel's status might make his casual sex pill easier to swallow, especially if he agreed to using condoms.

"And if we both come out clean, you'll cancel the dates Taddy got for you and we'll do your list."

"You know about that?"

"Yes. I don't want you going out with them, ever."

"I haven't been with anyone other than Diego in almost a decade. And what we did between the sheets the last few years wasn't anything to write home about." His psyche became zany, jumbled with hope and fear. "I haven't had much practice." He doubted whether he should've made such an admission, but he wanted his friend to know what he was getting into. He'd been told over and over again by his ex that he was a horrible lover.

Miguel didn't appear phased. "Noted." He put his hand on Blake's shoulder with reassuring confidence. "For the last six months, my sex partner has been Mr. Right Hand. Our STD results will be one hundred percent accurate, and let us know where we both stand."

"Yeah, but Mig, you have experience oceans-deep and wide. I don't."

"I'll coach you." Miguel shook the aerosol can from side to side then squirted a foamy, thick lather into his big hands. He jacked Blake up then down, up then down, intentionally building the erection so as not to cut him with the blade. "I have my own list you're going to carry out for me in return."

"Such as?" he asked, his voice rising in surprise. It was unimaginable what he'd be able to do for him. "A four-way? An S&M club? Drug exploration?"

Eyes rolling, he responded, "Nope. I've done it all, minus the drugs."

"What then?"

"You have your *Seven Desires*. I have my *Seven Needs.*"

"You do not."

"*Sí*, I do."

Upper East Side

Why were Taddy and Irma Brillford listed on a paper with her father? Lex couldn't make much sense of it. The only thing which stuck out to her was *probability of paternity.* Was Taddy, her lifelong friend of twenty-nine years, the girl she'd gone to boarding school with, a savior who'd helped her start her fashion business...also her half-sister?

Her fiancé sat at the kitchen table studying the paper.

"Masi, what do you think?"

"Appears your father attempted to have a paternity test." Massimo didn't seem as fazed by this as she was. If anything, he seemed annoyed, like this couldn't have happened at a more inconvenient time.

"I have to go downtown and talk to Mom." She pushed her chair out from the table. The legs squealed loudly against the floor.

M2 was awake in the stroller. His big brown eyes, the ones which had hints of green fading each day, grinned up at her.

"Hi, my baby." Lex pulled him out of his seat and into her arms. "There, there." She bounced him on her hip.

"Go back to bed. I'll handle this," Massimo said firmly as he reached for their son.

"I'll only be gone an hour. I'll take M2 with me." Anger was starting to fester inside her. She knew none of this was her fiancé's fault, but she didn't need him getting in her way. *Not today.*

"M2 stays here, with you and me. Birdie will stop by later. We'll talk then."

"Masi." She gasped. He did what she'd feared, overreacted to what the doctor said.

"Get back in bed."

"No."

"What about your blood pressure?"

"I'm fine."

"You're not going anywhere." The deep drawn brows and frown on Massimo's face worried her. She didn't want him to be concerned, but she felt fine.

"Please, Masi." She turned her back on him right when he was getting ready to speak. She'd never disrespected him like that before.

I'm sorry. She headed for their bedroom. At the dresser, she reached for a wrap dress with one hand while holding her son with the other. Looking down at her legs, she realized she hadn't shaved, so she grabbed a pair of jeans instead.

M2 started making those fussy noises, the kind which let her know he wasn't happy she was going somewhere. For only six months old, he was rather perceptive. Though she wanted to spend time with M2, she had to see Birdie. Lex couldn't ask her mother about this over the phone. Birdie would most likely hang up on her if she tried. Or avoid her 'til the wedding started. She didn't want that. The paternity test question had to be dealt with in person.

A thump came from behind her.

Startled, she turned around to see Massimo rummaging through their sex chest.

"What are you doing?"

"Looking for these." He held up a pair of twenty-four-karat gold handcuffs. They were from Tittoni's Gems of Distinction, his sister's nearby jewelry shop. A gift made for Lex for Valentine's Day.

"Oh, no you don't." She realized she couldn't take her son with her. He was hungry. "Feed M2 for me please. There's breast milk in the fridge. I won't be gone long."

Lex had to act fast. She gave her son a kiss on the forehead and placed him in the crib near their bed. The second she let him go, he started to cry.

I'm sorry, little guy. God, she hated to hear him cry. There was nothing worse than those tears. Except maybe finding out her father had kept a secret from her. She turned to run out the door.

"*Bella.*" Massimo stepped in front of her. "Don't disrespect me."

"We're not arguing. I'm leaving. You're staying here." She flirted with him, reached up to kiss him and wrap her arms around his broad shoulders. "I need answers," she whispered in his ear.

Taking her in his arms, he kissed her and lifted her up; her feet didn't touch the carpeting.

"No, Masi." Lex hated when he'd manhandle her around as some kind of puppet. "Put me down."

"*Sì.*" Massimo carried her over to the bed. "Light as a feather." He placed her gently on the mattress.

Lex sat up, inching her way off the bed, but Massimo playfully crawled on top of her. He sat on her legs.

"You're hurting me," she lied. Usually a little pain made her nipples ache with need.

"Never." His hand lightly came over her midsection. "We have another baby growing in here. You must not upset yourself."

"Too late. I'm more than upset. I'm livid. Now, let me go." Normally, she would've been turned on by his controlling ways, but right then, she needed to get downtown and see her mother.

"I will handle Birdie." Massimo grabbed her right hand with his left. He used his right to pull the handcuffs from his back pocket and latch them around her wrist with one loud clink.

"This isn't funny. Don't—"

"Listen to me and listen well."

He tried to cuff her other wrist by grabbing onto it, but she was too quick.

"Lex. Stay still." He tried again and cuffed her left hand, looping it through the headboard with rope. The rope was also from their sex chest, but it wasn't from some fancy jewelry store. He'd purchased it at Home Depot; he loved tying her up. Only that time, they wouldn't make love.

"You are to stay in this bed 'til tomorrow. No stress. No family drama. Just you and some rest." He lifted himself off her, smiled as if proud of his capture, and got to his feet.

"Come on…"

"No."

"If you don't untie me right this instant I'm going to…take M2 and go live in California." Lex couldn't think of anything. Her man wasn't threatened easily.

"Oh, yeah, with who? All of your friends are here with us."

She screamed in frustration. "Masi, I swear to God."

M2 started to cry.

"Don't cry, baby. Mommy's okay. Daddy and I are just playing a game," Lex said in her baby-talk voice, all the while giving her fiancé the evil eye. Unbelievable that he'd done this. "What if I have to go to the bathroom?"

"I'll bring you a bedpan."

The way he spoke to her, she knew he was serious.

"Birdie will only be hurt by whatever comes out of your sharp mouth."

Damn him. He was right. He was always fucking right. It wasn't her intention to hurt her mother's feelings, but sometimes it just happened. The more Birdie had sobered up, the more sensitive she'd become.

"I need to know."

"You knew your father and Irma had an affair, *si?*" Massimo went over to the crib, putting his hand down for M2 to hold. It took both of his little hands around just one of Massimo's fingers.

"No."

"Lex...."

"We knew my dad screwed around. We knew Taddy's mother did, too. We never figured it was together. At least, I didn't."

"Why not?"

"Have you met Mrs. Brillford?"

She had last seen Countess Irma when they were teenagers. It was during Taddy's emancipation trial at the courthouse. Irma was the wife of Joseph Graf, part of the Brillford elite who'd emigrated from Austria at the turn of the century. The woman was stuck up and wasn't anything like what her father had screwed around with in the past.

"You never questioned why Mr. Brillford abandoned her?"

"I knew he wasn't her father, we all did. But I never figured it was *my* dad."

For the first time in their relationship, he looked at her as though she were naive. That hurt her feelings.

"It's true, Masi. How could I? Who the hell would think such a thing about their own father?"

"The test was inconclusive. The blood sample was contaminated." He scooped up M2 as if he was going to leave the room.

She'd be stuck on the bed, alone. She laid there, handcuffed. What the fuck could she do?

"This isn't about you. And it's not about Birdie, either."

"Of course it is. How could Mom keep this from me?" She thought the pain from her past, the hell of her childhood was over. She'd buried it when she put her dad to rest in the Queens cemetery.

"Birdie, I'm sure, has good reason." He came over and caressed her cheek as he leaned over her. "You don't get it, do you?"

Massimo's stature intimidated her. But holding her son added a sweetness to him that she adored. "No. What?"

"This is about Taddy," Massimo said softly.

M2 squirmed in his arms, whining. Massimo lowered him down to Lex's level. "Kiss him *ciao*. His *madre* needs her nap."

Lex touched her lips to his as she thought about her BFF. She didn't want to hurt Taddy. Her life had been the hardest out of everyone's. The cry which burned in the back of her throat for the last hour finally broke.

"When will you talk to her about this?" Massimo seemed to soften up a bit when he noticed she was crying.

"I don't know. Tonight. Tomorrow. After the wedding? I wish Warner was in town." Warner was Taddy's globetrotting billionaire boyfriend and her rock.

"He's still in Paris?"

"Yes, for the week." Lex didn't want to dump this on her best friend without Warner being there. She was tempted to call him, but knew that would be breaking all friend codes. There wasn't any easy way around this.

"I'll call Birdie and tell her to come back uptown."

"Please, let me call Vive before my mom gets here."

"Why?"

"I need to ask her if Taddy has ever mentioned anything to her." She was her only hope. That wasn't breaking friend code. Vive was hers just as much as Taddy's. "She'd be the only friend who would know."

"*Sì*, you got it. They both can come over. You three can talk."

"Uncuff me."

"No." Massimo closed the door. "*Bella*, rest!" he shouted from the hallway.

Chapter Eight

Miguel's Seven Needs

Lower East Side

You have a list, too…

Terrified Miguel would push him to the brink, Blake didn't know what to say. He was going to back out of this, for sure. His friend remained a man-eating player by most standards, including New York's. But Blake was indeed curious as to what his list could be. He'd entertain this, at least for the day.

"Okay, let's hear 'em." Lying down, he blinked his eyes shut, feeling the shave of his scrotum. The pit in his stomach sunk deeper.

"*Número uno*, you'll move in with me while we do this list together."

"You want me to live with you in the Lower East Side?" He didn't expect to hear such a demand. Shit, the hipster area was absurd.

"*Sí.*" Miguel glanced down sternly.

"Why can't you live with me in Chelsea?" His hands flailed midair. "You'll have the guest wing all to yourself." Though, it would be nice to get away from those bad memories. No matter how many coats of paint he put on the walls, or new furniture he bought, his penthouse still haunted him with bad dreams from the past.

"Cool it." Miguel reached for him, placing his hands palm down on his heaving chest. "You know I work from home. Moving to your penthouse with my art supplies isn't going to happen."

The disagreement, which was ready to that boil over, expelled on a loud sigh. "Okay, fine." He realized it might be nice to stay someplace else. Maybe he'd finally get a good night's sleep.

"My driver will take you to work."

"Good. I'm not riding that subway." Going underground wasn't a consideration. He hated mass transit. He hated mass anything.

"Plus, I don't want to *siesta* in your guest room. We're going to share a bed, night after night. That's *número dos.*" Miguel seemed to study him, giving him a once-over in his usual suave manner.

How sweet. "Do you snore?"

"I'm a quiet sleeper." His large, almond-shaped eyes shot up studying Blake's face. "But the first night you'll only sleep in my arms. We won't have sex."

"Sounds easy enough…" He was all too familiar with sleeping next to someone and not having them touch him. "No problem." Though, if he was being honest with himself, he did for a split horny second think about burying his face in his friend's crotch. Yes, getting face-fucked was on the *Seven Desires.*

He tried to envision tasting Miguel. Would he be spicy? Hot tamales and cinnamon candy perhaps? Or would he be saccharine and creamy? A flan, sweet, lapped up as dessert.

"*Número tres*, I have to babysit my two nieces Cierra and Ofelia tomorrow along with M2. You're going to help me with them."

There went his free Sunday leisure—Barneys with Taddy, mimosas with Vive, and reading over the *New York Times* with Thor. He didn't have much experience with kids, though he'd always wanted a family. "Okay, we'll take them shopping—The American Girl store or FAO Swartz. This'll be fun."

"No." Miguel bowed his head. "Inez, my sister, won't approve. The girls are not into Barbie, Disney's Princesses, or anything pink."

"Snow White or Cinderella?" he asked in confusion.

"Afraid not."

"That's silly. What about the new ethnic protagonists?" Blake noticed Miguel's full lips purse together in confusion as if he didn't follow, so he added, "Jasmine or Pocahontas?"

"Mr. Morgan, no princesses."

"Inez is one of *those* types of mothers?" He'd heard of them; they lived near Lex on the Upper East Side and sent their kids to The Spence School.

"*Sí*. We'll have to do arts and crafts. Maybe take them to the science museum after we go to church."

"Church? Oh, for Christ's sake." He didn't care for the sound of that, either. God hadn't answered his prayers in recent years no matter how hard he'd tried. No one had helped him at his darkest hour. "Number four?"

"You'll clean my apartment, cook our meals, and do the laundry." Miguel lifted his nuts and gave him one final swipe with the blade. His feet arched in a pleasant response.

"That should count for three things, not one." His mind jumped to calling a cleaning service, ordering Thai food for delivery, and sending the laundry out to be done. The Lower East Side should have those accommodations, right? Blake was many things—a marketing executive, a good friend to many, a great son—but domestic wasn't one of them.

"It's all under household chores. Your rim job checklist should be accompanied with fisting. Your domination is combined with being tied up. Those are two for one."

"That was Thor and Vive's doing. All of this is." He couldn't believe he was going along with it. "You won't be fisting me any time soon, okay?"

"*Sí*, I will. We'll be getting to it"—Miguel held up his hand, large and surely capable of a basketball slam—"right before I top the shit of out of you," he finished with an uncompromising intonation.

Jesus. He about came in his ears hearing Miguel's determination. But it also terrified him. Was it all talk, or could his friend do this for him? "Number five?"

"You're to walk and feed Brutus, my pooch, in the morning and at night." One final swipe then Miguel tossed the razor into the steel bowl. He grabbed a towel and wiped him down.

Blood pounded in his ear as he touched the scar on his face. The mark always tensed up whenever he was stressed. Hearing he'd be taking care of Brutus terrified him.

Scarred in a plane crash the summer after graduating from Avon Porter, it took two cosmetic surgeons eight hours to reconstruct Blake's face. He never recovered on an emotional level. The traumatic ordeal caused him to flinch, tense up, and vacate areas where his face would be under bright lights.

Though he'd been told time and time again his features were perfect, so much so that Ford Models recruited him in college as a catalog model, he never got over the accident. How could he?

"Your dog terrifies me. Brutus is no *pooch*." He heard his own voice become thick and unsteady. He inhaled and argued, "*It's* a pit bull rescued from some Long Island fighting farm, bred to eat little kids."

Before attending Avon Porter he'd been attacked by a pack of dogs. His classmates had sicced them on him as a lesson to stay in the closet.

"I remember your trepidation about my dog." He leaned into Blake's face and stroked the hair away from his eyes. "I remember everything about you. And don't call my Bru an *it*."

His thigh stung from the sudden swat his friend gave him as punishment. Why was that suddenly turning him on?

"Let's put *Brutus* in doggie day care while I live with you. You know, that place on Park and Sixty-something, where Vive puts Hedda when she travels. " He smiled, trying to sell it, and suggested, "Your dog can get a massage and take obedience classes."

Miguel frowned. He leaned his face directly over his. An intimidation tactic, no less, but it worked. Blake tried to giggle but couldn't. All he could do was smell the spearmint coming off those juicy lips.

"Brutus lives with us."

"I'll pay for it."

"He is *mi bebé*. You'll feed him, walk him, and love him—as I do."

Impossible. "What if he bites me?" Blake's fingers trembled over his face. He realized he'd be walking on eggshells the entire week and his face would freeze up, making him look weird. The scar wasn't visible to most. But he sensed the area where the Air Carribea shrapnel had torn at his skin as if it were yesterday. His pointer finger ran up and down the thin line where the doctors cut and stitched. If he pressed hard enough, the scar tissue underneath felt hard. Often in February, when outside temperatures dropped, his face's right side would tighten. Migraines followed.

I can't do this.

"He won't hurt you. I would never let anything bad happen to you—ever."

Somehow, Miguel's words mended his shot nerves. A reassurance he'd never heard from his friend. He sensed his Latino spoke about more than just Brutus. Blake got the sense that he really cared about him. A part of him wished he'd let his friend in on what went down when he was married. *Maybe I wouldn't be in the mess I am now.*

"But I've never fed a dog let alone walked one."

"I'll help you the first day. After which he'll be your responsibility until we're done with our lists." He reached for his hand and encouraged, "Hanging with Bru is the best way to conquer your fear. You've been afraid of dogs for as long as I've known you."

Bru shmu. "How many days do you think we're going to live together?"

"One week."

"Seven days with a pit bull." *Fuck. You better be worth this Hell.* Could his *Seven Needs* get any worse? What was next, retiling the bathroom? "And number six?"

"I want you to go as my date to Lex's wedding."

He exhaled a reprieved sigh. *At last something easy.* "Sure, we're all going together in the limo. We're in the wedding party together. You, me, Vive, and Thor. We'll get dressed at Vive's. She's hosting a pre-cocktail mixer to get us all loaded." He laughed nervously as he still didn't want to be in the wedding. He didn't think Vive did, either.

"We're *not* going with the usual group," Miguel ordered.

"Why not?"

"It'll be you and *me*, as a couple." There was a maddening, arrogant gist to his tone, one which Blake had never heard from his friend before.

A tingle sparked his stomach. "Okay." *Since when did he become so possessive?*

"Get dressed. We're done," Miguel bossed in a tone which suggested he'd enjoyed himself. He laughed, probably because he'd gotten away with it, then dried his hands and threw the wet rags onto the countertop.

"Right. This was incredible." Lightheaded from the experience, Blake sat on the table's edge sensing Miguel's gaze was *still* on him. He slipped on his Burberry briefs and looked up to confirm his suspicion. "Stop looking at me like that."

His best friend's attention focused on his body. Embarrassed for wearing designer underwear, the most expensive money could buy, he figured Miguel was a 2xist or Jockey wearer. With his mocha-fucker cock, he probably wore boxers affording his girth room to breathe.

He continued with his slacks, buttoned his shirt, and slid his feet into his favorite Ferragamo loafers.

"I'll look at you however I want. Got it?"

"Ah-huh." He loved it. There was a part of him which was ready for this, a part which wouldn't think about the past and go solely on instinct and embrace this. A man, one who was dominating, in charge, an alpha, a top, the pig who would do whatever he wanted to him. But the other part, the practical, slightly jaded, very hurt part of him, said no.

"You have some dried wax in your hair. Let me." Miguel ran his hands through Blake's hair.

"Thanks." He smiled, turned to face him, and realized his friend really did care.

The dark eyes stared at him as if he had something else he wanted to say. Something he had to get off his chest. "What?"

"And now for *número siete...*"

Blake gave him his full attention. "Yes?"

Miguel vacillated as the ceiling fan above them kept the seconds passing with a repetitive swoosh. "My parents will be in town this week from DC, staying at their apartment uptown. I want you to come with me to dinner." His chest rose and he blurted, "To meet my family."

"Sure, I love your sister. I've always wanted to meet your folks." He couldn't remember why Miguel never brought his parents into their circle. Lex's mom was active with the group, so was Vive's. But Blake remembered, with good reason, why he didn't pry. His father worked as a Mexican diplomat who retired from a post in Washington, D.C.

"You don't understand." His developed arms crossed over his broad chest. "When you come home with me, I'll come *out* to them." A whisper broke from his tense, full lips. "It's time to tell them I'm gay."

Catching air in his throat, he nearly coughed but swallowed instead, remembering his friend wasn't out. He always forgot. Miguel was so at ease being gay with his friends. Closeted to him was unimaginable.

"I'm honored." Stepping forward, he pulled him into an unyielding squeeze. He'd do this. He wouldn't back out. His friend was serious and he wanted to help him come out. Possibly, when all this was over, he'd be able to trust Miguel enough to tell him what was really going on. The truth.

Over the years, he'd observed his friends' stress. Their throats sore at times, ulcers in their stomachs, and constant unease—all from being in the closet. Miguel was no exception.

"I'll be with you through each step," He vowed his support as he then reared his head, suddenly Miguel's lips locked with his into one passionate kiss.

Exciting him all the more, Miguel pushed him against the table. His friend's actions may have been plain old-fashioned lust, but someone sought him, in the flesh. Not for his monetary assets, but for his ass. "I want my tongue inside your hot mouth."

He wrapped his right leg around his friend's tight waist. The warm friendship blanketed them, making him feel desired. He'd never been kissed by anyone but his ex-husband before. This felt different. Real. Mutual.

His buddy tilted his head to the side. Bit by bit, Miguel gazed down over his forehead and finally rested upon his eyes, almost speaking intently, as if saying, *I'm going to give you the passion you've always wanted. I'll fill your need.*

Miguel brought his tongue to a long-stroked lick over Blake's bottom lip before plunging into his mouth, deep and hard with a grunting moan.

Breathless as a teenager kissed for the first time, his cock stiffened all over again.

"You're going to be my *niño* this week," he muttered in a thick accent. "All mine."

Relishing in the forceful kiss, exhilarated in agreement, he forgot the Hell and nightmare he'd been living in and answered, "Yes, I'll be your *boy* this week." Blake wondered how he'd ever be able to walk away from him once the lists were completed. Would they be able to go back to being best friends? More importantly, if he told Miguel the truth, could he keep it a secret?

Chelsea

At the clinic where they both tested for HIV, Miguel seized Blake's right hand, terrified into a sweat as if he'd finished the New York marathon. His tricks and fuck-fests flashed through his memory at warp speed.

If we're okay, I promise, Blake will be my last sexual partner. Please, let us turn out okay.

The Gay Men's Health Center physician assured them not to worry as both oral swabs came back negative.

Muchas gracias, we're clean.

On the way to pick up Blake's things for the week, he insisted they stop off at a sex shop called The Pleasure Chest in the West Village. He purchased a Manuel Ferrara Realistic Dong and a famous straight porn star's prosthetic penis. Blake asked the clerk for silicone oil lube, edible body chocolate, a butt plug, anal beads, and nipple clamps. The list came via text earlier by Thor.

Giving in to his amusement for his new submissive, he let Blake buy the toys, but Miguel's cock warranted assurance no man in his presence required toys of any kind.

They went to Blake's Chelsea apartment, and he helped him pack up his work and casual clothes, shoes, and grooming supplies required for the week ahead.

Always in awe over the space, he appreciated Château Morgan. A three-thousand-square-foot, full-floor Manhattan penthouse with top-of-the line finishes, adorned with marble floors and large-scale oil canvas paintings on the walls. The eighteenth-century antiques and four sweeping balconies provided panoramic Hudson River views. Obviously, Blake came from money, but he was never smug about it. Miguel found his many qualities endearing.

Sure, he could've loaded up his art supplies and spent the week there, but his goal was to make his blonde friend squirm. Having him at his mercy for seven days, on *his* terms, removed from his lavish comforts and being in his bed was his ultimate fantasy.

After all, his objective was to break him in, if it was the last thing he'd do.

I'll make Mr. Morgan mine once and for all.

He'd heard Blake's cry earlier that day at the spa when he'd touched him. His instinct was to stop the manscaping, turn him over, and hug. Nevertheless, his bud's body spoke to him and told him to keep going, and so he did. Blake worked through whatever pain he was feeling as Miguel fingered his tight ass. He understood this was only the beginning. They were on a long, erotic journey together. He wondered what MLD had done to him. It became obvious Blake hadn't been touched in a physical, emotional, or intimate way in years. But why?

Blake's walls were up in full fortress mode. Maybe they shouldn't be shopping for sex toys. No, Miguel figured he'd need a jackhammer to get his friend's walls down.

They took his limo to his Bowery and Bleecker Street loft. Blake had brought four oversized, Louis Vuitton monogrammed suitcases with two garment bags.

"Did you have to pack so much?" he griped as they climbed up the narrow stairs to his fifth-floor loft. The pre-war building was inspiring for him to work in, but sometimes unpractical.

"I forgot your building doesn't have an elevator." By the time they reached his floor, Blake looked breathless. "I…hope…" Unable to speak, he paused, inhaled, and continued, "You bought this at a good price…with this setup." He coughed. "Now I know why you have such nice legs…and a football player's ass. It's…these fucking stairs."

Flattered, he hadn't didn't realized Blake had noticed his legs, let alone his ass or any other part of his body. He unlocked the dead bolt and opened the door, stepping inside. His guest followed behind him. Turning back, he witnessed his apparent revulsion.

The apartment was one immense open space, maybe two thousand square feet. There was a mattress on the floor near one window, sink and counter space against one wall with a stand-up shower, and a toilet in a water closet.

Miguel's easels stacked with his canvas artwork were scattered all over. Maybe this wasn't such a good idea.

A strained smirk crossed Blake's model-like features, oblivious to Miguel. "This'll be fun. Either we'll fuck our brains out or kill one another. Where should I hang my clothes?"

He pointed to the closet. From the opposite side of the loft, Brutus ran up to him. *Sniff. Sniff.* Then he barked.

"Hey there, fella. We have a visitor with us this week."

The smoky-ash-colored pup turned and faced Blake.

Frozen, his gorgeous eyes glassed over in fear. This was a new, freaked-out level for his friend.

"Pet Bru," he ordered, hoping Blake wouldn't cry. Was pushing him to do this wrong? The last thing he wanted was to be a dog owner who forced his pet on someone who didn't care for him. But Brutus was his confidant. He *must* love him, too.

Terror, stark and vivid, glittered in his baby blues. "I—I can't." Blake's hands balled into fists. "Please, Miguel. Don't make me." Sweat beaded on his forehead.

"Vive has a dog and it doesn't bother you." He made his jealousy obvious. He hated when his friends played favorites. They partied at Taddy's penthouse, worshipped Lex's man, and cooed over Vive's dog. His Latino pride couldn't help but get envious.

"Hedda Hopper is a ten-pound, sixteen-year-old cashmere pillow. Poor girl is deaf, blind, and toothless. She drinks Perrier from a Waterford bowl and naps eighteen hours a day." Blake pointed at Brutus and declared, "There's a big difference."

A soothing proposal came to mind. Miguel went into the kitchen, pulling the junk drawer open. Buried under his paintbrushes and notepads was a nylon muzzle. "I've never put this guard on his snout. It's cruel, no?"

"I suppose." Blake crossed his arms, hiding his apparent tremble.

"The building's super made me buy the mouth guard when I adopted Brutus. Mrs. Garfieldo on the third floor almost experienced an aneurism over a pit in the building." He knelt down facing Brutus and apologized, "I'm sorry, boy. It's temporary."

Brutus sat on his hind legs, stifled a low howl, and lowered his ears as he snapped the shield around his mouth.

"I'll keep this on him 'til you're comfortable. *You* are going to have to make an effort."

"Thanks." The fear was replaced with gratitude.

"Lean down, extend your hand, and let Bru sniff you."

As instructed, he placed his agile hand down and opened his palm.

Wagging an excited tail, Brutus nudged his snout against Blake's arm, his way of saying, *Hello.* The dog made a licking sound through his muzzle.

His iced-up exterior, which no more than a bonfire could warm, softened. An affectionate glow cast over his symmetrical features. His broad forehead furrowed. A smile, Miguel hadn't seen on his friend's face in a very long time, dawned.

"Bru wants to be your friend."

He jerked his hand back in denial. A loud bark erupted in response through the guard.

"The dog assumes I'm Kibbles 'n Bits." His chiseled jaw muscles set.

"Address him by his name and not *the dog*."

"Have you fed him?"

"Yes, Brutus wants to go outside. Do you want me to walk with you?"

"Thanks for asking, but I'll manage," Blake said full of pride. "What if Brutus…shits?"

"Pick it up."

"Do you have a pooper scooper?"

Realizing it would offend him, Miguel tried not to laugh at his question. "No, I use disposable waste bags."

"*Baggies*? So I have to touch his…*shit* with my hands? My skin and his crap separated only by a thin plastic layer?"

"*Sí.*" From the table, he threw him the leash and the plastic roll. "Have fun, and don't get any on ya."

"Not funny, Mig."

"Here are your keys." He tossed him the spare. The keychain, a plastic square an inch and a half around, read '*I* ❤ *N Y*'.

He'd never shared his keys to the apartment with anyone. Ever.

"Thank you." Blake slipped them into his front pocket.

"When you return, you may start to tidy up this place and make us something to eat. I'm starved." Looking around, he noticed the dirty cereal bowl in the sink and the previous day's boxers on the floor. He was embarrassed with how he'd left his apartment that morning, but figured the sooner Blake started his domestic duties, the better.

He exhaled an irritated moan. "Oh, you're pushin' it, aren't you?"

"Hey, if I'm gonna rim you again *esta noche*, you'd better earn it. You haven't shot your load yet today, have you?"

That shut him up quick. He leashed Brutus's collar and headed downstairs.

Watching with admiration, Miguel realized his friend was awkward when it came to doing anything which didn't revolve around himself. *He'll learn who comes first soon enough.*

Avery Aster

Chapter Nine

Betty Crocker

Lower East Side

His friend had bought his loft years before, yet he'd visited him only once. Miguel never hosted or entertained. *Now I knew why.* The space was as homey as a block of ice.

How will I survive a whole week in this hellhole?

Wasn't he loaded? His art showings made fortunes. Blake was dumbfounded as to why he never did anything to make it more of a home. Such a bachelor.

Brutus led him to what he assumed was the dog's favorite oak tree to piss, the preferred wilted grass to shit, and his most wanted dirt mound to dig.

The dog was a cakewalk. *He* walked Blake. Typical, that a top such as Miguel would own a Dom-ish dog.

Optimistic he'd turn the art warehouse into a home, he called Merry Maids upon returning to the apartment. He'd given his own housekeeper the week off and didn't feel right about asking him to forgo his impromptu vacation and come back to work, so he scheduled a housekeeper to clean.

Miguel, unfortunately, overheard the conversation and made him call Merry Maids back and cancel the appointment. "You're going to clean this apartment without anyone's help," he said critically.

He didn't argue but rather mumbled, "Okay." The apartment was too big for him to clean by himself.

"You're going to cook us dinner, not order to-go food." He pelted the order without patience.

Blake nodded in agreement, realizing he'd underestimated him. "Yes, sir," he voiced in a submissive tone, oddly getting turned on by being told what to do.

"And you'll do the laundry, not send it out."

"Where's the laundry room?" Turning around, he searched for a washer and dryer.

"In the basement."

The very way Miguel stood, in command, revealed he'd thought out the fantasy all right. It was Butler Morgan III at his service.

"No banging your Levi's against the rocks in the Hudson River then, I take it?" He glanced down at Miguel's crotch. Unsurprised to see it swelling through his pants, he confirmed, "You love being Mister Boss Man."

"Don't be fresh." He pulled down his upper lip as if fighting the urge to reveal his trademark, attention-getting smile.

Did Miguel find this funny? Was he as turned on as Blake was?

Nevertheless, he was busted. *Fuck.* Traipsing up and down those stairs with Miguel's dirty clothes over and over again would become unbearable. "I won't have time to get to your laundry 'til tomorrow."

"We have my nieces and M2 all day tomorrow, remember?"

"Right." *Mr. Mom, here I come.*

"You'll have to do it tonight." His sexy Mexican lips curled up into a smile. "Let me help you."

"I'll manage." He sighed, wishing he could send it out as everyone else in town did.

"We'll do it together. Okay?"

"I'd like that." Blake couldn't help but grin. They'd always gotten along as friends. There was no reason to start arguing just because they were living together that week. Who knew, maybe all this housework would give him a juicy ass, too. "Do you mind if I call my mom?"

"Mrs. Morgan is *not* coming over to help you."

"No, certainly not. She'd be appalled at how you've decorated the place." He grimaced and continued, "I need to ask her for some recipes." And a prayer he'd get through the week without flipping his shit on Miguel's demands.

"Recipes for what?" His eyes studied him in an adorable way.

"A home-cooked meal isn't something I've ever prepared. Mom will walk me through what to make." He admitted, "I don't cook. I may have relationship experience, but my marriage didn't domesticate me in the least." He remained modest, but couldn't figure out why Miguel didn't have meals delivered or his own chef. Was this his *Seven Needs* game? He'd go along with it until his friend came out to his parents. That's all he really cared about, having his friend be true to who he was about his sexual orientation. But was Blake being true to who *he* was? Not at all.

"Okay, call her." He chuckled and then mumbled a few words in Spanish.

"Don't laugh at me. I don't see the *Joy of Cooking* or Betty Crocker's latest laying around *your* loft." He did, however, notice the *Jock XXL* magazines, graphic novels, and porn DVDs stacked on his bookshelf. "I could research suggestions online, but Mom's recipes are scrumptious." He was also afraid he'd find Miguel's cyber buddies lurking. Blake didn't want to know if his friend met guys online, and if so, what that routine entailed if he had one.

"Sure, tell your parents I said *hola*."

He'd tell them. His parents worshiped Miguel. After all, according to *Manhattanite* Magazine, he ranked as a top gallery attraction. With his exhibits scheduled during the year in Barcelona, Toronto, and Los Angeles, the Morgan's acquired his abstract works for their homes in Palm Beach and Sedona. Room after room at his parents was decorated in his artwork. Lex, Taddy, and Vive also decorated in Santana...so why his loft was so bare remained a mystery.

The second he hit the sidewalk to get groceries, he smelled downtown's piss, spiced street meat, and vomit. He knew one person might sympathize with him—his gal pal who wouldn't be caught below 42nd Street. He pulled out his iPhone and called Vive.

"Bottom boy," she answered on the third ring.

He laughed at his new nickname and asked, "Gossip Queen, have you been to Miguel's loft?"

"Nope. Lex goes over to the Lower East Side all the time. She and Miguel work out together. She mentioned his place is…sparse."

Blake gave her the *Seven Desires* to *Seven Needs* update. "Can you imagine?"

"Gorgeous, you've met your matchie-poo. Thor and I knew he'd be a challenge for you, but in a good way. A hung, Mexican, 'throw you over his knee and split your ass open' kinda way." Vive made a gulping noise over the phone.

"Getting fucked is so much work." He paused, realizing she sounded tipsy, and asked, "What are you doing?"

"While you're making mystery meat buffet for your *new* man, I'm having myself France's carbonated finest from a bottle. My meal is ready after I uncork, no cooking required."

"Booze is your dinner?" He remembered their talk earlier at the spa. What would it take to get her to quit drinking?

"Champagne puts about seven hundred calories in me. I can't afford to be my usual editorial self and have food to boot." She burped. "*Excusez-moi.* Listen, back to your Latin cock. Miguel is worth every ounce of blood, sweat, and tears you're going to shed this week. Mr. Santana is the most wonderful man I've ever met. And I know you agree." Vive sipped loudly then came a break on the line.

"Hello? You there?" He thought she'd hung up or the line had dropped. The cell provider had bad service on the Lower East Side.

"I'm here. That was Lex beeping in. She's called me a million times today. I'm ignoring her."

"Why?"

"After our spa treatments, I went to Easton's showroom and picked up my bridesmaid's dress."

Hearing about the wedding made him stop and stand still for a minute. "Are the gowns that hideous?' He couldn't help but think of that movie where the girls started having accidents after being food poisoned. They couldn't get out of the dresses fast enough.

"No, they are lovely. Jemma created them in Milan. I look ravishing in mine."

"Then what's the problem?"

"I'm too old to be a maid. Wedding parties are for kids. Who does this shit anymore?"

"My sentiments exactly."

"You mean, you don't want to be in the wedding either?"

"At this phase in our lives, who wants to be in a wedding?" Blake felt horrible for his comment the second it came out of his mouth. But it was how he felt.

"Did you get your tux?"

"Yes, and Vive, like it or not, we must do whatever Lex wants. This is her week." He tried to redeem himself from the previous remark. Vive had a big mouth—fuck, she was a gossip columnist. If Lex knew how Blake felt, she'd die. He was genuinely happy for her and Massimo to be getting married. Did it have to happen the week his divorce papers went through? No. But this wasn't his wedding.

"Agreed. Hence why I'm avoiding her call. I don't want to hurt her feelings. You know how insensitive I am." Vive laughed. She was good at ripping on herself, but she was right. "Enough of that. Let's get back to your hunk. I love Miguel for you."

"He is a great guy." Blake didn't believe otherwise. But he remained complex, a brute, and at times a challenge. Miguel treated Vive, Taddy, and Lex as ladies, but he felt as if Miguel resented him. He couldn't figure out why his friend always gave him a hard time, more so than even he gave Thor. And everyone gave Thor a hard time.

"I need your help." He elaborated on his chores and requested some advice on cleaning supplies. "Seeing as Taddy has a live-in maid and you are my only friend who does her own laundry. I'm lost."

"Suck my tits, bottom-boy. Though a maid is in my budget, I don't want one. I don't have the energy to hide my paraphernalia when they come over. This is my excuse as to why I never bring cock home, either." She snorted. True, Vive had more money than all of them put together; after all, she was the heiress to the Farnworth Firewater liquor company. Yet, for whatever reason, he'd never known her to have a housekeeper.

"I don't understand."

"Taddy spends about two hours a week hiding her sex toys from her butler. What am I going to do with my bong? No time for bullshit." Vive paused and the phone line crackled again. "Damn. Lex is calling in again."

"Do *not* tell her what I said, please. Just pretend we never talked."

"I won't. I better take this. It's not like her to keeping calling."

"One day of bed-rest has probably made her crazy. That girl can't sit still for more than a second."

"True, Miss Easton needs to learn the art of leisure." She laughed. "Give Miguel a big wet kiss for me."

"I will. Tell Lex I'll see her tomorrow when we pick up M2 for babysitting."

"Will do. Bye, gorgeous." Vive clicked over.

When he turned the corner, a large sign read, "*If It's Goya It's Good.*" Inside, he purchased veggies, fruit, and various meat selections. He included Formula 409 to wipe down the kitchen, Clorox to disinfect the bathroom, along with a mop and scrubbing sponges. Also, faux silk curtains in gunmetal gray, which he hoped might add some sophistication, and matching new bed sheets. They weren't to his liking, but it wasn't as if there was a Barney's nearby. He also picked up some potted houseplants and tipped the bagger at the store twenty bucks to help him bring the items home and walk them up the stairs.

"Blake, *mira acá*. You've gotta be joking." Miguel shook his head.

"You didn't expect me to carry nine bags up those stairs by myself did you?"

"No, but I didn't ask you to buy the kitchen sink."

"You needed it." He placed the clear plastic bags on the counter and felt Miguel's stare upon him. This was simply the beginning. His shopaholic talents forecasted new pillows, a shower curtain, and contact paper for the drawers on the near horizon. But he didn't want to insinuate a complete home makeover, not on the first day. "Wait 'til your washer and dryer arrive tomorrow," he muttered in a low voice.

"¿Qué?" Miguel wasn't having his generosity.

"Nothing."

"Don't buy me shit I don't ask for. I have my own money, understand?"

"I couldn't help myself. I went to this bodega store." He held up the VIP card the cashier gave him. "You know they have everything under the sun there. I could've kept goin' and bought rugs."

"Blake." His irritation over the shopping was palpable.

"Understood." *WTF?* He scratched his head realizing he didn't get a haircut at the spa.

He found a pot under the kitchen sink. Blake prepared a New England boiled feast with corned beef, cabbage, potatoes, white turnip, rutabaga, carrot, onion, and parsnip. A conventional dish, it was devoured on many occasions in the Morgan household.

One hour passed.

An apprehensive bite confirmed no zest or zing. Edible? Yes. But not by much. With caution, he studied Brutus under his feet and made a mental note to give the dog the scraps. There'd be oodles.

He wondered if Miguel, raised by Mexican parents, ever ate anything as insipid as corned beef. What was he thinking? The overcooked dish featured carrots, which in theory glowed orange, but instead gave off a lucid hue.

Miguel cleared his plate. Going for a second helping and obviously grateful for the effort put into the dinner, he didn't seem to mind. In fact, he appeared happy just to have Blake around.

"What's for dessert?" He placed his empty dish in the sink.

A cake or pie would have been nice, but he didn't think far ahead. "I'm your sweet treat tonight."

An unexpected frisson of arousal ran through him. He hoped Miguel was kidding earlier at the spa when he demanded they sleep next to one another without having sex on the first night. He wanted them to kiss again. God, he was the best kiss ever. It felt safe being in his arms. But deep down inside, he knew he couldn't do this for too long. Diego would stir up trouble again. His ex-husband always did.

Upper East Side

Over on Park Avenue, Lex was *still* chained to the bed, Massimo cuddled against her captive body. Earlier, her fiancé had fed their son and played with him for a few hours while she slept. Then he'd put M2 in the nursery.

On the Nanny Cam's monitor which sat on the nightstand, she could see her baby. He was on his back staring up at the Fisher-Price mobile of animals. The elephant, lion, and horse danced around and around in circles. Often, M2 kicked his legs in a twitch, right before he zonked out. Any minute he would be asleep until sunrise. She was also able to get some rest. After seeing that letter, she didn't think she'd be able to nap. But her body kind of gave out the minute she'd put her head on the pillow.

"Birdie should be here by now. What's taking her so long?"

Her mother had texted Massimo that the flower arrangement design took longer than expected. Thor had to draw up an entirely new concept, something he called the Juliet Rose. A rare and special flower, he declared the arrangements would secure her position in New York society as a trailblazer.

Vive had told Massimo, after his third attempt to reach her from Lex's phone, that she was preoccupied with other plans. What the hell did that mean? She didn't know what her friend was up to, but she should've come over when asked. She needed to talk to Vive in person about Taddy. But her talk would have to wait until tomorrow.

"You're getting off on this, aren't you?" she asked Massimo whose large brown eyes were starting to flutter shut. He'd better not fall asleep.

"No, *bella*. I'm worried for you. I want you to think about how you are going to approach Birdie. Do not go off on her. I don't want her to be a mess."

"I'm fine, Masi."

"Ha." Her fiancé didn't appear to buy it. "Tomorrow, you shall spend the day in bed again." He brought his body over hers and kissed her gently on the forehead, then the right cheek and the left.

"Dr. Cedar said twenty-four hours."

"I'm the doctor of you. And I say one more day in bed."

"You're being ridiculous." She loved him for it, but enough was enough already. "Jemma will be here soon with more dress options. I have the Poppy White TV Show taping in the morning. I can't miss it." She ran her schedule in her head. The hours were closing in on her.

"Don't overreact, *bella*."

"All I'm going to do is *ask* my mother about the papers. They could be made up or from a tabloid story."

"Is that what you're thinking?" His forehead furrowed slightly. "That they are fake?"

"They can't be real. As drunk and high as my mom was during my childhood, I can't imagine her keeping this quiet."

"Hasn't your father had many women come forward claiming that he fathered their children?"

"Yes."

"How many?" His brows shot up higher.

"I don't know. Half a dozen or so. None of them panned out."

"Right, so why do you think your mom kept this from you, if it wasn't real?" Massimo stroked her hair, trying to reason with her.

"Like you said, I think this has to do with Taddy."

There was a noise at the foyer. "Guys, I'm back."

"We're in here!" Massimo shouted. He sat up on the bed.

"Lex, honey, the flowers are—" Eyes wide, Birdie froze at the entrance to the bedroom.

"Come in, Mom."

"Am I interrupting something?" Her forehead wrinkled as she focused in on the handcuffs. "I'll come back later."

"Mom, no. Massimo was just going to uncuff me. Weren't you, Masi?" Lex was so close to punching him, but her hands were tied.

"*Sì.*" He pulled the key from his front pocket and unlocked her arms. "*Bella*, why don't you tell your mother what's going on."

"Tell me what?" Birdie held on to the shoulder strap of her purse, clearly uncertain what to make of this.

She grabbed the paper from the nightstand and handed it to her. "Here."

From the look in Birdie's eyes, Lex realized she'd read the paper before. A paleness, one she'd never seen on her mother's face, except when she'd overdosed, washed over her.

"Well?" She needed to know and couldn't wait another second.

"Where did you get this from?"

"It was in one of the boxes."

Her mother raised her hands in the air as if asking for a minute. She took the chair next to the bed, folded her arms, and mumbled something. Lex realized she was having one of her conversations in her head with her father.

"Mom, stop it. Tell me."

"Tabitha, that poor girl..." Her voice became shaky as she came over to the bed. She held Lex's hand.

Birdie's eyes were wet with tears and wide with sadness. Lex knew she was about to say something she might not want to hear.

"Taddy *might* be your father's daughter."

"Can our week get any crazier?" She sunk her head in Massimo's chest. How was she going to tell Taddy the news?

Chapter Ten

Pillow Talk

Lower East Side

Taking Miguel's cock in his mouth was all Blake could think about. This was such an unexpected distraction from all the negative shit going on in his life over the past few months. His own dick grew hard over the idea of jacking off in his friend's presence. Earlier memories—Miguel playing with his ass, fingering him, rimming him—consumed his every thought. The *Seven Desires* danced in his head on repeat.

The day's butt play had sparked a deeper hunger in him, one he'd never had before. He had no idea he'd enjoy being touched then licked down there, like that, but he did. He loved that tongue-fucking thing. He was getting more comfortable with the idea. But common sense told him not to. Common sense told him to run for the door, even though Miguel said they wouldn't do anything until the next day.

Naked, Miguel lay next to him. This was torture. He could've at least put on a pair of boxers, something…anything.

Exhaustion eclipsed every being in his newly domesticated body. Other than buying pre-made meals and making them appear homemade, Sandra Lee-style, he'd never prepared a dinner from scratch before. Shit, he'd never cleaned an entire apartment from top to bottom, walked a dog, or washed and dried then folded laundry. Growing up with maids and chefs in Fairfield County, Connecticut left no reason to. He didn't think he was better than household chores; he just didn't have the need to do them. *Until now.*

He did notice the more he cleaned the happier Miguel became. It sort of brought him pleasure to see his friend letting someone else do something for him. Nothing he did at home had ever made Diego happy.

Pulling him close, Miguel whispered in his ear, "Blake?"

"Yes?" He rolled over and admired those molten eyes. They were warm and inviting. He was used to keeping his eyes shut tight in bed. His friend's face was a welcome change.

"What was being married like?"

'Hell' was the first word which came to mind, followed by 'isolation, sleepless, loveless nights', and—according to his recent divorce papers—'abandonment'. He'd been tempted to have the lawyer declare cruel and inhuman treatment, but he didn't possess the urge to rouse danger. He chose the easiest reason for the courts to grant a divorce. His lawyers expedited the separation papers with an alimony agreement giving his life savings to get Diego as far away from his life as possible. He would be starting over in many aspects, including his finances.

"You and I haven't talked much since my separation." Blake realized they'd both avoided each other. It wasn't Miguel's fault. He should've reached out to his best friend much sooner. Depressed and ashamed, he hadn't seen anyone, including his closest friends in months.

"Sorry I wasn't there for you. I didn't know what to say or do. How to react…"

"It's fine. Diego is now living over at the Worldwide Plaza."

"That's rather *extravagante* for someone who does not have a job."

"I paid for it." He felt used by even saying it, but he had to get Diego out of his life and getting him a new place to live in was the best start. "My ex is getting alimony." He sat up and placed the new bed sheet over Miguel's groin to concentrate. The gray fabric decked out the place better than he'd expected. "Diego never got back on his feet after the recession. I don't know many guys who got jobs after Lehman Lynch closed. Do you?"

"No. Most in finance moved back to wherever they came from."

"After he lost his job, he gave up on Wall Street. We sorta collapsed from there."

"You never told me you were unhappy. When Thor called and mentioned you two split up, I felt bad. Getting married was your dream." He put his warm hands in Blake's lap.

A magician at hiding his real emotions, Blake acted all along as if he'd married Mr. Wonderful. Even weeks after Diego moved out, he pretended everything was status quo.

He worked in advertising and PR, and gave good face. Plus, he'd learned from his mom to never speak ill about your spouse to your friends. She'd say, "It'll haunt you when your social circle reminds you what a nincompoop your husband is."

He forced a smile to clear Miguel's worry. "I went into the marriage with the best intentions. We both did." He couldn't bring himself to tell Miguel everything. He'd sworn to Diego and himself he'd never speak of what really happened.

"And?" Miguel leaned his face in closer, almost touching his nose with Blake's.

"One month before the ceremony, I cancelled."

"What?"

"Called my folks and told 'em to stop the plans." He paused. "I've not shared this with anyone. Not even Thor." Saying it out loud felt agreeable against the disquiet growing within. Though this wasn't the real story as to why they divorced. Sure, it was a good one, one which was true and put a wedge between them, but it wasn't the final straw.

"Why did you call the wedding off?"

"We'd been in pre-marital counseling with our vicar at the Episcopal church. It came up in one of our sessions that Diego pulled away in bed—not making eye contact when we made love." *Here comes the embarrassing part.* "He'd often face the wall and check out. My ex treated me as if I were some trick, a stranger. He didn't even want to kiss me."

"Earlier today, when I frenched you, it was your first kiss in how long?"

He'd opened the can of worms, might as well tell him the truth. Well, some of it. "Five years."

"*Lo siento*, I didn't have any idea," Miguel repeated again. "I'm sorry."

Miguel's face didn't seem as shocked as he thought it would be. Then he remembered he'd cried at the spa earlier that day. His friend may not have seen his tears, but he'd heard his sobs. How could he not? He was embarrassed for blubbering like an idiot.

"We weren't growing on an intimate level. Or, at least the one I'd hoped for." Sanity required serious concentration on his part as the rejection increased year after year. Lovemaking, which had died in his marriage, felt at times as a white noise—a fixed bandwidth with grave density, and no matter how hard he tried to turn it down, he couldn't.

"What made you change your mind and move forward with the wedding?" Miguel traced his fingers over his arms, maybe to soothe him.

It worked.

"Empathy, I suppose. I assumed I'd be able to help Diego. Change him. If I presented a committed marriage, knowing I'd be with him for life, along with a good home, he'd open up and be vulnerable, and love me how I needed." His words sounded desperate the minute they left his lips, but he didn't care. It was the truth.

"Even if it's for the best, you can't change someone. They have to do it themselves, because they want to." His black eyes narrowed. "You know that, right?"

"Trust me, after five plus years, I know better," he replied as if the truth was the final kick to his head to end the relationship. "I'm an optimistic person, always have been. I believed Diego would get better. Not worse." Blake wondered if he'd ever regain the hopefulness for his future he'd once had.

When he spoke his vows, his enthusiasm and spirits flew high, en route as the perfect couple. They owned a penthouse in the city and a summerhouse in the Hamptons. He envisioned working part-time from home to raise their kids, while spending time with his folks who'd dote as loving grandparents. All those fantasies were smashed to pieces by his ex-husband's hunger to live dangerously. Years since taking his vows, he'd come to the conclusion, after Diego had moved out, that the divorce was a blessing. He learned to accept things for how they were and not to strive for perfection.

"People can change if they want to, Blake."

"I know…Diego didn't want to, not for me anyway."

"MLD loved you."

"As a friend, sure. Not as a husband or a lover." The oversight was mortifying. "Diego cherished the security and what a relationship offered on paper. But he didn't care for the day-to-day actions, which made the union possible." He felt stupid for going down the aisle. What was he, some Disney princess? He was a man, a gay man.

The marriage act seemed absurd now. "My ex is damaged beyond repair."

"Why is Diego damaged?"

"He'd been molested as a child. I knew about his demons when we met in college. He'd sworn he'd moved past them." Shaking his head, he realized his ex had never gone to therapy for his abuse. How did anyone heal without ever talking about it? "Once we made the wedding arrangements, he started acting out to me at home." Tears welled in his eyes. Blake didn't want to cry about Diego again, but he did. "Sorry." He reached for a tissue from the nightstand and blew his nose.

Sitting up, Miguel leaned in and hugged him. "Let it out, it's okay."

His friend held on to him until he was able to speak again. He swallowed the knot in his throat, tucked the Kleenex between his fingers, and sat back, staring at him. "In college, we took Intro to Psychology together."

"*Sí*. Professor Litchfield was quite the quiz giver. Why?"

"Remember a Sigmund Freud exam which you aced and I failed?" He wiped his eyes.

"MLD has the Madonna-whore complex?"

"Bingo. Who knew gays could get such a thing?" *Poor Diego.*

"Wow. So, you represented his dad after you married."

"Or his mother. I never figured out which. His scars run deep. He couldn't let anyone in for intimacy once he loved them." *Here comes the dreaded part.* "When Diego realized he loved me, he couldn't make love to me anymore."

"What about having another boyfriend?" Miguel reached for his hand.

"Jury's out on having romance." Blake frowned at his friend's hand, palm up and fingers out. He didn't take it. "A husband isn't in my cards. I don't think I can do it again." He debated if he'd ever be in another relationship. The marriage had almost ruined him. Almost.

"It's getting late. We better get to sleep." Miguel moved his body alongside his. He then lay next to him and pulled the sheet over them, pulling him close.

He noticed the time on the alarm clock and heard the garbage trucks rattling down the alleyway. "We've chatted the night away."

"I'm glad we're doing this."

Miguel exhaled a soft breath down his nape, sending an erotic charge over his entire body.

"Me, too," Blake confirmed. He hadn't spooned with anyone like that in forever. Even cuddling was far more intimate than what he'd ever shared with Diego after they'd married.

Slowly, Miguel pressed his hard cock between his ass-cheeks.

After a few minutes, his friend was asleep. He snored a little in his ear. It was cute, but kept him awake. He lifted his friend's heavy arm from around his waist and tried to roll him over to his other side. He was too big to move. While they were both the same in height, Miguel had muscle mass—dense, thick, delicious muscle mass.

Miguel was finally on his back, breathing softly. Blake sat up in bed and studied him. *God, he's so beautiful.* He laughed to himself. He couldn't believe he might do the *Seven Desires* with his best friend, Mig.

Any guy in New York would jump at the chance to have the sexiest man agree to do it with him. He knew he was lucky, but he was also scared of Miguel. He kept reminding himself the week would be a non-thinking, non-feeling fuck fest. He couldn't think or feel; he had to turn his brain and heart off. Just let his body do its thing. But would he get hurt?

There was no one better to do this with. From the stories he'd heard over the years, Miguel was a talented sex machine who could top and not feel a thing for the bottoms. His track record proved that. But fucking and not thinking was what got Diego in trouble. Blake put so much thought into everything he did. He knew his actions had reactions and those lead to repercussions. Sick ones. Deadly ones.

With his hand, he grazed Miguel's arms, admiring them. They had to be the size of his legs.

Miguel had that kind of skin which gave off a cinnamon-bronzy hue. If that wasn't enough, every inch of his body always had that 'Yo, dude, I just lifted' look. Juiced? Nope. He was a natural body builder by design, and the universe had done an amazing job.

As he sat taller, taking in the view, he noticed his cell phone was glowing on the counter in the kitchen. The area illuminated, causing Brutus' eyes to open.

Lord, he didn't want that dog to wake up. He was nervous about getting out of bed and walking over and turn his phone off. What if Brutus attacked him? He'd heard of pits that'd behave one way in front of their master and acted the complete opposite when they weren't around.

He looked back at Miguel who was sound asleep. The corners of his lips were curled up. Whatever he was dreaming about made him smile.

"Aww," Blake muttered and quietly slipped out of bed. The glossy cement floors were cold against his feet. He wasn't used to that. Grabbing his phone, he glanced at the screen to turn it off.

Diego. Damn. His message read, *Where R U?*

A deep sigh in frustration came from his lungs. His ex must've come by his apartment. He'd told the doorman not to let Diego up anymore. It was too painful to hear his voice or see his face. The locks may have yet to be changed, but he no longer had a key to Blake's heart.

He texted back, *Mig's loft.*

NYPD is asking questions.

Good, he hoped they'd arrest him, and get this over and done with. He typed, *Confess.*

Never, his ex-husband shot back.

He prayed his ex would burn in Hell. In fact, he knew he would one day. *Ur cell might be traced. Stop texting!!!* Diego was so paranoid. Suggesting his messages were being read by the authorities would certainly make him stop. He hoped.

U tell Mig?

God, did he want to. He felt horrible for not telling Miguel the whole story. He'd only shared part of it, the safe part. But it was the same reason why his parents, and Thor and Vive, weren't being told either. Some things were too fucked-up for people to put their heads around; this being one of them.

T & L know. That's it. He'd only told Taddy and Lex because they were the two who had seen what Diego's actions had done to Blake. It was Taddy's private investigator who'd told them. Ironically, the investigator tailed celebrities for Vive's articles at *Debauchery*, but the P.I. was a professional and wouldn't tell a soul.

Keep ur trap shut.

Fuck u! We R divorced!

Ur still mine.

No…I'm not.

Ur dead if u tell.

Christ. He was going to have to power down his phone. He didn't respond well to threats, especially not from Diego. He knew in the morning he'd have to go to the NYPD and file a restraining order. My, how everything had started off so well: drinks with Thor and Vive, and the wonderful surprise of Miguel and his offering. But his week had just been turned to shit. Diego had that way about him; he ruined everything he touched.

Well, no more. If the divorce wasn't enough to get that douchebag out of his life, he'd tell the authorities what he'd done and they'd lock him up for good.

Right before he shut off his phone, he texted Taddy. *Please bring Fendi to work.* Then he cleared the phone of all messages and tried to sleep.

Upper East Side

In the middle of the night, Lex had awoken to M2 screaming at the top of his lungs. He'd been hungry, again. Massimo had been up with her and she could see he was stressed, too. Her son could always pick up on her moods. He shared her sentiments with gas.

Little belly full, M2 rested in her arms. Together they rocked, back and forth. She enjoyed nighttime with him.

"Hush little baby, don't say a word..." Softly, she sang, hoping the baby couldn't detect the turmoil going on in her own mind.

She thought about the baby growing inside of her, M2's brother or sister. What would it be like for her son to grow up not knowing he'd had a sibling? How could her parents not have told her that she and Taddy could be sisters? Why did they keep this from them?

"*Sì?*" Her fiancé dimmed the lights above M2's crib. Made of mahogany, the furniture was used in Massimo's own nursery when he was a child, and his late father's, King Umberto, before that. The royal Tittoni family crest was painted on the arm of the chair. "Have you heard from your mom?"

"No. She's probably sulked herself to sleep. I wasn't hard on her, Masi. I just asked. That's all I did was ask." Then why did she feel as though she'd shot Birdie in cold blood?

"You did good, *bella*. I cannot help but feel bad for your *madre*."

Birdie had fled in hysterics. She wasn't able to speak about that paternity test. She offered no insights or excuses other than Eddie had never been retested and she'd promised Irma they'd never speak of the matter again. If Lex wanted the truth, it would be up to her to ask Taddy to get tested with her.

A noise came from the hallway.

"Could you please ask Jemma to keep it down? She's going to keep M2 up," Lex asked. Clearly, their house guest wasn't familiar with newborn rules. Jemma lived life in the glamour lane of Russian caviar and French champagne, not Lex's breast milk or cloth diapers. Yes, Massimo refused to allow his son to wear disposable Pampers.

Jemma hadn't adjusted to the time change yet and obviously couldn't sleep, either. She was chatting on her cell phone at the end of the hall to someone in Los Angeles or possibly Tokyo. Lex could hear her say, "My darling this," and "My darling that."

Loud and dramatic, the photographer was starting to get on her nerves. Her two boyfriends, Luigi Bova, who ran the European division of Girasoli Garments, and Rocco Cazzo, who managed Massimo's Milan estate, were scheduled to fly in the day before the wedding. Tempted to put them up at The Plaza, Massimo said they'd be offended if they didn't get to room at their penthouse and spend time with the baby. Again, he'd accused her of being too American when she'd offered a second time to get them a hotel room.

More guests would be trickling in over the next few days. She hoped she could keep her cool until then.

Massimo knotted his robe and left the room.

Next to the chair, her cell phone vibrated. The screen glowed soft blue, causing the room to light up eerily.

A text from Vive. *Busy today. Sorry. C U @ 9 w/ Taddy xo.*

It was the middle of the night…was Vive drunk?

Days before, her friend had agreed to come over with Taddy to help style her hair and make-up for the Poppy White Sunday Morning Special Edition Show taping. The program would air live. Usually Vive's role played with her as a journalist, while Taddy coached her along, as well.

Poppy didn't throw tabloid-style punches at Lex, because she knew better. But she hadn't even thought about what she'd say about the wedding. There was no theme other than love. The guest list included everyone from Beyoncé to Gaga. All of Birdie's rocker friends, too. Most importantly, her group: Taddy, Vive, Blake, Miguel, and Thor. They were joined by Massimo's sister, Paloma, and Jemma, who'd been a part of his life since they were kids.

Lex texted back, *Come @ 8…alone.* Time with Vive, if only for a few minutes, would clear up whether or not Taddy knew and had ever said anything to her in the past.

Sure. U...OK?

She thought about what she should say. If she replied no, Vive would be in a limo on her way over. That was how their friendship rolled. If she texted yes, then the woman would strut in whenever she felt like it. With that understanding, she stood her ground and typed, *Yup c u @ 8.*

"Mi scusi, mi scusi," Jemma chanted outside the door. *"Buonanotte."*

Suddenly, her guest was quiet. *Thank God. Clack! Clack!* Her heels went to the guest room and the door closed.

The penthouse shifted into that quiet state where Lex could hear Massimo walking around on the hardwood floors. He shuffled his feet when he wore his slippers. She could always tell where he was, and right then he was in the kitchen, most likely getting cookies.

Again, Vive texted. *Why so early? Need to sleep in. Will be there w/ Taddy.*

"Jesus, Vive. Work with me here," Lex mumbled. She adjusted M2 on her chest and thumbed the keys, pressing hard. *Come alone at 8. Need to talk privately. Thanx, Viveca.*

That should do it.

The nursery door opened. "Are the boys picking M2 up in the morning?" Massimo asked as he came in with a plate full of pastries.

It wasn't fair that his body wouldn't be changing like hers over the next few months. His stomach would remain flat, his legs and arms would stay strong.

"We're all set." She took a bite of the dessert as he put a piece in her mouth. Careful not to get a crumb on M2, she covered him, lowered her voice and said, "Thank you for agreeing to do the taping with me."

"You know I'd do anything for you. Even TV."

Previously, she had always hated the press, but in the last year, the media worked more and more to her advantage. Between the fashion covers, latest reviews of her collection, and the pre-wedding releases, the publicity had overall been positive.

"Blake has not watched M2 before, has he?"

"This will be his first day babysitting. You nervous?"

Massimo shrugged. "Miguel will be with him, so he'll be fine. If anything should happen, they can call my *sorella*."

Having Massimo's sister, Paloma, offer to help was great, but Blake had to take to M2 if he ever wanted to be a dad one day. It bothered her that Blake hadn't spent much time with her son. *He might as well start tomorrow.* If he stepped it up just a bit, she'd ask him to be the godfather of the next baby. Even with all the drama going on, her escape was thinking about their second child. She was getting excited.

Her cell phone vibrated again. Massimo picked it up and looked at the screen. "Hmm."

"Tell Vive to fuck off." Lex laughed from exhaustion. She rocked the chair faster. "Come on, baby. Go to sleep."

"*Bella*, it isn't from Vive."

"My mom?" Maybe Birdie had some long confession she wanted to get off her chest and had decided to use text messaging to do it.

"No. It's Taddy." He held up the screen for her to read as she nibbled on another cookie.

What's wrong? Vive said something is up w/ u.

"I swear, nothing is private around here."

Lex didn't know what to do.

Chapter Eleven

Morning Woody

Lower East Side

Restless, hot, and aroused, Blake slowly opened his eyes. He was in Miguel's bed, being watched by his friend who lay next to him.

Miguel's black eyes focused on his body where his hand was stroking his cock, tugging at his balls.

His breath caught in his throat. He licked his lips. Miguel lowered the sheet which separated them. Thick and beautiful, his erection grew. Blake watched in awe as he scooted closer beside him.

This was just a dream, he told himself. But it felt real.

"Don't worry. I'm here now. I'll protect you. I won't ever let anything bad happen to you," Miguel said confidently, his voice rough and low.

He tried to say, "Yes...Mig," but could only manage a whimper. Unable to answer, he wasn't sure what safe felt like. He tried to speak again, but his friend's lips met with his, kissing him passionately.

"Give yourself to me."

"I...can't."

"Submit to me, to us. I know you want to."

"Mig, I'm nervous," Blake murmured in Miguel's ear, knowing his friend was right. He wanted to give himself, all of him, to this man. He wished he was as free as Thor and Vive were about sex. But he wasn't. "I can't do my Seven Desires. *We shouldn't have agreed to them. They're wrong for me."*

"They are perfect for you. Let me have you. I won't hurt you."

The safety of being in his arms caused every nerve in his entire body to prickle. Maybe he could *trust him.*

He brought his hand over to Miguel's cock and slowly stroked him, up then down, up then down. "You're so sexy, Mig."

"And you're handsome," Miguel complimented.

Blake became intoxicated by those words, as he'd never heard him speak that way about his appearance before. Instinctively, he brought his hand up over his face, the scar, and his ugliness. Miguel pulled his hand away and kissed his face, kissed along his imperfections.

"I hate that you hide behind your hair. Let me see you."

Blake kissed him.

"I'm sorry I didn't come for you sooner. I didn't know how bad things were for you."

Miguel played with his nipples, possibly to make him smile.

He felt a tear. He'd cried so much he couldn't remember what laughter felt like anymore.

"I can't talk about it. I don't want to get you in trouble."

Blake started to pull away, but Miguel brought his body down on top of him. "You'll talk when you're ready. I won't rush you. I want you to trust me." His big hands slid under him and massaged his ass.

God, his friend worked his body in all the right places.

Miguel lowered himself down to Blake's cock. The heat from his open mouth warmed the head of his dick as he licked and sucked. All of his fears started to melt away. Was he desperate to be topped by Miguel?

His face came up as he asked, "Do you trust me?"

"I want to, Mig." It would take time. He realized this, but in order to take the next step, he had to let Miguel in. "Fuck me now. Mig, do it now," he urged, rolling over onto his stomach, acting as if he'd done it a million times and wasn't an anal virgin. After all, this was his dream.

"You want it doggie style?" Miguel joked, climbing on top of him and the back of his neck. "This is going to feel so good, for us both. My cock inside of you is where it belongs."

He arched his backside into Miguel's erection. "I want to be a part of you. I want to share myself with you."

"Me, too."

"Put a condom on!"

The deep, hot penetration of Miguel's cock suddenly burned as it found its way inside him. His hands wrapped tight around Blake's neck as he sunk his flesh in.

"I said, put a—"

Everything became black. He could no longer see the morning sunshine as his face smashed into the pillows and dark.

"You want my gift?"

That voice.

"Mig, I changed my mind." His cries choked his throat. *"We can't. I don't wanna bare back."*

"Shut the fuck up, you bug chaser."

The nightmare returned. *"Stop!"* Blake screamed.

"I should've bred you a long time ago."

It wasn't Miguel. Those weren't the words of love he'd been hearing from his friend.

"You little bitch." Diego, his ex-husband, his demon.

The dream came crashing around him. It was over...

He awoke Sunday morning to searing breath smacking his face. *Diego?* No, thank heavens. Brutus. The dog panted in hopes to secure his attention.

"What do you want?" He wiped his eyes, realizing he'd been crying.

It was only a nightmare, he reminded himself. He was safe. Miguel was a good guy. He was asleep right next to him. The heat off his friend's body gave him peace.

Brutus licked his arm. The alarm clock on the nightstand blinked 5:58 a.m.

"Go lie down," he pleaded, pointing the four-legged, not-yet-a-friend canine to his corner. He snapped his fingers, but the dog didn't budge. "Damn you, dog…"

Rolling over with a yawn, his friend's pecs became exposed. He stretched his developed biceps over his head with sternness in his eyes. "Brutus goes out at 6:00 a.m."

Christ, you are a sexy beast in the morning. "For Pete's sake, you didn't tell me I'd be taking him out this early." Coffee. He needed it strong, black and caffeinated.

But something told him Brutus wouldn't be able to wait that long.

The dog sat at the door, staring at the knob intently.

"Go walk him." Miguel kissed him on the cheek then tore off the sheets, kicking him, jokingly, from the bed.

Groggy and stumbling, Blake dressed into sweats and left with Brutus on the leash, but didn't put the muzzle on him. It did feel cruel. The dog had been nothing but a big teddy bear with him.

Twenty minutes later, he returned and went to scrub his hands in the kitchen sink. "Mmmm." He inhaled sharply. *Cinnamon? Vanilla?*

Something simmered on the stove.

"*Buenos días,*" Miguel called from the bed, in the buff, stroking his cock.

How did he miss the view when he came back in?

"I made *atole* for you on the stove."

"That's what smells so good."

Frozen by the view of his erection, he remembered his friend's penis outlined at the spa, playing peekaboo from his pants. *Now it's here in plain sight.* But there was nothing plain about that dick. It was fucking gorgeous.

Putting his earlier nightmare behind him, he didn't know what to do. Run to his bedside, or wait to be invited? Turning the stovetop's heat off, he grabbed the saucepan and poured himself a cup. Stirring the brown froth with a spoon, he gave it a quick blow before sipping. *Atole* tasted similar to rich hot chocolate. "*Delicioso.*" He laughed at his Spanish. He knew very little. How could he sip a hot beverage with a Latin stud on the bed?

Silence filled the air.

Miguel sipped from his own mug.

Blake mirrored his actions.

Christ, they could be at their stand-off for hours.

"*Atole* will give you energy for the day ahead." Miguel set his cup down on the floor beside the bed, making a loud clink. He then tugged at his cock.

"And…why would I need energy, Mig?"

He kept his cool and swigged the warm confection, allowing it to seep over his tongue. The thick drink stayed in his mouth for a few seconds, and then he swallowed. But on the inside, there was a firecracker going off. He didn't think he'd give in to the *Seven Desires*, or want them to happen as strongly as he did right that very second. But it was all he could think about at the moment.

Miguel smirked in response, but said nothing. He played with Blake's resistance.

Bastard. He set his cup on the counter and crossed his arms. He cocked his chin up, not taking his eyes off him. He'd wait this out. Nothing was going to happen. This was merely teasing him.

"Come, lie with me," Miguel ordered.

"What?" Were the *Seven Desires* really going into motion?

"Get naked and bring your hot body the fuck over here."

Blake had never been told he had a hot body before. He enjoyed being told what to do. The commands were quite different from his former docile, unassertive experience.

He went over and peeled his nylon sweats off as Miguel watched, then dropped to his knees on the mattress. *Game on.* He lowered his shoulders and crawled forward, palms out as a panther approaching a meal. Hungry, reaching for his friend's cock with his right hand, Blake stroked his shaft with his left. He witnessed his friend's eyes roll back in pleasure. Other than his own, he hadn't held a cock in his hands in years. Miguel's pink head deserved his attention. A little freaked out by how easy this was, by how natural it felt, Blake tried to stay calm and just go with it.

Miguel moaned louder in Spanish then ordered, "You're going to be a good *niño* and suck my cock."

Nodding in agreement, he asked, "And then?"

"Don't use your hands." Cupping his fingers around Blake's *jawline*, Miguel brushed his thumb over his lips.

"I'll keep my hands behind my back." He clasped his palms by the floor.

"Once I'm nice and hard, I'm gonna face-fuck you, hard." He glanced down at his dick. "When I come, you'll swallow me—whole, understand?"

"Is there anything else, boss man?" He pretended he'd swallow, but would spit it out, like they did in adult films. Yes, that was what he'd do. Or take it on his chest, or maybe his face. Maybe.

Miguel rested himself on the mattress. "Get started."

Supercharged with enthusiasm, he leaned forward and nipped at Miguel's dick. He ran his tongue in long strokes along his shaft. Spice, sweet and exotic, enveloped his senses. By far the biggest he'd seen, the dick was thick, too. Licking under the shaft, he produced enough lube to do his duty.

"Taste good?"

"Ah-huh…" He couldn't believe he was doing this.

"Let me watch you. Take me. Come on, boy."

First, his lips glided down. The satiny penis head hit the roof of his mouth. He opened wider. A dive down further pressed his face all the way up against the crotch. The black pubes tickled his cheeks.

"Doing good, boy."

The cock twitched and slid in more. *Deeper.* Careful not to scrape the skin, his two front teeth rested at the base of his dick.

He looked up at his Latin God with a grin.

Miguel blew him a kiss and seduced Blake to continue. As their playfulness increased, he wondered for a split second what else he'd do for his best friend.

His tongue laced the nuts as he took him in further. Still nervous to pump the dick with his mouth, he continued to suck, sweetly. His nostrils burned. He thirsted for more.

"Fuck!" Miguel shouted. "Take my entire cock, *chico guapo.*" He pressed his body against Blake's face. "*Caliente.*"

He jerked back.

His top became more fired up.

"I—umm." He wasn't confident he could take any more.

The very way Miguel sat up from the bed and then stood, demanding to be worshiped, it wasn't like anything he'd ever encountered. Ever. He fucking loved it. But he didn't want to disappoint his friend. Inside, he felt unsure about his capabilities. Miguel was the polar opposite. He wondered what it felt like to know you were desired, wanted. Blake hadn't a clue but it was obvious Miguel owned it, at least in the bedroom.

Eyes, midnight as the dark skies, flashed a quick fury. Miguel scooped him up and slammed his backside against the wall next to the mattress.

Christ, you're strong. The coolness from the plaster wall braced Blake's head as he found his footing in the corner. He tried to act nonchalant. As if it was status quo for a gorgeous hunk to pick him up, ragdoll-style, and throw him. At over six feet tall, this wasn't normal.

Miguel lowered him to the floor to kneel at his feet. He dug his knuckles through his hairline and pressed his body, hard.

With a cry, he whimpered and noticed it turned Miguel on. Acting submissive—was he acting? Or was it real? He felt vulnerable. He wanted to be overpowered. He didn't want to be a victim, not any longer, but this was different. Something about this gave him a freedom and a power he'd never known.

"Is my boy okay?" Leaning down, Miguel licked his lower lip.

"Get rough with me." Blake kissed him. He let his guard down a little. Miguel had tested negative at the clinic. He was okay. They were good.

Miguel grabbed his jaw, staring into his eyes as if he was drunk on adrenaline and asked, "You sure?"

"Yes. Dominate me."

"Hmm." Miguel seemed to register the hunger he felt for domination. "Get ready." He slapped Blake across the cheek.

Oh, my God! "Mig!" He didn't expect to be hit, not like that. It stung, but the pain felt good. In one small way, it filled his need.

"Open your mouth, pretty boy."

Blake was going to orgasm right there. This was the hottest thing. Shocked to arousal, he'd been shut up. Blake released his mouth. *"Ahhh."*

Miguel closed the small remaining distance between them. "So obedient. I like this side of you." He shoved three fingers into his mouth. Forcefully, he shook Blake's face from left to right. "I want your sweet lips blistered up when we're through." Withdrawing his fingers, playfully he slapped the other side of his face a little harder than before.

Astonishment heated Blake's body as if he'd stepped inside a tanning bed. It scared him. He didn't know why, but he wanted more. This pushed him to his limits. As far as he could go, his friend will take him to a place he never thought possible.

One more strike came down his face. That time it was open-palmed and stung his right cheekbone. It didn't hurt, not badly, but rather it felt...good. Yes, his cock ached for release as he stroked himself.

"Down, boy."

Miguel pushed him to the floor and shoved himself in Blake's throat. Immense pressure filled his mouth.

"Hold it." He moaned in Spanish and pumped. "That's it."

He swallowed up the pre-cum as Miguel held the base of his cock and retracted.

"You gonna puke, pretty boy?" Miguel gripped onto his neck as if he'd snap it in two.

He went for it. He could do it. This was how it was supposed be, right? He'd never wanted anything more in his entire life so he replied, "No." Feeling a little bit more confident, he urged, "Face-fuck me harder."

Blake was in sex Heaven. His encouragement seemed to make Miguel wild, insane with determination. It felt amazing to forget the Hell he'd been subjected to in recent months. If just for an hour, he'd go with whatever Miguel wanted. Then they'd have to talk, seriously.

Miguel fucked his mouth with such force. He did this repeatedly, stretching his lips wide, filling his mouth to the brim.

On the last thrust, he withdrew and said, "You love having your mouth worked over, huh, *bebé?*" He shouted things in Spanish, tightening the hold around his neck.

Swallowing, he encouraged, "Don't stop. Keep going."

"*¿Sí?*" He stood at attention.

Dominate me. "Show me what you got." Blake felt empowered. He taunted his alpha to control him. His friend's reputation was true. He was good. Damn good.

Miguel pulled his hair, gliding his body from the wall over to the mattress. "Lie flat on your back." He hoisted a pillow under his head and shoulders. Standing, he squatted over Blake's face. Again, he buried himself down his throat with one deep plunge.

His gag reflexes subsided; Blake was learning well. He studied his face.

"Take my cock." Miguel grunted with each thrust and picked up speed, pumping faster.

Tears found their way down his cheeks. *Are we going too far?* He loved every minute. His nose caught a pheromone whiff as they oozed sweat. The man was so attractive to him. He trusted him with his body. Could he start to trust him with his heart?

Bottomless in him, his top was smooth yet rough, sweet but brutal.

Mine. He held on to Miguel's butt cheeks as he plunged again and again. Fucking his face.

"No limits this week." Miguel gripped onto his hairline with his knuckles. Looking deep into his eyes, he said, "Understand?" He pulled his cock out, demanding a response.

"Yes, Mig." His eyes watered as he let his guard down. He couldn't believe he'd agreed to this.

He leaned down and then licked Blake's tears. "No crying." Miguel kissed his lips. "You'll do whatever I say. I want no secrets between us." It was as if he knew something bothered him.

"Mmm." Feeling the most vulnerable he'd ever been in his entire life, he nodded. He'd try. He would.

"Now open, boy. I'm going to come down your throat."

Dropping his jaw, Blake responded to the command.

Over his tongue, the cock slid in. "Imagine, in a few days, I'll be in your virgin ass. You ready for it?"

Quickly, he nodded, starting to like the sound of that. Their exchange was intense and special. He kept reminding himself that he was just a friend, that this was one week and wouldn't go any further than his *Seven Desires*. And even some of those acts he was still on the fence about.

Blake shuddered, closing in on his climax. Miguel distended and grasped his hair tighter through his knuckles.

He garbled a scream.

Eyes squinting to focus, he was concerned he'd get scalped bald if Miguel didn't hurry up and come. The grip on his hair kept getting tighter. Man, did he need a haircut.

On the final cry, Miguel pressed his shins up against Blake's torso. The long cock buried bottomless down his throat.

"I'm gonna come." His friend quivered, hovering over his friend. "Ready?"

The power-heavy frame pinned him down. He blinked his eyes with encouragement. His body pressed further onto the mattress.

Upon the first squirt, he realized he'd swallow the orgasm. He hadn't intended to as he figured at the last second he'd pull out and take it on the face. But he didn't expect what came next as the hot liquid shot down his throat.

Miguel squeezed his nose shut. "Take it. Don't breathe. Just swallow."

Nostrils pinched, unable to inhale, he swallowed.

At high-speed he jammed, getting into his orgasm. The cock didn't permit air into his taut mouth to breathe. In a longer shot, more cum spurted.

He swallowed again.

Miguel shouted several things in Spanish which he didn't understand, but he knew what they implied. Climbing off Blake, he wiped his forehead. Strands of his wavy hair were wedged between his dark-skinned fingers.

As he lay in awe over what had transpired, he wiped his lips dry with his hands, rubbing them, sort of in shock. Okay, a lot in shock. He'd gone there. He'd given him a blow job, and not just any blow job—Miguel came in his mouth, a notable first, for sure. Oddly, he didn't feel as freaked out as he thought he would. They weren't in college exploring their man-love. This was strictly an act of sex, possibly with the hottest man on the planet, who just happened to be his best friend. A good guy, a little crazy on the domination thing, but sincere.

Switching his alpha behavior to omega compassion, Miguel kissed his face and chest, slowly and romantically.

"I didn't think you'd be able to take my roughness." He pulled them closer together, skin to skin, as one. "Was I too much?"

"You were...perfect." He didn't know what the fuck else to say. He thought he would've told him to stop before he came...so much for that. *Perfect* was it. Oral sex with *Señor* Santana could not have been any hotter if Vive and Thor had been there to choreograph every move.

194

"Is this how you want the week to play out? This intense?"

He didn't want to want this. But what just happened, that right there, was probably—no it was *for certain*—the best time of his life. "I'd love nothing more," he panted, realizing he hadn't come yet. On the norm, he masturbated once a day, sometimes twice. He needed to release, so he tugged. "Now it's my turn."

"No, Blake."

"Mig, yes."

"Your load belongs to me. I'll say when and how you'll come. And it's not …time…yet." His voice was thick and in control as he sneered. Then he burst into laughter. "We gotta go pick up M2, and we're going to be late. No orgasm for you today, *amigo*. It's babysitting time."

"Aren't we lucky?"

His jaw softened as his face fell. He also wasn't going to have any time to go to the police station. Not unless he wanted to clue Miguel in, and he didn't. His friend was in such a great mood with his upcoming Barcelona exhibit to work on and his parents to come out to. The last thing he needed was to help Blake clean up his messy past. A past even he and his lawyers were unsure how to fix.

Upper East Side

"How do you think Miguel and Blake are getting along?" Lex rolled over, facing Massimo who was getting up to feed M2.

The previous night, she didn't sleep very well. How could she? She'd spent the entire day in bed, dozing off. Plus, her life was upside-down.

"I bet they're screwing each other's brains out."

"You men. Such pigs."

"*Sì*. Imagine *deux* pigs together." Massimo made an oinking noise as he put his robe on.

Her fiancé was cute with his deep baritone voice and Italian accent making animal sounds. As serious about appearances as he was, deep down inside, he was a kid at heart. That's what she loved about him most, his playfulness.

"I can be piggy with you," Lex joked. The pregnancy news, DNA letter, and the TV show taping had involuntarily caused them to put sex on hold.

"Tonight, you and me."

"Seriously?"

"Cancel Poppy. Let's spend the day in bed together, *bella*." He turned to face her and opened his robe.

The man could get a hard-on in a millisecond. She had never seen anything as splendid as Massimo before.

"Masi." Lex threw a decorative pillow at him.

"*Bella*, its Sunday, *per favore*." This was his day to be treated as a God.

"Okay, tonight it is." Lex laughed. She didn't think they'd ever be one of those couples who needed to schedule sex, but it appeared so. "I'm sorry we're taping, but this morning was the only slot the producers could fit us in with our schedule."

The Poppy White Show was owned by Gotham Media Group, who'd acquired Vive's *Debauchery* magazine. Poppy aired weekly at 4p.m. with holiday and Sunday specials on the Lifestyle Channel. The Tittoni royal wedding was expected to be the network's highest-rated show for the year.

"Espresso?" Massimo smiled then looked at her belly. "Wait, the baby can't have caffeine."

"Chamomile tea with lemon." She noticed the time. "Vive and Taddy will be here soon. I'm going to get in the shower."

She went into the bathroom and undressed. Her best friend had texted her a few more times the night before, worried about the wedding. She didn't have a clue what was really going on with her. And how would she? What she couldn't figure out was why Vive's behavior was growing increasingly erratic. Blake was skittish enough as it was about being in the wedding. She sure as hell didn't need her getting all maidzilla. The Easton Essential showroom manager had told Massimo that Vive had come in to try the dress on with a bad attitude, cussing up a storm, anti-wedding this and anti-wedding that. Aside from embarrassing herself, she'd hurt Lex's feelings.

At first, the showroom manager thought Vive was just plain rude until she found her passed out in one of the dressing rooms, wasted.

An hour later, Lex opened the foyer's French doors, seeing Taddy smiling and Vive frowning.

Massimo and Jemma were in the kitchen. Miguel and Blake had just left with M2 for the day. The Poppy White Show preparations were full steam ahead.

"Morning, Easton." Not making eye contact, Vive strutted in right past her and plopped Hedda on the white carpeting.

"Hi, Viveca." She addressed her by her full name when she was pissed off, and she was. Why Vive couldn't have come earlier, alone, was anyone's guess.

"Taddy." She hugged her friend who always smelled of tuberose.

"I'm wearing silk. Don't squeeze me so tight, I'll wrinkle." She let go of Lex and stepped through the entryway. Her long, ginger hair was pulled up by her oversized sunglasses. A pair Lex had purchased for her when they were shopping while in St. Barth last winter. "What's up with you?"

"Nothing. I'm fine. As I told you two in my texts, I'm A-Okay."

Typical Vive, she fixed herself a cocktail at the bar on the far side of the living room. The dog followed her, as best as she could; Hedda couldn't see, but got around okay.

"Can you please wait 'til after we're done taping to get trashed?" Lex inhaled deeply through her mouth and then tried to force a smile. She wasn't kidding.

"No, I can't. I'm stressed out as it is. I need a bloody Mary, or two, to take this edge off." Vive filled up a glass with ice from the mini fridge. The cubes clinked loudly against the crystal.

"Please, Vive, prep me on this interview." She hoped to win her over, put her in a good mood, make her feel important and part of the wedding process. Was that what bothered her friend? Did she feel left out?

"Taddy has the preliminary questions. It's mostly about who's in the wedding party, what we're wearing, your music selection, the usual bridal mumbo-jumbo."

"Right, of course." Lex motioned Taddy over and whispered in her ear, *"What's with her?"* It saddened her to see their friend acting up. She thought back over the week. Had she done anything to tick Vive off? Not that she knew of.

"Beats me. She picked up her bridesmaid's dress yesterday. That's all I know." Taddy shrugged.

Lex could usually tell when she fibbed to keep the peace; she wasn't.

"And?"

"Talk to her."

"Vive…" She stepped closer, picking up fluffy Hedda and giving her a hug. Lex waved the dog's dainty paw in Vive's face and asked, "What's wrong?"

"Why did you ask me over here an hour early?" Unscrewing the blue lid from a Grey Goose bottle, she poured the clear liquid into a glass.

"To talk and catch-up." Lex didn't want to state her reasons, not in front of Taddy. She realized she'd have to talk to her best friend directly. Trying to get Vive to weigh in on the matter was a huge mistake.

"My champagne toast is written. I have my plus one. I'm all set."

"The tomato mixer is in the other fridge." Lex went to get it for her, giving up on trying to keep Vive sober for today. "Who's your date?"

"Warner's brother, Sheldon," Taddy interjected.

"Studly Sheldon." Lex thought they'd make a great pair. They both loved booze, sex, and parties. "You two will be a hit." She handed the mixer to Vive.

Warner and Taddy had been dating for a few years now. Warner was a busy billionaire, but he always made time for Taddy. Sheldon, on the other hand, was trouble. Hot, yummy, fuckable trouble were the words Vive used when anyone mentioned Sheldon Truman.

"Thanks, I'll drink it straight." Vive raised her glass in the air and downed it as a shot.

Oh, brother.

"That's better." She adjusted her pink lip-gloss. "Lex, I have to ask you something?"

"What?" Confusion irked her. This was supposed to be about her and Taddy. How did Vive's drama get into this?

"Did you talk to Blake? Did he tell you I didn't want to be in the wedding? That's it. Isn't it? That's why you wanted me over here so damn early to tell me what a bad friend I am to you."

"What? No." She felt slapped across the face.

"Why don't you want to be in the wedding?" Taddy asked.

"Come off it, Brill, and you do?"

"Yes, of course." Taddy didn't waver.

"Why don't you want to be in my wedding?" Feeling a burning streak down her spine, she folded her arms and tried not to lose it.

"I'm too old for this."

"Too old?" her BFF repeated.

"To be a bridesmaid. I'm practically thirty, for Christ's sake." Vive's face reddened as her voice became louder. "Isn't that why you wanted me over here bright and early this morning, to go off on me? I told Blake—"

"No. That's not it at all." Lex knew the wedding would be hard for Blake, but she didn't imagine Vive would be at odds. It didn't make any sense. "I asked you over so I could talk to you about something else, privately. It's not important now." She held her friend's hand and said, "If you don't want to be in the wedding, you don't have to be. Leave."

"What?"

"You heard me. Go." Lex dropped her hand slowly, as if it was the last time she'd ever touch her. "You're not needed here today. You can go get wasted somewhere else."

"Lex," Taddy scolded.

Tears glistened on Vive's striking features. "I didn't realize the wedding was going to be such a big production. I mean, Saint Patrick's Cathedral and The Plaza? Jesus Christ. Who are you, Princess Kate?"

"Sort of." Taddy glared at her. "She *is* marrying a prince."

"The dress we have to wear goes to the floor."

"Most black-tie affairs require gowns as such. You're a Farnworth. You've been to a million of these types of events. Vive, what is wrong with you?"

She put her hands in the air and raised her voice. "This isn't you, Lex. You used to be so low-key. Ever since you met Massimo, you've changed."

"Well, this *is* me now. And if you don't want to see me happy then you don't have to come at all. Blake, too. The both of you. I'm done."

Taddy tried to step between them. "Lex doesn't mean it."

"Yes, I do. Get out of here, Farnworth!" She'd had it. Lex had heard of brides who lost their cool and fired their maids days prior to the ceremony. God damn, she'd become one of them. "Over the years, I have bent over backwards for you."

"Who asked you to?"

"*You* did!" she shouted.

"I have not."

"Vive, you are delusional." Her temples pounded. "Who was there when you buried San? Took you to rehab for pill addiction? Helped you sell your magazine?" She slapped her own mouth. Did she really just say all of that, out loud? Oh, no. The second the words came out of her mouth, she regretted them. She'd crossed the line.

It took a lot to make Vive cry. Over the years, she'd flown first-class to Hell and back. She choked back the sobs and said, "You, Lex. You will always be the friend I look up to, my role model. But I have news for you, girlie. I'm...not...*you*. I don't keep a scorecard. But if we're tallying up...*who* was the only girl at Avon Porter who talked to you because you were so fat?"

Lex felt her jaw drop.

"Me. That's who."

Vive eyed her up and down, making Lex feel thirteen all over again.

"And *who* was the only woman in this city who stood by your side privately and publicly when your father whacked himself and you lost everything, including the shirt on your back?"

She still didn't have a word for her. Vive had never spoken to her like that before.

"Again, it was *me*." Vive stepped in her face. Her black pupils swallowed her gray eyes. "And *who* was the first journalist to give your not-so-special fashion designs a glowing review?"

"Get the fuck outta here, Farnworth!" Lex had heard enough. "I don't need this shit from you. I don't need you in my life, Vive."

"That's obvious, isn't it, Princess Tittoni? You have yourself a very special wedding." With that, her shaking hands picked up Hedda and she stormed out.

Massimo came into the living room, face white as snow at what he had obviously heard. Jemma stood behind him, her mauve, glossy mouth hung open.

"Fuck. I didn't mean what I said. I just flipped." Pinching the bridge of her nose in frustration, she realized how hard she'd worked over the years to not lose her shit, and she had just blown up all over the place in a monstrous way. "I don't understand Vive. What's going on with her?"

"Vive has her good days and not so good days, Lex. You know this." Taddy put her arms her around her. "Jemma has your designs. I've drafted your talking points on index cards." She pulled the papers out from her Birkin bag and sat them on a nearby end table. "If I know Vive, she's headed to The Pierre to drink. Can you handle Poppy without me?"

"Go. Be with her. I'll call you if there's a problem."

"Know I'm not taking sides. I'm just nervous Vive might..."

"Me, too."

The last time Vive hurt herself was when she'd learned the little baby girl she'd been forced by her parents to give up for adoption, the infant she'd always wanted to see again, had no interest in ever meeting her. The adoptive parents had reinforced a closed-adoption policy even as the child grew into her teen years.

She turned, facing Massimo and Jemma. Her wedding seemed frivolous right then. "Can we cancel? Please."

"*Sì*. I will call Poppy and tell her no show for today. She will understand."

"No, I don't mean the show, Masi."

"*Bella*?"

"I want to call off our wedding."

Stunned, Massimo asked, "Are you sure, *bella*?"

"I'm sure."

Lex didn't see the sense in celebrating without all her friends. If Vive and Blake weren't happy for her, she wasn't going to rub their noses in it. From the start, her wedding had been what everyone else wanted. She was over it. Maybe Vive was right. Maybe she was becoming to frou-frou for her own self. Well, not anymore!

Chapter Twelve

Madeline's High Tea

Upper East Side

Miguel's expectations of Blake lending a hand babysitting his nieces ranked at about zero. But to his surprise, Ofelia, age four, and Cierra, age six, adored them together.

Blake treated the girls to Madeline's Tea Room at The Carlisle Hotel, an Art Deco institution on the Upper East Side. M2 slept in the stroller; Ofelia and Cierra were in wonder over the 24-karat gold leaf-covered ceiling. Studying the mural depicting the tales of Madeline's adventures, the imagery featured illustrations by Ludwig Bemelmans. He pointed to each drawing and educated the girls on the wall's story. They munched on raisin scones spread with clotted cream and raspberry jam. Miguel never saw his nieces as captivated as this before, let alone eating anything other than cheese pizza.

A pianist, who stirred memories of his late grandmother, played nursery rhymes from Mother Goose. Cierra knew the words and sang along while Ofelia clapped, swaying her shoulders and bumping into Blake, then him, then back to Blake.

"*Tío* Miggy," Cierra whispered in his ear, chomping on a pink jellybean which she'd screamed tasted as yummy as a real watermelon. "Me and Ofelia like *Blakey*." She popped another candy in her mouth. "He's fun."

He grabbed the bag of sweets from her sticky hands. He hoped to have the kids back to his sister before their sugar crash arrived. "I like Blake, too."

"*Tío* Miggy?"

"*Sí,* Cierra?"

"Is he coming to *Papá*'s for dinner?" she asked as her brown eyes widened with anticipation.

Cierra possessed an inquisitive side. Her intelligence was from her grandfather, his father. He noted how alike they were. His father always asked a lot of questions.

"Blake will be there for dinner." The fact he'd be coming *out* to his family was an abdomen-jolt he'd not forgotten. He never thought he'd have the support to come out to his parents—until then.

"Yeah!" Ofelia overheard and cheered on. She reached for his hand and squeezed it.

Her little fingers in his hand reminded him how unconditional love felt. He never wanted to not have his nieces in his life. The girls were so very special to him. He hoped his sister wouldn't react negatively to his being gay and do something drastic, like not allow him time with the girls.

After tea, they walked to his sister's condo near the Whitney Museum, returning his nieces to their nanny. They then headed over to Central Park for a walk, pushing M2 in the stroller.

North of the Conservatory Water at East Seventy-Fourth Street, they stood facing Alice in Wonderland. A bronze sculpture featured Miss Alice atop a large mushroom surrounded by the Cheshire cat, Dormouse, Dinah, and the Mad Hatter.

"Ever imagine yourself with kids?" He knew Blake's response but wanted to ask to be certain.

"Sure, all the time," Blake answered without any hesitation.

"*Really*?" He heard his own voice crack. Miguel remembered Blake wanted kids when he was married, but if he was so uncertain about romance a second time around, wouldn't his desire to be a father change, as well?

"You sound surprised." Blake slowed his pace to walk in tandem with him. He looked a bit silly with the stroller. He was so tall and uncomfortable with it. "Diego and I were looking into adopting. We both knew our marriage wasn't going anywhere, though, so we stopped."

"A boy or a girl? You have a preference?"

"Nope. As long as he, or she, is healthy, that's all that matters. And you?"

"Same. I'd love to have a baby." He wanted children. This was his first time articulating it to anyone. Not even Lex or Vive knew. To his revelation, his response came out with natural ease.

"*Really*?" Blake mimicked the tone he'd heard moments before.

"Don't be sarcastic." He pulled Blake into him as they picked up speed, pushing M2 through the park.

"You didn't strike me as relationship-bound, let alone the fatherly type, 'til today." Blake grabbed his hand and complimented, "Watching you with your nieces was sweet."

Honored to be holding his buddy's hand in public, the sensation felt good, but different for him. His insides tingled with excitement. Guys from Miguel's past shied away from public affection. Not Blake. In the group, he hugged everyone as he greeted them. His arm at a party held friends' hips, as he laughed and carried on. It was odd to think that behind closed doors, a man so giving would receive so little. He remained natural at being himself in any setting. Always comfortable with being gay, even effeminate at times, he didn't hold back. He wasn't affected, but expressive, and in touch with his emotions. It struck him as refreshing.

"I've helped raise the girls since they were born. Inez's ex-husband lost custody last year when his money laundering surfaced."

"I'm sorry. You never talk about your sister's life. I remember one tiny blurb about it in the Wall Street Journal, but that was it. Lex said you didn't want to talk about it, so I didn't pry."

"My dad tries to keep us as media-free as possible."

Unlike the rest of his friends' families, the Santana's avoided scandals. Looking back on that statement, he realized it was one of the reasons he'd never come out. He didn't want to bring shame to his family.

Miguel pointed to a bench for them to sit. The plaque on the backrest read, *"Madeline Kahn, 1942-1999, A brilliant actress and lovely soul who loved this city and this park."* He continued, "The judge wasn't lenient on him in regards to grand larceny, falsifying business records, and securities fraud." His ex-brother-in-law was such a pompous ass who never thought he'd get caught. "He's locked up for the next two decades. The girls don't have a father who's around." Resentment entwined inside him.

"I feel ridiculous about the tea room." Blake's cheeks reddened.

"Don't. Today was great. The girls loved it and they enjoyed you." He couldn't remember the last time such happiness had decorated their sweet little faces. "Cierra sang and Ofelia danced. Granted, their good moods may have been from too much candy." He beamed, holding his hand tighter.

"It's frivolous."

"My nieces don't have to live in a constant reminder their dad's a con and Mom's caught up in her career."

"I see…Inez isn't home much, is she?"

"No. It makes me *loco*. But I'm not their parent, she is." He studied Blake's eyes for a second to see if he followed. He did.

"Does your mom help out?"

"*Mamá's* preoccupied with my *papá*." Apprehension swept through him.

His high forehead rose up a fraction. "What's wrong with your dad?"

"Let's change the subject, okay? Why spoil a perfect day?" He shuddered at the thought about telling him about his father's health or how they left Mexico the way they did. His family never talked about it; he wasn't sure he even knew how.

"You're not spoiling anything by telling me more about your folks. You never speak about them." Blake pressed on. "We've been friends for ten years, yet I feel as if I'm meeting you for the first time. You don't go deep with *anyone* about *anything*."

"Ouch." His words hurt. He spoke the truth, but Miguel had never heard his standoffishness packaged as his demise.

"Take your birthday, for example."

"Don't start."

"Taddy nor I, not even Lex or Vive, have a clue when it is."

He put his hand on Blake's leg, nudging him to change the subject. His attention shifted to M2 in hopes he needed care. Nope. The infant was zonked out. *Darn*. Miguel didn't want to go there with him. His friend had revealed so much about himself already. He hadn't shared as much. He just couldn't bring himself to do it.

"Why?" He crossed his legs.

"I don't celebrate my birthday, you know this."

"The Santana's are Catholic, not Jehovah's Witnesses."

"Meaning?" He tried not to laugh at his friend's sarcasm. It was always light and funny.

"You have no reason not to have a cake and let us celebrate you. Even if for a day."

"Stop. I don't care for the attention."

Blake rolled his blue eyes dramatically. It reminded Miguel a bit of Thor.

"You never talk about your childhood. None of us know much about your life before college. You have no friends from when you were little," Blake listed as if he'd stored the items away, waiting to unleash them over the last ten years. "I don't know what your favorite meal was growing up."

That last one was a stretch, but he'd entertain it. "I hear you." Opening up for him wasn't natural. Miguel knew as a boy he was different. He didn't make much of an attempt to have friends. Artwork was his focus and what he enjoyed. It was his haven to escape. "I'm flattered you'd take an interest. No one ever does. Most guys who come out later in life, or those who don't come out at all, don't have real friends, ones they can be themselves with."

"I get that. But you've always been *out* to me, Lex, Taddy, and Vive. Thor, too."

"*Sí.* I'm thankful every day to have you all. But before college, I only had Diego in high school as a friend. We had a connection because we both knew we were different. Not like the other boys in class. We became friends, but Diego and I never really talked. Not the way you like to talk."

"I was married to the man. I know what you mean."

"After you two got married, Diego and I didn't speak anymore. And you were busy with your career at Brill, Inc., and I had my art."

"I'm sorry we grew apart. But please, share something." Blake grabbed at his arm.

He realized his friend didn't just *want* to know something about him, he *needed* to know.

"My favorite dish is chicken mole. What's yours?"

"Hmm, Eggs Benedict for breakfast, a good BLT for lunch, and for dessert, it's—"

"Angel food cake." Miguel remembered because he'd watched him eat it every summer in the Hamptons. He thought it was the blandest thing he'd ever tasted. "I don't talk about my folks. You know I don't celebrate my birthday." No cake meant zero wishes. Why set up false expectations?

"Why?" Blake's eyes hooded with hawk-like intensity, trying their best to get him to open up.

Miguel was close. He wanted to share, but he couldn't. "Stop." He didn't know where to start. He didn't seek pity as a kid or now. Talking about his early years was something he just didn't do.

"Fine." He sighed with defeat and slouched back against the bench. "Tonight, I'm cooking us pork loin and corn on the cob. But I'm happy to try and make your chicken thing."

He understood that all Blake ever wanted was for Miguel to feel as if he belonged and was cared for by the group. But what about his friend without Taddy, Thor, or Vive? Just the two of them. Would they stand a chance?

"You reminded me. I'm giving you the night off from all household duties and cooking us dinner."

"Why the change?"

"I figured we'd take turns." He didn't have the heart to tell him his cooking sucked.

M2 started to cry. Without being asked, Blake reached into the stroller and picked him up. "He's wet."

"Here, let me." He grabbed a diaper.

"I got it." More confident than he was that morning when they'd picked M2 up, Blake took charge of changing M2.

I'm impressed.

Lower East Side

That evening, Miguel did as promised and made chocolate chicken mole with yellow rice. He'd dropped M2 off with Birdie who'd called and asked that her grandson come to her place. She said Lex and Massimo wanted privacy after their long day. He figured the TV show taping must've wiped them out. Poppy could be exhausting when she wanted to be.

After supper, they watched the movie *Y Tu Mamá También.* He pressed his naked body against Blake's backside and started to give him a hot oil massage scented in vanilla.

Brutus laid by the window asleep. In thirty-second intervals or so, he released a windbag of air from his flapping jowls.

"I've never seen a dog snore before." Blake smiled warmly toward Brutus.

Could that be affection he caught in his friend's blue eyes?

"Do you want me to wake him up to stop?" Miguel asked.

"No, it's fine. He's growing on me." Blake started to laugh. "He must get his snoring from you."

"I don't snore."

"Yes, you do. None of your boys who've stayed the night ever told you that before?"

"No. No one sleeps over." He realized the guys he'd hosted in the past came over, got fucked, and left. Blake was possibly the first guy ever to sleep on his pillow until morning. He pressed his friend's shoulders firmly. "How's that feel?"

"I've never had a massage in bed."

His body responded to every touch. "Your shoulders are tense. You anxious?" He pressed his fingers harder, sensing worry between his fingers.

"Watching this erotic movie and straining my eyes to read what they're saying is stressing me out," he joked.

Turning his head on the gray pillow, Blake revealed a sweet grin. On his stomach, he stretched out, comfortable in Miguel's arms. He felt his friend's entire body go limp. He worked his thumbs down the spine toward his ass and realized he should have a bigger TV. His small screen was from way back. Then again, he wasn't one for sitcoms or at-home movies. Not when he was in bed with the hottest blonde he'd ever known.

Blake arched his ass upward for him to play with. He spread the buttocks wide with his slippery hands and admired the tight pucker in the center.

"I can't wait to be inside you." He settled his cock between the ass cheeks and ground.

"I'm nervous."

"Don't be. I'll be gentle." He wanted to bust his nut inside him right then. Their ten-year sexual build-up was enough to make anyone explode. Blake was worth the wait. One more day and his friend would be his.

"You, gentle?" Blake tightened his ass cheeks and hugged Miguel's cock as if it were a hot dog enclosed by a bun and said, "Yeah, right." He shuffled his legs and hands under his frame.

"You'll see, my *bebé*. I'll make you hum." He finished the session with reflexology to the feet.

In approval, Blake arched his heels and asked, "Who taught you the pressure points of the feet?"

He hesitated. He'd never kept anything from his friend, so why start now? "My lover from last summer, the one who worked at The Healing Institute down on Canal Street."

"The tall Irish guy who lived in the East Village? The one with the orange hair?"

"*Sí*, the dirty ginger," Miguel confirmed. "Gillian Neeson."

"What happened with you and Gil?"

"It ended."

"Why?"

"New York has a lot of men to choose from. Gil got what he wanted and then went on his way." Miguel didn't examine men's actions too much. What was the point? He didn't love them. He only loved one man.

"Mig, what happened to all these lovers?"

"What do you mean?" he asked as if the answer was obvious.

"You've had your handful over the years. I've seen guys throw themselves at you over and over again." Blake flexed his toes.

"No one's ever stuck around long enough to get serious with me," he replied huskily in his ear.

Miguel's cock swelled thick. *I must fuck you soon, buddy.* Dipping the head of his dick against Blake's anal starburst, his asshole closed tight. Taking his hands, he split the ass cheeks wide and rubbed his cock vertically against his crack, teasing him.

"Ooh," Blake moaned as he pressed deeper. "You have magic hands."

He leaned down and kissed his friend on the ass cheek. "*Muah.*" It was a sweet gesture and created a loud sound against his skin.

They laughed.

The tune changed as he spat a wad—dead center—into the asshole. He buried it further with his fingers.

"Mig?" Blake squirmed.

"*Bebé,* I'll give you a sample for what's to come." Miguel kept him flat, chest down, and sat on the backside of his legs. He slid his cock alongside Blake's crack, building up friction.

Gripping down on the pillow underneath, Blake prepared to be impaled. "Put a condom on."

"I'm not going to fuck you." *Not without a commitment.* He leaned forward and prodded his cock at his friend's opening. He'd never gotten that close to raw sex. "Keep still," he ordered and pushed the head of his dick in, just a little. "Yeah, you are…tight."

The pressure against the asshole felt wonderful. He sat there for a second, taking pleasure in having his friend under him, watching his cock's head press shallowly into his asshole. The temptation to drive his cock to the core was strong.

Blake's ass rose higher, causing his cock to swell and sink further into his ass. He arched himself under Miguel. "Mig…get a condom."

"Hot." He pulled his head out.

Blake dropped his head back down onto the pillow and mumbled something, but he couldn't understand what he'd said.

Ass cheeks squeezed together, he rested his cock on Blake's crack. He placed his hand over his cock while his base grinded against the asshole. Humping him, he sped up as his nuts slapped back and forth. "My cock rubbing your virgin ass is intense."

Reaching under himself, Blake started to jack off.

"No, *bèbe*." Miguel grabbed his hands and pulled them up behind the small of his back, holding him down.

"I have to come tonight."

He shook his head. "I want your load full for tomorrow."

"Why?" Blake turned back, staring up at him in confusion.

"For extra lube." He humped him, not giving in to his friend's urge to jack himself off. "Your virgin hole is going to require a lot of elbow grease."

"Please," Blake cried in need.

He could hear it in his voice. His friend wanted to be pounded so hard he was aching for it.

"I said no." Miguel let go of Blake's arms and lowered his lips to Blake's ass, rimming him for a few minutes, ramming his tongue in and out, going deep. "You enjoy getting your ass eaten, don't you?"

"Fuck, Mig, yeah," Blake encouraged, screaming in pleasure. "I can't wait to have you inside me." He reached behind him and held on to Miguel's hand.

No one ever held his hand when he was in bed with them, 'til then. *Sweet*.

Finished rimming, he pulled on Blake's hair, holding his head back and pressed into his body. He shifted under him, possibly trying to position his ass to take Miguel's cock. He humped his cock faster, going back and forth against the crack.

"I'm going to come." He lifted his body up a bit then shot his hot seed over Blake's back.

He leaned over him. "Let me get a towel and wipe you down."

As he went into the kitchen, he thought about what Blake asked him, about the guy from the East Village, convinced he'd given other guys a chance. Maybe he'd gone after the wrong men in the past. Guys sought him for his cock and alpha intentions. Bad habits remained his demise.

He'd do whatever was needed to put a stop to it, hoping his friend felt the same way. Hard to tell; he wasn't the best at reading people. Everything about Blake's body said why not? Yet, the previous night's conversation rang caution in his mind. *"Jury's out on having romance. But I don't think it's in my cards."*

He couldn't make sense of Blake's behavior. At times, he was resistant, not wanting to be intimate and struggling with his walls, with letting him in. He could tell. But then they'd get comfortable and there was a hunger inside of him, emptiness, a desire to be loved and wanted so badly. It almost pained him to watch it. He'd do whatever it took to fill those desires, but his heart had to come with the entire package. Miguel needed his love; more than ever before, he wanted his friend to love him, and be in love with him...only him.

When he went back to clean Blake up and turn off the television, he was curled on the edge of the bed. He'd dozed off. He noticed he always slept with one foot off the mattress as if he was going to get up suddenly and make a run for it. Did he sleep like that at home, too? And if so, why?

Miguel held him in his arms. *I love you.* If he spoke out loud, he'd choke.

He thought about what would happen if Blake said no to a relationship with him. He'd have to end the friendship. Seeing him would be too complicated as friends. He wouldn't go through it again. The week required courage to carry out the *Seven Desires*. They'd barely gotten the list started, and already he'd fallen harder for him, more than he imagined.

He was in way over his head with this one.

Part Two

I Love Blake

THE MANHATTANITES

love, friendship, scandal, and drama to the hilt

"Whoever said 'speak your mind' was high, drunk or partying with our girl Vive Farnworth. Sentiments like 'I'm in love with you' are better left…unsaid."—Miguel Santana, kinky bastard, dog lover.

Chapter Thirteen

Gin Showers

Blake was on his back, looking up at him.

Miguel hovered over him. Intent with his stare, focused with his control, his shoulder muscles appeared tight. His arms were flexed, ready to move into action.

"I want you and me to be as one."

He was the most gorgeous man he'd ever seen.

They kissed, sending a chill over his body. He spread his legs wide.

"To have a family together. To make babies together," Miguel said as his full and hungry lips glistened.

"Silly, two men can't make babies together," he said, though he knew this was just a dream.

He wanted...babies.

He wanted...a family.

He wanted...love.

Unconditional. Accepting. Forever.

"We can try," Miguel joked then pulled his long legs up over his shoulders. He stroked his cock, telling him how magnificent his body was and how sexy his muscles were.

Was this his second chance at love? If so, he'd get it right this time. Blake felt reborn just being with him.

"Relax." He massaged the tight puckery rim of his asshole.

"I will. Give me time. I need more time."

"Let me inside you."

"Now?"

"Sí, right now." His lips curled up with encouragement. He was going to top him that time. Slowly, he inserted one finger. "Bébé, you are a tight ball of nerves."

"I want you to..." He swallowed hard at his friend's determination.

"Will you let me cum inside of you?"

"Never."

Reaching for a condom, Miguel sheathed his cock, pressed at the tip, and repositioned himself over Blake. His mouth tightened into a tense smile as his eyes glittered for him. "You belong to me. I'll take care of you. Let me love on you."

"I'd like that, Mig. I want that. I do."

"Do you want me?"

"Yes, I do."

"You are so fucking sexy," he almost growled as he penetrated deep.

"Mig..." He shuddered. He'd never had a cock inside him. It was as he'd always dreamed: full, warm, and intense. Though he knew this was a dream, it still felt real. "I want to know more about you."

Thrusting up inside him, Miguel suddenly became quiet. His face hung low at Blake's nape, kissing him while he focused.

"I need more time with you. Share with me."

He shushed him to be quiet. His body picked up speed.

Feeling the moan from the back of his throat, he held on to him. This was special.

"I'm going to come." His friend grabbed him by the hair. Hard. Unexpected. Almost violent, and not in a hot-please-dominate-me way.

He felt the burn and unexpected wetness shoot inside him.

A haunting laugh erupted, filling the room with a grave intensity.

His hand went down to his ass. "You came inside of me," he cried, sitting up to see the condom on the mattress, torn off and unused. "You tricked me."

"Stupid faggot."

That voice. Demented and twisted. Miguel brought his face up. It wasn't his friend at all.

Diego. It was his ex-husband laughing again.

"You wanted my seed, my gift, and my love. You got it."

This is just another bad dream, *he told himself over and over. A nightmare.*

Again, he woke to Brutus. The dog edged himself onto the mattress. His snout licked Blake's fingers which hung off the bed.

He pushed the furry alarm clock away. He wasn't keen on cuddling notions with the dog just yet. Not even after the nightmare he'd just had.

He turned around on the pillow to see Miguel wide awake and staring at him.

"Morning," he said softly.

"You okay?" Miguel pulled him in for a kiss.

His lips felt dry. "Yes, why?" He played dumb.

"This is the second night in a row you've had nightmares."

"Oh…they're noticeable?"

"You scream horrible things."

"Hmm. Maybe it's from watching TV. Or…I was reading a Stephen King novel last week, so I bet that's it. Yes."

"Nice try. There's something you're not telling me. What is it?" Miguel wrapped his muscular arms around him, pulling him on top of him.

God, he felt strong and supportive.

"Nothing," he dismissed him, realizing the Barcelona exhibit was the following week, Lex's wedding was coming up and Miguel had to come out to his family. This could wait until Diego was behind bars. It had been going on for well over a year; a few more days without his friend knowing would be fine.

Brutus barked.

"Duty calls." Blake never thought he'd be as relieved hearing his howl as he was just then. He rolled off him, laced up his sneakers for a jog and went to take Brutus downstairs.

When he returned, Miguel started the shower, so he fed Brutus breakfast.

Hot steam came from the door crack as it opened, "Get in, the water's *caliente*."

Sweaty from the run, he stripped naked with enthusiasm and stepped into the stall. He'd never taken a shower with another guy before.

Miguel kissed him, hard on his lips. He pulled him closer into an embrace and then ordered, "Get on your knees."

Squatting, water beaded along Miguel's magnificent chest. His nipples grew hard visibly. A slight fuzzy patch over his six-pack went from dry fawn to wet sable. His legs were bronzed and firm as tree trunks. His cock became eye level, soapy foam decorated the skin. His morning woody grew harder by the nanosecond.

Cock shuddering, he held on to his shaft and pointed his dick at Blake's face. "Close your eyes, *bébé*."

A second later, his penis shot gold. First a slow squirt, then a steady stream.

On delay, Blake shut his eyes and realized he'd get a different shower, a golden shower.

A warm stream inaugurated his forehead, trailing his left cheek then his right, and then over his lips. The watercourse beaded stronger onto his skin. He inhaled the piercing ammonia tang. He hadn't thought he'd like this, but he did. It was...different.

"Open your mouth."

Unafraid, he parted his lips. Miguel decorated his tongue with his steam. His mouth filled to the brim then the hot piss dribbled down his mouth.

"Spit."

Leaning forward, he did as instructed.

"Good boy." He lifted him, guiding him to stand. "Keep your eyes shut."

He smelled green apple as cold gel covered his face. Miguel's long fingers ran over his eyelids, cheeks, forehead, and neck, intensifying the fruity aroma. Sultry water rinsed him clean. Fresh.

"Okay, open."

Blake looked up, not quite forgetting his friend's beauty. His black pearl eyes raked over him, full lips and dimples received the gesture.

"Has anyone ever told you that you are the spitting image of Mario Lopez?"

"From *Extra* TV??"

"Ah-huh." He always appreciated his friend's sex appeal, but he'd never noticed how gentle and caring he was until that moment. He could be super sweet.

"Every day," Miguel returned, the smile accentuating his dimples to further resemble the TV actor. He handed him a toothbrush topped with paste and instructed, "Brush."

Scrubbing the toothbrush in his mouth, he cleaned over his top and bottom teeth, then his tongue back and forth, spat on the shower floor next to their feet, and rinsed his mouth in the shower.

A creamy shampoo was applied to his curls while standing under the showerhead. With a bristle brush, Miguel scrubbed his shoulders and back counterclockwise, followed by his chest, arms, legs, and feet clockwise.

He'd never had anyone wash his hair except at the salon. Overwhelmed by how the simplest gesture made him feel, he closed his eyes and tried to stand tall. In silence, he observed their closeness. *You...treat me as a gift. Make me feel special.*

This shower brought the intimacy between them to a newfound intensity.

Reaching down, Miguel grabbed him close, groin-to-groin. Their two cocks touched. "We're about the same size."

"Not quite," he corrected, believing Miguel to be bigger. He wasn't sure why, but he'd always felt so much smaller around him. Maybe it was his dominant personality, his confidence.

Miguel held onto his cock and rubbed his palm over the tip. He then circled his hand over his own. His dimpled grin increased.

He squirmed but stood his ground, looking his friend deep in his molten eyes. He wasn't backing down. Not then.

The challenge must've motivated what came next for Miguel reached behind him and grabbed his ass.

His mouth leaned up to Blake's right ear. "Tonight, I'm going to fist you. I want your ass clean." He buried two fingers inside him.

"Mig!" He loved this.

"Understand?"

"Yes." He was tempted to say, *No. No way in Hell*, but his friend seemed intent on fisting. He'd brought it up a few times. Who knew, he enjoyed his face fucking and golden shower, so maybe the pleasures would continue. "This morning was the hottest thing ever."

"I'm glad you're enjoying yourself." After grabbing the shave cream canister, Miguel lathered his scruff.

"I am, very much so."

Miguel popped off a new disposable razor lid from the shower caddy. Starting with Blake's right cheek, he glided the blade down, top to bottom and said, "Such a pretty face, for a man." He studied his eyes for confirmation.

"Oh, please…" He looked away knowing he wasn't one for compliments, especially about his face.

"Why do you dismiss what I say?" With an owner's grip, he turned his chin and shaved his upper neck.

"I wasn't raised placing an emphasis on looks." He felt the shower's heat steal into his pores. It was hard to listen to the compliments. Ever since that plane crash, back in college, he never thought of himself as attractive.

"You'd never know with the way you carry yourself."

"What do you mean?" He drew his upper lip down, enabling Miguel to shave under his nostrils.

"You take pride in the way you dress, the clothes, fit body, perfect teeth—"

"Thanks. I work in advertising. It's my job to look good."

"It shows."

Miguel pressed his lips against his mouth. He slid his tongue into his mouth and kissed him deeply, pulling his body in tight. The shave foam residue lubed their lips. Blake's backside rested against the tile wall, his torso buried deep in his friend's embrace.

"Why do you look away when I compliment you? Do I make you uncomfortable talking about how attractive you are?"

"No. I, ahhh…" God, how would he answer that? He tried to smile. "Mig, no one's ever said that to me before is all."

"Well, it's true. You're the most attractive guy I've ever met." Dropping the razor onto the ledge, he wrapped his arms around him.

With relentless enjoyment, he pressed into Miguel's rock-hard body. "Thank you." He saw acceptance in his friend's eyes. He'd never noticed it until then. Had he always looked at him that way and he'd just not seen it before?

The shower suddenly felt too small. He could barely breathe. "I better get dressed. I have some errands to run before work."

Miguel squirted shampoo onto his own hair as he stepped out and toweled off.

"Blake…"

"Yeah?"

"There's money on the counter to cover the items you bought for the apartment and for the lunch with my nieces. Take it."

"No."

"Take the money." There was no reasoning with Miguel.

"Fine. Enjoy your day." Blake wrapped a white fluffy towel around his torso and went to get dressed.

Downtown

Blake walked into the Family Court Clerk's Office even though he'd promised himself he wouldn't do this. Diego's actions weren't his to face. After the divorce, he hadn't expected to hear from him again. His attorney had suggested not talking to the police, not to tell them what had really gone down. He didn't have a case. No witnesses. No one had come forward.

He knew this. But he needed to be sure.

It was up to the victims, the people who Diego had hurt, to come forward and press charges. Blake felt terrible for them. Too ashamed by what his ex-husband had done, and there'd been no reports. How could they? He hoped, though, one of them would, and soon. Last he heard there were thirteen guys who'd fallen prey to Diego Oalo's erotic acts gone deadly wrong. One of them *had* to come forward. When he was alone and quiet, he thought about the men Diego had slept with. They were faceless, most nameless. But he had known a few of their names. Some were even his friends at one time. Were they under medical care? Had they told their loved ones? Or had they crossed over to the dark side with him, causing harm to others?

Diego's threat to kill him was a new act of desperation. Blake figured his ex-husband must be losing his head. He ought to be. He should lose a lot more than just his mind for what he'd done to those guys.

He needed to do what he'd always done: protect himself.

"I'd like to file a restraining order, please," he said to the woman who sat behind the desk chomping on a piece of gum. It was bright yellow, probably banana; he could see it swirling around in her mouth as her lips opened, crackled the gum, and then closed.

"One sec." The officer looked him up and down, as if he was too big and too male to be filing a restraining order.

But he was. Maybe that was his own paranoia, but he had to do what his gut told him. And that was to fill out the paperwork.

She turned around and shouted, "Hey, Chauncey, what file is the abuse relief application under?" Her Staten Island accent was thick.

"Oh, boy," he muttered. Hearing her say those words made his skin bump.

Another female detective approached. "Mornin'."

Wide-hipped, she had a coffee in her hands. The way she carried herself told him this Chauncey was the go-to lady for most things around there.

"I need to file a restraining order."

"Have you been hurt?" Chauncey stepped around and gave him a once-over.

"No. Not yet."

"Is the person you're seeking protection from a family member? Your brother or father?"

"My ex-husband."

"Interesting." The two women glanced at one another. "Was *he* arrested?"

"No. And he doesn't have a record. Not that I know of…not yet, anyway."

"Are you pressing charges against him?"

"We recently broke up. He's dangerous. I need to make sure he stays away from me."

Her head tilted to the side. "Sorry, but unless he's physically come after you or hurt you we can't file a restraining order with the courts."

"So…I have to wait for him to do something to file this?"

She pressed her lips together then muttered, "Afraid so…"

"What if he kills me?"

"Call nine-one-one if he attacks you. Then we'll file a report and the restraining order." Chauncey didn't seem fazed by the question.

Unbelievable!

"Thanks," he said sarcastically, wishing he hadn't deleted those darn texts from the night before. He would've showed them to her. Instead, he turned around and stormed out.

Would Diego try and hurt him?

Blake wasn't sure. He gave him almost his entire life savings to go away. He had no idea what he'd spend it on. He hoped it would go to the guys he'd fucked over, as he'd heard a few had asked for money, but he doubted that. He wanted to help everyone Diego had wronged. Like them, he was innocent. Hell, he didn't even know *it* had happened until a few months before. That was when his dreams of starting a family all came crashing down around him. They'd cancelled the adoption process and called their marriage quits.

All he could do was wait, see if one of them would come forward and tell.

He headed uptown to Brill, Inc. and twenty minutes later, he arrived at his office.

Taddy's personal assistant, Kelly Ivy Kailyn Izatt, who Taddy had nicknamed Kiki, and his assistant, Duckie Capri, stood in the hallway as if waiting for trouble. Duckie's appearance bestowed an all-knowing, all-gossiping, 'I have shit on you, boo daddy' face. And Kiki's sweet, innocent Mormon grace, which became more corrupt the longer she lived in Manhattan, spoke, 'Do tell, do tell'.

At twenty-two, Duckie was the youngest guy on the marketing team. On a good day, he stood at five-foot-ten with a tight bubble-butt and a young, round face, which he imagined most gay men dreamed about shooting their release over. He'd found his assistant while shopping at Barneys. A cosmetics queen behind the fragrance counter, his outgoing personality and recent degree from Pace University compelled Blake to offer him a job as his executive assistant.

The temptation to fuck him was also another factor. He'd dreamt of taking his assistant into his office, throwing him over his desk, and topping him. Married at the time, he never cheated. Plus, Duckie soon proved himself to be too annoying to screw. Looking back, he wasn't the best executive assistant, either, and he remained gifted in stirring up drama.

"Good morning, boss."

Duckie held the door wide with a Cheshire cat smile, making him suspicious.

He returned the greeting.

"Happy Monday, Mr. Morgan," Kiki enforced as Duckie's backup.

"Hello, Miss Izatt." He headed for his desk and set his briefcase down. Blake hoped the two returned to their cubicles. He stared up at his assistant when the man stepped closer, leaning in the doorway. "Yes?" He nodded him in as she followed behind.

"I received a text late Saturday evening from my friend Bobby who's been topping Jason who's bottoming for Ernie who said that my boss—that being Y-O-U—visited Exhale Bliss Spa and got your cannoli cleaned." Duckie smiled with a proud face for letting it rip in one breath.

Kiki giggled nervously and crossed her arms.

He wondered how long they'd waited to share their news. Seventy-two hours? Surprised their heads hadn't combusted from having kept it in for so long, he held his breath, attempting not to make his reaction obvious. "How would your friend know this?"

"Ernie manscaped you." Duckie and Kiki sat down in the chairs near his desk as if they were all in for a long, fascinating conversation.

"What exactly did Ernie say I had done?"

"Ernie reported your legs and chest were clipped, nuts shaved, and ass sugared."

"And what if I did?" Blake sat across from his assistant. The large glass desk between them protected him from the vicious gay drama brewing. He didn't like how comfortable the junior staff was making themselves when it came to personal matters.

"I want to go with you the next time, Mr. Morgan. I'm curious." Kiki, who came from Utah and started at Brill, Inc. about two years before, was up to her tits in sex talk from the staff. But as far as he knew, she'd remained a virgin, though they were all waiting for her curiosity to get the best of her. It would soon enough.

His assistant reached across the desk, straightening out the papers before them. "I'm happy for you, boss. You've been unbearable since your divorce."

"Have I really?"

"Painfully so." Duckie nodded. "If you're paving the road for traffic, does your spa service signify happy trails ahead?"

"Perhaps." He appreciated the sincerity.

"I also heard..."

"What?" Blake couldn't imagine anything else.

"*This* is where it gets *good*, Mr. Morgan." Kiki sat on the seat's edge as if she were getting ready to pull back some fantastical curtain to a freak show. "Go on."

"Ernie stated there was moaning coming from your treatment room. He also mentioned a special guest popped in...to massage you." Duckie crossed his legs as if he'd planned on serving up the dish for a long time.

"I'm going to get your little friend Ernie fired for spreading rumors."

His assistant tossed that morning's *Manhattanite Times* on his desk. Inside, a two-sentence blurb read, *"New York's gay socialite Blake Morgan III returns to the single scene. According to Exhale Bliss Spa, he's quaffed and raring to go."*

He gasped. "This is unbelievable. Why do they keep writing about me?"

"Ummm, next to Anderson Cooper and Andy Cohen, you're the most established and cutest gay in town," Duckie complimented and held a picture frame from his desk. It was a snapshot from a charity event with Taddy, Vive, and Lex. "You run with an elite group. Lex and Vive both make the papers week after week."

"I've never thought of myself that way."

His assistant stood, and Kiki rose to follow. "I've already taken four calls this morning from Perez Hilton's camp on *who* they believe your tall, dark stranger is. They're convinced he's topping you."

"First…I've never bottomed." Blake grabbed the paper from his hands. He didn't want it circulating; Taddy would have a field day. "Second, the mysterious man who came into the room is a dear friend. If his name is leaked out in the papers, he'd kill me." Thoughts about Miguel coming after him for spa rumors scared him, but also turned him on.

Duckie leaned over his desk, shoving his young, hairless bird-chest in his face. "Ernie told me who *he* was…"

"Oh, no."

"Our lips are shut tight, Mr. Morgan," Kiki reassured him and added in a lower voice, "Manhattan knows Miguel Santana is a Latin closet-case whose family has ties to Mexican government officials who'd have us killed for talking."

"Ernie identified Mr. Santana?" Blake's stomach flipped. If Miguel knew, he might not speak to him ever again. Then again, his friend had come to the spa on his own accord. This really wasn't any of his doing.

"I promise I won't tell Taddy." Kiki smiled. But who were they kidding? Taddy Brill was the mother hen. She knew everything about everyone at all times.

"Seeing as how he's your best friend, and Taddy's, too, we know Miguel is off-gossip-limits." Duckie rubbed his palms together.

"I love how the *Manhattanite Times* smears my name to pieces but never reports on *Taddy's* lifestyle. Why's that?"

"Miss Brill uses an alias when I book her spa appointments, such as the one you've had," Kiki replied. "At Exhale Bliss Spa I book her under *Mademoiselle Red*."

"Noted." Blake eyed his assistant to make sure this didn't happen again. And he needed to get on with his day.

"I didn't make your spa appointment, sir." Duckie's right eyebrow rose, signifying none of this would've happened if it had been left in his hands.

He pulled up his morning's schedule. "Call Thor and confirm my lunch with him. Also, pull the file on the Baden Cosmetics account. We should review the strategy for their new wrinkle cream. Taddy's going to want to do a press launch."

As they scampered out of his office, he couldn't help but feel attacked. First by his ex-husband, then the media, and finally his own staff.

A few hours later, Blake was hunched over the computer screen in disbelief. He sunk himself further into his Herman Miller chair. The morning's *Manhattanite Times* article prompted him to do internet research on various socialite articles from years past.

Will the online wedding announcement to Diego from forever ago ever vanish?

He scrolled to yet another tabloid website displaying photos from their wedding ceremony. Both he and his assistant had called the gossip rags pleading with them to eliminate the posts when Diego moved out.

No luck.

Any time someone would do an online search for him, there they were. The online wedding photos and articles celebrating his union would haunt him forever. What made it worse were several gay, New York bloggers posted in recent weeks follow-up articles announcing his divorce. One entry read, *"First Young New England Gay Couple to Wed, Now First to Divorce."*

Ouch.

For cyber eternity, he'd be known as a gay divorcée. He felt as if he were damaged goods. Worse, he was pretty sure Diego would be arrested soon. He had to be. And then his name would *really* hit the papers.

Shit.

A knock at the door.

"Blake…it's Taddy."

Carrying a package with her left arm and flipping her red hair back with the other, his boss pushed her way into his office, closing the door behind her. Pulling the box which appeared to be some type of a lush gift into her breasts, the Fendi was slung over her shoulder.

"Your text message has me worried. You sure you know what you're doing?"

"It's just a precaution." He filled her in on the morning's attempt to get a restraining order.

"The gun is locked and loaded, darling." Taddy dropped her arm, allowing the bag to hit the desk. "Safety switch is on. The last one to use this was Vive."

"Why was she using your gun?"

"Apparently, her penthouse has mice." She laughed.

He stared at the bag and hoped he wouldn't have to use it.

"When was the last time you fired a gun?"

"Hmm, with Thor and Vive last week at Lipstick & Lead rifle range." He thought back to his last round. "My aim is getting better. I'm not as good as you, mind you, but no one is."

"No doubt, but I'm not worried about that. It's your target I'm concerned with. MLD is quick on his feet. Do you think you'll keep the gun loaded or just use it to scare Diego away?" Narrowing her eyes, Taddy cursed Diego's name under her breath while stroking her bag as if it was her pet.

"I'm at a friend's this week. Diego texted me. I'm pretty sure he was at my condo, hiding from the police, I assume. So, I'll keep it loaded."

"Would you kill MLD if you were given the chance?"

"An eye for an eye, a tooth for a tooth—isn't that what the Bible says?" Blake thought about her question. He hated violence, but he also wanted to live and he'd do anything to get a second chance at happiness again. "Without a doubt, I'd kill him. I'm afraid he won't stop otherwise."

"That's what I thought, too. I admire how strong you've been through this."

"I get my courage from you."

"If I can do anything to help you, tell me." She nodded and forced a smile. "So, where are you staying if not at your place?"

"A friend's."

"Friend, huh? Have you told Miguel about MLD yet?"

She knows.

"No, and I won't. You know how he is. He won't rest 'til he's seen Diego behind bars. Miguel needs to focus on his exhibit next week. This is my mess to clean up, not his."

"MLD's actions are *not* your mess. You aren't responsible for what *he* has done." Taddy sighed heavily.

His ex's name had that effect on people. "So…no one has stepped forward then?"

"Nope. I have a few names, but if I tell the police who they are then I'd be exposing them, their health, their families—they don't want that. I can't say I blame them. Only you and Lex know what Diego did. I'm going to keep playing along as if everything's fine, because if I don't, I'll go insane. Okay?" Blake didn't want to talk about it anymore. Taddy was right. This was Diego's mess, not his.

"Agreed. Well, if you need protection, Vive can stay with you when you go back to your place." Taddy laughed. "That woman could scare the devil away. Speaking of which…"

Glancing back at the monitor, he hit the OFF switch, giving Taddy his complete concentration. "What's up?"

"In addition to dropping the Fendi off, I need to speak with you about a professional matter." She held up the gift box and continued, "As well as a personal one."

"Okay, personal first."

"We'll get to this box in a few. Now, did Duckie schedule your lunch with Vive today?"

"Yes, usual time and place with Thor. Why?"

"Vive and Lex sorta got…*into it* over the weekend."

"About what?"

"Let's just say, Lex cancelled the wedding."

"Shit. No."

"Yes, but no one knows. Not yet. Massimo is keeping a lid on this one from the press." Her green eyes narrowed. "Is it true you don't want to be in the wedding?"

"Damn Vive and her mouth. I, ahhh…" He didn't know what to say. His love for Lex went without question but no, he didn't want to be in the wedding. As selfish as it sounded, it was hard for him to be happy for someone else when he himself was so unhappy. But he'd planned to go, paint on that smile, and do his best.

"Blake, I know this year has been tough on you, but you have to put that aside, for one day, and be happy for Lex."

"I cannot believe Vive threw me under the bus and repeated what I said." He wanted to strangle her gin-soaked neck.

Taddy leaned forward. "I don't care what you and Vive want to complain over with each other, but keep it to yourselves. Don't screw this up for Lex."

"We just—"

"Shut up. Fix Vive before I *fix* you. *Capice*?"

"Got it. I'll talk to Vive." Blake inhaled a deep breath. "How's Lex? Can we get her to change her mind and go on with the wedding?"

"I'm heading over to Easton's office later today, hopefully to stop her before she sends out her cancellation notices. Massimo won't let her near the phone or computer 'til she calms down."

"That bad, huh?" One thing Lex had was a temper.

"Yes. She said she wanted to talk to me about something non-wedding related. Any idea what it might be? Anything else you or Vive did to set her off even more?"

"Nope. Other than when I picked up M2, we didn't really connect this weekend. I was busy."

"Get ready to be even busier." Taddy grimaced evilly. "I'm putting you on a new flanker label from Baden Cosmetics."

"Are you punishing me?"

"No, *darling*," she replied sarcastically as she tapped her nails on the box.

"I have too much on my plate as it is." He gritted his teeth.

"Ha." Annoyance shadowed across her face. "You'll manage. It'll easily bring in a mil."

"Whoa." Blake didn't snub opportunities to make money. In the dire market, he knew better, especially since Diego had taken his entire life savings. He'd been saving up for surrogacy but hadn't told anyone, not even his folks. However, his past weekend with the kids made that urge in him to be a dad all the more real.

Between the cost of an egg donor and carrier, he calculated the nine-month process to be a six-figure investment. Working on the new Baden line could easily move things along again.

"We've been assigned an extraordinary mission." She toyed with the gift box in her hand. "I know you're going to gay-it-up into something more fabulous than anyone else on our staff may envision."

Not caring for how it sounded, Blake didn't think his queer eye was any better than anyone else's—straight, bisexual, or gay. "What's the project?"

"Baden wants us to restage their market potential for branding, marketing, and public relations, the whole nine yards."

"For which Baden brand?" His voice rose in hopes it may be enjoyable. Perhaps perfume, or their yummy energy drinks.

"Baden Puppy." Taddy followed the response with a woof, then a snort in her own amusement.

"You want me to do *dog wash?*" He didn't hide his vexation. First he was Brutus's caretaker—now this. Since when did he become a canine aficionado?

She turned on his desk, cleavage in full view. "They're looking for something original and atypical for the puppy line. I'll e-mail you the brand brief to read up on."

Blake rolled his eyes.

"Spare me your tantrums?" Taddy pointed a glittering artificial fingernail in his direction.

He gave a fake smile. "Sure thing."

"Now, so we're clear, I'll work on Lex today and see if we can keep the wedding scheduled. You get Vive on board with being a bridesmaid. Okay?"

"Deal. I wouldn't miss Lex and Massimo's wedding for all the cock in Chelsea." He tried to make a joke of it, but Taddy didn't laugh, so he asked, "How is Warner? Is he coming, too?"

"Warner will be back from Paris just in time for the wedding. I've missed him."

She perched herself on the desk's edge and leaned in. Her Christian Louboutin stilettos smacked the wooden floor as she slid them off. He admired her pedicured feet. Probably Mr. Kim Lee's work.

"Good, I can't wait to see your Big Daddy." Remembering Miguel's *Seven Needs*, he said, "I'm bringing my own date, too."

"*Hmm*. It couldn't be Nello. He said you cancelled. Did you go straight for Gunter?" Taddy's glance broadened in approval. "Is this date the reason for your face being all aglow?" She pointed at his cheeks.

"I don't know what you're talking about, Miss Brill."

"The water cooler was abuzz this morning in regards to the new spring in your step. Something tells me it isn't from Gunter, either."

He thought about Miguel and it warmed him from the inside out. "Thank you for setting me up with them, but something came up and I couldn't make it." He didn't think anyone noticed his cheer. Though, he was confident the newspaper article had circulated amongst the office. "Maybe it's my new Gucci loafers." Blake could never outdo Taddy's footwear, but he tried. He needed to respect Miguel's privacy and not tell her anything. *Not today. Maybe tomorrow.*

"Hoochie-Gucci-Pucci-Fiorucci," she mocked. "Shoes have nothing to do with your glee. I think it's this gift from our friend…Miguel." She released the lush wrappings from her grip and placed it on his desk.

The mysterious, medium-sized, black satin box covered in dark roses sat waiting for him to open. A gold-etched hangtag hung off the side...

To Mr. Blake Morgan III, from Señor Santana.

Chapter Fourteen

Phone Fucked

Heart racing, Blake untied the satin ribbon and took one of the roses in his hand. Inhaling sharply, he said, "These smell wonderful."

"I've never seen roses so dark before." Taddy eyed them jealously.

He had to know what was in the little black box. Whatever was inside must be expensive. The wrappings it came in were lush. "Don't play dumb. I know Vive and Lex filled you in on what Mig and I are up to."

Her face flushed. The glued lash extensions which shadowed her high cheekbones flew up. "True, but I wasn't expecting this. By mistake, I thought the box was for me."

"You opened my present?" He popped the lid off, silently questioning her with heavy irony.

"Kiki assumed the package was for me. Seeing as how I'm the only one around here who receives roses—let alone black satin boxes—I can't blame her."

"Then why didn't your assistant bring me the package?"

"Kiki mentioned being over here earlier. She figured you had enough of her and Duckie for one day. She asked me to do it."

"That's bullshit."

"When you see what's inside the box, you'll understand why Kiki shied away." Taddy laughed. She handed him a card from her breast pocket and made no apologies for opening it. "I didn't see the tag. I assumed the gift was for me, from Big Daddy...until I read this card and realized it was for you."

He glanced at the envelope. Peeking in the package, he divided the purple tissue paper with his thumbs and let out an unanticipated scream. "*Oh, my God!*"

"Ironic, those exact words came flying out of my mouth, too." She stood into her couture pumps. "I know Miguel's game. You sure you know what you're getting into with your *Seven Desires*?"

"*Taddy*." Blake pleaded with her not to press the issue.

"Are you and Miguel finally having sex?"

"What do you mean by *finally*?"

"Uh-huh. I knew it." She rattled her red acrylics over his desk. "In college, I always thought you should've married Miguel, not MLD."

"Did everyone think this?"

"Yes, including your parents."

Errr.

"Are you nervous about being with him?"

"Very. I don't know if I can go through with it."

"Try, for me, please." Taddy hummed, *"Miguel and Blake sitting in a tree, makes me so happy."*

"I'm thinking about it." From Blake's view, her nipples pebbled underneath the sheer red blouse. Was she getting turned on?

"My two favorite gays fucking. How glorious!" Her green eyes squinted. He wasn't surprised by her arousal. He just hoped she wouldn't come on his desk.

"Don't start."

"Do you think you could make me a few videos to watch?"

"Videos?"

"Home movies with Miguel topping you," she said with a dead-shit-serious face. "I didn't think any of this was true when Vive told me. I thought you'd gone celibate."

"It's real. I'm staying at his place this week."

"What did he do with his pit bull?"

"Brutus sleeps on the floor."

"Wow." Her forehead shot up in surprise. "Someone's gotten over their dog phobia."

"Not quite, but I'm working on it. I'm working on a lot of my issues."

He'd never get over being gay bashed as a kid and the cruel joke of having those dogs attack him, but it was time to move on. Not all dogs are bad. Right?

"That's good, darling. I'm proud of you. Speaking of dogs, the girls mentioned fisting is on your *Seven Desires*. I must see the footage, you animal."

Oh, mah gawd.

"I'll play your videos in slow motion while I'm on the elliptical. I've always wondered how hung Miguel is and—"

"No friggin' way." Blake refused to feed her ravenous appetite for sex. "You have Big Daddy to satisfy your porn addiction."

"Big Daddy travels. I'm often alone, and I'm horny. A girl can't help herself." She gave him a perverted smile and headed for the door. She clapped her jeweled hands in approval. Her signature tuberose aroma lingered behind. "And PS, it's nice to see you in high spirits again. It's been too long since happiness decorated your gorgeous face."

He winked and mouthed, *Thank you.*

She closed the door behind her. Her heels clacked down the hall, and sounds from keyboards resumed as employees scuffled for cover typing.

His desk phone chimed through the speaker. "Mr. Morgan, your mother is holding on line one."

"Great, got it."

Thank heavens Blake was already sitting down when he opened Miguel's package. His legs would've buckled if he'd been standing. Pulling the present from the box, he caught his breath. *Miguel, you're a dirty pig.*

"Happy Monday, Mom…"

Lower East Side

Unsaid

Sitting at the work station, Miguel glided his paintbrush with exact precision over the multimedia canvas. The Mexican pop culture icon lacquered his trademarked enamel, which had made him famous. After a month-long brainstorming session, image sourcing, and sketching to the point where he thought his fingers might fall off, the oversized canvas was coming together. *Almost finished.* This would be his final piece for the Barcelona exhibit.

His cell phone rang and he answered, "*Hola.*"

"Darling, it's Taddy-licious. How are things?" She giggled in apparent amusement with herself.

"*Bueno.* I'm looking forward to Lex's wedding." He wondered if Blake had picked up his tuxedo.

"Me, too." She paused. "Listen, I just came from Blake's office. He mentioned that he was staying with you this week. You wanna fill me in?" She acted as if she were leading with something.

"*Sí*, that's what friends do." *Back off, Brill.* He'd been raised to be discreet.

"Did you catch the *Manhattanite Times* today?" A crinkling paper sound came from behind Taddy's voice.

He laughed rotating in his chair. "*Sí.* Nice to see Blake is putting himself out there again."

"Any idea who for?"

"You should talk to him." He wasn't going to speak for Blake.

"Let me be a little more direct with you," she hissed.

"Uh-huh." He hadn't a clue where she was going with this call.

255

"By mistake this morning, I opened your goodie box."

"I see." *No, no, no.*

"My first thought was you and Blake would always be an item. I do, however, have one cautionary request for you."

This wasn't her fucking business. Nevertheless, he humored her. "What's your demand?"

"If you hurt Blake, I will ruin you, Miguel."

"¿Perdón?"

"I'll call art galleries from here to Timbuktu and have your paintings pulled, shredded, and mailed back to your loft in a Ziploc bag." Taddy's voice sounded tight and loud as if she'd held up the receiver to her tonsils. "You and I both know my connections run from the Louvre in Paris to the Metropolitan Museum of Art here in New York, so help me, sweet Jesus, I will."

"It's not what you're assuming." This wasn't just sex. He had tried hard not to allow his feelings for Blake to get in the way, but he realized he'd failed at the no-feeling strategy so far.

"I mean it, Miguel. Blake's been a mess for months. You haven't seen him on a day-to-day basis as we have at the office. I sent him to Secrète de St. Barth to get healthy with Lex after MLD moved out." The crinkling paper turned to a ripping noise. "I'll be damned if he reverts back to being sad."

"Meaning?"

"Today is the first time I've seen his face have any semblance of happiness."

"Is that so?" His heart melted.

"Yes and if you hurt him in any way, shape, or form similar to what that Diego bastard did, I'll come for you as you've never imagined. We clear, *Papi*?"

"Very." He hated when she called him *Papi*. Miguel respected Taddy for as long as he remembered since she was self-made and ruthless. Her friends were her family. She was protective. "Perhaps you know more than me about their marriage. What exactly did MLD *do* to Blake?"

"To quote your earlier remark, *you should talk to him*," she mocked in a Mexican accent.

Miguel laughed as another call came through his line.

"Taddy, I have a call coming in."

"I love you, darling. Big Daddy and I can't wait to see you at the wedding." Her voice flipped back to its usual high-pitched, love-you-more-than-Coco-Chanel tone.

"*Adiós*." He clicked over and greeted the next call.

"*Hola*," his sister Inez cheered. "Miguel, the girls adored their time with you yesterday. They loved your friend."

"*Maravilloso*." He kept working.

"What are you doing?"

"Getting ready for the Barcelona opening." Sensing he was being disrespectful, he turned his attention away from the canvas. "I'm putting the finishing touches on my main piece."

"When is the Spain *exposición*?"

"Next week."

"Wouldn't it be great if *Papá, Mamá*, the girls, and I came to your show?"

No. It would be stressful. Dad will be sick and Mom'll drive me insane. Covering for his delayed pause, he raised his voice with fake enthusiasm, "Sure."

"We can dream, can't we? I'd love to take off work and come with you to Spain."

He glanced at the kitchen clock. "Are you at work?"

"I'm between meetings. You know these shareholders are up our asses to see profits this year."

"Everything okay? You never call me during the middle of the workday."

"Sí, fine. Cierra and Ofelia mentioned you're bringing Blake to the house for dinner."

He paused and elected to be honest. "*Sí.* He's coming with me." Where was she going with this? A knot twisted behind his belly button. "You've met Blake. We went to college together. Last name is Morgan, from Greenwich, Connecticut."

"I remember. I've always enjoyed your friends, in particular Blake." Her rapid inhale echoed. "Cierra came home after your day with her and said, and I quote, '*Tío* Miggy has a boyfriend'."

Flat on his feet, he stood from the chair, ready to hit the ceiling. *¡Ay dios mio!* Brutus followed, jumping to all fours in response to Miguel's stance.

He huffed. In his twenty-nine years, Inez never asked him *the* question. "Where would Cierra get such an idea?" *She's a smart one.*

"Cierra's classmate, Rose, in her nursery school has two daddies." She laughed. "It's quite the trend at her school."

"*Bueno* for Rose."

"Cierra goes over there to play sometimes when I can't get home in time to pick her up after work and the nanny is running errands."

"What does her classmate have to do with me?" *It has everything to do with you, you ninny.*

"Cierra mentioned that spending Sunday with you and Blake reminded her—" Inez stopped.

Her evident hesitation in her communication caused him to hold his own breath.

"It reminded her of hanging out with Rose's two dads."

Damn that little Rose. "Did she now?" He tried to laugh it off but couldn't. He wanted to hang up but wouldn't. He'd love to yell at Cierra and her little friend Rose, but shouldn't. "Just because two men hang together doesn't make them gay."

"*No chingues.*" She lowered her voice, taking on that big-sister tone, and repeated in English, "Cut the shit. Are you and Blake lovers?"

"*¿Perdón?*"

"Are you gay?" Her life-size, superior pitch amplified. *Are you gay? Are you gay? Are you gay?*

Inez's question echoed as a scratched vinyl in his ear. "I'm not having this conversation over the phone." He didn't want to have it in person, either. Blake would point the finger at him for being lazy in the emotional and feelings department. In reality, he detested confrontation. He also didn't want to disappoint his sister or have her worry. Her plate was packed full with other matters to attend to, matters more important than his desire to suck cock.

"I don't have the luxury of time that you do. This is your chance to talk to me. Otherwise, I'll see you at the dinner." She always used a backhanded tone, which remained supportive yet a little threatening.

He glared at Brutus for encouragement to answer the question. His orange, love-you-with-all-my-heart eyes were ogling back up at him. If his family abandoned him, there'd always be Brutus.

"*Sí*, I'm gay," he answered without any misgivings. *It's now or never.* Coming out that week was in the cards. He'd wanted to do this more than anything. Granted, not on Inez's work break, but still…

He heard her crying on the line. He felt selfish, stupid for not doing this ages before.

"I'm sorry we're doing this over the phone. I love you."

"*Te amo*, too, sis."

"I'm fine with…" Her voice trailed off. He heard her blowing her nose in the background.

He wondered if she'd say it.

She cleared her throat. "I'm okay with you being gay."

His cheeks rose into a smile. Hot tears stung his face, and the tightening in his chest released. His sister was never one to mince words.

He released his right fist and rubbed his clammy palm up and down his jeans. "I'm telling our parents at dinner."

"With Blake on your arm? I figured as much."

"Do you think *Papá* will freak out?"

"I can't answer for him."

He wanted his sister to confirm that their family would understand. "Right." His chest retightened as his scalp and cheeks began to sweat. He felt as if he'd sucked on a habanero pepper marinated in Tabasco. He couldn't breathe. Was he doing this?

"It's time you told them. They deserve to know what makes you happy." There was dead silence on the line for what felt like eternity. "If they choose to support you, great."

"And if they don't?" he asked, besieged in doubt. *They won't love me anymore. I'll be a failure to them.*

"We'll cross that bridge when we come to it."

"Meaning?" He weighed the possible ramifications.

"Papá's illness has given him lucid thoughts. Issues which bothered him in the past, today he may be at peace with."

That's because Papá is ready to die. "And *Mamá?*"

"You'll have your work cut out for you with her." She shared a laugh with him, breaking the uncomfortable tension. "Let me ask you, does Blake make you happy?"

"Sí." More than ever if they solidified their relationship. "Very much so."

Going through the *Seven Desires* and *Needs* motions had its advantages—Blake in his arms night after night, the kissing, and the discovery of each other's bodies. But there wasn't a guarantee he would be his, *all* his. Forever wasn't on the list.

"My next meeting is here. Thank you for telling me. *Te amo.*"

"Te amo," he echoed.

In disbelief he'd come out, Miguel set his cell phone down on the kitchen counter. "One down, two more to go." To his surprise, his sister didn't rush over when she'd heard he was gay and throw holy water on him. She didn't scream he'd go to Hell, or even hang up on him. Inez continued her love for him and went back to work carrying on with her day as if it were any other.

Would telling his parents go as easily? Did they already know? Close to thirty, and not once did he ever have a girlfriend. They had to suspect. But then, the mind believes what the heart wants it to.

He picked up his cell and texted Lex. *I just came OUT to Inez.*

Lex replied, *And? What did she say?*

He typed back, telling her the good news as, ready for his walk, Brutus swaggered over with his leash in his mouth.

A few minutes later, Lex texted, *I cancelled the wedding.*

What? Why didn't Taddy say anything to him when they spoke? Maybe she didn't know. Was this because of the hospital? Was she okay?

He didn't reply and instead picked up the phone.

"Lex, *qué pasa*? What's going on?"

Bryant Park

"I haven't come in four days," Blake confessed in a low voice as he stared at Vive and Thor for sympathy. They sat in close proximity to Condé Nast, Heart and Fairchild media personalities by their table. The ever-popular Koi restaurant in Bryant Park was, as usual, crowded. But leave it to *Debauchery* Magazine's connections to get them a table. He picked at the blue cheese-stuffed olive in his gin martini and gave Anna Wintour a wink a few tables over.

"Miguel's making you earn your mangasm." She reached across the table, jabbing her sterling fork into his calamari salad.

Decked in a Dior suit, she came from her last gossip interview with actress Anne Hathaway. Tired and over the day's drama, Vive said she didn't want to talk about Lex, Massimo or the wedding. So he kept the conversation on the subject she loved most—sex.

"Not since I was fourteen have I gone this long without masturbating." He remembered his middle school subscription to *International Male* catalog showcasing guy's buns and gorgeous chests. Those images had confirmed his sexual tendencies. "My cock is going to burst."

"You can make it. Hell, you went half a decade without ever experiencing bonafide intimacy, *boo*," His friend reminded him as he sipped his cocktail.

"This should be a walk in the park and it is. I'm having a great time." Blake pinched his chopsticks together, scooped tuna tartar from his plate, and swallowed. *Yum.*

"Are you falling in love?" Thor's right eyebrow jumped.

"*Love?* Heavens no." He'd always adored Miguel as a friend. This week he might be fighting the urge to see his friend as a boyfriend. They'd agreed to sex, nothing more and even that was a big step, one he was still on the fence about doing. A risk to be heartbroken again wasn't on their lists or even on his mind. It would destroy him. No more husbands.

"Gorgeous, don't say *no*," she pleaded.

He didn't like where this conversation was headed. "I'll say it again…no"

"Blake, we watched you suffer with MLD for years and if we can bring you happiness, otherwise known as Miguel's heart, we will." Thor's gaze settled on his with an unapologetic glare.

They remained clueless as to what really happened in his marriage. It was hard not to tell them since they were always so honest and upfront with him about everything.

"Love? What are you talking about? That wasn't on the list."

"Oh, spare me." Vive's voice cracked.

"I've always pictured Miguel as a sex machine, never a boyfriend." He wondered if he'd just lied to them as he'd denied himself true love for the last decade.

Thor's lips pouted into a sulk. "*Shit. Shittt. Shiii—it.*"

"I second your shits." She glanced over her shoulder to make sure no one heard what they were cussing.

"What are you two triple-shitting over?" Blake scooted his chair in closer to them. They were up to something, they always were. He could tell by the way the little hairs on his arms stood up.

"I told Miguel you'd had the *hots* for him," Thor confessed.

"Who hasn't? But for sex." He bit down on crispy wonton. The crackle sound brought a serious ramification ring to his *Seven Desires*.

"We even bet money on it." She shook her blonde bob.

"How much?"

"Ten grand…that you two…would be living together within the year,"

"You guys are nuts. An actual relationship? With Miguel Santana?" he blurted aloud, and realized what he'd gotten into and glared at them across the table. "Oh, boy…I don't know about this."

"Miguel may have taken your *Seven Desires* as a ticket to boyfriend land." Vive treaded the topic without calling him a dumbass. Though even through a dozen or so Botox injections to her forehead, he could tell by the look on her face, she wanted to.

"Why? It's S-E-X?" That alone was more than he thought he could give.

"No, Blake. This is a lot more for Miguel than just sex and you know it." Thor laid it out on the table. "Grow the fuck up."

"Wake the fuck up!" Vive snapped.

Chapter Fifteen

Lemonade & Lycra

Mixed emotions surged through Blake as he tried to understand Miguel's intentions better. Though he'd been hesitant of them from the start, they made sense now—a *Seven Needs* list.

Of course, his friend was testing his waters to see what a real boyfriend felt like. Why didn't he see these objectives earlier? But did Miguel possess the capabilities of sustaining something long-term, going beyond a week, a month, or a year? His dating history said no way.

His cock always stood to attention whenever Miguel walked in the room. What about his heart? Was love possible again? He worried he'd need a jumper cable to get it going. "Why hasn't he ever told me this?"

"Do you have any sense how intimidating you, Blake Morgan the Third, are?" Thor asked.

"No." Just because he came from money didn't mean he was hard to get. He wasn't easy to be had, either.

"You know what I mean. You're *scary* to most guys."

"Scary?" His mind reeled with confusion. "As in the movie *The Exorcist*?"

"No, not demonic scary. Scary as in you're hot, chic, and loaded. We all have a defect. But you, you're kinda perfect. It terrifies most gay men who are riddled with insecurities and doomed for rejection."

"Spare me." No one was perfect.

"Okay, let's put your perfection aside. Look at it from Miguel's vantage point, shall we?" Vive asked, attempting to help Thor with his clarity while she poked at his meal.

"Which is?"

"He's afraid you'll reject him as you did in college," she reminded.

"Rejected?" Blake repeated. "Try being married to a man who won't touch you for half a decade. I ooze rejection." He hated to bring a negative back to his failed marriage. It was his only barometer. "And besides, Miguel is one of the most confident men I've ever met. If he wanted me, he would've grabbed me by my hair and pulled me into his cave a long time ago."

"Diego never stepped up to the plate and enjoyed your cave. He realized he'd never be your equal." Thor always acted as if he knew the answer.

"Money and cave aside, Miguel is my equal, if not more so. Didn't you two see *Manhattanite* magazine last week? They're touting him as the next Salvador Dalí," Blake added. "And I do, too, have my faults." He knew his shortcomings. Shallow at times, often one-sided, but he was working on it.

"Taddy secured Miguel that art-ranking editorial. His press never goes to his head the way your stupidity goes toward yours."

"Ouch, Vive! That stung." Blake moved his plate away from her reach as punishment for calling him a dummy.

"You two belong together," Thor stated without any expression on his face.

"Once again, I'll second him as your top love interest." She threw her napkin on the table, focusing on her cocktail. Lifting the crystal with both hands to her lips, she gulped the gin. She squinted as she crunched down on the ice, shaking her head in disappointment in his direction.

Two against one, he was outnumbered. They'd known him since the ninth grade. The communication between them at times could be described as telepathic.

He grabbed his bleached white cotton napkin and twisted the starched fabric through his knuckles. "I don't want another relationship. It was too hard, too much disappointment." He promised himself he wouldn't go through another Diego nightmare again.

"Sour much?"

"As a lemon," he answered with a snap. "And I have a right to be." He wasn't over his divorce. Another commitment on the horizon was unthinkable. "I want to be single for a while, at least a year." He sipped his drink.

"It's time for you to make some effin' lemonade," she suggested.

"Why? My lemons are fine the way they are." He grimaced. "Doesn't your misery love my company?"

She rolled her eyes and replied, "Not always." Apparently, she was still pissed off about Lex's wedding. It wasn't his fault her lips got loose.

"I know you better than most. You're *not* the kinda guy to be single forever." Thor kept social behavior notes on his buddies when it came time for hooking up.

"You've both been single forever. Why can't I?"

Thor held his hand over Vive's and responded, "I'm designed to be a solo act. When I tested positive for HIV back in college, I made a promise to live my life with no apologies. I go to clubs. I pick up men. I have consensual casual sex with other poz guys and I party the night away. You, however, are not designed for those activities."

"Oh, no?"

"You want monogamy and all that happily-ever-after stuff. I sure as hell do not and that's okay, Blake."

"And I attract the wrong men," Vive interrupted. "I want a man. A hairy-chested gorilla who's going to throw me over his knee and—"

"*Vive*, enough." He forgot any topic going off Viveca Farnworth caused her to fret. Domination didn't play into her loneliness, either—booze did. He turned to Thor and asked, "What am I designed for then?"

"A husband, kids, house in the country, sporting J. Crew, not Lycra. Don't you see? It's who you are," Thor declared.

"I'll have a baby without *another* husband. I'm looking into surrogacy."

"Oh, Jesus," Vive snapped. "Why don't you take Hedda Hopper for a week? You'll learn the TLC demands for my furbaby before you go off planting your seed in a surrogate's womb or picking up a kid from China." Her Scandinavian, ice-blue eyes rolled around clockwise then counterclockwise in annoyance.

Done with their lunch, Thor sat back in his chair and crossed his arms. "The longer you stay on the market, the deeper and faster your stock'll depreciate."

"Stock?" *First it was lemons, now the stock market.*

"Listen, a certain *hot factor* arises when you're first single. You'll see it at Lex and Massimo's wedding later this week. The men at the reception will be all over you, like flies on shit."

"Don't you mean bees on honey?" Blake smiled. "That's assuming there's even going to be a wedding." He shot Vive a snide look. "Besides, Mig will be glued to my hip." He shared with Thor the *Seven Needs* list Miguel had counter-proposed. Vive, who'd been previously briefed on the *Seven Needs,* asked the waiter for a gin refill.

"Are you nervous about meeting his dad?"

"No. Should I be?"

"Mr. Santana is"—a faint sadness threaded in Thor's throat—"not well."

"What did Miguel tell you guys?"

"He's dying."

Shocked, he dropped the glass from his hands. "Why the frick didn't you two tell me this sooner?"

Fashion District

Against Massimo's wishes, Lex went into work. She had to; it was who she was. Birdie agreed to watch M2 for the day.

At her desk, she sat, toying with who to call first to cancel the wedding. Over two thousand people had confirmed. Guests coming as far as Sydney and Massimo's royal associations from the Mediterranean, but they didn't mean as much to her as Vive and Blake. Massimo's parents were both deceased, and she debated if the wedding was that important to her fiancé or if she'd gone off her rocker and overreacted.

Her interoffice phone light lit up. She pushed the button and said, "Yes?"

"Miss Easton, Taddy Brill is here to see you," her office coordinator announced.

"Send her in."

Lex stood. On her desk, the City DNA Lab letter stared back at her. She picked it up. Then put it back down. God, there were no rules or etiquette on how to do this. In her head, she'd gone over what to say at least a million times, maybe even two million. But right then and there, she couldn't remember what they were other than *you might be my sister.* Which sounded so dramatic and made for TV. Was this really happening?

"Darling." Taddy came in as her office coordinator closed the door behind her. Kissing Lex on both cheeks, she took a seat by the desk, crossed her long legs, and asked, "Feeling any better about the wedding?"

"No."

"Vive and Blake will come around. They're at lunch today. In fact, they should be eating and talking right this very minute about how they're going to help make this the most amazing wedding ever. So please, don't cancel."

"I haven't called the wedding planner yet. So, it's *not* official."

"Good girl."

"Masi won't let me." The control that man had over her drove her crazy. "But I'm going to, you'll see." When her mind was made up to do something, she did it.

"He's a smart guy."

She licked her lips, trying to find courage. "Taddy, do you remember the summer we were sent to live at Avon Porter?"

Her friend's forehead wrinkled as she shifted in the chair. "How could I forget? Jesus, did my parents fight that year."

"Right. Joseph Graf fought with Irma over your paternity test."

"Yup, I'm not my father's daughter."

Taddy spoke about it as she always did, matter-of-factly. The love she had from her boyfriend Warner enabled her to heal. Lex understood this. Her friend was a better woman for having Warner in her life. But why didn't her friend yearn for answers as she did?

"Haven't you ever wondered who your *real* dad is?"

"When I was younger, sure, all the time. Irma even offered to tell me. But as I've gotten older, I'm not interested."

"But why? Don't you want to know?"

"It won't change anything." She paused. "Lex, why are you asking me about my birth father? Is this what you wanted to discuss today?"

"Sort of..." She spoke so quietly, she wasn't sure if Taddy heard her.

"And here I thought we'd be talking about sending Vive off to rehab or something. I went by her place last night. She wouldn't answer the door."

"Why not?"

"The doorman let me in. I found her on the living room floor, passed out cold."

"Drunk?"

"Last night was the worst she's been in years. She'd apparently thrown up." Taddy shook her head and closed her eyes then muttered, "Vomit dried on the floor around her. Poor Hedda was shaking in the corner. What if Vive had choked on her own bile? She'd be dead right now."

"Taddy, why didn't you call me?" Lex couldn't help but get upset.

"You have enough going on with the wedding. I thought I could manage Vive. But I don't have the detox contacts you do, so I'm telling you now. We have to try one more time. Can Birdie get her in to Hampton Horizons?"

Hampton Horizons remained the only facility Birdie was able to get dry from after Eddie died. She was such an advocate of their innovative therapy treatments she signed on to be a spokesperson and do all of their commercials. Granted, they'd paid her three million dollars for the endorsement, but Birdie had been desperate to get sober.

Making money along the way was a great bonus considering she'd been broke.

"Let me make a few calls to Mr. and Mrs. Farnworth and see what we can do." She thought back to how their friend had failed rehab a few times.

"Vive most likely won't talk to us ever again if we push for this. Will she?"

"Not if it backfires. Hampton Horizons is hardcore and experimental, but worth it. I'll let you know what they say." She almost forgot the reason she'd asked her to come. "But it's not Vive I wanted to talk about. It's you."

"All right." Taddy sat back in her chair. The tension on her face subsided.

"Mom brought over some old photos the other day. I found *this* in one of the boxes." She picked up the paper and handed it to her.

"City DNA Labs," Taddy read out loud suspiciously. She opened the letter, and her jade eyes scrolled from left to right. She glanced up at Lex and then back down at the paper and gasped. "Jesus Christ, Lex."

"Did you ever think my dad…"

"Never. *Shit!* I mean, I knew Irma cheated. Why didn't they just tell us? If not them, why hasn't Birdie said something after all this time?"

"At first, Mom wouldn't open up to me about it. But this morning, when she picked up M2, I got some answers. She said she'd made a promise to Irma never to talk about it. Mom wanted to tell you when you were older. Then older came and went, and you filed for emancipation from Irma. She was going to tell you a few years ago, and then

Dad died, and she felt too bad about not telling you and thought it would only make matters worse, because he was, well, gone."

"This is all suspect, right? It's not for sure. Eddie was supposed to get the test, but according to the letter, he didn't."

"Right. But, Taddy, come on. We're both tall. Our voices sound alike on the phone. My father and your mother were lovers. It makes sense."

"Okay, so Eddie is my father. Big deal." She tossed the letter back on the desk.

Taddy didn't seem to care. Was she only putting on an act as a defense?

"Don't you want to be certain?"

"No, I don't. It won't change a thing between us. For once, I agree with Birdie."

Lex couldn't believe what she heard. "You're as crazy as our parents."

"For wanting to keep my sanity? Perhaps." Taddy got to her feet. "My life won't be any better because of a test, only worse. Besides, my love for you and our friendship won't change either."

"How can you say that? We could be sisters."

"You've *always* been like a sister to me, Lex. I don't need a blood test to tell me how important you are in my life."

"Well, I do." She had to know.

"Why?"

"Because I just do, Taddy. I can't explain it."

On the inside, Lex felt this was a piece to her which was missing. After all the years of secrets and lies from her father, this could be the one truth, the one real thing she might have to hold on to. Since his unexplained suicide, she didn't have any answers. Eddie did overdose, but he'd done drugs for years; she couldn't figure out how or why he'd gone to the point of no return.

"It's that important to you?" Taddy's face sunk.

"Yes—more than anything. I'll never ask for another favor."

Her bestie smirked. "Can I get that in writing please?"

"City DNA Labs merged with GeneLynx. I called them this morning and made an appointment for us to get the test."

"Oh, really. Wait 'til the press gets a hold of the news. You have no idea what can of cray-cray you're unleashing when Eddie Easton's fan club hears about this one."

"They won't know. GeneLynx agreed to do it tonight, after hours. Their chief counselor and medical physician will supervise the test."

"Your father was—correction, is—the biggest rock-n-roll star in the world. This *will* get out. It always does."

Taddy spoke about the press' actions confidently. It was, after all, her career. She knew what she was talking about. Suddenly, Lex questioned if she might be naïve to think otherwise. Had Birdie done them all a favor by keeping this quiet?

"There's no way around this, Taddy. We must."

"I hate needles—"

"It's an oral swab."

"Can't this wait until…after the wedding…after your honeymoon…after I've had some time to think?"

"No. *Thinking* only makes it worse. It's been tearing at me for a few days now. Trust me, I'm on the verge of freaking out. Look at what I did to poor Vive."

"The results could take weeks to come back. We won't know tonight."

"One hour. The appointment is at seven this evening. By eight, we'll know if my dad is your father."

Standing, Taddy cursed under her breath a few times then reached for her Birkin.

Was she going to leave? Lex needed her to agree to this.

"I'll do it under one condition."

"Anything."

"You make up with Vive, we get her into rehab, and move on with the wedding as planned."

"Geez, Louise! You're asking for a lot."

"Then I'm not doing the test." Taddy headed for the door. "Enjoy your day, darling."

"That's blackmail."

"Call it whatever you want, coercion, manipulation, I don't care. I have to get back to work. Baden Cosmetics has a wrinkle cream launch. My reality TV star, Neve Adele, is coming—lots to do. It's a big production over there." Taddy turned her jaw up.

Lex couldn't tell if she was fighting back a tear before she said, "You let me know what you decide. Seven tonight we test or not. But the wedding goes on as planned, and you and Vive have a heart-to-heart. If we're going to get Vive sober, she'll need you more than ever. I, on the other hand, don't *need* this test. *Capisce?*"

And just like that, Taddy was out the door. She didn't wait for a reply; she never did.

Lex picked up the phone. "Can you get me the number for Hampton Horizons? They're out on Long Island. It's a…rehab facility."

Bryant Park

Blake couldn't believe he didn't know Miguel's' father was ill. Was that why his friend acted aloof about his family all the time? "Tell me, what's going on?"

Biting his lip, Thor lowered his voice. "I may be a gossip about who's banging who in this town, who's filed bankruptcy or been dumped. But there are some things you'll never hear roll off my tongue."

"Those being?" He clenched his mouth tighter.

"People battling disease, facing death, or swimming upstream away from grave misfortune." His dark eyes squinted as if Blake should know better.

Snubbed, he sat back in his chair. "My apologies. I didn't mean to imply you're a bigmouth. But you are." He couldn't help himself. Thor was the male equivalent to Cindy Adams or Vive Farnworth. He wasn't *a* bigmouth, he was the *biggest* mouth.

"Ask Miguel yourself." He glanced down at his plate. "I made a promise I intend to keep."

"I respect your position and won't pry." He'd never known Thor to be so tight-lipped. It must be more serious than he realized. Nevertheless, he turned to Vive for an answer.

She offered, "I will say I don't suppose Miguel's father has much time. If you know what I mean."

He nodded in agreement; he'd drop it. Blake respected Miguel's privacy. But it was odd how his friend never shared childhood stories from his days in Mexico. He never shared much about himself at all. It was what prevented them from getting closer.

Thor, on the other hand, was an open book about his life, including his diagnosis with HIV a few years back. Vive spoke often about her addictions. The dialogue and sharing created a bond between them all, which he'd always wanted with Miguel. He just needed to figure out how to make it happen. How did one get a guy to open up when his only vice was keeping quiet?

Blake remembered the park bench conversation. He knew if he asked or forced any issue with Miguel he'd be shot down. No one would ever tell that Latino what to do. *It's infuriating!*

"I'll be there for Miguel, in whatever capacity he wishes. When he's ready to share the information, he will. Okay, on to lighter subjects." Blake reached down into his Jack Spade tote and pulled out *the* black box.

Thor sat up in his chair with excitement. "*Ooh*, this sounds like it's gonna be fierce."

"This morning, I get into work and not more than an hour into my day, the messenger service drops this package off." He placed the box on the table. "Taddy thought it was for her, so she's seen it."

"What is it?" Vive asked.

"It's from Miguel? Open it up." Thor reached for the box and tore the lid off. "My. My. My." His eyes were sharp and assessing. "You must've died knowing Taddy saw this."

"You gays are unreal." She laughed so hard the editors next to her sat up in their chairs to look in the box.

Inside was another, smaller white box with green lettering from the drugstore: *Fleet Enema.*

"I've never used an enema. I don't even know what to do with one," he confessed.

"Enema virgin here also, honey," she added.

Thor held the box up and pointed to the illustration on the side under the directions. "Kids, you don't have to read English for directions. They're drawn on the box's side with pictures." He snickered. "I use this brand all the time. Right before I get gang-banged."

He gulped. "What do I do?"

"Leave work a lil' early. Go by your apartment and shove this plastic nozzle up your who-haw." Thor lowered his voice. "You lie in the fetal position on your bed and rock back and forth, back and forth."

"And then what?"

"Hold it for about five or so minutes and then go to the bathroom and…" He dusted his hands off.

"*Gross!*" she screamed.

"Right." Thor placed the enema box back into the wrapping. "What's this?" He reached for the note inside.

"The address where I'm to meet Mig at tonight. I've already texted him and told him I'd go."

"Do you know what location this is?"

"No. Do you?"

"Umm…yeah." She snatched the card from Thor's hand and fanned herself. "It's The Dupree Club."

"Where you girls go to exercise?" he asked.

Thor snorted and corrected, "Workout their pussy maybe."

"Yes, it's where we attend dominatrix classes. The BDSM class after work is on Thursday nights. I bet Lex gave Miguel the idea. It's an infamous sex club."

"Oh." His attendance to the city's gay clubs and bars were minimal, let alone a sex club. In the office, he'd heard Taddy talk about Queen Dick Dupree often, but didn't put two and two together until that moment.

"Perhaps he rented a room," she added as Thor licked his lips.

"Room?" *Lordie*.

"Miguel's going to throw you into a sling and fist you." Thor's mouth quirked with humor.

"A fist up this ass?" Blake shook his head. "I've been thinking about it since this morning. I can't do it." He wanted to bottom, yes, but not this.

"You'll be surprised what will go up your tiny hinny when you do it." Thor snatched the note back from her hand and read it again. "Says you're to meet him there at six."

"Right after work. No dinner, no romance. Rather wham, bam, thank you, ma'am."

"Don't you mean 'sir?'" she corrected. "That's the language lingo Queen Dick Dupree teaches us to use to call our doms."

"Miguel wants you on an empty stomach. That's why he's having you meet him so early."

"Thor." Blake tried to suppress a giggle as Vive let her laughter cackle.

"Don't finish your lunch. Drink hot water with lime when you get back to your office." Thor reached over the table, taking his tuna from his mat. "We'll finish your lunch, *boo*."

What on God's Earth had he gotten himself into? He didn't want to be fisted. He also now knew Miguel went along with his acts for a relationship. He'd have to put an end to his sexscapade. He'd tell him he didn't want a commitment, not yet.

The whole *Seven Desires* to *Seven Needs* was off!

Chapter Sixteen

Sling Time

East Village

Miguel received a text from Blake confirming the package had arrived. Doing as instructed, they'd meet at The Dupree Club at 6:00 p.m. He rented out the entire establishment from Queen Dick. There'd be no distractions.

Geared up for action, he studied his reflection in the mirrored hallway. His head sported a muir cap with a sable peak, and gunmetal veiled his groomed brows. Latigo, tough cattle hide strapped across his chest with a nickel-plated O-ring over his pecs. It felt icy against his nakedness. The hardware joined at his nips with Chicago screws and roller buckles. His legs were covered in jet-black, split leather chaps with poly-mesh lining. Each pant leg featured a vertical front thigh vent allowing his skin to breathe. Up his calf muscles were knee boots, each with a steel toe. Out in the open, his dick was displayed, getting hard from all the inspiration. Ready to top, he went into the sling room. He'd been waiting for this moment for over a decade.

He tested the electronic BDSM contraption. The device could keep Blake on his stomach while he'd anal bead him and whip him. With a button flip, he'd elevate his boy-toy higher or lower, where he'd fist and then top him.

Let's get this domination started.

A swooshing sound made Miguel turn in response as the steel door opened. Blake entered. Fear overstated his usual collected expression.

"Hi there." His voice resonated with an uncertain tone.

"You're on time. Such an obedient sub."

"*Sub*—very funny. I tried calling you after my lunch."

"Once you texted back and confirmed, I powered down my cell to focus on getting ready." He looked around. Everything was in place as he planned. The night would be perfect.

"Miguel, we need to talk about our agreement and this whole week."

"Don't worry. You're here now." Kissing him on the forehead, right by the scar he always covered with his wavy hair, he hoped to put Blake's nerves at ease. He'd seen those terrified blue eyes earlier in the week when Brutus approached. "I'm going to take good care of you." He went to his toolbox and withdrew what he should've taken out the minute his friend walked in the door.

"I lunched with Thor and Vive today and they suggested you might be—"

Whap. He slapped black vinyl tape over Blake's mouth.

"No more talking." Miguel figured he'd try and negotiate his way out. "We have the club only for a few hours. Get naked."

Blue eyes rolling, he put his hand up to the edges to tear it off.

"Remove the tape and I'll never speak to you again." He reached for his sub's zipper, yanking it down, almost knocking him off his feet. "Get your virgin ass onto the sling."

Chest heaving, Blake kicked off his beige penny loafers. Pushing down his chino slacks, he drew up his thin, navy-colored summer cardigan then unrolled his checkered-pattern socks. His gaze dropped from Miguel's eyes to his exposed cock.

The rubber cock ring he'd cinched around his shaft earlier doubled his natural girth. Blake seemed in awe. "This here"—he grabbed his cock—"is going to drill you, boy, for hours."

In response he stirred his hands, covering his own groin.

A tingle sparked inside him. He nodded encouragement for him to continue stripping. "I'm going to tear you apart tonight, *bebé*."

Blake shook his head.

"Do you want to call this off? Move back to Chelsea? No sex. No me?"

He shook his head again, a little slower than before.

"Then do as I say. I promise, in the end, you'll get what you want."

His sub glided his thumb along the elastic band of his underwear as if uncertain whether to get undressed or not.

"Trust me."

Blake flung off his briefs, throwing them to the ground in one pile against Miguel's boots. He kicked them to the corner. Naked and exposed he stepped forward, mumbling what sounded like, "Okay." Hands on his hips, they examined each other with intent.

He appeared to be trying to cover his erection. Stiff as a rock, cravings clear as day, he wanted this. He loved this. Miguel could tell and he was going to get this.

"Since I've found a way to shut you up, you won't have a safe word."

Arms crossed in apparent annoyance, he shrugged. His erection bounced up, making it obvious to them both what he wanted: to be dominated.

"If you want to call our Dom-sub session quits, make the peace sign with your hand. I'll stop. Understand?" He demonstrated, raising his right hand, pointer and middle finger in the air.

Holding up a peace sign, he nodded.

"Sí." Miguel patted his right hand on the sling's shiny backrest. "Lasso up, my li'l sub."

On all fours, he crawled onto the bench, lying flat on his stomach. Resting his head between the harnesses, he stretched his limbs out, fit to be tied.

Fastening his sub's left wrist to the strap, Miguel crossed over to the other side and kissed him on the forehead just as before. He felt like kissing him all over, but there'd be time for that later. He had to pace himself.

Eyes fluttering nervously, Blake shut them. Perhaps he didn't want to see what was going to happen, only feel it.

He went to fasten the armband on the right limb and became annoyed that his sub's eyes were still shut. He pulled inward, catching his sub's skin into the buckle.

An earsplitting shriek erupted. Eyes snapping open, Blake jerked his head, accentuating the purplish veins in his neck. A rapid dart came from his restrained hand; the attempt to punch Miguel failed.

"Don't close your eyes tonight."

Recovering, he opened his baby blues wider. He rolled them from left to right, top to bottom, blinking Kewpie doll-style in sheer sarcasm. Making a gesture that he understood, he resumed his cradle rest facedown and with a slight sob.

Was his sub acting? It was just a pinch. He couldn't be hurt.

He loosened the strap, releasing Blake's red flesh from the buckle and tying it shut. He rubbed the tender spot with his thumb, "There, there, *bebé*." He kissed him with a lick.

His sub glanced up with an apologetic pout radiating from his eyes.

"Don't defy me," he ordered in his ear.

His cheeks rose as if smiling under the tape. Was he turned on by the punishment? Did he like the feeling of pain?

"Tonight, you are my sub. My property. Mine."

Starting with his lobe, he traced his sub's curved ear cartilage outline all the way to the crown. He planted his tongue in the middle of the ear. Exhaling through his nostrils, he calculated the faint discharge would drive Blake wild. Shocker, it was he who was stimulated.

"You want more?" He knew he did.

Blake squirmed on the bench. He inched his neck toward him for more. Without a doubt, he'd forgiven him for the skin-snip.

Before going any further, he had to test his sub's threshold for pain. A quick bite would do the trick.

Withdrawing his tongue from the ear, he enclosed his lips once again on his friend's lobe and bit down—hard.

"Hmm," Blake moaned, not out of pain but pleasure.

"My good boy," he reminded him once more from behind his clenched teeth and noticed his cheeks rise, like before, smiling under that tape. He bit down harder, not breaking the skin but close.

"Ahhh." His face became motionless.

One second passed, and then another. Legs kicked, and then his body went still as he released his bite. Was he giving in to submission? He nodded up and down in encouragement.

The boy got into biting.

He kissed the mark his teeth left and then traced his tongue over his sub's taped lips. "You're learning. You enjoy submission. You like pain."

Becoming more comfortable, Blake stretched his body out on the table as he nodded in agreement.

Moving from the shoulders down to his legs, he massaged Blake's left foot. He tied one ankle to the post while palming his left hand up on the other leg. With a tight grip, he squeezed the calf muscles, releasing the tension. Applying pressure over the hamstrings, he watched the leg spasm into relief. "Good boy."

His sub's rapid breathing calmed into a slow cadence.

Turning his attention to the right leg, he repeated the ritual and admired his sub's ass. It was poised, ready for attention.

"You're hot as fuck." He encouraged with compliments, telling him how beautiful his body was. "I love your ass." His palms rubbed over the supple bottom. "I've waited so long. You have no idea." Squeezing the electro-conductive, water-based lube onto his sub's backside he then massaged the cheeks. He wanted to eat him out first. His sub's skin became warm to his touch. Soft. Ready. The white and pink skin glistened in response to each rub.

In his side pocket, he wrapped his fingers around the string and withdrew the plastic beads. Several balls varied in size from itty-bitty to busta-nut-big. Pulling up a stool, he sat between his sub's feet and focused.

"My sub is still tense." He rubbed the feet, lending a hand toward his relaxation. Memories from the previous night—Blake sound asleep in his arms—danced fresh in his thoughts.

Lovable. Mine.

Blake's shoulders dropped to staid calmness, showing his faith in him. *Tonight may take our friendship to a new level.*

The urge to rim was all he could focus on. Burying his face in his sub's asshole, he licked the puckering and traced his tongue up the crack's right side. He slowed down as he hit a dry spot then sped up. His sub's hands grabbed onto the poles as if accelerating on a motorcycle. He spit in the crack. Bull's-eye. His tongue stiffened, jabbing his taste buds into his tightness.

Teasing Blake with a rapid tongue-lashing, he pulled out and wiped his lips with his fist. "I own this ass. You hear me?"

My sub is lovin' this...

Moaning confirmed Blake's enjoyment. He hoisted his ass up for more. Miguel buried his face deep, stretching the hole. His tongue hammered at the crack, down the left side to the bottom, to finish his tongue-thrash in a complete circle. Scraping the pristine skin with his teeth, he licked a second round. Heat emitted from his oral trace.

Blake whimpered again and again. His hole opened. The attempt wasn't enough, not for what Miguel intended.

Top. Love. Forever.

Jerking his head back, he reached under Blake's ass for his dick and took it tight in his hands. He stroked the thickness as it pulsated hard. "I want your cock in my mouth."

His sub nodded enthusiastically.

Miguel spit on his thumb and pointer finger and cupped his sub's cock. He tweaked his fingers over the mushroom head. Admiring the slit decorating the center tip of his cock, he nipped the skin with his tongue. The shaft continued to swell.

"Want your cock in my mouth, *bebé*?" A true top never sucked dick. He was no exception. No man had ever been worth it...until that moment.

Right thumb up, encouraging him to continue, Blake arched his feet and attempted to push himself up on his knees. When that didn't work, he lowered his ass, dropping his cock further into Miguel's grip.

He leaned under, kissing Blake's dick. He couldn't let his friend suffer anymore. Aching for attention after several days, his sub's dick deserved TLC.

With anticipation, he licked his lips then angled his face and scooped Blake's dick up in his mouth.

Fuck, he's thick.

An oxygen rush stung his nose. Exhaling, they became one. Blake smelled citrus fresh; it was how his sub tasted, too. For the first time, he sucked his best friend.

He pulled his mouth back and said, "I own your cock. Do you understand me?"

"Yes," Blake answered through the tape, squeezing his hands into fists.

Dropping his jaw further, mouth wider, tongue wetter, he paid special attention to his gag reflexes as his mouth filled with Blake's dick.

Yeah. Sub's a grower. He bobbed his head back and forth. His eyes stung as he increased suction.

Muffled sounds grew louder from Blake as if he'd blow the guard right off his lips.

Pulling back, he opened his mouth wide, gunning for cock.

So beautiful. So hung. So Blake.

Euphorically, he licked the slit and then guided Blake's shaft in. His sub's thickness slid over his tongue. The velvet smacked his throat. This was exhilarating. He cupped the nuts in confirmation he'd taken his entire cock in his mouth. Jerking his erection further down his throat, salty pre-cum laced his oral cavity ready to receive pleasure.

"Mmm," Blake mumbled through the tape, egging him on to continue.

He stroked under the pelvis, milking him. His sub's ass danced in slow, receptive circles.

Sucking tight at the base, he held the cock at his throat muscles as his tongue massaged the shaft. Tears of pleasure found their way to his eyes as he almost gagged on the girth. Blake's moans encouraged him to glide his tongue back and forth.

Quickly, he took more. Slowly, he pulled back out. Back and forth, he sucked hard. Just like its owner in every way, the cock was perfect. He'd waited a decade to have his lover's beautiful dick in his mouth. He felt, for the first time, that he was worthy of being a lover to the man in his arms, not as a friend, but as a boyfriend.

Gasping for air, Blake breathed heavier as his cock grew harder and thicker by the second. Was he close to coming?

Once more, he released his friend's soon-to-orgasm cock. It bounced up, and Blake slowed down his hips' gyration in obvious frustration. He moaned something, probably to tell Miguel not to stop.

"You're almost there, boy." His attention went back to Blake's ass. Addicted to the unmarred asshole, he sunk his lips in deep with fury, splitting his flesh apart, ramming his tongue in and out from the ass. "You enjoy this?"

His sub rotated his hand as if to say, *so-so*.

Miguel laughed. "Liar." His teeth nicked the flesh. Following the beet-colored scrape was an intense craving to bite. He licked his lips then nipped playfully at the ass cheek.

He bit hard. Harder. Hardest.

Groaning against the tape, Blake jerked his right foot back as if attempting to hit him in the face to stop. The restraints held his sub down.

"You okay, *bebé*?" He checked his sub's hands—no peace sign.

Blake nodded, declaring he was good.

The saliva from his lips connected love-strings to his sub's ass as if spinning fine silk. For a second, Miguel examined the bared skin. There were no permanent marks, only a flash of a crimson ring. Down his swelled nut sac, Blake oozed pre-cum, clear as water with a milky center.

"You fucker. My bite made your dick harder." A smack to the ass with his right hand seemed fitting. Then he grabbed for his cock again, guiding it up with his left hand. Swiping Blake's pleasure onto his thumb, he rubbed the pre-cum between his fingers similar to a Texan finding oil. With a compliment, he licked his digits clean. "You taste sweet." He dropped his head and ate the pre-cum, which laced his sub's nuts. "It's time to stretch you out."

"Aaaah," Blake muttered.

He grabbed onto the purple plastic beads and doused them with lubricant. Placing the beads on the bed and massaging the ass cheeks with both hands, he rammed his long tongue in and out of the asshole. He blew an air stream over the virgin skin. His sub's flesh goose-bumped.

"You wanted to play with toys, *bebé*. This was your idea, remember?"

"*Uh-huh.*" Blake nodded through the headrest.

His asshole opened a little.

He picked up the smallest plastic bead at the end of the string, about twenty millimeters or so in width. He pressed it into the anus. It popped in as if it was a marble.

Once halfway in, his ass sucked it right up. Blake whimpered.

"Good, *niño*," Miguel whispered. He kissed the ass cheeks, pushing the string further down the opening followed by another sphere. This one was double the size from the previous.

His sub didn't flinch.

"Two more beads left, *bebé.*" He rubbed the ass cheeks, extending his hands down the calf muscles to relax him.

His sub's body was stunningly taut. Spitting into Blake's asshole as it puckered out at him, he inserted the third bead. It was at least forty millimeters in width. He could only insert half the ball in.

Damn, this boy's too tight even for the ball.

He pulled it back out. "You're doing good, boy. Take a deep inhale for me."

Blake's lungs filled with air.

He squirted more lube onto the string and inserted the globe in full. He didn't wait this time for the ass to

---

subside. Without haste, he followed the third bead with the fourth and final ball, twice in size as the third.

Hearing Blake shouting through the tape, he leaned to the side and checked for the safety sign.

No peace sign; his sub's hands lay flat. His bottom's ass opened again with a little more ease...and a lot more trust. Good, very good.

Miguel finished pushing the final one through. He imagined his cock buried deep into that ass versus the toy.

All four plastic balls were strung inside his sub. *Hot.* He went back to his toolbox and pulled out four transcutaneous electrical nerve stimulation pads, otherwise known as TENS.

Gramercy

Anxious, Lex couldn't sit in the lobby of GeneLynx, so she stood at the reception desk and filled out the paperwork. Her heart beat in her ear and her stomach was in her throat.

Name: Easton, soon to be Tittoni.

Profession: Fashion designer turned professional worrier.

Relatives: M2, Birdie and…Taddy?

Reason for Visit: Confirmation of sisterhood.

Taddy wasn't there yet. She'd promised if Lex kept the wedding as scheduled and agreed to meet Vive and make up, she'd be there. She and Vive were booked for dinner the following night. All of the requests were made, so why wasn't she there?

It was ten past the hour. It wasn't like her to be late for anything in her life.

She has to come.

She handed the clipboard back to the woman behind the desk. "Umm, my friend isn't here yet."

"Miss Brill could mail us her oral swab or hair and nail samples if she likes," said the woman whose nametag read *Danita*.

"Hmm." Something told her Taddy wouldn't be up for that. "Mind if I wait a few minutes?"

"Sure."

Danita didn't look perturbed to be working past closing to get this done. But Lex felt a little guilty anyway. What other choice did she have? She was an Easton, daughter to the late icon who may have fathered her best friend. The last thing she needed was *OK! Magazine* showing up with a camera because a patient in the lobby tipped them off. They had to do this after hours.

"Take a seat, Miss Easton."

She selected a chair in the corner near a philodendron.

A brochure on the table in front of her was on DNA testing. She eyed the picture, a man, presumably a father, holding up a toddler a little older than her own son. The copy read, "Discreet and accurate answers await you."

She knew who her father was. Her life wasn't uncertain. So, why did she care so much? The DNA test was all on Taddy, not her. Feeling silly to have come, she grabbed her purse to leave.

"Easton," a voice called out. "I'm here, darling. Now what?"

"Hello, Taddy..."

Dressed in the same Chanel suit she'd had on at her office, her red hair was up in a tight bun. The opaque lenses on her sunglasses prevented Lex from seeing her eyes.

"Sorry I'm late. My Baden Cosmetics account is going to make me jump off the Brooklyn Bridge. I've been with their CEO all day. The damn cream isn't FDA approved, and we're supposed to do a press launch with Elle, Harper's, and Allure. Can you believe it? Baden also wants to brand a pet line I'm dumping on Blake."

"Thank you for coming."

She pointed her in the direction of Danita who held the paperwork out, all ready for her. Her bestie went on and on about her day, all irrelevant to what was about to take place. She was babbling, a sure sign Taddy was nervous as she filled out forms.

"Will you be taking us back at the same time to take this test thingy?" Taddy asked Danita as she handed over the paperwork.

"We can if you'd like us to, Miss Brill. It's a very simple test—"

"Yes, please." She held on to the counter.

Lex reached for her hand; she was shaking.

"Follow me," Danita said as she brought them past the security check point and into an exam room. "This is Dr. Kenzik. I'll see you back in the front when you're through."

"Hello, ladies."

"Hi, Doctor." Lex shook his hand.

"Miss Easton, it's an honor to meet you." He smiled eagerly. Bald, short and in his late sixties, he looked her up and down.

"Thank you for taking us so last-minute."

"My pleasure. I was a huge fan of your father's." He started to talk about Eddie's music and how wonderful it must have been to have had him as a dad.

Lex frowned. Was this really the right time or place to be going through the Rock-n-Roll Hall of Fame? She was used to it, but come on; she was about to find out if her best friend was her sister. "Thank you," she forced.

"Eddie's the reason why we're here," Taddy snarked.

"Right. Okay, ladies. I'm going to ask you some additional questions for clarification on the paperwork and then explain how the DNA matching works. We're testing to see if you two are related, correct?"

"Yes, sisters," she admitted.

"Now, you both note different mothers. You believe to have the same father, right?"

"Yes, Eddie Easton, rock-star, remember?" Taddy rolled her green eyes.

Dr. Kenzik's mouth hung open over her flippant comment. He glanced at Lex and then tightened his jaw. "We'll be doing what's called an X-chromosome test. It's ninety-nine-point-nine percent accurate. Men, like Mr. Easton, all have one X-chromosome. That chromosome is passed down from father to daughter. You each have two X-chromosomes."

"Meaning?" Taddy removed her sunglasses. Her eyes were smudged in mascara.

"If you two are sisters, your X-chromosomes will match exactly the same. We can also do a full sibling test to make certain. Are either of your mothers here?"

Taddy laughed. "God, no."

"I didn't know—" Lex panicked. Birdie was aware she'd be there, but she didn't think to have her join them. "I could call mine and ask her to come. She's watching my son."

"Is that necessary, doctor?" Taddy asked.

"We like to look at many factors of your DNA as it will help us assess your relationship." Dr. Kenzik went into the cabinet and pulled out some cotton swabs. "But it's not necessary. Who would like to get swabbed first?"

Lex raised her hand and opened her mouth. Her eyes wandered over to Taddy, whose forehead was starting to shine. A tiny beat of perspiration dotted her upper lip as she wiped it with her finger.

"I'm not taking your saliva as much as your cheek cells. You'll feel a slight scrape." Dr. Kenzik swabbed her, put it in a vial and sealed it with a label.

A minute later, he turned his attention to Taddy. Knuckles white, she hugged her Birkin bag tightly as he took her sample.

"There, we're all set. Ladies, Danita will call you back in about an hour when we have the results." Dr. Kenzik left the room.

As if in a hurry, Taddy followed right behind him.

She wasn't leaving, was she?

"Good night," Taddy said to Danita as they passed the front desk.

"Taddy!" Lex grabbed her arm. "Aren't you staying?"

"No. I told you I'd do the test, and I did. But I don't want to know the answer. I respect that you do. Enjoy your night." She pushed the door open after Danita unlocked it for her and left.

Lex couldn't believe it. What was the big deal? Okay, this was a *huge* deal. But how could Taddy not want to know? She thought she'd had her best friend of twenty-nine years all figured out, but Taddy's actions had just confused her more than ever.

Chapter Seventeen

Electrotica

Miguel peeled the gel sticker tape guard off the first pad. He was careful not to touch the device with his left hand. His right smoothed the conductive adhesive gel over Blake's skin. He layered the goop in the desired area where the pad would give the most muscle relaxation, and positioned it on the ass. He placed the second pad right about an inch below the other. He duplicated this on his sub's other ass cheek. Blake was encased in four pads. If that didn't loosen him up, nothing would.

At the headrest, he kissed Blake's shoulders and then his nape. His sub rose for more affection.

"I'm going to turn the anal beads' vibration on first. It's going to stimulate your sphincter. They aren't attached to the pads, so you'll feel each one separately."

"Mmm."

"Then I'm going to turn the electro pads on."

"Huh?"

He'd forgotten to show his sub the full gamut of tricks when they started, and realized Blake didn't have a clue what was stuck to his own ass. *Poor sub.*

"You're going to sense a prickle at first, then more prickling. The pads pulsate the muscles. You *will* open up."

Middle finger risen high, Blake laughed through the tape. Miguel walked around to face him, to check on him.

His forehead arched up as if to say, *Bring it on, Sir.*

"Two lashings, noted." He returned to his sub's backside. Holding the ring which tipped the balls into Blake's ass, he flipped the small switch on. His sub's toes curled as Miguel said, "One down, one more to go."

He turned on the electrical pads.

Each fiber of Blake's body was on edge, alert and stimulated. His flesh goosed up; the little blond hairs on his legs and arms stood on end.

"*Bueno. Y*ou enjoy this, *bebé*?"

No peep from him. His hands were composed into tight fists in an apparent attempt to contain his arousal. One glance down and he knew his sub was having a pre-orgasm. Toes curled, he was grinding his groin into the board, humping the bench to release.

He walked over to his toolbox and pulled out electric clippers. He put them up to Blake's face.

Blake's humping ceased. His sub's glittery eyes opened in alarm.

"Last time I face-fucked your pretty mouth, you screamed when I pulled on your hair. I don't want to hurt you again. I only want to give you pleasure. Tonight, I'll buzz your hair off."

Head jerking up to attention, the whites of Blake's eyes enlarged as curls of his blond hair shook, curls which always covered his face and his scar.

"No more temptation to pull your hair again."

He muttered his resistance through the tape.

"I thought we agreed you were going to trust me. Let me do whatever I want to do. Give yourself up to me completely."

He closed his eyes as if contemplating everything.

"You wanna continue?"

Blake didn't reply.

"You trust me?"

A quick nod confirmed Miguel could continue.

Plugging the clippers into an electric outlet on the wall, Miguel clamped on the number three guard. He footed the clipper's fork under Blake's neckline and ran the sheers up the lower hairline toward his forehead. Light-hued locks twisted against the blades almost as if fighting to be cut. Some stood straight up while others jimmied under the cutter. His first swipe turned to two, then three, then four. Fresh-cut hair floated to the cement floor.

He stepped back. Blake's face rose for approval. *So hot.*

"Let's go shorter." Going back to his bag, he grabbed for the number one guard and replaced number three.

Another nod of agreement came from his sub.

He grabbed his sub by the scalp with the only remaining hair, packing it in his fist. Squatting down face-to-face, he pressed his lips over the tape and kissed him.

Staring into his fears, he promised, "I won't shave you. No skin, okay?"

His sub nodded.

Miguel rolled his lips over the taped mouth again. "Good, *niño*," he whispered. "You're learning to submit."

After repeating the same process with the clippers, he was soon finished. His sub resembled a United States Marine ready for duty.

"There's my man, hotter with buzzed hair. You're butched up. Who knows? Maybe you'll be topping me soon enough."

Blake put a thumb up in the air to confirm the idea.

"Me bottoming?" He smirked. "Will never happen. I'm a top one hundred percent. About time I showed you."

He went over to the wall, setting the clippers on the counter. Short and long gleaming chains hung on the left; to the right lay the whips, polished to perfection. He reached for the flogger first. The suede tassels spun out around him as he pulled it over with a tight grip.

Starting off easy, he tickled the leather straps down his backside. Blake's shoulders were unblemished, as perfect as whole milk. He flipped his wrist down fast and with a quick turn. The black straps snapped across his sub's backside.

Blake moaned.

"You like?"

"Sss," he muttered through the tape, his eyes glaring up at him eager for more.

Miguel went harder and faster, flogging his backside...one, two, three strikes.

His sub's ass flinched as the asshole opened wider. The anal beads and electro pads performed magic.

"It's time to remove your toys, *bebé*. My cock's getting jealous. It wants inside." He returned the flogger to the wall. Standing over his sub, he flipped the vibration off on both. Removing the pads from his sub's pink ass, he looped his pointer and middle finger through the loop on the anal beads. With a gentle tug, the first ball came out.

Blake cried as if sorry to release them.

With his right hand, he pulled on the second, third, and fourth. He massaged his sub's ass with his left palm, sliding his middle and ring finger into the asshole. It was tight, but not as impossible as before.

"Your ass is ready…for my…fist."

Thrusting his feet, Blake shook his head back and forth.

His refusal angered him. *Dammit.* "You promised you were gonna be a good lil' *niño*. You deserve a spanking." He returned to the wall, grabbing the paddle.

Crack. The wooden handle went down on his ass. Hard.

Blake flinched. Up to that point, everything radiated pleasure, but this was pain, discipline, respect.

"I'm taking your tape off. I wanna hear you moan."

Miguel walked around to face Blake and kissed the tape covering his lips. With his right hand, he pulled on the upper left edge of the black sticker. It felt welded to his sub's face. "Ready?"

His sub's eyes shut tight.

"Open your eyes, *bebé*."

He did as he was told.

"*Uno, dos, tres.*" He slowly peeled the tape off.

Gramercy

"Taddy, stop." Lex ran after her out onto the sidewalk. They were on the corner of Irving Place and Fifteenth Street where her mother once worked. Birdie had a recording studio she'd rented for a few years when she was trying to make a comeback album. She hadn't been to the neighborhood since.

Her friend's feet came together and abruptly stood still. One of her hands went up in the air as if asking for a minute. She didn't turn around. "Don't…"

In silence, she waited. The cabs and buses traveled north. Rush hour was over. The sun was setting. She inhaled the night spring air, not sure what to do. "Please say something."

Taddy turned around. Tears rolled down her cheeks, her eyes more emerald than usual. "I don't want to hurt your feelings."

"Try me."

"I'm better than this. We both are."

"True." She'd heard it all before. "My father is no different than Bob Dylan with his rumored handful of unclaimed kids. Or Daddy's friend, Steven Tyler."

"Oh, God!"

"Remember, poor Liv didn't know Steven Tyler was her father 'til she was about nine."

"I'm a lot older than nine. Eddie is dead and my mother wasn't some *Playboy* centerfold like Liv's mother, Bebe Buell."

Taddy never prided herself on her Austrian roots of nobility, but maybe she didn't want to be associated with the Easton's after all. It was all starting to make sense to Lex.

"No, but my mother was. We are not any more or less special than Steven and Liv are and I'm sure this caused the Tyler's as much pain as we're feeling right now. If not worse."

"I'm not in pain, Lex. I'm pissed off. I'm mad."

"Come on, sit and wait with me inside."

"I'm too upset. I didn't think I would be, but I am. I went back to my office today after you showed me that letter. Irma had to know we were related while we were growing up."

"Countess Irma isn't a good woman, Taddy. We know that."

"How could they not tell us? How could they have kept this from us? I don't want my life to change. I don't want to be—"

"Sisters." Lex gasped. "You don't want this to be true."

"I didn't say that. This has nothing to do with you. I hate to say it, but it doesn't. I don't know why you're pushing for this." She crossed her arms. "My life is pretty good right now. I have Warner, and he loves me. Brill Inc.

is doing well, too. I have my friends. I have you. I don't need to know that Eddie was my father. *My father*, Jesus Christ. I can't even imagine."

"Why is *that* so horrible?" She loved her dad.

"I grew up with your family. Eddie came to my birthday parties. Eddie stood trial and testified when I was emancipated. But I'm not mad at you or him."

"Then who are you upset with?"

"Irma. This is her last laugh, isn't it? Her big *fuck you*. I thought I'd washed my hands free of my mother's wrongdoings years ago, but here we are, almost thirty years old and getting a DNA test to see if we're related. This is going to change our friendship forever. I don't want that. I've already lost so much in my life. I can't go through something else like this. I just can't, Lex. Don't you get it?"

"You could see it that way, sure." Lex put her arms around her. "But I see it another way." She turned her friend back toward the clinic and waited for her to take the first step.

Taddy stepped forward. "I'm getting a sister?"

"Yes, you'll be an aunt to M2 and a sister-in-law to Massimo. You'll be part of my family like you were always meant to be, as you've always been."

"What if the results come back that we're not a match?"

She laughed. Who were they kidding? She didn't think that was possible. "You'll always be my BFF."

Arms locked together, they walked back in to GeneLynx and waited for their test results.

East Village

Miguel put his hand over his sub's mouth to ease the sting, and then he removed it.

"You had to cut my hair?" Blake shouted. Drool and spit came down the corners of his lips.

"You ready for your spanking, *bebé*?"

"Fuck you, Mig! You're going too far." He kicked his legs, but they were restrained and only smacked against the table.

Enough! Miguel grabbed his sub's jaw, sliding his thumb inside that perfect mouth. White glue traced the corners of his swollen lips.

"You wanted this."

Tense, Blake's choppers bit down on his thumb.

Ouch. Withdrawing his hand, he slapped his sub's face. "Don't bite me."

Turning his face back, crimson droplets streamed down Blake's left nostril. Blood. "Being tortured wasn't on my fucking list."

"*Sí,* it was, *bebé*. Call it submission. You're getting some bonus items with your list today."

"I don't want any *bonus items*." He exhaled. "Untie me. Lesson finished." Dropping his head back in the cradle as if the session was over, his impatience was evident.

Open-palmed, he seized Blake's scalp, lifting his head up basketball-to-dribble style and stretching out his neck. He put his face right up to his sub's and stared with possession into his eyes. "We're just getting started, *mi amigo*. I owe you some more lashings."

Licking his lips, Blake met his gaze. His lips puckered with a clicking sound from his throat. He spat in Miguel's face.

What the hell has gotten into you? He wiped off the spit with one swipe. The sticky goo wadded in his hand. Smacking his face open-fisted, he let him have it right back. He couldn't help himself. Every muscle in his sub's body spoke disobedience and arousal at the same time. How was this possible?

"Let's see if you have it in you. Give me those three lashings."

He reached for the paddle and cracked the punishment on his ass again. "Take it."

"Yes, Sir." Blake mimicked the serious response.

He noted his sub's nuts swelled tighter under his shaft. *You're getting off again.* If Blake wanted to play, he had a list of things from their past he should be spanked for.

"You thought I'd let you get away with such horrible cooking?"

"No, Sir," his sub answered in a coy tone, mostly annoying and yet very cute.

"I won't let you get away with shit, ever." He put the paddle down and stood staring at his sub. "Understand?" He held on to his dick then shoved it down his sub's throat.

Blake nodded. His eyes rolled in ecstasy then closed shut as he sucked on Miguel's dick.

He thrust again and again, admiring Blake's ability to take it.

When he withdrew his cock, he clubbed Blake's face with it. His shaft silhouetted itself over the cradle rest. "You love abuse—dirty little pig boy." Striking his cock across his sub's face again, he whipped him over and over again until his dick throbbed in pain. It felt so good.

His sub didn't answer, rather opened his mouth wider, resembling a ravenous bird waiting for his mother to drop a worm. His cock clobbered against Blake's scarlet features.

Enough. If a beating was what his sub wanted... He returned to the wall for the longest leather whip they had. A layer of dust roofed the strap. He assumed it was there for decoration and that no one had ever dared try.

Blake's gaze filled with horror. He wrenched his head back. "No, Mig, not the..."

"*Sí*." With a wrist flick, he tested the whip against the cement floor, watching in awe of its magnificent strike. Dirt rose in a razor-thin line. "Forget the bad cooking. Let's get real. Let's be honest."

"What are you talking about?"

"You think it's okay for us to be best friends for ten years. Ten fucking years and not once did we ever try to be lovers?" he shouted as he swung his right arm over his head. The whip climbed higher, lassoing over his sub's body.

"*No.*"

His sub's screams were the last thing he heard as the whip cracked in midair, above Blake's backside. It didn't touch him. Please, a bullwhip would've killed him. He was dominant, but not destructive.

Blake coughed into a guffaw and muttered, "You fucking asshole."

"You're laughing?" *Nothing will break this little bitch.* The desire to shove his cock inside his sub's ass grew stronger, but his sub hadn't earned it. Not yet. Blake must say he loved him. That was the only way.

"Sorry. I didn't understand 'til today you felt this—"

"Now you do." Miguel reached down and picked up an oversized cement brick from against the wall. "Take a deep breath."

Blake wiggled his body as if trying to get comfortable.

He placed the brick over the shoulders and back, right in the center.

"You're killing me!" Blake screamed. "You're fucking—"

He laughed and corrected, "Nah, I'm showing you how I felt when you married MLD and not me."

"What?"

"You've weighed on me like this brick will weigh on you. My heart was set on you—"

"*Mig.*" He wiggled his backside to get the brick off. No luck.

"You should have been mine." He tapped his fingers on the brick's surface.

"I'm sorry." His sub's intonation lowered as if he was being squashed.

"Are you?" He pressed down on the block. "You have stomach support. This isn't hurting you. Don't be a pussy."

Blake turned his head, revealing a pleasurable grin. "This rock is nowhere near the weight of Hell I carried during my fucking marriage." His condescending snicker returned. "You're clueless to commitment."

"Is *that* so?"

"Your relationships don't last longer than a weekend."

"Shut up." How infuriating. He had no idea Blake thought this about him.

"Your boyfriend's name is Brutus."

"My pet." Pissed, Miguel stalked over to the control panel and punched the lever.

The supporting bench pulled out. Blake's arms and legs stretched apart. The brick on his back hit the floor, breaking into two stones.

A bloodcurdling yell erupted. A noise in the vein to a *Friday the 13th* slasher film.

"Such a scream queen. You may want to audition for a horror flick. Pity no one will hear you. This room is soundproof."

Suspended in midair, hands and feet still tied to the four poles on the corners, his sub's body was extended and stressed, glossed in adrenaline. He was gorgeous, resembling a virgin up for a sacrificial offering at the altar.

"Help me out, sub. Was suspension on your *Seven Desires*? I can't remember." Miguel walked around the captured prey.

"Shit." Trying his hardest to keep his head up, Blake jerked on his arms, perhaps hoping to untie himself.

"I've never seen the sense in having a relationship with somebody simply to fill my time if I didn't love them. I've only wanted one guy my whole life."

"You are—*so* full—of it." His voice strained as his limbs turned white.

"Do you remember the night we met? At Vive's party."

"No. Not really." His face dropped.

"We saw each other for the first time."

"So."

"You rejected me." Miguel and Diego met him at the exact same time and Diego secured the attention, and Blake's heart.

"Such a victim," his sub snarled. "You didn't try hard enough."

"I'm sick of your mouth." He reached for another brick from the corner and placed it over his back.

Inching toward the floor, Blake moaned. Sweat dripped off his chest, forehead, and crotch into a shallow puddle beneath him. "My wrists are gonna break." He turned with a begging look on his face. "Please."

But his cock grew harder.

You fuck, you're enjoying this.

Ignoring the pleas, he asked, "Who taught you how to fold clothes?"

Blake mustered a response. "I'm not your effin' maid."

He turned on his heel, coming around his sub's backside. Circling him once more, he admired the view. "Indeed, Mrs. Morgan would be appalled." He reached for a smaller whip, one he knew was safe and pleasurable. Snapping the leather against the cement floor, the crack jerked Blake's body in response. Bouncing off his back, the bricks crumbled to the floor.

"Ready?"

"Always." Blake faced him with a bold grin.

Miguel snapped the whip down as fast as possible, lashing his sub. "That's for not remembering and for picking MLD." An odd feeling of sadness and relief came over him for telling his friend the truth, that his past actions had hurt him. He'd never told Blake how he'd felt about him picking MLD over him. The release from getting his frustrations off his chest was too much.

"Let me hold you." Blake's vocal chords were stifled. "Untie me."

He threw the whip down. "Ready?"

"Yes."

Miguel flipped the lever up. The leather bench came up from below. Blake's body shook with relief. His sub's back muscles relaxed as he closed his eyes.

He went over to a towel caddy plugged in by the door. Taking two cold wash cloths, he rinsed Blake's back, wiping him clean. The burning red glow subsided to a soft cherry. He kissed his shoulder blades, forearms, lower back, and hind legs.

"Amazing. Thank you." The heaving chest slowed as the words caught in his breath.

"You okay?" Afraid he'd been too rough, he could see that Blake's gratitude proved otherwise.

"Hells yeah! I played the tortured prisoner well."

Miguel untied his arms and legs. "You enjoyed being my hostage?"

Rolling over onto his backside, Blake faced up. "Of course." He expressed amusement. "I want more."

His response put Miguel's concern that he'd gone too far at ease.

"My sub is testing me to go further?"

"Uh-huh. I'm feeling sinister."

Unfathomable. "You sure?" He'd misjudged Blake's resilience.

"Child's play was fun. Now show me what you really got." He nested his arms behind his neck and issued a fake yawn.

Who knew Blake was a power bottom? Miguel enjoyed watching his friend come out from his frigid shell. He'd been pent-up for far too long. "Don't get too comfortable, *bebé.*" He reached down and kissed him on the lips. "This was only round one."

Chapter Eighteen

The Donkey Punch

Blake never imagined he'd be enjoying BDSM play as much as he was right that second. Especially, considering he hadn't wanted to come to The Dupree Club in the first place. Man, he was happy he'd changed his mind and stayed. He pushed his buddy to extremes. Unaware these desires existed, he didn't think they'd feel so good. Once tied up, anal beaded, electricity padded, flogged, whipped, then suspended, though it was strange at first, the discipline might become addictive, nonetheless. Something about being made into a sex object was so fitting. His ex husband considered him a roommate, bill payer, a means to an end. In no way a submissive bottom—and especially not after Diego crossed over to the dark side, he couldn't.

His reflection against the mirrored walls motivated him to carry on with Miguel. The muscles he'd worked so hard to build in recent months were being put to the test. Up to the point where his Dom put a fucking cement brick on his back, he'd relished in Miguel's domination.

Getting sentimental? *WTF?* He'd forgotten about the lunch with Thor and Vive. They'd warned him that Miguel might've put more at stake than he'd realized.

He respected Miguel for letting his true feelings for him out, at long last. But why did he have to be tied up and weighed down to listen? He should've confessed his feelings years before.

Or maybe not.

Time gaps flashed in his mind as Miguel walked over to the wall and pulled down more toys. He realized his friend didn't know how to communicate how he felt. Hell, the man wouldn't tell him when his birthday was, let alone profess his emotions.

Hmmm. He pondered two questions. One, would he have married Diego if he'd known Miguel wanted him? Two, once married, would he have asked for a divorce sooner if he'd come for him? He didn't have an answer for either.

He was snapped back to reality by the strident sound of a smacking noise, as if his Dom had put on a rubber glove. Spreading his legs, he glanced between them and asked, "*What* are you doing?"

Miguel squatted and reached under the table. He pulled out a tub. *Crisco.* "What does it look like?" Unscrewing the lid, he dipped his rubber-gloved hand in.

"Not gonna happen, Mr. Santana."

"Back at this again, are we?" His Dom rubbed the lard, glossing up his fist.

"I'm not playin' the tortured prisoner routine this time. I'm being serious." Closing his legs tight, he said, "You're not fisting me." *I can't do this.* "Vibrating anal balls— electric butt pads—enough." *Fuckin' just fuck me already.*

"*Yes*, I am." Miguel held on to Blake's knees and pried them open, pulling his ass closer to the table's edge. "Don't overthink this. Just go with it. You'll thank me later."

Screw you.

He kicked his leg up to escape his Dom's capture. His leg rose higher than expected, and with his size twelve feet, he struck Miguel's face. *Whack!* Blood splattered the wall mirrors next to them.

"Sorry. I didn't mean to—"

"Asshole."

He squeezed Blake's foot with his right hand while wiping his bloody nose with his forearm. The blood must've flipped him out because with a slow force, he twisted the ankle in a direction Mother Nature hadn't intended.

"Break my bone, go ahead." He lifted his left leg to kick Miguel's face again, that time with more force.

"*Ha!*" Miguel blocked the subsequent hit, gripping both feet. Pushing Blake's legs into his chest, he pulled up on his ass, bringing his body closer to his own. The Crisco fell to the floor, spattering beneath them. "Forget breaking your ankle, *bebé*. I'll shatter your legs."

"Stop!"

Miguel drew him tighter into his frame, unaware he wasn't kidding.

I can't. Blake reached for the bench's edge to get away.

"I'm going to top you senseless. You'll be unable to get up to do anything about it."

Wrists too sore from the recent bondage to hold on, he lost his grip. He put his palms over his face in defeat.

He kept his body heavy in Miguel's arms. "We're going too far." He understood his Dom didn't intend to hurt him, but his ankle throbbed. "We're destroying one another."

Miguel returned his legs back to the table. He straightened them out as if he was putting him down for a nap. Rubbing the feet, he kissed his two big toes. "We're cool."

Frozen, he didn't take his hands off his face. He was finished. His own nervous breath bounced back onto his cheeks. "I can't."

"Blake?"

He shook his head, unable to respond. *This was a mistake.* "Take me home to Chelsea."

Miguel chanted his name in an extended baritone influence, accentuating his Latin accent. His body weighed the bench down when he sat on the edge. His left thigh touched Blake's shoulder as he removed the hands from his face. "You're shaking," he whispered.

Too scared to face him, he inhaled and swallowed, unsure how to respond.

"Look at me," Miguel commanded.

Squinting, he witnessed the Mario Lopez grin, beaming as if everything was hunky-dory. "Don't you *dare* give me *that* smile." He touched his friend's lips, testing the authenticity.

Miguel leaned down with a nudge and kissed him. "I promise I won't hurt you. Put your trust in me."

He resisted his friend's kiss and kept his lips pressed together. Uninvited. He shook his head.

Repositioning himself with more intent over Blake's face, he asked, "Rejecting me again?" He licked his sub's lip in one long stroke.

"Mmm." Mouth shut, he fought the temptation to smile.

A second lick to the top lip radiated a tickle, causing him to drop his jaw. Opening his mouth into a grin, he signaled he was okay.

Permission given, his Dom slid his thick, wet, powerful tongue in. He kissed him with a force as if he was trying to apologize, to ask for a second chance and to say they were indeed all right.

"I'm sorry." He brought his legs up around Miguel's backside, holding onto his friend's shoulder while kissing him.

"Do you trust me?" His Dom nuzzled his neck and lowered his lick-kiss-suck technique to his right nipple.

Oh, my sensitive nips. He squirmed. "I do. I trust you. I always have."

Miguel locked his lips over the areola and tugged on the nipple with his teeth.

Blake pressed his backside into the bench, relaxing as his friend feasted on his pecs.

"*Bebé*, I love the way you taste." He switched his focus to the other pectoral muscle and hunkered down on his sensitive flesh.

He arched his chest up, wanting more. "I had no idea I'd enjoy *this* so much."

"I did."

His Dom removed a string from his left pocket. Nipple clamps. He traced his left nipple and flicked with his tongue. He then clamped one down.

Shit. Tight. Love. A twisting sensation enhanced every fiber in his body.

He reached down Blake's torso and jacked his dick. He lapped up the clear liquid. "I love your pre-cum, *bebé*."

Returning his focus on the nipples with his right hand, he stretched his other nipple flat and pinched the tip, hooking it up to the other clamp. Blake's nipple clamps were connected by a steel cord. He pulled back on the string, watching in fascination. Blake's nipples lifted. His cock hardened.

"Your body loves torture." Miguel leaned down, taking Blake's cock in his mouth.

"Fuck, Mig, yeah. Honey, suck. That's right." Ramming his groin into his Dom's mouth, he pumped and pumped his cock down his friend's throat. Miguel tugged onto the string, bit by bit, tighter, distending his sensitive nipples. *Oh, my!*

Miguel stood hovering over him. Caressing his face with his left hand, he kept the string taut with his right. "Do you still want to stop and go home to Chelsea?"

"No." He exhaled, lifted his legs, arching his ass and welcoming everything his Dom intended.

"Let me fist you." Miguel's chin rose in confidence.

Slowly, he nodded in agreement. He was ready. He wanted to trust him. It was time.

"Rough sex is your favorite. You enjoy acting resistant. *Sí?*"

Again, he nodded. "Who knew?"

"You play the part. Tell me to stop all you want." He wrapped his hand around Blake's neck and applied pressure as if to choke him. "I'm going to give you a safe word." He leaned down taking his mouth with a savage intensity.

"No tape over my mouth?" Tension around his neck grew tighter.

"We've gotta talk our way through the fisting."

"Okay." This was going to be extreme.

"Eyes focused on me. I'll guide you."

"What's my word?" Blake sat up.

"Your safe word is MLD." Eyes squinted, a muscle in his jaw twitched.

"Not funny. But I get it." He wasn't going to shout his ex-husband's acronym for Missy Limp Dick during his euphoric inauguration. *Damn, Mig, you're good! You're pushing my body and my emotional buttons all at the same time.*

Resuming the position between his legs, Miguel sat on the stool. He slid his fingers into Blake's ass. "Three fingers, *bebé*. You're doing good. Deep inhale for me." He pushed in more. "Four fingers." He stood, rolling his shoulders back. Massaging Blake's inner thighs with his free hand, he encouraged, "Doing great."

Fuck. "Feels...like I'm split in half."

"Love your ass." Miguel held onto his nuts with his free hand and pushed his fisting hand into his asshole.

"Make me come. For Christ's sake, let me come."

He felt Miguel's fingers slide deeper. Intense pressure built. His asshole was in ecstasy. "Give me more." He smiled up at his Dom. "Get your fist in there, Mig."

Gramercy

"Ladies," Danita called them back up. "Dr. Kenzik will see you now."

For the first time since finding the DNA letter, Lex felt better. She knew this happened for a good reason. A blessing after all their parents had put them through, the verbal abuse, the drugs, and neglect—sisterhood was a gift.

"Ready?"

"As ever." Dry-eyed, Taddy seemed relieved they'd talked moments before.

Dr. Kenzik greeted them as they came into the room. Paper in hand, his face didn't reveal their test results one way or another. *He must do this every day. Just not with Easton girls.*

"Miss Brill." Dr. Kenzik turned his attention to Lex. "Miss Easton. The results showed that you two are...an exact match." He handed them each a paper.

"Oh! My!" Taddy shrieked happily.

"I get this is the news you were hoping to hear?" Dr. Kenzik put his hand out to congratulate Taddy.

"You mean we're sisters?" Lex said. Overwhelmed, she gulped hard as hot tears slipped down her face. Happy ones and yet, she felt so confused. At the first idea of them being sisters she'd been sick to her stomach over it. But since they were indeed related, she was angry at her father.

"Yes, I hope this helps." Dr. Kenzik extended a handshake. "I'll leave you two to talk. Danita will meet you up front with your bill. Take your time."

Taddy inhaled and wiped her eyes. "You okay?"

"Why do you think our parents never said anything?" She felt like such a fool. "I don't know what to say. Are you glad you know?"

"Ummm…yes and no. I'm relieved and yet perplexed as to why Eddie never went to get retested."

"Drugs, probably. Dad hated going to the doctor's office. He hated to be sober. Anything like this appointment would've forced him to dry out for a few days."

"Eddie was so selfish."

"He was an addict, Taddy." It had taken Lex years to come to terms with what her father was, but she did. "Look on the bright side."

"What's that?"

"You won't have to share the Eddie Easton estate with me," Taddy joked.

"Right. Dad died bankrupt. There isn't one. He signed his music rights away, too." Lex tried to laugh with her. She couldn't. "The only thing you're getting out of this is knowing I'm your half-sister."

"That's more than I could've ever asked for. Well…I'd suggest we go get a few drinks with Vive to celebrate, but you can't have a cocktail for like seven more months and Vive needs to quit booze altogether."

"Thanks for reminding me." Lex realized, with all the drama going on, that she was already so blessed with friends and family. Now, there was another baby growing inside her. "I don't know what I'm going to say to Mom." And how would she tell her fiancé? "Massimo must think my family is crazy."

"Yes, I'm sure he does." She put her arms around her. "DNA or not, you're still my sister. We don't need GeneLynx to tell us who our real family is."

"I love you, Taddy. I love you so much."

"That's the first time you've ever said…you loved me." She smiled.

"It is not."

"Darling, it is. The only person who has ever said they loved me is Warner."

"I didn't say in love with you." She laughed, though her mind raced for a second. Maybe her bestie was right. "Are you trying to make me feel worse?"

"No, darling. But if it got you to finally wake up and count your stars and say you loved me, I'd go through this GeneLynx test again."

"You would?"

"Sure. I love you more than anything. You may be a pain in the ass, but I can't imagine my life without my best friend."

"You mean your sister. I'm upgrading my BFF status."

She paid the bill, put Taddy in the SUV, and headed home to be with Massimo and her son.

East Village

His Dom tugged at his ball sac with one hand and plunged in his ass with the other. His right hand pushed in further and with each millimeter inside his ass, Miguel's smile broadened.

You get off on being in control over my body. You want to own me.

With a tug at his cock, Blake started to jack off. He found it helped relax his ass. "Intense. So tight." He reached down, grabbing onto the string to tug at his nipples. "Fuck!" he shouted and pulled harder to prevent himself from a panic. He let go from the emotional resistance. "Take me."

"I'm in mid-hand, *bueno*." Miguel's thumb massaged the scrotum, dancing a fire around his G-spot. "Let's do breathing exercises together. Relax more."

"Can't. This is as good as it's gonna get." He felt his ass cheeks tighten.

His Dom frowned. Any hope to avoid a panic was waning.

"*Blake*," he called to him in a tranquil voice. "Trust me. I'll make this your best experience yet." His hand pushed in further. "On three, I want you to clamp your asshole around my hand and hold it for ten seconds. Ready?"

"Uh-huh."

"*Uno, dos, tres.*"

Blake's ass filled with pressure. His ass cheeks tightened.

"*Ocho* more seconds."

He screamed. "Shit. My ass is closing."

"Look at me."

Miguel's controlling words with his hypnotic stare possessed him into further submission.

"Release. You did it, ten seconds." He grinned.

Taking a deep breath in then out, Blake released the constricted muscles in his asshole. The second he gave way, Miguel slid in further, deeper. Blake held on to the string between his nipples and shouted, "Fuck!" *I can't take it anymore.*

"Let me in." Miguel wedged his wide hand in further.

He felt as if he'd been sawed in half.

"I love you how you're giving yourself to me, *bebé.*"

In a flash, he experienced the full fist, causing his body to tremble. The fine hairs on his chest stood on end. "You're in!" he screamed.

"*I'm in.*"

Letting the nipple clamps go, he held on to the table's edge, arching his back. "Mig."

His Dom hoisted himself up onto the bench under his legs. "I love your body." He moved his fist in and out of his ass with care. His other hand jacked the cock.

"I'm going to come." He pressed down with his feet and arched his legs as he pushed into his back.

"Come for me, *bebé*." With his free hand, Miguel pumped his cock with feverish intent.

Raw with desire, eager to orgasm, he hadn't cum in four days. It was time. "Ohhhh," he trembled, starting with his toes, sending a spiral up his back. The first squirt came with a liberating, giddy laugh. A second, larger pump ejaculated up high, reaching his shoulders.

"*Bebé*'s a shooter."

"Yeah, fucking jack me harder." He rolled his eyes, seeing black. Heaven.

Miguel tugged down, yanking his cock with one final thrust, sending him into ultimate release. Hot liquid singed his chest as it rained.

"*Mágico*." He retracted his fist from Blake's ass.

He shook, too tongue-tied to speak. He'd given up control. He gave in to his senses. He'd allowed himself to be stripped of his defenses, weak to his Dom's touch.

I did it.

Sudden coolness washed over him as his body separated from Miguel's. His ass felt as if it had been dipped in ice and set on fire. It was a heady mix.

His Dom cheered him on. "The best." He licked Blake's release into his mouth.

He noted he didn't swallow, but stuck his covered-in-white tongue out at him. *Piggie.* Lapping up his second release then third, Miguel's mouth cheeks were full. He tried to sit up as his best friend pushed his legs back into his chest, ass out.

Miguel spat a wad into his hole. "Using your cum for lube," he chimed.

Bigger pig. The cum pelted down his ass, ready for his friend's cock.

Standing, Miguel wiped his lips with his forearm. "It's my turn to come." Pulling his body to the edge of the table, Miguel hoisted himself on top. He rested between Blake's legs, up over his stomach. He pulled out a condom and sheathed his dick. Slowly, his cock started to penetrate him. "I've been waiting to fuck you since the day I met you," he whispered in his ear.

Guilt consumed him. A flashback to the brick on his back and the weight of what Miguel had carried for the last ten years.

Miguel lowered his face, resting his lips upon his in a kiss then slid his tongue in with one powerful push. Their mouths danced.

He repositioned himself beneath his friend's weighted frame, trying to get comfortable. *You can do this. It's just sex. Miguel will be fine.*

He couldn't.

He wouldn't.

"Enough squirming, *bebé*. Let me get my cock inside." He held on to Blake's hips, ready to penetrate all the way. Staring into his eyes, Miguel appeared drunk by the passion. "I love you, Mr. Morgan." His kisses were weak, confused. He pulled his head back again, waiting for a response. "I always have."

I can't. "I love you, too." He must end this. "My love for you is why we must stop now."

Reacting as if Blake teased, he nodded dismissively. "Prisoner, I'm releasing you from your captivity. You may be my boyfriend now. Not my sex slave." His dark eyebrows rose, posing the question, waiting for his response.

It was the first time he'd ever seen his friend appear so vulnerable.

Boyfriend? For gay Heaven's sake...no fucking way. "What?"

"I'm in love with you. I want you to be mine. Forever." Miguel moved his groin in closer. "I want us to be together." He pushed his cock into Blake's ass.

"Ahhh…" He held on to Miguel's shoulders, ready to be impaled. So tempting, being with someone he trusted, who loved him, who he'd have great sex with. Be best friends with—an ideal relationship.

But what if his friend changed his mind as his ex-husband had and went against his word? Riddled with relationship fear, he *couldn't* go through that again.

"M-L-D," he affirmed and attempted to push Miguel away from him.

Miguel's cock disengaged. His movie star smile faded, brows furrowed, and shoulders dropped. Pulling his body back, he asked, "What?" He kept his arms over Blake, pinning him down for an answer.

"I can't be in a relationship. I don't want—"

Eyes glazing over, Miguel said, "You're selfish. You love yourself too much to allow anyone to love you back." He pushed his body down further. "That's why you picked Diego over me. You knew all along he wasn't your true love. Diego couldn't hurt you. You were safe with him as long as he did what you wanted."

Oh, Diego hurt me all right. Like I never expected. "You don't understand." *Do not do this to us, Mig.*

"Can't risk getting hurt?" His arms and legs enclosed Blake's body.

Miguel wouldn't let him go without an answer.

"Not exactly," he grunted. He never imagined himself emotionally unavailable. When his friend posed the question, he became conscious of the possibility.

"What then?" He blinked. Drops of sweat clung to his forehead.

"I need time to think, to process this."

"You've had ten years."

He raked the Latin's chest with his fingers, hoping the conversation wouldn't get worse. "I assumed a crush, or a fuck. Never love. Not this."

"Now you know." Miguel cupped his hands around Blake's face. Leaning in, he gave him a kiss on the forehead then on the left cheek. He crossed over and pressed his lips against his face's right side.

He felt as if the oxygen in the room was burned up by the fire between them. "I'm sorry."

"I'm over your apologies. Give me an answer." Miguel kissed his chin. "Right now." He planted a final kiss on Blake's lips. Eyes open, he stared down at him.

Too intense. Too much. You'll destroy me if I agree to this. Blake pushed his friend's mouth to the side. "I can't." He needed Miguel off him.

"Can't give me an answer?" Tears dropped from his shadowed eyes. "Or *can't* be in a relationship with me?"

"Both."

I'm so confused. How did this get so messy?

Defeat eclipsed Miguel's body. His skin was so tight you could bounce a silver dollar off his chest. Standing without acknowledging Blake, he grabbed his trench coat, covering his leather attire. He picked up the toolbox.

"Don't leave, please…" He sat up off the bench and ran toward the door.

Miguel didn't face him. "Find someone else to finish your *Seven Desires*." A repugnant tone laced his voice as he muttered over his shoulder, "Fuck you, Blake." With that, he stormed out.

After sitting there for a few minutes collecting his thoughts, and his things, Blake slipped his pants and shirt back on, ashamed he'd let the week go as far as it did. He knew better. Nothing good could come from sex, casual *or* committed. It wasn't worth ruining his friendship. It had already ruined his marriage and Diego's life.

Out on the sidewalk, he rubbed his tender wrists. The night's damp air made him feel even more alone than he'd already felt on the inside.

A text came through to his phone. *Morgan, stay in Chelsea. I'll messenger your shit to your doorman later. Take care, Santana.*

'Take care'? That was worse than 'eat shit' or 'drop dead'.

He'd be safe at his Chelsea penthouse. Diego hadn't been there earlier when he'd stopped by. Maybe a night alone would help him clear his mind and think. Everything seemed to be compounding and getting worse. First Diego threatened to kill him, then Lex canceled her wedding, and it looked like he'd just lost his best friend.

I wanted to be punished for picking the wrong guy, but not this. You don't understand what Diego did...

Part Three

Just marry me already

THE MANHATTANITES
love, friendship, scandal, and drama to the hilt

"When a girl is in love you can see it in her smile, like me with Masi. When a boy is in love you can see it in his eyes, like Masi with me. When two boys are in love with each other, they both can't see shit, like Miguel and Blake."—Lex Easton, mom, wife, fashionista.

Chapter Nineteen

Cagney & Lacey

Midtown West

In the limo, Miguel exchanged his leather gear for jeans and a t-shirt. At the suggestion of Madam Queen Dick Dupree, he went to the only place in town he could have a drink and let out his frustration while wearing his leather ensemble.

The Eagle.

Divey and dark, The Eagle was situated in the West Twenties. Close to the gay neighborhood of Chelsea but set away from the main avenues, it made sense why guys went there to be…mischievous. At least they were that night. As he walked into the bathroom to piss, he noticed a guy taking a leak down another dude's throat. He laughed, thinking about his and Blake's shower together.

Thirsty, he went to the bar and ordered a Corona with lime. The DJ spun a heavy metal classic. Birdie Easton's *Lucifer's Mistress*, *"Take me, take me tonight, take me now…"*

"Miggy." A familiar voice called out over his shoulder as he took a seat.

He turned to see Gillian Neeson, the guy he'd dated the previous summer. "*Hola,* Gil," he greeted, admiring his rust-colored hair and light skin. Freckles spattered across the bridge of his nose, the ones he'd given nicknames to, appeared to have darkened since the last time they'd been together.

Gillian tried to kiss him but he turned his face, planting his lips on his cheek. He took the stool next to him.

He didn't like that. He didn't ask for company. He wasn't up for small talk, either, especially when Gillian's hand grazed against Miguel's leg.

"True or false—"

"I'd rather play truth or dare."

"Ha." Gillian laughed, making himself comfortable. "Rumor is…you're living with Blake Morgan. Is that true or false?"

"Gil, what biz is my life of yours?"

"It used to be."

"Nice try. Who told you?"

"Duckie Capri."

"Blake's assistant is gossiping about his personal life? Talk about career suicide." If he didn't fire Duckie, Taddy would, for sure.

Gillian huffed. "Everyone in town is talking about Blake and you." Without asking, he took a sip of Miguel's beer. "Hard to believe you've *settled* down."

He didn't care for the way he stressed the word *settled*. Like Blake was beneath him. His friend was one of, if not *the,* best catch. Period.

"Ya know, I still think about you." Gillian winked.

"Bullshit." One, no one in town talked about him and Blake as a couple because they weren't an item. Two, Miguel wasn't really out of the closet yet, so no one could say much about him. Three, no way Gillian Neeson thought about him as he was only capable of thinking about himself.

"I do. At night, alone in my studio, when I'm jacking off, I think back to us last summer. About me coming over in the middle of the night, climbing in that big bed of yours, kissing you, getting under your body." Gillian ran his arm up a bit too high on his thigh. He was way past grazing.

He pushed his hand away. "All we did was fuck."

"It wasn't just a fuck. No. No. No. It was the best…sex…ever. Besides, what else is there? You and I both know gay relationships in this town don't last."

"Oh…" He'd never heard anyone admit that one before. "Why's that?"

"Too many options." Looking out at the dozens of men who circled them like sharks, he realized Gillian was right. There were many men to choose from. Maybe that was the problem, there'd been too many. The gays were kids in a candy shop, and in this town, it wasn't possible to have a relationship, at least not a conventional one.

"We had fun," Miguel complimented, realizing he was being a jerk.

"I mean it. Hands down, bar none…you're number one, Miggy."

Why was Gillian pursuing him again? He didn't care for aggressive bottoms. That's what he found endearing about Blake. His friend let him lead as the natural dominant. There was none of whatever this dude was trying to serve up right then.

"Maybe you should try a few more guys."

"You have a nice cock, Miggy."

"*Gracias.*" Nothing new there, however that night, he enjoyed the compliment. Returning the favor, he conceded, "You're a good bottom." He felt a little cheap for saying it. Almost as if he wasn't being loyal to Blake, but his friend could go fuck himself as far as he was concerned.

"What else?" Flirting hardcore, Gillian leaned his muscular body against his and licked his lips.

His eyes were blue as Miguel liked. But not the Blake Morgan III blue. The kind which hinted of flecks of gray and sparkled aquamarine hues when he'd blinked. Void of any real life, Gillian's eyes were a flat navy. The ones where you couldn't tell where the pupil ended and the iris began, as if painted onto a plastic doll.

"That tight ass of yours milks a dick just right." Putting blue hues aside and facing facts, Miguel was pissed off by the fact that Blake broke his heart, ten years before and again that night. If Gillian wanted to play with him, as well, someone was going to get hurt, and it wasn't going to be Miguel. Not anymore. He didn't believe the ass sitting next to his was all that, not compared to Blake's, which to his knowledge was still a virgin bottom.

While Gillian rambled, he couldn't help but think about his friend and his tight body. How Blake had trusted him, allowed him to fist him. God! His warm hole, feeling inside him. That was the most intimate moment of his life. He thought about how he even told him he was in love with him.

"Where's the famous Mr. Morgan tonight?"

"Huh. Oh, ummm, his place, I imagine."

"Great. Take me home to yours."

"*¿Esta noche?*"

"Right now."

Gillian stood. He seemed shorter than Miguel remembered.

"Come on."

"My beer." He held the glass bottle up and slowly sipped. "I'd like to finish." It tasted warmer than when he'd first ordered. He picked at the lime wedge, not making eye contact with Gillian.

"The best sex of your life is standing before you…and you're sipping beer as slow as breast milk."

"*I* never said *you* were the best sex I ever had. *You* did." He was over Gillian Neeson long before then. Sure, he could've taken him back to The Dupree Club, tied him up and got rough with him, but Gillian would've loved it too much. This ginger was easy with his body and his mind? Well, he'd forgotten how shallow, horny, and dumb the guy was—until that moment.

"Don't play me. You want me. I want you."

"*Ay puta.* Get lost."

"What…did you say?"

"I wouldn't top you if you were the last piece of ass in Manhattan. Tight or loose, you're too easy. I wouldn't even let Brutus take you for a walk if his bladder depended on it." *That should turn Gillian off, for now.* He didn't know what else to say other than, "*Adiós.*"

"Asshole!" Gillian turned dramatically. Before he went, he brought his mouth back over to Miguel's right ear and snarled, "That's always been your problem, Miggy. You're moody, you care too much about that damn mutt, and you don't accept our lifestyle for what it is…"

He met Gil's angry glare and asked, "And what's that?"

"Just sex."

"That's always been *your problem,* Gil. I want more than *just sex.*"

"Appears you'll get a lot more than that with Blake. From what I've been hearing, you'll get the bug, too."

The bug? He grabbed Gillian's leather shirt before he could walk off. He stood over him. He didn't like to use his height as an intimidation tactic, but he did so now. "What did you say?"

"I always knew you were a freak in bed, but I never figured you for a bug chaser, Miggy. You have gone and lost your gay mind."

The edges of Gillian's mouth curled up as if he'd let some big reveal out of the bag because clearly his own response was utter shock.

"Blake is negative. We tested together this week."

"How cute. He may test negative as some poz guys do who aren't detectable, but he's poz. You will be, too, if you don't wrap it up, Miggy. Literally." Gillian marched off, leaving his jaw hanging wide open.

He slouched back on the stool, feeling as if the air had been sucked out of him, while Gillian's words reverberated over and over again. Could Blake have tested negative with him, but actually be positive? Rubbing his palms over his face, he closed his eyes, inhaled deeply, and tried to make sense of what he'd heard. Gays in the city didn't joke around about this. It was too taboo.

Think!

He replayed the past few days in his mind. For a second, he took the probability of Blake being positive off the table and asked himself, why would his best friend lie to him about this? Come to think of it, Miguel hadn't asked, "Are you HIV positive?" when they were at the Exhale Bliss spa. Rather, he just said they'd go get the test, and they did. Negative. He'd dated poz guys in the past; he didn't discriminate, but he'd double-bagged it. He wasn't big on sucking cock, so that part didn't matter. Blake's cock was the first he'd put in his mouth in years.

Thor was poz. Blake could easily come out about his status. The group wouldn't turn their back on him. Taddy gave millions for AIDS research every year. HIV wasn't something to be ashamed of in New York or with their friends.

Why would Blake create his *Seven Desires*, a list of uninhibited acts, if he was? He'd heard of poz guys who'd re-tested negative. Medically, it was possible with the right pill cocktail. But would he put his health at risk by engaging in oral sex? Though the community had told them they couldn't get HIV from oral sex, some health experts argued they could. Was that why he wouldn't let him fuck him?

No. This didn't make any sense.

Instead, he thought back to his rejection. At first, he questioned if he'd been too rough with him. That wasn't it. He could tell by the way his friend's body responded he'd loved it. Blake was a masochist, no doubt.

Their week had been progressing nicely. Opening up more that week than ever before, Miguel became comfortable about his feelings. Then everything seemed to hit the fan when he'd confessed his love.

Surely Blake was comfortable with love. He had to be. He'd gotten married and given his vows in front of hundreds of people. Christ, he'd cried in his arms earlier in the week about the disappointment over his failed marriage and not being able to start a family. None of those actions seemed in line with someone who didn't want love in their life. Blake Morgan III believed in love. He was romantic; it was who he was.

Diego.

What did that guy do to cause him so much pain? He'd seen sadness on his face for months. Something happened. Diego cheated, that was obvious. But it felt, at least to Miguel, as if the damage was worse than an infidelity. Maybe Diego had fallen in love with another guy?

Shaking his head in confusion, he couldn't think of anything else other than Blake being positive. He didn't want to, but he'd love him regardless. HIV or not, it didn't matter as long as he was okay and knew his friends were there for him. He loved him no less.

He reached in his wallet and placed a ten dollar bill on the bar. There was only one way to find out. Outside, he found his driver and said, "One Worldwide Plaza." If he couldn't get the truth from Blake, he'd get it out of Diego.

Eleven traffic lights and eight minutes later, he was at the three-tower, mega-block building situated in Hell's Kitchen. The Worldwide Plaza was a massive residential and commercial building. With fifty floors, he wasn't sure which unit Diego owned. Miguel walked into the main security area of Building Number Two.

Behind the hotel-like oak reception desk the guard greeted him.

"*Buenas noches*," he replied. "Diego Oalo lives here, but I'm not sure which unit. Can you help me, please?"

The guard cleared his throat. "Mr. Oalo lives in this building. He isn't in and hasn't been seen for a few days."

"Hmm. Do you know when he'll back?"

"Sorry, no. The police asked the same thing. He must be in demand...*aye*?" The doorman gave him an annoyed smile.

"*¿Policía*? Were here? For Diego?" Miguel suddenly felt a spike of adrenaline.

"A few times. First a detective, yesterday in fact, named Shiloh something or another. Then a squad of officers came in today."

"Do you know why?"

"Nope. Other than Mr. Oalo is a wanted man."

"*Gracias.*" Miguel headed out and jumped back in the limo. This was crazy. He had to get to Blake's apartment.

Upper East Side

Lex invited Taddy to come over after their GeneLynx appointment. She figured Jemma and Massimo would be hungry and want to go out to eat with M2. But her friend declined and headed back to work to finish the press details for Baden Cosmetics. Taddy informed her Warner would be getting back into town the following day, and her schedule needed to be cleared so she could spend time with her man.

When Lex arrived home, she passed Jemma in the lobby. She was off to a party downtown at some Italian Cultural Institute of New York shindig. Notably, her two boyfriends Rocco and Luigi hadn't flown into New York yet, leaving her to her own mischievous devices.

Looked like her evening would be spent alone with her own two favorite men. She was excited to spend some alone time with them. It would probably be their only evening together until after the wedding.

A sense of home and love filled Lex's heart as she walked in and spotted Massimo preparing supper. He'd even put M2 to bed.

"Thanks for making dinner." She stared at him, allowing his gaze to meet hers. His presence alone gave her comfort. She *was* the luckiest woman in the world.

"My pleasure, *bella*." His voice was as silky-smooth as ever. Massimo was suave. He made everything appear so damn easy. The yummy garlic aroma confirmed he knew what he was doing in the kitchen.

She wavered on whether she should tell him, especially when she saw the pity he had for her in his eyes. He knew. "Did Taddy call you?"

"Texted. She told me about the test results, said you were as happy, mad, and confused as ever. How do you feel now?" Massimo set the spoon he was using to stir the tomato sauce on the counter. His forehead rose in inquiry.

"I'd feel better if you apologized to me for thinking the DNA test would come out any different."

"Scusami, amore mia." He took her in his arms.

His touch was reassuring. Inhaling his usual muskiness, Lex played with the buttons on his Oxford shirt.

He squeezed her tight. "I don't know what to say."

"It's bittersweet, I suppose." She shrugged to hide her feelings. There was a pain and sadness swirling inside her. Lex couldn't figure out why, but there was.

"Nothing has changed. You, Taddy, and your *madre* are all okay."

"You spoke to my mom?" she asked, suddenly feeling worse.

"*Sí.* Birdie rang here about ten minutes ago. I told her. I thought I'd save you the trouble."

"What did she say?" Her spirits quieted and she hoped Massimo wouldn't notice the tremor in her voice. How her mother would respond to this was one thing she was uncertain about. The last thing she wanted the DNA test to do was hurt her mother.

"Your *madre* sounded relieved and was happy it's all out in the open. Vive called, too. She said you two are all set for dinner tomorrow at her place."

"Don't remind me." She had yet to deal with her Farnsworth drama. Slipping off her Manolo Blahniks, she grabbed the salad bowl from the counter, gave Massimo a nod, and went into the dining room. He'd even cut the cucumbers in those thin little slices she liked so much. *God, he's good.*

Two candles, one at each end of the table, were lit. The overhead lights were dimmed.

Quietly, she took her corner seat at the rectangular table, while her fiancé brought in a plate for each of them and took his seat at the head place setting. Date night. She loved it.

She took a small bite. The pasta not only smelled delicious but tasted good, too.

"Talk to me." He poured her a glass of Pellegrino then served himself red wine. "What's going on in your pretty head?"

"Masi, I'm fine."

"*Bella...*" He gave her that 'we have no secrets' face.

"Oh, all right. I wronged my dad by doing this DNA test. I wish I trusted him more. He's been dead for almost four years, and I'm still angry with him."

"Eddie killed himself, left you and Birdie bankrupt. Lex, if anyone has the right to *not* trust Eddie, dead or alive, it's you. It's okay to be mad."

"It's not the way he died or what we were left with or without, but his past. Daddy has so many skeletons in that closet, and they keep popping up. What's next?"

Massimo didn't say anything, just listened and nodded for her to continue.

"Dad's gone. It doesn't matter what I thought about him then or now, does it? Regardless of what my father did, nothing will erase his bad deeds. Nothing. I guess I hoped in some way to make him right, at least with me, in my head. Justify his ways."

His full lips drew downward into a frown. "Everyone has a past. My *padre* wasn't perfect, either. I don't remember my *madre* much, but I'm sure she and Birdie could swap stories." Massimo's father, the late King of Isola di Girasoli, had affairs, producing another family in America, including Massimo's half-sister, Paloma. He smiled, took a piece of bread from the basket and set it on her plate. "Eat."

Sick with the emotions inside her, she took a bite, hoping to feed the emptiness plaguing her. Chewing, she let the bread sit in her mouth for a minute while she thought about her father.

"Eddie's letter gave you every right to assume what you did. Taddy now knows who her father is. You did nothing wrong, Lex. Don't beat yourself up over the DNA test. If Eddie were alive, he'd understand."

Massimo caressed her arm. His very touch was medicine for her fears.

She swallowed. "Maybe knowing that Taddy is my sister will turn out to be something good for me to remember him by, not just the bad stuff."

"You have many good things to remember him by."

"Such as?" Right then, she honestly couldn't remember any.

"Lex, your father's songs are played everywhere we go. Birdie's are, too. His face is on TV and used in many commercials. He is part of American history. You have many things to remember him by. How can you say that?"

"Masi, that's not my dad. That's Eddie Easton, the rock star. I mean *my* dad…the guy *behind* the voice and guitar, the *real* Eddie."

"I see." His voice sounded concerned. "You have M2. Birdie says he has Eddie's eyes."

"M2 does have Daddy's eyes, doesn't he?" Her heart lifted every time she thought of her baby.

"*Sì.*"

Massimo blinked dramatically, showing that M2 didn't have his eyes. She knew it pissed him off. But M2 did have his name.

"I wish my dad spent more time with me growing up. I don't have many memories of him when I was little. The bad ones are so vivid and hard to put to rest."

"What was the longest he was away from you and Birdie on tour?" Massimo asked.

"About five years. He came home…twice." Anger flushed her cheeks as she spoke. How could any parent leave their child for half a decade? Oh, right, his excuse was in two simple words: world tour. The one the record label called the bestselling show in music history. Why bother having a baby at all if you were never going to be home to be with them?

Suddenly, M2 cried from the nursery. It was as if on cue. She went to jump up to get him but remembered what her fellow new mom friends had said: "Don't run to the baby the second he fusses. An experienced mother waits it out. The baby will stop."

"M2 heard you when you came in," Massimo said.

His scream wasn't the 'hungry' cry. It wasn't the 'need to be changed' or the 'waking in a dark room alone' cry, either. It was the 'Please pay attention to me, be here with me' cry. It broke Lex's heart to hear M2 scream and not run to him. A chill ran through her.

"Was M2 like this earlier?" she asked her fiancé. Lex had never heard her son wail so loudly. She sat on the edge of her seat.

"Go…M2 hasn't seen his *madre* since this morning. He misses you. He needs you." Massimo spoke without judgment. But there was a thread, albeit slight, of concern in his deep voice.

Lex stood and made her way to the nursery.

The sweet whiff of baby powder filled her nostrils when she entered M2's room. Just as Massimo overdid his cologne when he dressed and the garlic when he cooked, she often found the nursery clouded in talcum even hours after he'd changed M2's diaper. Heavy-handed, in a loveable way, was one of her fiancé's strong traits.

"Masi Junior…hi, baby."

On his back, his mouth opened into the perfect 'o' as he caught his breath between cries.

Reaching for him, she reflected on what her mother said earlier, about being more available for her son. Should she resign as President and CEO at Easton Essentials? A company she'd brought to life? Right then, as M2 made eye contact with her and gave her a gummy grin, big and wide, she realized she was fortunate to be able to afford to stay at home if she chose to. Not every woman had the financial resources which were afforded to her. Lex figured she wasn't resigning as businesswoman but taking on the role of mom.

Her career could wait for her.

Her little guy could not.

Chelsea

"Get out, Diego. You don't live here anymore." Blake couldn't believe his ex-husband had gotten past security. Apparently, he knew the doorman on an intimate level. He was shocked when he had come home from The Dupree Club and found him in his gourmet kitchen, wearing his Gucci clothing and eating his Pringles. *As if tonight couldn't get any worse.*

"Fucker, I told you I can't go back to my place. The cops are lookin' for me. I'm staying here for a while." Diego locked the double doors which separated the foyer from the penthouse elevator. He stalked over to the living room windows, which illuminated an Eighth-Avenue view, and brought down the blinds as if he still lived there.

The penthouse, with its open floor plan and always-airy feel, suddenly filled with enclosing darkness...and fear.

"Did one of the guys come forward?" Blake held on to the granite counter for support. He didn't know what to do, other than scream.

"A few have, yes."

"Good," he snapped, feeling a slight bit defiant.

"You wanna see me in jail?" Diego met his accusing words without a flinch. He brought his face in close, nose-tip to nose-tip. "Nice haircut."

His breath reeked of the scotch Blake stocked in his bar. But it didn't have the usual vanilla-caramel aroma he liked. The one he'd kiss him with after dinner back when he thought he was in love with him. No, Diego's skin smelled of another kind of sweetness, the one which came when he smoked crystal meth.

"Don't get in my face." Anxiety chilled the angry fever boiling inside him.

He stared up and down at his ex-husband. Unrecognizable, Diego's tall frame slouched forward, and his muscular body wasn't as aspiring as it used to be. He wasn't the Ivy League graduate who'd swept him off his feet ten years before, working a high-powered job on Wall Street, caring what people thought about him, and loving him. Now, his ex-husband appeared gaunt with sunken eyes, and it wasn't the disease making him appear sick.

No, it was the drugs, the guilt and the erotic game he'd played and so murderously lost.

"You're not staying here."

"Shut…up."

Smack!

His cheek exploded with the burning sting of Diego's hand across his face.

Instinctively, Blake's stomach clenched tightly as sourness came over his tongue. But he reminded himself why he shouldn't be afraid. Not anymore.

Taddy's Glock pistol.

Disguised in a candy apple, vintage red Fendi Baguette, the gun was on the kitchen table, close and loaded. He'd never fired a Glock outside of their usual Lipstick & Lead Rifle range before.

In hope it wouldn't come to threats of violence to get Diego out of his life, he opted for a less dramatic approach first. "If you don't leave, I'm calling the police." He pulled his cell from his back pocket, the screen light up.

Diego grabbed his wrist with one hand, sending a sharp pain up his arm. He snatched the cell with the other. Surprisingly, his grip was still strong.

"You aren't callin' anyone." Thrown across the room, the LCD screen cracked on the marble floor. The bright neon light faded to black. "Why won't you help me? What's wrong with you? It's not like you to turn your back on the ones you love!"

"I don't love you. I can't…help you." Biting his lip, he looked away and hit the light switch by the overhead chandelier. The formal living room glowed brightly. He wasn't going to be alone with his ex-husband in the darkness. Not when Diego was high. He knew better.

"Let me stay here 'til I figure things out. A few days."

"You're killing people." He swallowed hard, trying not to show the anger boiling inside him. The sweat around his hairline dripped down his face.

"No one is...dead." Diego chuckled nastily. His wide, once-engaging eyes darkened into black dots.

"Not yet, but they will get sick."

His words shamed Diego as his attention shifted to the floor. Seeing that as the opportunity, he made a run for the front door. His heart raced as he ran as fast as he could.

Diego came up right behind him, almost embracing him.

Trying to think of what to do next, he couldn't give in. His hands held on to the doorknob as he faced the door. He wanted out. *Please, just let me go. I'm going to kill you if you don't.*

"They begged for it." Diego's voice was unapologetic and steady.

Breathing down his neck he spoke into his ear, saying things which made him sick.

"My sex was hot for them. Why don't *you* get *that*?" The denial flew off Diego like bullets ricocheting. His hands grabbed Blake's shoulders, squeezing them painfully, right when he unlocked the deadbolt.

Blake turned around while opening the door. "You stay. I'll leave."

"No." Diego slammed the door. Pulling his body into him, he groped his chest and arms.

Closing his eyes, he missed when those touches were good. When as a couple they were great together. But they weren't anymore. The embrace felt cold to the touch, strange and threatening. "Don't…"

Diego pulled him tighter into him.

In return, Blake pushed him, hard. Diego flew against the hallway wall, taking down a few hung photos. A picture of Vive with Thor at the beach in the Hamptons cracked when it landed on the floor. Impressed with his own strength, he'd never fought his ex-husband off before with such strong resistance.

Tall and angry, Diego stood there, no longer slouching but laughing. It was the evil cackle he'd heard in his nightmares.

"You wanna *play*?"

"No…"

"You got turned on when I got rough with you, didn't you?"

"Never." Blake shook his head vehemently.

"You always did like it dirty."

Lunging for him, Diego grabbed him by the neck. His anger focused as his grip tightened.

He couldn't breathe.

His head shook as his back was slammed up against the very wall where the pictures once hung. The plaster dented as a rush of pain shot through his head. He kicked Diego in the shin and then closed-fist punched him across the face. He'd never hit him before. Perversely, it felt good. Damn good.

Diego brought his right hand back and punched him in the head. Bright white, brilliant stars danced in his sight.

"You like it dirty. Admit it," Diego hissed and slapped his face.

Copper, the taste of bitter metal filled his mouth as he swallowed. *Fuck that hurt.* "No one wants that..." He spit at him as his tears fell.

"Once you're bred, there's nothing anyone can do for you." Diego wiped the phlegm off his face as his jaw set. "You have to live with it, make the best of it."

"By infecting others? You're crazy."

He went to spit at him again, but Diego slapped his face harder than before. A circle of iciness then heat ringed his mouth.

"Stop hitting me." Blake swung at him, but lost his balance. He grabbed onto Diego's shirt as they fell. His shoulder smashed against the floor and his breath flew from his lungs as Diego landed on top of him. Smothering him.

Gun. He had to get the gun.

"Get off me...Diego," he grunted, trying to get free.

"I should've bred you when I had the chance."

The intercom buzzed from downstairs. It filled Blake's with hope. The lobby must've been trying to reach his condo. Thank God. Someone was there, for him.

"Help me! We're in here. *Help*!" Blake screamed.

Diego tried to silence him by putting his fist over his mouth. His hands tasted like that chemical he shoved up his nose.

No one came.

With his free hand, Diego unfastened his belt and tore it loose. He wrapped the black leather strap around Blake's neck so tight, so fast.

"Aah." He tried to wedge his thumb under the leather strap. It was so tight. Too tight. *Shit!*

Fury blazed in Diego's eyes as he choked him harder. "You are no different than me. You like it. Say it."

Diego slammed his head against the marble floor. A piercing pain shot through him.

"No." He sobbed, wanting to claw at Diego's face but feared drawing blood.

"Say it."

"Stop."

"Say it!"

"I—like—it," he appeased, hoping he'd get him to calm down. Then he'd make a run for it. But first he had to get Diego off him.

Unable to inhale, he couldn't breathe. His lungs constricted with a tight pressure. Lightheaded and dizzy, he was about ready to pass out; he couldn't take much more. But, did he have any energy left to fight? Absolutely. He rolled over onto his side and tried to get up.

Diego grabbed at him and held him down. "Not so fast."

The pit in his stomach deepened. He elbowed Diego's side with all his might causing the belt to come loose around his neck.

"You can't leave," he blew out a shallow breath, and hugged his abdomen.

Inch by inch, as best he could, he crawled toward the dining room table.

"Come here." Diego jumped on his back, pushing all of his weight onto him.

Feeling defeated, he screamed as loud as he could. It was the only thing left to do. He'd worked out and lifted weights at the gym in hopes to overpower him, one day, but he couldn't. Dammit, he couldn't.

"Leave—*stop*!" he shouted louder.

Blue buttons popped, and the back of his shirt ripped off him as it if were a piece of paper. Something was suddenly stuffed in his mouth, the material drying up his tongue as it was wedged down his throat then knotted behind his head.

A burst of oxygen went through his nose as he tried to inhale. Tears choked him.

He's going to kill me.

Diego wouldn't quit. Not then. Not ever.

The front door slammed open and next thing he knew, the pressure of Diego was lifted from his back.

Blake despair transformed into relief when he turned. "Miguel." His best friend picked Diego up as if he were a throw pillow.

"Santana." On his feet, Diego acted meek and curled into himself.

Without any warning he suddenly turned around and punched Miguel in the face, striking his right eye. He fell back against the living room wall. One of his paintings hit the floor in a loud crash.

The gun. I have to get the gun.

Trying to get his footing, his body aching, he went for the Fendi. Together they could take Diego down.

Miguel lunged at Diego and punched him back. Loud thumps echoed in the room as he beat his face over and over again.

Blood spurted as Diego backed up, putting his hand up for him to stop.

"Come on!" Miguel shouted for him to continue. "Let's go."

"Stop, Mig. Don't touch him. He's bleeding."

Diego's face colored fiercely beneath the bruising coming out.

"So what?" Miguel's brows came down in puzzlement.

"He's positive."

Miguel stepped back. His face twisted. "He has HIV?"

"Yes. Don't touch him."

"Call the police, Blake," Miguel ordered.

"Don't fuckin' call anyone!"

Just as he started to retreat, Diego picked up a crystal lamp with a solid brass base from the nearby end table. He brought the fixture up high in the air. The cord snapped free from the outlet and the light blinked off as he swung at Miguel as if he were lightning striking.

"No!" Blake reached for the Fendi. Opening the zipper, he couldn't pull the Glock out fast enough as he heard the loud thud of the lamp against Miguel's skull.

Diego's arms came wide for a second swing, Miguel lying limp on the floor.

"I'll shoot you."

The cool metal tightened in Blake's hands. He released the safety switch.

Frozen, his ex-husband glared at him. He wiped the blood from his face, his expression growing serious. "You can't shoot me. *It's me*...you love me."

"Drop the lamp and get away from Miguel."

Imposing iron control over the gun, he approached Diego with a new level of confidence. He was no longer his ex-lover. He was a target.

He cocked the pistol and aimed for Diego.

"It's loaded, you piece of shit." He grinned with even more confidence when the whites of Diego's eyes widened.

As a kid, his favorite TV show growing up was reruns of Cagney & Lacey. He used to pretend to be Christine when he played guns with his cousins out in the Fairfield County woods. Often they picked on him, had called him a faggot for wanting to be a female cop. That night, the spirit of Christine Cagney was in hands. He was in charge now. "I said move!"

Avery Aster

Chapter Twenty

Diego Oalo's Demise

Miguel's head throbbed. An intense pressure in his ears made it so he could barely hear. Shaking his head in dazed confusion, he caught Blake shouting. That much he could make out.

He sat up. The room lit florescent and bright. A gun—pointed at Diego. Instantly, he came to with a tight panic. *No, Blake...*

The crystal lamp hit the floor and broke. Diego put his hands up and stepped forward. "You love me. You'd never shoot me." Ridicule loaded his words.

Diego had been playing Blake for quite some time. He seemed to enjoy the emotional struggle Blake was having with himself. He was so very fragile, and Miguel could see it now, in that moment. Mad at himself for not fully grasping this earlier, he realized his friend had been breaking down for some time. His demons were unimaginable. He wasn't sure he still understood them fully.

"Don't talk to me about love! You don't know what *love* is." Blake stared at Diego as if he *was* going to shoot him. "Look at our lives! You've ruined them." He lowered the gun, squinted his left eye, and said, "I'll never forgive you for the harm you've caused."

Was he aiming at Diego's cock?

"Here's a favor for all the boys in this town!"

No doubt Blake wanted him to pay for what he'd done, but he couldn't hurt a soul. Could he? Revenge and murder didn't embody Blake Morgan III. He was gentle, caring, and right then, hurt. Miguel, however, was more worried about Diego at the moment. If he gained control of the gun, there was no telling what would happen.

"Give me the gun." Miguel broke the concentration of their argument. Slowly he approached, putting himself back in the situation.

Blake's eyes widened, glancing up at him as if unsure of what he was doing. "You have no clue what Diego did, hosting those breeding parties."

"They wanted—"

"Shut up! You went *too* far. You always do. So help me God, I've let this go on for far too long."

Bam. Blake's right hand jerked as the gun fired a bullet. It grazed Diego's thigh.

"*Fuck! You faggot!*" he screamed. His weight shifted onto one leg.

Miguel saw the bullet stuck in the white wall behind him. He'd missed. Well, sort of. The front of Diego's pants darkened as the smell of urine filled the air and the man cried for Blake to stop.

Okay, Blake *would* kill him. This wasn't murder or revenge, but justice, at least from his point of view. Miguel was wrong. He *did* have it in him. *Shit!*

"I'm going to blow your cock off, Diego." Blake's fingers tightened on the trigger as his arm straightened.

"For me, *bebé*, don't." Miguel took another step closer. He couldn't let his friend spend the rest of his life in jail.

"Move, Mig. Get out of my way. I have to."

Click. Blake cocked the gun.

All he could stare at was the barrel of the gun as he closed the distance between them. "*Sí*, give me the gun." He lowered his face to Blake's. "Look at me." He needed to see his friend's blue eyes making contact with his. They were possessed, filled with rage. It was as if Blake didn't recognize him. Miguel surely didn't recognize *him*.

"I want Diego to turn himself in." Pupils dilated and cheeks reddened, Blake bit down on his lower lip and gasped loudly, shaking his head as the tears fell.

"That's it, *bebé*. Breathe. This isn't your fault."

"Diego, did you fucking hear me?" Blake wiped his nose with his forearm while holding on to the gun. Diego stood perfectly still, crying. "If Mig won't let me shoot you, I want you to turn yourself in to the police station."

"You win…I'll turn myself in," Diego said.

"I'm right here. You're okay. Give me the gun."

Blake surrendered the gun into Miguel's hands. The steel felt foreign and odd.

As Miguel's concentration focused on turning the safety on, he heard Diego making a commotion.

"He's getting away!" Blake shouted.

"Let him. This isn't your battle." He hugged Blake tightly. "Diego won't get far." Pulling out his cell, he called 911. He gave the attendant on the line all the pertinent information and then hung up. Checking the halls, he noted Diego was long gone, so he returned the gun to the Fendi and put it on top of the fridge.

Blake put his arms around him as he came back into the kitchen. He could almost smell the fear coming off him.

"You need to leave. I'll take care of the police."

"I'm not going anywhere. I'm staying here with you." It was where he belonged.

"Your name. You gave the operator your name. This'll ruin your image in the art world, Mig, and your parents. Please go—"

"I don't care about that." He couldn't believe Blake said that. "I care about *you,* Blake. I wish you would've told me all this. I only want you safe."

"I couldn't…"

Minutes later, the NYPD arrived. When Blake gave them Diego's name, a special agent by the name of Detective Benson was called in. He came in about an hour later and introduced himself as an undercover officer who'd been working the breeding parties for the past few months. Jacked with muscles, he insisted they address him by his first name, Shiloh.

The detective took control of the situation. If it wasn't for the silver briefcase he carried, the badge he flashed, or the gun and its holster over his shoulder, he would've never figured Shiloh Benson for a cop. In sweatpants and a hoodie, he only stood at about five-ten. He reminded Miguel of a hustler who worked down on Christopher

Street. Shiloh exuded Jersey Shore Guido. He couldn't figure out if the cop was gay or not. As he rolled up his sleeve, his forearm sported several tattoos, which weren't the gay norm, per se, of perfectly drawn barbwire or Chinese words, but something he'd seen on the gang members turned convicts when visiting his brother-in-law in prison with his nieces. The shapes of numbers, names, and symbols were poorly drawn, homemade dots of ink scattered across his tan skin.

Miguel poured Blake a glass of water from the kitchen sink and sat with him and Shiloh at the dining room table. Blake seemed calm, almost sedate as he gulped on the water.

"Mr. Morgan, you were married to Diego Oalo, correct?" Shiloh asked.

Blake felt as if he was going to throw up. How did he and his ex-husband get to such a low point in their lives?

"We married five years ago and divorced last week."

His life was over. He couldn't believe he'd tried to shoot him. A part of him wanted to be locked up, too, for not ending this sooner. Thank God Miguel was there and saved his life. What would he ever do without him?

"We've been investigating Mr. Oalo for a few weeks." Shiloh pulled out several photos. The five-by-seven and eight-by-ten glossies made this all the more real. Diego would be the face for this crime. It was time for this to be brought to everyone's attention.

"How many men have come forward?" he asked, staring at the pictures.

God, his heart had broken for his ex-husband so long ago. He didn't think he could feel any worse. But he did. Uncontrollable tears came. He didn't stop the cry as he recognized Mike, Scott, and Jason in the photos with Diego at what looked like Battery Park. They'd all been his friends at one time, too. Mike and Scott attended their wedding. Jason came to their housewarming dinner. This was all before they started gravitating to the dark side. Late-night calls, scheduled outings while leaving him behind and the inside jokes, which he never found funny about boys, sex, and the parties.

"We have fifteen victims who've given a statement about their infection. This is an HIV related offense and a crime."

"*If* you catch Diego, what type of penalty is he facing?"

"*When* we catch Mr. Oalo, he'll be tried by a jury of his peers." Shiloh glanced to Miguel. "The DA will prosecute to the fullest extent of the law."

"What's the punishment for this type of crime?" Miguel asked, reaching for Blake's hand.

The detective eyed them both and replied, "Life."

Lord. He died a little bit more hearing that. His ex-husband was guilty, no doubt, but 'life', whether it was spent locked up or in the electric chair was unreal. If only he'd acted sooner. He blamed himself. He always did. If he'd only gotten Diego treatment, he couldn't help but wonder if this could've been avoided. Yet, how could he have gotten someone help when they'd refused it? His grip tightened on Miguel's hand

"Why didn't you arrest him sooner?" Miguel asked. A greenish color washed over his complexion. This had to be causing him a lot of pain, too. He'd been high school friends with Diego.

"Until a few months ago, no one had come forward. This isn't a typical case for us. We needed time to collect the evidence. The judge issued a warrant for Diego's arrest this week, and here we are."

"Right, here we are." He spat out the words contemptuously. The anger inside him for himself, for Diego, and for what happened was overwhelming. How could any sane person process this?

"Any idea how this started?"

He inhaled loudly. He hadn't spoken about this—ever. Never putting the horror into words, he'd strung together a few ideas which Taddy and Lex became privy to, but had never given an actual picture, until then. "It started in the financial district."

"How?"

"There were a few unoccupied corporate apartments owned by his former employer. They'd gone vacant after the recession. That's how it began."

Shiloh withdrew a notepad from his folder and gripped a ballpoint pen in his hand. "Tell me what happened."

Miguel leaned forward, as if he'd finally have some answers for what happened. He didn't have a clue. That was obvious by the questioning gaze on his face.

"Lehman Lynch underwent several rounds of layoffs. Diego wasn't making his goals and was the first to be let go. Initially, I didn't know. Every day, he acted as if he'd gone to work. One week, he started coming home about two to three hours later than usual." Blake remembered that feeling in the pit of his stomach as if it was yesterday. Bitter acid, slow and churning, festered inside when he realized something was wrong. "Then the following week, he came home in the middle of the night. It was shortly thereafter he stopped coming home at all."

Miguel studied him as if he searched his face for answers.

"Diego was using meth."

"Had Mr. Oalo used crystal meth before?"

"Not that I know of…" Anxiety charged through him as he recounted the events which led up to this in his head. That was when the word 'party' became deadly. "I've said enough. I should call my attorney."

"Blake?" Miguel appeared all the more confused.

Hesitating about what to do or say, he sat there staring at them both.

"Mr. Morgan, your openness to share and be honest with us will make our case against Mr. Oalo solid. You may call your attorney right now or answer these questions and get this over with faster. What'll it be?"

He didn't want to go down memory lane with Shiloh. Not in front of his best friend, a man he respected. Miguel was upstanding. This would ruin any goodness he had for him, for sure. Then again, he didn't care what people thought about him anymore. He was way past the stage where of reputations mattered; lives were at stake. He felt as if his life was already over. It didn't matter anymore.

Thick and obvious, the silence loomed over the table like a heavy fog. It felt impossible to steady his erratic pulse, but he knew he had to come clean and tell the detective everything, even if he didn't want to admit it to himself. In his heart, he'd always been afraid he was guilty by association. His mother used to say, "Birds of a feather flock together." He didn't want to flock with Diego. He certainly didn't fly high with him, but somehow he was stuck with him as bird dung which would never come off. He'd take the blame then, maybe, his pain might end. "Am I going to be arrested?"

"No, Mr. Morgan, not if you cooperate and tell us everything."

Other than shooting that gun, Blake wasn't a criminal. He reminded himself he'd done nothing wrong, except to stand by his man longer than he should have. But that alone was what made him feel so much of a criminal.

"Okay, ask."

"Did you use drugs with Mr. Oalo?"

"Yes." He hesitated. Needing to clarify, he added, "But not those kinds of drugs." God, he heard his own hypocrisy. Drugs were drugs, regardless.

Miguel let go of his hand.

A tremor of fear rocketed through him. He tried not to lose his mind. He couldn't imagine his life if Miguel wasn't by his side.

Covering his face, Miguel muttered to himself in Spanish as Blake feared he might wind up with nothing in the end. He'd already lost his husband, most of his money and sanity. Was his best friend next on the list?

"The most we'd ever done together was a joint on New Year's Eve, and again at a few Halloween parties." He heard his own voice become smaller as he talked about smoking pot.

"Anything else?"

"Umm, well…we tripped on acid and took a few hits of ecstasy in college with our friends. We were nineteen then." He looked at Miguel, remembering their academic years together. Miguel had refused to join in the party. If he was being honest, and he was, he might as well tell them everything. "Once, on our honeymoon cruise to Greece, we tried cocaine together. I was sorta drunk. It made me sick. Diego knew I didn't care for drugs as we got older." He couldn't listen to the words he spoke. He heard the sigh, saw the disgust and felt Miguel's disappointment in him. "My ex liked cocaine. He thrived on speed and never really stopped since that vacation. Shortly after we got back from the cruise, he lost his job. That's when he started smoking meth." He paused, his eyes stinging with tears. "He was hooked. I couldn't get him off it. I tried and tried. But he loved meth too much."

"Please, go on," Shiloh encouraged.

He couldn't make eye contact with Miguel. He could only feel him staring, surely glaring at him in horror.

"Diego got into group sex with one of the meth dealers. He asked if I wanted to join. When I refused, he got angry and accused me of being unsupportive and called my love for him conditional." At the time, he couldn't believe he was being shamed, but he was. "Diego took my resistance as a challenge. He thought he could get me to change my mind, so...he invited the party here. They'd fuck in front of me."

"Blake." The veins on Miguel's neck purpled.

He focused, looking at the tabletop, and continued, "I couldn't get into it. Diego wanted an open relationship, so he did as he does with everything: he took one. I remained celibate. We hadn't been having sex for a few years anyway, so I can't say I missed it." He turned to Miguel. "I wasn't lying to you about his issues. He has the Madonna-Whore Complex. We didn't have sex once during our marriage. Diego could only screw strangers. Looking back now, I realize that was a blessing. I'm not sick—I *am* negative. I was never infected or at risk."

Miguel's hard features softened.

"Regardless of your status, *bebé*, I'll always love you." Miguel reached for his hand again, intimately, as if Shiloh wasn't sitting in front of them.

"When did things escalate?"

"Right after he tested positive last year. He was on the medication. When I found the bottles, I asked him. I told him I'd stay with him, see him through if he got off the drugs and went for help. In a way, I thought him being positive would be a reality check, like maybe he'd turn his life around. You *can* be positive and lead a healthy life."

"And did he?"

"No. His desire for self-destruction only escalated."

"How did it get worse, Mr. Morgan?"

"Can I have a minute, please?"

As Shiloh nodded, Blake reached for the water glass and took the last sip. What he'd shared already was horrific, but it was nothing compared to what was about to come next. He inhaled, hoping he wouldn't puke and tried to focus on telling the facts—not how he felt about them, but the events which had taken place. "Diego said he got an erotic thrill off bottoming for positive guys."

"What?" Dramatically, Miguel threw his back into the chair.

"Diego liked the rush he got from it. The danger turned him on. When he tested poz, he flipped and started topping negative guys who sought the same thrill. He said the negative bottoms loved the excitement of having sex with him not knowing if they'd get infected."

"They bare backed?" Shiloh asked.

"Always. Diego claimed it made him feel more desired, more like a man."

"Some *man*," Miguel grumbled.

"I didn't find out until right before we separated that he'd taken this a step further and topped guys while lying about his status."

"He *purposely* infected people who had no idea?" Miguel slammed his fist down on the table.

"Please, Mr. Santana," Shiloh warned in an attempt to get control of the situation. "Blake, how did you find out Mr. Oalo was doing this?"

"A private investigator my friend uses told me. Initially, I'd hired him to follow Diego at night and see where he was staying. To figure out what was going on."

"Can you give me his contact info when we're done here?" Shiloh asked.

"Sure. Oh, he smashed my phone. But I have his info at work. The PI is how I knew he was infecting guys who didn't know about his status. He only admitted to it after I asked him." Blake hesitated for a minute. "His name was Garrett Lochte."

Shiloh's face lit up. "We already interviewed Mr. Lochte. He's been a great help to us. Odd, he didn't specifically tell us you hired him."

"Garrett promises full discretion with his clients. I called and asked him a few questions. He told me Diego lied to others about his status." He wiped his eyes. "That was the day I asked him to move out. I asked him to leave. I wanted to go to the police, but Garrett said it was the victim's responsibility, not mine. He warned me I couldn't give names of those infected."

"Mr. Morgan, there isn't always a good way to handle a bad situation. But in this case, you did the right thing. I hope this brings you some peace by me saying this: you are *not* at fault." Shiloh handed Miguel his card. "Call us if Mr. Oalo contacts either of you. I suggest getting a locksmith to change the locks."

"Blake won't be sleeping here tonight." Miguel reached for a pen and notepad, wrote down his number and handed it to the officer. "Call me if you need anything."

"Thank you, Mr. Santana. We will."

Drained and exhausted, he said his goodbyes to the police and let them out.

"I'm so ashamed I let it get this far out of hand, Mig. How could I? Fifteen people's lives are ruined because of me."

"No. It's not your fault, *bebé*. You heard what the detective said; you handled it the only way you could." He hugged him. "Do you want me to call your parents? Or Taddy?"

"No." He buried his face in Miguel's chest. "I only want to be with you tonight."

"I am here for you, always. They're going to catch him. You'll see. He can't run forever."

Chapter Twenty-One

Loving Miguel

Upper East Side

Lex opened her heavy eyelids to find her fiancé standing above her. Massimo whispered in her ear to wake up. She glanced around; she'd fallen asleep with M2 in the rocker. The moon bounced off the city's skyscrapers, reflecting shades of night into the room.

The penthouse settled with quietness. Knowing Jemma, she'd come in around sunrise as they got ready for work.

Massimo picked up M2, kissed him on the cheek, and put him in the crib with a few Italian words of love.

"Does he need changing?" she asked instinctively.

"He's dry." He came over to her in the chair and lifted her up into his arms. "Let's go to bed, *principessa*."

Massimo was strong; he held her as a feather in his hands. God, he still made every inch of her body come alive as he pulled her close. His exhale as he carried her into the bedroom exhilarated her. Her appetite was back—not for dinner, for sex.

She kissed him, remembering those jitters which exploded inside her when they'd first met. Surprisingly, he still made her heart race. Massimo placed her on the bed, and she said, "I'm going to stay home with M2 more."

"Good. You make me happy."

"I love you, Masi."

"*Ti amo*," he said and kissed her neck as he undid her blouse.

She reached down to unzip her skirt.

"Allow me."

Smoothly, Massimo's big hands slinked her body free from the outfit. He was good in the kitchen, but superb in the bedroom. His right hand tugged at her panties which also came off with one swoop. He buried his face in her pussy, growling and grunting, somewhat playful yet focused. "I'm going to make you come, *bella*."

His lips found their way over her clit. His beard stubble grazed her flesh, sending an erotic chill up the back of her spine. Turned on, Lex arched her back, burying her head into the pillows while he sank his face further between her legs. Fucking her deeply and passionately with his tongue, he lapped up her cream as an orgasm came over her. She closed her eyes, getting lost in his arms. Enjoying every second, she begged him not to stop.

"*Magnifica.*" Massimo came up to kiss her, and she tasted herself on him. With hunger, he pulled out his cock, burying it deeper than his tongue ever dreamt of being before. Holding on to her by her shoulders, he filled her, completed her.

Spreading her wide, he fucked her balls-deep, burying his face between her breasts. Massimo must've forgotten her nipples were off-limits and sunk his lips around the areola of her right breast while loudly humming to himself.

"Masi!" she cried out in pleasure, recognizing the tingly ache as he fed on her. Her breasts were sensitive, more so because she'd been breastfeeding nonstop for the last six months. In recent months Massimo had done his best to not touch them, but it was obvious he couldn't hold back any longer. Lex didn't deny him as he tugged at her nipple. Perversely, his cock swelled as he became more excited.

His face came up revealing his sharp Mediterranean features, wiping his lips. "My *bella* tastes sweet." He sucked on her other breast for a second longer than the first while drilling her pussy hard.

She needed him. She loved this man.

With jackhammer-like strokes which parted her spasming flesh, she clenched her cunt muscles, holding his fat cock inside her. She didn't want the feeling of him, of her, of them together as one to stop.

"You milking my cock, *bella*?"

"Bone-dry," she replied playfully.

Sensation slammed through her as he came inside her. She couldn't articulate the love they shared. He was hers forever and always. How could she not marry this man?

Together they laid there while he held her in his arms. He didn't pull out. No longer erect, his cock was still hard. *"Incredible."*

"I needed that."

"You feel better?" he asked, knowing full well she did.

"Yes, every time you fuck me—"

"*Love*. Every time we make love," Massimo corrected.

She laughed remembering he hated when she used the word 'fuck'. It was too crude and American for his taste.

"Every time we make *love*, I feel all the worry in my heart and mind disappear."

"Are you worried about the wedding?"

"Not the ceremony or reception, but us, our family and friends. I don't want anything to change, Masi." She didn't want to lose her friends and the thought of them all going their separate ways tore at her. But she'd hope for the best. She didn't have much choice.

"*Bella*, life changes. It moves forward, and together, we'll make the best of it. *Sì*?"

"Yes, we will. We'll have two babies to look after, soon."

"Maybe three." Masi tickled her.

"Don't get ahead of yourself. You always want too much."

"And you always expect so little."

Lex kissed him on the lips then looked at his brown eyes. "Is it wrong to have expectations for our family?"

"I have them, don't you?"

"Subconsciously, I guess I do."

"What are they?"

"I don't want us to ever be apart, not for an extended period of time. Not the way my parents would go months without seeing one another."

"Agreed. What else?"

"I want the babies to grow up here, not on a plane."

"We already talked about this, Lex. You will have New Yorkers as children during the school season. Then they'll summer in Italy. What else?"

"I'm only…oh, forget it." She felt silly for saying what she was thinking. It was judgmental and pessimistic.

"Speak."

"I only want to get married once," Lex blurted, watching Massimo's face respond in confusion. She elaborated with an example. "Look at Blake. He's divorced and once you're divorced, you're more likely to get divorced—again."

"Says who?"

"Statistics."

"*Bella*. We're hardwired for commitment and marriage. Our parents weren't, but we'll make those vows to one another, for M2 and the baby on the way, that nothing but death will part us."

"Good, because if you ever give me cause to divorce you, it'll be over your own dead body."

"Do not talk like that." Massimo shushed her.

"You still don't get my humor sometimes."

Pulling her body against his, Massimo told her to sleep.

As Lex drifted off, she thought about what their forever would look like. She wondered if Birdie had the same ideals when she was getting married to Eddie. Did Taddy's mother have them as well when she married Joseph Graff? What about Blake when he married Diego? Did they all, at that moment, days before their wedding, think in their heart of hearts their marriage would be forever? Or was Vive right? Had Lex's fairytale romance changed her for the worse? Was Vive's negative outlook on love a hard reality or just a jaded view on real life?

Lower East Side

A heavy rainstorm started to fall the second the Mercedes left Chelsea and passed Twelfth Street, making it hard for the driver to go any speed other than slow. Blake brought with him some of the Baden pet products for Brutus, which Taddy had given him to test. He couldn't believe it, but he was looking forward to seeing that dog.

Putting his head on Miguel's chest, he waited for him to say something, anything. But he didn't speak. Ever since the police left, he'd grown quiet.

"Are you mad at me?"

"No. Never."

His body felt cold and unwelcoming, though he could hear Miguel's heart beating rapidly.

"Tell me what you're thinking."

His friend's hands bawled into fists. He squeezed them tight then released. "It doesn't matter what I think. We're not boyfriends."

"Not yet..."

"Don't tease me, Blake. I'm here for you as your friend, nothing more. Respect that."

"Is that what you want?" He sat up, looking at Miguel who wouldn't make eye contact with him.

"It doesn't matter what I want. It's not important now."

He grabbed at Miguel's square jaw, forcing him to make eye contact. He raised his brow. "Maybe if you told me, you'd get more of what you want and less of what you don't."

"That's rich coming from you."

"What's that supposed to mean?"

"You're the one with lies and secrets." Miguel's tone had changed since leaving his place.

"Ouch, that hurt." He knew he deserved to hear a lot worse. "I've never lied to you. I just didn't tell you."

"What's the difference?" Miguel took Blake's hand off his face. "You should be able to tell me everything."

"My marriage was *my* business, *my* mess. Not yours and don't go thinking you could've done something to stop what happened. No one could, not even the FBI."

"Tonight, you almost killed him. You were out of your mind."

"No. I wanted to shoot him in the leg so he couldn't run."

"I could've helped you if you'd told me about this sooner." Miguel's chest rose as he inhaled through his nose. "I'm not mad at you for not telling me. But if you want this friendship to continue, you won't keep anything from me, ever. Got it?" He stroked the top of his hand.

Miguel's touch drove Blake crazy. Seeing his friend so caring and possessive was annoyingly hot.

"I promise."

"This isn't over with Diego. They'll catch him. You heard what that officer said; he'll pay for what he's done."

"I'm ready for the worst." He slid his right hand over the seatbelt and started to play with the belt buckle.

"For Diego, yes, but for yourself, *bebé*, hope for the best. You deserve to be happy again. All I want right now is for you to be happy."

"To be honest, I've forgotten what happy feels like. It would be nice…"

"I'll do everything in my power to bring joy back into your life again, as your friend. All of us will." Miguel spoke with such seriousness. "But I meant what I said at the club. You're going to have to find someone else…to finish your *Seven Desires*."

"What? Why?" He pulled away, sitting on the edge of the leather bench.

"I told you already, I can't have sex with you."

"What's changed since the other day at the spa when you were ready to top me and show me who was boss?" He wasn't sure why, but the rejection caused a sick feeling to swell in his stomach. "It's because of what's happened with Diego, isn't it? You don't want me now. You don't look at me the same way, do you?"

"No, not a damn thing has changed. My feelings for you are still the same. I thought I could go through with our *Seven Desires*, but now I know I can't."

"Why? I want to be there for you when you come out to your parents." He was losing him. This was exactly what he was afraid would happen. Air, he couldn't breathe. He cracked the window. The fresh night was thick with rain, spraying his arm. "We don't have to finish my list. But we're going to finish yours." He wouldn't budge. Life without Miguel was unimaginable.

"No we won't."

What point was there in staying at his loft if they weren't going to work on their lists? How would they ever get closer? "You're serious?" he asked Miguel for confirmation as his friend nodded a reply. "Okay. Then this is all pointless." Blake leaned forward to the driver. "Sir, can you take me back to Chelsea? I won't be staying here—"

"Ignore us, *por favor*." Miguel balked at the driver who'd parked the limo in front of his building. He directed his attention to Blake and glared at him, the pity in his eyes evident. That made Blake livid.

"You either stay here with me tonight, or I'm taking you to the police station and they'll put you in protective custody."

"I don't need you. I can protect myself."

"Is that so? What would've happened if I hadn't shown up tonight?"

"I still would've wounded Diego..."

"Or he might've killed you. You're staying here tonight, *bebé*. Don't argue with me."

"Spare me. I'll walk."

He opened the limo door and jumped out into the storm as Miguel tried unsuccessfully to grab at his waist so he'd stay put. This was such bullshit. How dare Miguel pull away when they were getting closer? He didn't need that shit.

"I'm not your escort!" Miguel shouted after him as he came out the car. His shirt was getting wet, revealing his insanely developed chest.

"Goodnight, Mig."

There was so much more to their lists than just sex. He didn't understand how Miguel couldn't see that. Ever since his lunch with Thor and Vive earlier that day, he'd thought differently about him and what his friend wanted and especially after the events of the evening. He wanted one more chance with Miguel to make things good. He wanted to try to give him what he'd wanted.

"Don't walk away from me. Stay here and talk to me."

"Talk?" He marched back to Miguel and got right up to his face. He hoped the rain covered his tears as competently as it got in his shoes. "You don't talk and now that we're getting close, you're putting distance between us. This is why we never go anywhere. You can be so giving one minute, but it's never unconditional as you get all high and mighty. You, Miguel Santana, are an asshole."

The damn smirk which he found so endearing graced Miguel's face. The street lights illuminated his profile making him all the more haunting and gorgeous.

"I've been called worse."

"Here." He shoved the Baden bag into Miguel's arms. "Give these to your dog."

Miguel ignored the bag and grabbed him tight, drawing him in even as he tried to pull away.

"Let me go."

"Listen to me, *bebé*. You want me to start telling you what I want?" His arms brought Blake in for a tighter bear hug.

He wasn't escaping the tight grip any time soon.

"Yes, you fucktard and you haven't even asked me what I want."

His feelings had changed since the club. He loved this man more than anything. But he still wasn't sure what he had left inside of himself to give anyone in the form of a relationship. Diego had pretty much bankrupted his spirits.

"I want you in my arms tonight."

"You do?" He felt a warm sensation tingling through him.

"*Sí.* I want my cock buried deep in your ass." Miguel's strong hands stroked his butt through his soaking-wet pants.

"Now we're talking."

"I want to pound you so hard you'll beg me to stop."

He kissed his lips passionately, and with such intensity, Blake could've sworn he had something wet in his shorts, and it wasn't rain.

"I want it rough and tender, fast and slow."

"I'm lovin' this rough stuff."

"I want to make love to you like I've never made love to any man in my entire life. Because if we're being honest…since we were eighteen, I dreamt it would only be you. I have to have you tonight. I want to feel myself inside of you where I belong."

For the first time in Blake's life, words escaped him.

"I don't care anymore, *bebé*, if you don't love me. I've resigned myself to the fact that I'll always love you. Tonight, I'll show you what love feels like. It's clear to me, after what happened today, you've never felt real love, either."

"Mig…" He still couldn't get the words. *Fuck.* He knew what he wanted to tell Miguel—he was in love with him, too. Miguel was right. He had never made love to anyone before.

"In the morning, we'll talk about our friendship. But tonight, I'm going to fuck you." Miguel turned him around to face the door of the apartment building. With a swat of his ass, he shouted, "March!"

He was more turned on than he'd ever been in his entire life. If he had a pussy it, for sure, would drip. At least that's what Vive would be screaming in his ear right then. Lord, Miguel had grown some serious balls and he was ready to suck on both of them. "Yes, Sir."

"Good boy."

Walking beside Miguel, he heard scratching at the door when they got close to the loft. "Did you walk Brutus today?"

"Not since early this afternoon."

Miguel unlocked the apartment. The pooch flew out into the hallway, chasing his tail and spinning with his leash in his mouth. Brutus went straight to him and rested under his legs for acknowledgement, barking with excitement.

"I'm sorry, Brutus."

Miguel stepped inside for a second then came back out into the corridor with a raincoat. "Here, you'll need to cover up. Want me to go with you?"

"No, thanks. I could use a few minutes alone to clear my head."

He zipped the jacket and threw up the hood, leashed Brutus then headed back downstairs. He'd never taken Brutus out in a downpour, but was surprised to witness the dog walk as if it was no big deal.

Head hung low, Brutus was as tough as Miguel. Rain pelted his furry back, matting the gray locks together. Walking faster than usual, Brutus stopped near the community garden to do his business.

Upon his return to the apartment, he heard Miguel in the shower, singing in Spanish to some flamenco music he must've turned on.

Unsure, he left Brutus at the door and leaned into the bathroom. "He's soaking wet and starting to shake. What should I do?"

Miguel's cute face popped out from behind the shower curtain. "Bathe him in the mudroom sink. Use the products you brought home."

"Gotcha." He grabbed a few towels from the rack.

"Be careful not to make the water too hot. Brutus has sensitive skin and don't get anything in his ears." Miguel went back to showering himself.

"No worries." Blake stepped closer, following Brutus. Miguel's backside was broad, his butt juicy.

Miguel whipped around, facing him, stroking that cock of his. "Thought you were gonna give Brutus a bath?"

"I am. I was just admiring the view."

Dripping in sex, Miguel tugged at his cock. It swelled. "You mean this?"

"Yes, that." He swallowed the lump in his throat.

"Don't take too long."

"I won't." Grabbing his bag from work, he pulled out the Baden products labeled *Dog Shampoo*. Once the water was set at a tepid temperature, he filled the basin.

Brutus swaggered over to the sink as if knowing the routine. He stood on his hind legs and leaned into him.

Blake lifted him into the sink. "Whoa, you're heavier than I thought." He scrubbed him from head to toe, remembering not to get anything near the ears. "I'm going to start feeding you Baden diet food. Daddy spoils you." He rubbed his belly with a washcloth, removing the city's grime from his fur.

When Brutus was nice and sudsy, he grabbed his iPhone and snapped a photo. The picture caught the dog's head covered in foam and cocked slightly, the brown eyes looking into the camera. A Baden shampoo bottle floated in the water beside him. He e-mailed the picture to Taddy and the manager of Baden with the message: *A pit bull needs Baden love, too.*

He sensed Miguel moving across the apartment behind him and quickly rinsed Brutus off.

The dog licked his hand in appreciation.

He'd bonded with him and realized his canine fear had subsided. He was no longer anxious when in the same room with Brutus.

Draining the sink, Blake squeezed the extra water out from his legs and tail. He looked over his shoulder to confirm he was alone with the dog. With a lean toward the basin, he talked to him for the first time. "I'm sorry I misjudged you." He kissed Brutus's black, wet nose-tip and added, "I was wrong about your daddy, too."

Reaching down, he grabbed a towel and dried the dog. He lifted and carried, then lowered Brutus back to the kitchen floor. He fed him his food, poured fresh water into the bowl, and waited to see if he'd eat the new stuff.

He did.

He caught his reflection in the kitchen window. A total mess, his eyes were still puffy from his crying earlier.

"¡Arriba, arriba!" a sexy Latin voice called out from the loft's corner. "I have a present for you." Miguel shot him a seductive glare from the bed. He'd lit votive candles alongside the bed's far wall and turned the lights down.

"I'll only be one minute." After stripping his clothes off, he showered quicker than usual. Drying himself he stepped out, anticipating it, needing it, and headed to the bed.

Miguel lay there as if he was an endangered gay god species to be admired, impossible to nail down. His long, thick, tanned legs were spread wide. A beautiful cock teased his appetite, half-covered by the sheets he'd purchased for him. A black trail came up from Miguel's pelvis to his belly button, dusting over his six-pack.

He realized he'd waited over a decade for that moment.

Quarter-size nipples decorated his friend's sculpted chest, and his face—

Are you kidding me?

The bastard was asleep.

In a huff, he crossed his arms and turned on his heel, ready to walk back into the kitchen.

A hand grabbed his calf muscle and yanked him onto the bed. He fell back onto Miguel as excitement pitted in his stomach.

"Psych," Miguel snickered. He held him down, stripping the damp cotton towel from around his waist. "*Bebé*, you didn't think I'd be asleep, did you?" His lips came over his. His tongue was playful with his kiss.

"I was going to get Brutus's leftover bathwater to throw at you if you didn't wake up."

Smothered in Miguel's love, he wrapped his legs around Miguel's side and held on to his cock—the joystick to his ass's pleasure zone. His top's dick was rock-hard, and he jacked it, up and down. Miguel's face radiated pleasure.

"Do you remember where we left off at the club?"

"Yes. You were going to fuck me."

"And what did I say to you?"

"Mig." They were back at the feeling stuff again. "You told me you were in love with me."

"*Te amo*." Miguel nibbled on his earlobe.

His body felt tingly all over. Having this man gnaw at his ear. Oh! God! He sat up in Miguel's lap, enclosing his muscled back with his arms. "I don't like feeling like this."

"Like what?"

"Emotionally naked."

"Is that why you've run from me for all these years?"

"Maybe."

"I can see right through you." Running a hand over his freshly buzzed head, he said, "I know you're scared. It's going to take some time, but we'll get there. I promise."

"Since we're not keeping secrets anymore, I'll admit…I'm in love with you, too. I've wanted to be with you since the moment we met."

"So, you do remember."

He nodded. "You were so nervous that night when you came up to talk to me. I felt something special between us right then. Didn't you?"

"*Sí,* of course! It was electric. I've been drawn to you ever since."

"It scared me, and when you just stood by and watched Diego talk me up, I went with him. Maybe that was out of spite." He hadn't thought about his motives until right then.

"Don't ever be scared of me again." Miguel rotated his body, placing him on his back. He lifted his right leg up over his shoulder. "Can I ask you something? You don't have to give me a response, but don't lie, *sí?*

He smiled and nodded, not sure what was on Miguel's mind.

"Thor tells many tales, but one he shared was about when you were dating MLD. Did you...shout out my name in bed a few times?"

"Yes," he replied truthfully. "Even in the last year when he pulled away. I was left with a void in bed, and I would often close my eyes and think about being with you."

"Tonight, I want you to keep your eyes open for me." Miguel kissed him all over. "Our bodies flow together like water over a rock." He pulled Blake by his whole body to his cock. "I'm your rock."

He smiled with excitement as Miguel reached beside the candles for the lube and a condom.

Taking Miguel's dick in his hands, he pumped as it swelled. The head thickened. The girth pulsated as if having its own heartbeat. Unwrapping the condom, he sheathed himself.

He raised the clear bottle high and let the silicone oil drizzle over his cock. Placing a dollop of gel on his fingers, his friend leaned in and kissed him. "I have to lube up my prized possession." He slid two fingers into his asshole.

"Ahhh." He looked into Miguel's brown eyes and grinned. He wasn't nervous. "I'm ready, Mig."

"Wait, *bebé*." He sat up putting Blake's left leg over his right shoulder.

He held on to Miguel's shoulders and lifted his head off the mattress an inch, allowing his body to fall back against the sheets. The physical pressure then increased.

Sliding his hands under Blake's knees, Miguel pushed his ass up from the bed, bending down to lick his asshole. He bit on the skin's tight edges.

"Ohhh." Grabbing the pillows around him to brace himself, he closed his eyes, enjoying every second.

Miguel's tongue sank deeper, and Blake started to jack himself off.

At once, Miguel grabbed his hands, holding them down at his sides. "Don't jack off. I want you to come without touching yourself. Relax."

Blake pushed his ass further into his lover's mouth, letting himself get into being rimmed. His scalp tingled, and sweat beaded over his upper lip. He felt as if his body was on fire. He went to sit up but Miguel held his body down, eating his ass and rotating two fingers between each tongue-lashing.

"Come on, *bebé*, come for me." Miguel spread his ass further apart with his fingers.

"Mmm." He felt his asshole open wide.

Reaching up, Miguel tugged at his cock. Blake came instantly. With no warning, he slid his cock's head inside Blake's ass while he quaked from his orgasm.

"Fuck yeah! Here we go." He pushed his cock further into Blake's asshole.

Blake shot out more cum.

Collecting the release in his hand, Miguel flicked cum onto his own dick. Fingering the rest of Blake's load into his hole, he said, "Your virgin ass is mine." And he dove his dick back in.

"Fuck." He grabbed the mattress corner and held on as Miguel drilled deeper and faster.

So hot, Miguel's cock felt perfect. His muscles and flesh separated then tightened.

Looking up, Miguel smiled at him while he impaled harder. "I love you, *bebé*."

"*Yes!*" He couldn't take any more. "I love you, too, Miguel!"

Miguel placed him on his side and kept his dick embedded in his ass. He pumped harder and harder.

"*¡Papi!*" Blake screamed.

His top laughed.

The resistance seemed to egg Miguel on. He inhaled a deep breath and allowed his body to get into his friend's machismo ways.

Miguel penetrated deeper. "*Bebé*—gimme." He grabbed his face and kissed him, thrusting his cock up and down, higher then lower into Blake's ass.

He held on to the headboard, to balance himself from Miguel's pounding. He reached down for his own cock. Hard again, he jacked himself off while his top pumped his ass and filled him with his dick again and again. If he could come again, he'd relax and allow himself to take more of Miguel's cock, so he yanked. The dual sensations were intense. Miguel's gaze confessed his arousal.

In a push-up position, Miguel encased him beneath himself and sank in deeper. "You're going to shoot your load for me, *bebé*. Give me more cum."

"Fuck-fucketty-fuck-fuck!" He tugged at his cock harder. "It's your turn to come."

Miguel shook his head. "Bottoms first." He lowered his head over Blake's and kissed him, then reared his head back and hammered on.

"Oh, my..." He shot off again. Cum came up over his chest, decorating pearl streams over his skin. He'd *never* orgasmed back-to-back before.

His lover screamed in Spanish and ended with, "Yeah, you're so fucking hot."

Remaining deep inside him, Miguel reached for Blake's ankles and then lowered his torso. His face became more serious than ever. His hips thrust from a rapid salsa to a slow, gyrating dance. His cock was imbedded deep. "Love having your ass hugging my dick." Miguel lowered his face to his, stared deep into his eyes, and smiled. "*Te amo.*"

"I love you, too," he said as he watched Miguel's eyes roll back in his head.

"I'm coming." His entire body spasmed.

Better than he'd ever imagined, they didn't need their *Seven Desires* and *Needs*, they just needed each other. "You got me. I'm all yours."

"All mine." Miguel forced his tongue into his mouth.

He hugged him, allowing Miguel to collapse on top of him. Burying his face in the nape of his neck, his breathing was heavy.

Lying back, he absorbed his lover's masculine energy. Glancing up at him, he noted his beautiful man didn't look away. He held his gaze, smiled, and tucked his legs next to his. In his arms, he listened to Miguel hum the song playing in the background.

He stared for a second at the blank walls ahead before he asked, "Why haven't you ever decorated your loft?"

"I didn't want to make a home without my boyfriend. It's an old Mexican superstition which states if you live alone and create a home, you'll be single forever."

"We need to decorate."

"We?" Miguel hugged him close. "Does this mean we're an item?"

"We're working toward that, aren't we?"

"You've sexually submitted your body to me." Miguel stroked his cheek. "What about committing your heart to me as your boyfriend?"

He wanted to. He was so close. He couldn't explain it, but fear held him back from jumping into another relationship, especially with Miguel. He didn't want to hurt his best friend, so he said, "I need a little more time. Can I tell you my answer at the end of the week?"

"Sí."

Miguel didn't seem as upset as Blake thought he'd be, but something told Blake he wasn't getting out of this one. Scarred and broken by Diego, did he actually see himself in another relationship with anyone, ever? One which worked out the way it was supposed to, delivering on all of its promises?

His answer deep down inside told him…no. Not again.

Chapter Twenty-Two

Secrets from Puberty

Upper East Side

The next day, Lex hosted an intimate get together with tea and pastries at her penthouse for Vive. Taddy agreed to come for emotional support, but it was so much more than that. She had spent the better part of the day talking to an alcohol specialist, mastering the conversation which was going to take place. If only Vive's parents were here with the therapist from Hampton Horizons. They'd promised they'd come. And Thor? Where was he? Massimo and M2 were in the nursery. Jemma was out at another event.

Declining on the Dammann Frères tea blend Lex had picked up at Bergdorf's a few weeks before, Vive sat buzzed with vodka in her hand. Hedda lay in the usual position on her lap. If she only knew her parents were coming, she wouldn't be so smug about tea.

Hell, she couldn't tell Vive they'd planned a surprise intervention, so she went along with her bridal party talk.

"I'm sorry for what I said to you the other day when you came over." She closed her eyes, trying to remember exactly what she had wanted to tell Vive aside from the fact that her butt needed to dry out. "I do need you in my life. You're one of my oldest friends. Massimo and I can't imagine our special day without you." She hated to lie. Vive wouldn't be there. After their talk, Vive would most likely never speak to her again, or be going away for treatment for a very long time. Either way, she wouldn't be at their wedding.

Vive rounded her shoulders and stared at Taddy then returned her attention back to Lex. "Honey, I accept your apology. But I'm not sorry for what I said, so don't expect me to return your sentiments."

"I don't *expect* anything, Vive."

"Darling, why can't you apologize, too? Then we can move on with this." Taddy's gold jewelry chimed as she handed Vive a chocolate pastry. "Eat." Her green eyes studied their friend's unfashionably thin figure.

"'Cause, girlie, I'm *not* sorry. Sure, I feel bad we fought, but I meant what I said." Vive's cheekbones appeared higher than usual. "You've changed now that you've got Massimo. Taddy changed when she met Warner. Blake changed when he married MLD. Relationships change people." She held her cocktail tight and sipped. "And stop pushing dessert in my face. I'm not hungry."

"I imagine when two people share their life together, they naturally evolve or—"

"Change," Vive interrupted eagerly, causing Hedda to stand up on her front legs.

The more Lex listened to Vive the better she grasped her friend's fears. Perhaps, Vive felt as if she was losing everyone around her. Not for good or forever, but a piece of each of them to their significant other. "Okay, we naturally change then. But it doesn't mean our friendship is going to stop or we won't be close."

"*Puhlease*. You say that now. We all know you'll soon be busy with your kids and your royal husband. Naturally, our friendship will fall through the cracks."

"I won't let it."

"That's why we're discussing this now. A preventative measure, darling, to make sure we all remain as close as ever." Taddy's tone became warm as she looked to Massimo who brought them in another tray of sweets.

Earlier he'd offered to sit in with them, but Lex feared Vive would keep her guard up with him at the table. The night was for girl-talk, then straight to rehab.

"Where are they?" Massimo asked quietly in Italian to Lex as she adjusted her plate.

Lex shrugged. "If they come, let them in," she whispered in Massimo's direction before he left the room.

Too busy seething, Vive didn't pay any mind to what she said to her fiancé. She still didn't have any clue.

The anger radiating off Vive consumed the passing minutes. Reaching over, Lex grabbed her hand. "I don't like seeing you mad at the world. You have so much rage inside you. Can't we help you get to a good place?"

"Ha." Vive laughed sarcastically, giving Hedda a love pat on the head to lie down. "Wave that magical wand. What's next, prince charming appears? Maybe whoever *he* is can wipe away my problems."

"No. You shouldn't be in a relationship, at least not right now."

"Lex." Taddy kicked her under the table.

Ouch! She held onto her chair. Lex didn't intend to go there until Vive's parents arrived. Unfortunately, the conversation drove itself in the direction.

"What?" Vive asked, petting Hedda more rapidly. "Why don't you think I should be dating?"

"Because you're an alcoholic." The words blurted out so effortlessly, she couldn't help herself.

"Here we go…" Taddy clenched her jaw and reached for Vive's other hand.

With Lex at her left and Taddy at her right, a fake gossip magazine editor smile curved her mouth. "A li'l vodka throughout the day never killed anyone."

"You promised us you'd get better. Not once, but three times."

"Are you keeping score? Why are you judging me?" Vive pushed her chair back from the table and crossed her legs.

Hedda again stood on her lap. For the first time ever, Lex noticed Hedda growl at Vive.

"Not at all. We're trying to help." Lex felt a cry swelling up in the back of her throat. *Crap, this intervention thing is hard.*

"Yeah, darling, we'd like to see you make more progress to get well," Taddy added.

Slouching, Vive palmed her hands over her face causing her gaunt features to redden. She chewed her bottom lip then said, "I'm sober."

"You must quit drinking." Lex felt a sense of relief as she spoke.

"Can't a girl have one vice?" Vive huffed in bright mockery. "Lex, why don't you give up Italian cock and Taddy can give up shopping at Chanel. Then talk to me about stopping the occasional drink. I don't have a damn problem."

"Don't lie to us." Taddy rose in one fluid motion and stalked over to the French double doors separating the formal dining room from the rest of the place. She closed them and rested her head against the wooden frame for a brief second, perhaps mustering enough strength to continue. Turning to face Vive, she flipped her long red hair back behind her ears, cleared her throat, and resumed her seat. "Finding you on the floor the other day unconscious, nearly dead, made me realize we've overlooked this for far too long. You are physically dependent on alcohol, are you not?"

"No." Vive shook her head. "I'm not. I can stop any time. The other day was a one-time thing. I've never fallen asleep on the floor like that."

Lex remembered back to what the Easton Essentials showroom manager had said about Vive's belligerence while trying on gowns. Obviously, she lied about how often she blacked out. Right then, she needed support and motivation to go to rehab. Attacking her wouldn't do any good. How could she not see she needed help? The counselor on the phone had said she must admit her problem before surrendering to treatment.

"In the last month, what's the longest you've gone without a drink?" Needing Vive to open up, Lex tried the new approach. She couldn't remember the last time she'd seen her without a drink.

"How the fudgeballs should I know?"

"Dammit, Vive, think." Taddy's voice carried a unique force.

"Maybe…six hours." Shakiness overcame Vive when she talked. "I, uhhh…I can get it under control. I know I can."

"Good. How?" Lex managed a small, tentative smile toward Taddy. They were making progress.

"I'll go see that doctor over on Madison near Barney's. He'll give me a prescription to stop drinking." She smoothed her blouse over her torso, which only showed her thinness.

"Absolutely not. Quick-fix doctors aren't going to work this time." Taddy's glossy red lips pursed.

Being the boss of her own PR firm had its advantages, but inspiring people to do things they didn't want to do wasn't one of them.

Lex went on. "In the past, you've tried group meetings and counseling. You know what has to be done."

"Rehab?" Vive's penciled taupe brows shot up in surprise.

Taddy shut her eyes tight. "It's the only way."

"It's what my mom did to dry out. To this day, she says it's the only place to go." Lex had to hand it to her mom. Birdie's rehab gave her experience to deal with Vive.

"That's a fucking month of my life away at some loony-bin spa. I'm not crazy."

"We know you're not. But you have to address the reasons *why* you drink so much."

Closed-fisted, Vive slammed the dining table. The bone china rattled against the sterling silver. "Why don't you try burying the only man you've ever loved, and then be forced to put your baby up for adoption and tell me how it feels? Like death warmed over."

"Avon Porter was a bad time for all of us, you especially." Lex never forgot the fight which had caused Vive's boyfriend's death. The police had ruled it an accident, but Sanderloo had tripped on LSD. Paranoid from the acid, he started gay-bashing Blake, accusing him of coming on to him when they were drinking in the woods. He'd beaten Blake until he blacked out. To this day, Blake maintained he couldn't remember. But Vive never forgot. How could she?

"I should never have picked up that shovel." Vive's pink face turned green.

"Sanderloo didn't give you much choice."

Vive had stepped into the brawl, fending him off by striking him. The blunt force trauma to the head had instantly killed him.

"Reliving nightmares won't inspire me to quit drinking. I was sixteen and five months pregnant with his baby. Sanderloo and our child are on my mind *every* day. They don't turn off in my mind. I can't go to rehab again. I don't want to deal with it. I have too much going on in my life now to dig up that past. Please, don't make me…"

Taddy swallowed so hard Lex heard it from across the table. She'd made everyone promise never to talk about that year at Avon Porter. Covering up the dead body had been Taddy's idea until Vive cracked and turned herself in, telling the Connecticut authorities where they could find Sanderloo.

"Other than facing the past, what's holding you back from going?" Lex wanted her to talk more as Taddy seemed in a haze. Hearing Sanderloo's name had that effect on them.

"*Debauchery* is doing great. We're outselling *People* magazine this quarter. I can't leave the publication for a month. It'll tank." From her satchel, Vive pulled out the latest copy and threw it across the table toward her.

On the cover were Lex and Massimo. The headline read, *"Royal Wedding Planned at St. Patrick's Cathedral."*

"Sure you can, darling. We'll help with the magazine while you're gone." Taddy's brief moment of distraught left as if a strong wind came through giving her focus to rejoin the conversation. Work talk remained her forte. "Kiki in my office will round up freelance editors to come on board. Blake and I will work to keep your ads up. Hell, most of your advertisers are my clients. It'll be easy-breezy." No doubt Taddy could run the magazine in her sleep. Kiki, too.

Squinting at Taddy's simplification of her job, Vive mumbled to herself, "Rehab didn't work last time. Don't you two remember? I'm immune to sobriety."

"They got you off the pills, but you never addressed the drinking. You went right back to vodka when you got home."

"So fucking what? I can't give up everything. Pick one: booze or pills."

"My mother says liquor is your pathway to other addictive substances. If Mom can do this, so can you."

"Birdie is stronger than me. I won't make it." Lowering her head to Hedda's ears, Vive spoke quietly to the restless dog. Hedda snarled, showing her teeth.

"So…you're going to live out the rest of your life drinking, being miserable and mean to everyone around you," Lex stated.

Wishing Blake was there to help, she noticed the time. He should've come. But the boys were dealing with their own drama. If he hadn't already, Miguel would be coming out to his folks soon. Afraid he'd chicken out, she and Taddy let them off the hook for the intervention.

"I promise I'll be more pleasant to be around. Give me another chance."

Her courage to see Vive through sobriety gave her no choice. "If you don't go to rehab, Taddy, Blake, and I can't be your friends anymore." That was the worst thing she could say, but the social worker had told her it was the only way. The intervention would work. It had to.

"Taddy?" Vive's right eyebrow arched as she glared across the table in denial of Lex's threat. "You can't be serious."

Waving aside any hesitation, Taddy said, "If you refuse to go to treatment, I will cut you out of my life."

Her best friend crossed her arms, hugging herself as if a chill had set in. It had—maybe not in temperature, but in determination. She admired her more for not breaking eye contact with Vive.

"Screw you both." Reaching for her purse, Vive jerked to her feet; Hedda bounced in her right arm. "Thor would never turn his back on me. My parents won't stand for this, either." Just as she grabbed her purse to leave, the doors behind her opened. Frozen, Vive's eyes widened in alarm as if seeing something, or someone, she didn't expect. "What the fuck are you people doing here?"

"Watch your tongue, Viveca," a Scandinavian voice scolded.

She turned around in relief to see they'd finally showed up.

"Sorry we're late, Alexandra. The midtown traffic was impossible. We should've taken the helicopter. Hello there, Tabitha," Mrs. Farnworth said.

With powerful hands, Mr. Farnworth yanked Lex to her feet. Mrs. Farnworth gave her a kiss on both cheeks. So did Thor who'd come in behind them. He introduced Vive to another woman. *Must be the therapist.*

For the first time ever, Hedda barked. She didn't stop yapping until Vive sat back down in her seat and held Lex's hand.

The therapist took control of the group. "Let's get started."

Upper West Side

Miguel couldn't feel his legs, but knew they were attached when he climbed the marble stairs heading to his parents' apartment. Holding on to the iron railing, he turned as Blake came up behind him. "I have to tell you something." He motioned him over to the rear stairwell and sat down next to him.

"What?" Blue eyes widened more innocent than ever.

"It bothers you I don't talk about my family. I understand your frustration." Dropping his tone, he said, "My parents are *different* than yours."

"I'd imagine so." Blake reached for his hand. "I'm confident you came from two wonderful people."

"*Papá* suffered a stroke a few years back, causing him to retire from Washington. His speech is slurred, right side paralyzed, tires easily, and becomes agitated often."

Blake gasped. "I'm sorry."

"He has a cardiovascular condition." He only hoped he wouldn't break his father's heart by telling him he was a homosexual.

"Understood."

"*Mamá* is a bully. A devout Catholic, she's stubborn, opinionated, and will cut you off if you say something she doesn't want to hear."

"Sounds like you two have a lot in common." His friend snickered.

"Ready?" He stood, wanting to get this over and done with.

"Signal me when to chime in." Blake studied his face. "You're going to be fine," he reassured.

"Never thought I'd be doing this." His sweaty hands gripped Blake's, pulling him to stand.

"We've accomplished plenty this week. Just think, it could be worse."

"How?"

"We could be with Lex and Taddy right now as they try and get Vive to go to rehab."

Blake knocked on the door then sidestepped, pushing Miguel front and center. As a rule, he went right in. With his lover on his arm, he felt as though he was a stranger at the door—one who didn't belong. He'd stood at the entryway a million times, but that night he felt would be his last. The entrance labeled *The Santana's* opened. A familiar smell of fried beans flowed out.

His mother, dressed in her favorite hand-stitched apron with her raven hair in a bun, wrapped her flour-covered arms around him. "*¡Hola, hijo!*"

"*Mamá.*" He hoped she'd still greet him that way once he came out. *I love you.* He held on to her a moment longer, as if it was their last moment together.

Blake coughed.

Seeing him over his shoulder, she released his embrace and faced her guest. "Blake?"

"Mrs. Santana, nice to meet you." He extended a handshake.

"Inez says you come." His mother smiled as her eyes studied him up and down.

Blake held out the liquor. "A gift for you and Mr. Santana."

"*Gracias.*" Miguel's mother clapped him on the shoulder and accepted the bag. "Please, call me Marisol. *Entra.*" She waved them in.

Miguel followed his mother down the long hallway with Blake close behind. Family photos taken during happier times decorated the walls.

"*Papá* slept earlier. He has energy for tonight." His mother chatted in Spanish under her breath, letting him know that since they were late, the food was getting cold, so they'd sit down and eat right away. "Cierra and Ofelia ate pizza earlier. The girls are in the back room playing with wooden puzzles you gave them for Easter."

He stepped into the living room. "*Hola, Papá,*"

His father stood slowly on his good side, putting pressure on his cane to support the bad. "Miguel." A smile caused one side of his face to jerk up while the other remained dead-still.

"Meet my friend…Blake Morgan. Blake, this is my *papá,* Teo."

Blake greeted his father with a handshake. A few words were exchanged in Spanish, which were impossible for him to understand, but his friend accommodated him with sincere engagement.

Inez emerged from the kitchen, wiping the oven heat from her forehead. "Hi, guys." She hugged them both. "Let's eat." She flipped the light switch on in the dining room, his favorite part of the house. Many Christmas dinner memories came from that room, and studying Algebra in the late hours with his father. No matter how busy he was with his political career, he always made time for him and his studies.

There was a long, oval table with two chairs on each side and one at each end. The tablecloth had stayed the same, Mexican embroidered linen made by his late grandmother. The design featured caracara birds flying in the center as Aztec dahlia flowers bordered the corners. The best china was out for the night.

Surprisingly, his father, who never took anyone's hand for support, leaned on Blake. They shimmied to his place setting. Falling in behind them, Miguel listened intently to their talk, paranoid about who'd be saying what to whom. His nerves clustered in a ball.

"Inez says you're in advertising, *sí?*" his father asked Blake as he held his arm tighter.

He could tell because Blake flinched.

Miguel realized his father's condition was deteriorating and Inez must've looked Blake up online to know what he did for a living and blabbed to his parents. He hadn't mentioned his friend's résumé during their talk on the phone. *Snoopy big sister.*

Blake responded with his usual spiel about his career achievements. They were impressive, even hearing them the tenth time around. He and Taddy had built Brill, Inc. together, starting from scratch and growing it into the millions in client revenue.

Entering the dining room, his father took the first seat. He patted the empty high-back chair and added, "Sit next to me, Miguel."

The lump in his throat thickened. "I can't do this," he whispered in Blake's direction as he sat beside his father.

"Yes, you can," Blake replied under his breath. "This dinner looks delicious," he said louder, over his previous words, and sat beside him.

His mother poured his friend a cocktail.

"Mrs. Santana, what's this?" he asked as he held the salt-rimmed glass.

She served her husband a much smaller glass. "Teo's favorite, *Micheladas*."

A lime beer mixed with Chamoy spices and Serrano pepper, Miguel knew it by heart. "Should *Papá* be drinking a *Micheladas*?" he asked with concern.

"Die in peace," retorted his father, holding up his tumbler for a toast. "*Salud por la Amistad, Blake.*"

"*Salud,*" Inez toasted, dipping her head with a smile at their guest.

"*Papá* cheered you," he whispered to Blake for clarification.

"Thank you." He swigged his drink. His light-skinned face beamed an immediate fire engine red.

"*Caliente,*" his parents responded in amusement.

Inez reached for a fresh glass, pouring him papaya juice and nudging him to sip.

Blake chewed on ice cubes, blotting his forehead and cheeks with the ivory napkin from his lap. "*Mecha-*whatever you called it is spicy. Not for the faint of heart."

The glass rose with another quick swig before his mother placed the beverage far from reach. "Enough."

"¡Ay, dios mío!" He rested his hand on Blake's leg under the table to try and get it to stay still. No one in his family could see the fear his hands were showing.

Blake raked his fingers on the top. He appreciated his friend's attempt to try and calm him.

"My daughters have a crush on you, Blake." Inez filled up his empty glass with a second nectar helping. "They insist you take them back to the tea room for scones."

"Scones?" repeated his mother with curious amusement. She stood and served the *chiles rellenos* dish.

"Cierra and Ofelia are wonderful girls."

"Gracias, Blake." Inez's pride for her two daughters radiated. "I wish I could spend more time with my girls. Work keeps me away from them."

"Any time you need a babysitter, I'm game."

Blake studied his plate. Miguel realized he might be unfamiliar with the red sauce covering the dish.

"I like him," Inez enthused to her parents over Blake.

"Sis'll put your digits on speed dial."

We're all getting along. So far, so good.

Around the table, his family quieted and ate their dinner.

"It's wonderful." He complimented his mother's cooking. He winked at Inez, knowing full well she'd made the meal. Everyone enjoyed their food, except for one person.

The uneaten plate in front of Blake was seized by his mother and loaded up with yellow rice. "This will calm the hot sauce." She returned the dish to his place setting and ordered, "Dig in." Her Mexican accent was thick but endearing when she became bossy.

"Sí, sí," chimed his father. "Miguel mentioned you met at the university?"

"We've been friends for about ten years—" Blake cut himself short with a forkful from his plate.

The homemade rice brought a smile to his face as he chewed. He hoped it would set his mother at ease since Blake was eating.

"¿Diez?" his father repeated, questioning the timeline and turning to Inez. He lowered his voice and mumbled in his disabled tone audible to his children.

"Blake, Papá asked since you two have been friends for a decade, why are we just meeting you now?" Inez's unease was evident. "Why not sooner?" She mouthed to Miguel, Tell them.

His mother placed her silverware down then folded her hands together. "Tell us what?" She hunched over her plate and leaned in.

"I can't." Panic rioted inside him. Sick, the room began to spin.

"About those ten years. I'm glad you asked," Blake interrupted.

He nudged his friend under the table. Stop.

Squeezing his hand, Blake continued. "Mr. Santana, Mrs. Santana, we came over tonight because Miguel has something to share with you." He pinched his hand hard and stated, "News which has been on his mind for quite some time."

"Sí. Ten years," his sister added.

"Inez," he hissed at her to shut up.

"What is it?" Bleak worry flashed in his mother's eyes.

"I was hoping to get you two warmed up on tequila then I'd share." He cleared his throat. "Nevertheless, *I'm gay*." He slipped the words out, immediate and unrefined. "I've known since I…well…since puberty, I suppose."

His mother made the sign of the cross. She recited a prayer verse in Spanish from the Act of Contrition.

Was the news too much to handle?

Chapter Twenty-Three

A Sobering Future

Upper East Side

Lex clung to reality, hoping she could keep her cool. "We're all here for you." Again, she encouraged Vive to admit she needed professional help.

"No…you're not. How can you do this to me?"

Just when Vive got close to agreeing to treatment, she reverted, claiming she'd manage her disease alone. For ten minutes, she kicked the table, threw her purse, and threatened that she'd move to Paris and never talk to any of them again.

Vive hated Paris.

Hedda licked the tears falling onto her hands after she wiped her face. Mr. and Mrs. Farnworth remained collected and strong. Clearly, they'd been down this road before with their daughter. Everyone stood their ground not giving in to her ideas for a second chance.

There'd be no retreats to St. Bart's for sun therapy or detoxing mud baths in Romania. Every whammy Vive came up with got rejected. Mr. Farnworth made it clear she'd be cut off from the family's fortunes and removed from all financial support first thing in the morning if she didn't go to rehab that day.

Head hanging low, Vive appeared worn down. Her body leaned in toward the therapist, possibly hoping for advice. Taddy and Thor listened on as the social worker, Georgette, explained the next steps and the program.

Hampton Horizons remained the most controversial rehabilitation therapy center in North America. The first phase prohibited patients from communicating with the outside world, reading or watching TV as they sought medical treatment. Once stable, Vive would be placed on a crop farm on Long Island where she'd work on the land and attend classes on addiction. After a few weeks, she'd be granted contact with her family and friends and allowed to use the phone while continuing to work the season's harvest. Though it was the furthest thing from the norm for Vive to get her billion-dollar hands dirty, this was her best hope for getting sober.

"Tonight you'll be driven to Hampton Horizons." Georgette sat on the edge of her chair.

"Who will ride with me?"

"Just me."

The conversation needed to come to a close. It was time.

Georgette pulled out the forms from the folder and spread them on the table along with a pen. "Sign here, please…"

"Who's going to admit me?"

"Since you didn't attempt suicide like last time, there isn't a court order." Mr. Farnworth's thin lips pressed together. "You will admit yourself. Now, be a good girl,

Viveca, and sign the papers agreeing to stay 'til the program is over."

"Meaning I may leave any time I like?" Vive wrinkled her red nose. "Right, Dad?"

Good Lord, Vive. Don't think like that.

"The doctors will decide when you're ready to return. That is, if you want to come back to Manhattan." Georgette moved the papers closer.

"Don't be ridiculous. I've never heard of such a thing." Vive thrust her fingers through her blonde hair. A bead of sweat collected on her forehead.

Please, sign the frickin' papers. Lex nearly chewed her bottom lip off.

"Viveca, if you don't finish the program and live a sober life, your mother and I will cut you off for good. For your *own* good," Mr. Farnworth said sternly, his patience fading.

"How long is the fucking program?"

No one spoke.

Please, go to therapy, Vive. The answer tore at Lex's insides.

Agitated, Vive grabbed her by the wrist. "Twenty-eight days?" she almost begged.

"Hamptons Horizons is *unique*."

Georgette's evasive response caused obvious concern for everyone in the room. Only Lex understood how long the program took because her mother had done it years ago.

"How much time is spent in treatment?" Raising her voice, Vive squeezed at her wrist for an answer. "This was all your idea. Answer me."

"Three months…to start." She saw fear in her face as she released the grip.

"No fucking way. Fuck that and fuck you!"

Rubbing her sore joint, she quickly banished the thought of Vive not going to rehab and asked, "Do you trust us?"

Vive swore under her breath. "I hate you so much right now. I'll never forgive you."

"You don't mean that," Taddy corrected her. "Answer the question. Do you trust us?"

The room's walls felt as though they were closing in on everyone. Nauseous, she didn't think it was her pregnancy making her sick. No, it was the thought of not having Vive in her life anymore. Were they making a mistake?

"Since we were kids, I've trusted you both."

She wouldn't look at her, which hurt. Instead, Vive turned her attention back to Taddy who held the papers in her hands.

Taddy handed her the pen. "Sign the papers."

"My stuff. I need to go home and pack first." Pushing the document away, Vive gave the room a tight smile.

"I did all that for ya, toots. That's why I was late." Thor earned her attention. Just his casual tone seemed to put her at ease. "Your luggage is out in the limo. I packed your best couture. You're going to be one fashionable bitch at rehab."

Everyone, including Vive, giggled. Even Mr. Farnworth, who for as long as Lex had known him never smiled. The release of the stress leading up to the night, along with the unease of how this would go down, made it easier for Lex to breathe for the first time in days.

"Thor, you did all that for me?"

"You bet, baby doll. I want this for you. We all do." Out of all of Vive's friends, Thor Edwards, fund-raiser, safe-sex advocate, and veteran party boy who'd gone to rehab for crystal meth addiction years before, gunned for her rehabilitation.

"Me going to Horizons means that much to you?" Her mouth opened to say more then closed without another word. Crouching, she buried her face in Hedda's fur and rocked from side to side.

"We joke about our booze, but this party has to end sometime, and that time is now. When you get back to the city, I'll be dry right along with ya." Thor nodded to reassure her. "Shit, if Marc Jacobs can get sober, so can you, Miss Thing. Think of all the weight we'll lose by giving up those extra carbs."

Lex mouthed a thank you to Thor. He was flawless as always.

Looking up, the worry in her eyes dilated her pupils. Vive asked, "What about Hedda? My furbaby is blind and deaf. She requires around-the-clock care. May I bring her with me?"

"I'm sorry, no," Georgette replied, holding her clipboard to her chest.

"Hedda and I have never been apart. Not since she was a puppy. She's all I have. Georgette, maybe you don't understand, but she's like a child to me. Please..." Tears streaked her face.

Crap! Her decision was heading back toward no.

Mrs. Farnworth got up from the table and wrapped her arms around her daughter. Kissing her on the forehead, she spoke in a low, loving voice, assuring her this was for the best.

"I'm going to take the best care of your pooch." Thor reached over and stroked Hedda's back. "We'll go to Doggie Day Care. I'll take her shopping and bring her to visit. I promise."

Earlier, Lex had called everyone she knew in their circle to see who could take Hedda for such an extended period of time. Thor was the only one who'd agreed. He'd do anything for her, including taking care of a special-needs dog.

"You'll come see me on the farm?" Vive asked.

"Every chance we get, we'll be there." She felt the weight coming off her, hoping Vive swung back to agreement.

"Will you be mad at me, Lex? If I leave tonight, I won't be in your wedding."

Kissing the top of her hand, she felt too choked up to speak, but she found her answer. "You're giving us the greatest wedding gift Massimo and I could ever ask for."

"What's that?"

"Sobriety. Your health. I can't think of anything I'd want more than to have this."

"More than a gift from Waterford Crystal?"

With such a shallow comment, she sensed her humor return. "Way more than anything on my silly registry."

"Okay…"

The room paused. Did they hear her correctly?

"What did you say?" Taddy asked with a sound of hopefulness in her voice.

"I'll go. I can't let you guys down anymore." Grabbing the papers, she signed on the line. "More importantly, I have to do this for myself, right?"

"That's our girl."

Hugging for what felt like forever, she soon found herself downstairs with everyone, including Massimo and M2, waving goodbye. Georgette and Vive took off, heading north up Park Avenue toward the Long Island Expressway.

She'd miss Vive and wished so much she could be able to share her wedding day with her and Massimo. Lex realized she didn't want Vive to miss out on finding her own chance for a happily-ever-after. Knowing sobriety brought better times ahead helped. No one deserved to love themselves, and possibly a man, more than Viveca Farnworth.

Upper West Side

Frantically, Miguel stared at his parents. They hadn't said one word after he'd told them he was gay. The silence about killed him.

"I fought being gay for years, 'til college," he added, hoping to get somewhere with them. A vulnerability he'd never experienced paralyzed him from talking any further.

Here it comes. They're going to disown me and ask us to leave.

Neither parent spoke. Rather they sat there, speechless, staring at one another from across the dining room table. Noise from the air-conditioner filled the silence.

Panicked, he turned from one to the other for a response; anything. The silence drove him insane. He'd do anything they wanted to stay in their lives, but he had to be true to himself. He'd spent too many years not celebrating himself with his family. Missing out on so much already, he didn't want to carve that part of his life out from them.

He swallowed, feeling the dryness from his tongue swelling in his mouth, and begged, "Say something."

"We've known," his mother said as his father nodded. A tense laugh followed.

"You have?" He released Blake's hand and leaned forward in his chair in confusion.

Inez gave him a 'you stupid fool' smile and confirmed, "Of course they have."

You knew they suspected and didn't tell me. You brat.

"Since you were a little boy, you were always special." Attempting to stand, his father grabbed at his cane.

"Too handsome to not have taken a wife." His mother went around the dining room table to help her husband rise.

Miguel stood, as well. "Because I'm not married, you two assumed..."

"Never *assumed*. We wanted you to tell us when you were ready," his father said while he held his wife's arm.

Inez studied Blake and then Miguel. "We figured you'd tell us when you were comfortable. They never wanted to ask you something you didn't want to share."

"Why?" He didn't understand why no one had said anything. So much time had gone by.

"Fear you'd stop coming home to visit." Tears brimmed Inez's eyes and she wiped them away. "They hoped you'd come out when you'd found someone special and wanted us to meet him."

"And you have Blake." Part of his father's paralyzed face stimulated to express happiness. He stared at his wife who admired her husband's strength and held out his arms for a hug.

"But, *Papá*, we are—"

"Taking our relationship slow," Blake interrupted. He leaned in, whispering, "Let them assume. Don't make them worry."

He nodded as he walked past his chair toward his father. He wrapped his arms around his parents. Miguel hugged them as they cried. Laughter followed.

"I'm sorry I didn't tell you sooner. I always thought with our religion, you'd flip."

"God loves everyone." She hugged him again. "This is your first time bringing anyone home to us. We're honored to meet Blake."

"Are you two living together?" his father asked, returning to the head of the table.

Shit, he didn't think his parents would be one step ahead. He returned to his seat and sank in his chair.

"We're still working out the details," Blake answered for him.

Miguel's mother sat across from him. She reached for his hand and asked, "Are you two going to get married? I hear a big white wedding is what the Manhattanite gays do these days." Though she laughed, her expression read across her face as serious.

His friend's jaw dropped and his mouth hung open as the words 'big white wedding' reverberated in his own ears. He could only imagine how they sounded to Blake. Probably like an atomic bomb.

Miguel reached for his friend's hand to comfort him, sat down in his own chair and responded, "We haven't talked about it."

"Speaking of weddings." Blake paused for a minute. "Our friends Lex and Massimo are getting married later this week. We'd like you to come."

"Are they gay?" his father asked.

"No, they are straight," he replied, unable to believe Blake invited them to the wedding.

"*Sí*. We would like to meet more of your friends." His mother looked fondly at them.

"Come on, let's eat." Inez urged them to finish their entrees.

Love filled his heart, making him feel complete for the first time in his life. He embraced this feeling. It was as he'd always prayed for, the happiest moment he'd ever experienced. His folks had suspected. *Why did I wait so long?* He should've come out much sooner. He questioned if he'd told Blake how he'd felt about him ten years before, if that would've saved them both so much heartache. A decade had been wasted on missed opportunities to share his real identity with his family, and be with his best friend.

I'm not going to waste another minute.

As dinner came to an end, he raised his glass to a toast. "To our health." He winked at his father. "To our love." He patted Blake's leg. "To our wealth and time to enjoy them all."

Once everyone sipped their drinks, his father added, "Miguel, we want to go to your exhibit."

"In Barcelona?" Miguel smiled.

"We're all going. We talked about it yesterday. The tickets are purchased," Inez confirmed.

He didn't realize coming out of the closet also meant he'd be sharing every aspect of his life. He wasn't used to this.

Blake put his hand over his and squeezed it hard. His bright blue eyes sparkled in his happiness for his friend.

"That would be great," he said.

Hand in hand, Blake left with Miguel at his side. They were almost giddy walking to the limo parked on Central Park West. Going over the night's conversations, he thought Mr. Santana seemed naturally at ease with the whole thing, and so did his wife.

"Now I know where you get your good looks from. Your dad is fucking hot. I mean, like really—"

"Silencio." Miguel balked as if he'd heard it his entire life. He held the car door open for him and swatted him on the butt as he got inside.

"I'm so proud of you, Miguel." He kissed him the second the sedan headed downtown. Tasting the night's dinner on his lips, he said, "You were…amazing."

"Muchas gracias. I couldn't have done it without you guiding me."

"Puhlease. My help wasn't needed. You had their approval before we even walked in the door." He thought about how frustrated Miguel must be with himself to have waited until he was almost thirty to come out of the closet to them. *What a jackass*, he chuckled to himself.

"Did you have to invite them to Lex's wedding? Won't Birdie mind?"

"Who do you think gave me the idea? Birdie told me to make sure your family had an invite. My parents are coming, too." He felt a warm tingle inside knowing his parents would meet the Santanas. The friendly introduction only took ten years.

"This seems too easy." Miguel grinned, showing his perfect teeth. His pink tongue came out to lick his lips.

Lord, he dripped sex when he was in a good mood.

"Or maybe it's from going with the flow. Isn't that what you always say?"

Lightness replaced the earlier dread in Blake's chest watching the Santana's love their son. The night couldn't have gone any better. "How does it feel to finally be *out* to your family?"

"One word: relieved. I made being gay a bigger deal than it really is. My parents always assumed... After all these years, I cannot believe they didn't ask me."

He hoped Miguel might one day get it. He wasn't quite there yet, which frustrated the crap of out of him. "Why should they have to? This goes back to what I mentioned last night. You gotta tell people what you want in order to get it. You can't just hope."

"*Sí,* I'm getting that now." Kissing him on his neck, he brushed his fingers along his cheek in a slow caress causing him to giggle and turn in to him. "That citrus smell of yours drives me wild. I love it. I always have."

Miguel's lips, followed by his tongue on his neck along with the compliments in his ear, made his cock hard.

"The cologne is called Happy by Clinique."

"*Perfecto* name. Whenever I catch a whiff, that's how I feel. You make me happy, Mr. Morgan." Miguel unzipped his fly and pulled out his cock. Stroking it slowly, almost in tantric motions, he said, "I want you."

"See, you're getting better at telling people what you want. First, you said you wanted me in your bed." He held onto his beefy right arm with his left as he licked his fingers and glided his thumb over the head of his dick. Catching his breath short, he continued, "Then you said you wanted to come out to your family, and you did. Now tell me what you want to do next." Lord, he prayed Miguel would say he wanted to get fucked. His desire to drill his friend's Latin ass grew strong. Could he get his dominant alpha to bottom for him?

"Have you given more thought to us?"

Like a splash of cold water hitting him, he sat up. Losing the sexy moment, he slid his cock back in his pants and zipped up. "Indeed. It's on my mind. Meeting your parents tonight helped me understand you a bit more."

"What's there not to understand?" Suspiciously, Miguel glared at him for taking his cock away from his affections.

"You're not easy to figure out." Crossing his legs, he tapped his loafer's heel against the door's armrest. He hoped the conversation wouldn't avalanche into an argument after having such a perfect dinner.

"I'm a simple guy with simple needs." His friend's strong hands grabbed both of his knees. "Spread 'em." From east to west, Miguel split Blake's legs wide.

"Simple, my ass." He shook his head, trying to close his legs. "This week's brought us closer together." *Lord, he is gonna fuck me in the car. He's going to keep fucking me 'til I give in and move in with him. I can't give in to what he'll really want. I won't share someone again. Your past only proves that possibility is too great to risk.*

"*Sí*, very much so." Miguel dug his hands into his waistline. His long fingers reached for his cock.

He tried to push Miguel's hands away. "These experiences…we'll never forget."

Determined, Miguel wrapped his hands around his nuts. "Don't you see? We belong together. We always have." His friend spoke with certainty. "Give me your cock, boy, and that ass, too. Now."

He covered his mouth to stifle an erotic howl when Miguel got to his knees, pulling his slacks to his ankles.

"Move in with me. Tell me you want that, too." Taking his cock in his mouth, Miguel hummed to himself. Sucking hard, going down and coming back up on his shaft, he kept his black gaze fixated on his. When he didn't reply, he scraped his teeth along the tip of his cock in a playful way. "*Papi*, answer me."

"I…" Ever since their moment at Club Dupree, Blake had tried to imagine how they'd be as a couple. Their private moments together felt as pure as New York City snow, but what about a month or a year down the road? Once his rose-colored glasses wore off, would Miguel's feelings change in time? More importantly, if he told him what he *really* wanted, monogamy forever, would he agree?

The limo turned onto Miguel's block.

"What's that detective doing here?" he asked, noticing him in front of the building.

Miguel zipped up his pants. He opened the door the second the Mercedes came to a stop and helped him out.

Smoking a cigarette, Detective Shiloh Benson sat on the lobby stairs.

"Evening, fellas." Shiloh stood as they approached and put the smoke out with his shoe. "I have good news and bad news. Which do you want first?" He reached into his pocket and pulled out what appeared to be a United States citizen passport book. It was blue with gold foil lettering.

"Did you catch Diego?" Screw the guessing game, he had to know.

"That's my good news. Yes. Port Authority Police caught Mr. Oalo at JFK airport." Shiloh handed him the passport.

It looked familiar. He flipped it open and saw it was his. "Where did you get this?"

"Brazilian Airways confiscated it from Mr. Oalo when he tried to pose as a Blake Morgan III boarding a direct flight, first class, to Rio."

"What tipped the airline off?"

"The ticket agent noticed the stamps in your passport never had you going to Brazil before. When the agent looked closer at your photo and read the description, she saw the ID had blue eyes. Mr. Oalo's are brown. The check-in counter called security who'd seen the FBI Most Wanted listing and called us." Shiloh didn't seem smug about it, rather more matter-of-fact.

Relief came over him. "Thank you." Blake leaned in to Miguel's strong frame for support, putting his arm around him. "This is such great news."

"Mr. Oalo will go before a judge tomorrow. We have a long road ahead of us if this goes to trial. I wanted to be the first to tell you he's behind bars."

Happy and sad, Blake couldn't breathe as he held on to Miguel tighter. "What's the bad news?" Blake asked, wiping a tear away from his face. He didn't know why he was crying.

Shiloh pretended not to notice. "The press is going to be intense. You work at Brill, Inc., so you know how the media can be."

"How big is this story?" He thought about all the good people's names which would be dragged into this. All those families of the victims coming forward for help. The boys who'd partied along with Diego would all be exposed.

"The story will make headlines in a few hours if it hasn't already. It's one of the biggest cases we've had all year. Port Authority has already released a statement. Our FBI office will do the same."

"What can I do?"

"Avoid all interviews until our office says it's okay. Tell your friends to do the same. We clear?"

"Very." No one better came to Blake's mind to manage the journalists than Taddy. The woman had her way with them. He thanked the detective and went inside with Miguel.

Taking Brutus out for a long walk while Miguel showered, he thought about what Diego's capture meant to him and the other victims. The beginning of closure. A time to rid himself of his demons and take faith in a fresh start. As a single gay man in Chelsea...or part of a new and exciting relationship in the Lower East Side? He wasn't sure. But he had to make up his mind and tell Miguel exactly what he needed. If he couldn't deal then screw him. If he'd learned anything during his past mistakes with Diego it was to never lower your expectations in yourself because those around you have lowered it in themselves.

Chapter Twenty-Four

Miguel's Bottom

Midtown

Blake dressed in his tuxedo at The Plaza suite reserved for them to get ready near St. Patrick's Cathedral. All traffic going north of Forty-Second Street and west of Madison Avenue had been closed off for Lex and Massimo's royal wedding.

Miguel had assured him how excited he was that his parents were indeed coming for the day's celebration. The Santana's acceptance of their son being gay gave him a new reason to whoop it up.

He studied his attire in the mirror, a midnight-colored jacket and slacks designed by Jemma. Proud of his accomplishments from the gym, he'd worked hard in recent months to have his body tight. That day was his first time getting formally dressed and showing off his physique in he couldn't remember how long. He turned, admiring his backside. Did he actually look better with the buzzed haircut? Or was it the love Miguel had given him throughout the week which made him all the more attractive. Even the scar on his face didn't seem as noticeable with his short haircut.

The bathroom door opened. "Jemma did a *bueno* job with these, didn't she?" Miguel stepped out. The suit framed his massive Latino physique perfectly.

He examined him. "So handsome."

Miguel's broad chest was decorated by onyx button covers. A black bowtie sat around his neck, and he wore the black loafers Lex insisted upon.

"You like?" He turned around and gave him a three-sixty inspection. His cock bulged a bit from the front when he turned back around.

"Very much." His gaze froze on Miguel's crotch as it continued to swell. As big as a garden hose, the cock stood up and over to the side.

"*Gracias.*" Miguel closed the distance between them. "Let's fuck before we go to the wedding."

He felt sex coming off him as he wrapped his arms around him. "I love you." Unzipping his pants, he looked down at his own cock. Hard, his dick inched up. The mushroom head's slit glistened with pre-cum.

"*Te amo* more." Spitting in his hand, Miguel tugged at his cock, tweaking the bulbous head with his fingers and gliding his other hand up the backside. Blake caught his breath in his throat. He could've orgasmed right then and there.

Bringing his dry lips closer to Miguel's for a kiss, he licked them wet and glided his tongue over his soft lower lip as his friend moaned for attention. "I love the way you touch my body." He possessed a euphoric, intuitive level over him. With a decade-long friendship, he instinctively knew which buttons to push to make him laugh, make him cry, and nowadays, turn him on.

Gripping his chin, Miguel stared into his eyes. "If you're going to be my boyfriend, that means I can take you whenever and however I like, *si*?"

"No way." He smirked as his cock ached for release.

"Don't tell me no."

"I was hoping we could talk about us being…versatile."

"No."

"Ha. Now look who's saying no. If you want an equal partnership then you will let me top you." His sexual self-confidence was in full swing.

With a snug nuzzle from his nose over to his neckline, Miguel brought his soft, warm lips down upon his while he jacked his friend's cock. "How about I think about it? I'll let you know my answer after you tell me we're an item, and when you're moving in."

"Fine."

"Now, I can't let you leave with this load." He hoisted him up against the kitchen table and asked, "Don't you agree?"

"Yes, Mig. Release me."

Dropping to his knees, Miguel pulled his shorts down. His dick shot straight up toward the ceiling. Getting comfortable, he spread his body out against the kitchen table. He let his mind wander with ideas about how he'd top him. Would it be theatrical like in a sling? Or more tender in his bed?

Squatting between his legs, Miguel took his cock in his mouth quickly. His head bobbed back and forth as if on a mission to make him come in a nanosecond. It was new for him, having someone care that much about his pleasure.

He brought his face up, his Mexican brown eyes seducing him. "Lay back, boy." He grabbed his nuts and yanked them down toward the floor, causing him to slide a little and release the air caught in his throat.

Oh, my God! He pressed his weight against the table as he gave in to Miguel's control.

Miguel's mouth went up and down over his dick as his Latin god dominated his cock.

Over the white cotton dress shirt, Blake pinched at his own nipples. *Ouch.* Still sensitive from the clamps the other night.

In and out, Miguel slid his fingers into his asshole. Twisting them back in then out from his tightness. "*Bebé*, look at how hot you are." His tongue traced wet circles around Blake's cock.

Receiving compliments on his sex was new to him, but he loved hearing them. He hadn't felt attractive and was never complimented. Often his ex-husband made him feel sexless. At times asexual. But his best friend constantly told him how turned on he was by him. How hot and sexy he was.

"*Bebé*, your pre-cum tastes good. You gonna shoot for your *papi chulo*?"

"You want me to?" he asked, hypnotized by the request. His cock was ready to fire off.

"*Sí*, right now."

He put his arms behind his neck, pushing his groin up. Letting the fire pass through his body and into Miguel's receiving mouth.

His lover held his legs down with his arms while he worked on his cock. *This man is driving me wild.*

He grabbed onto his broad shoulders. Digging his fingers into his black curls, pushing Miguel's face deeper onto his cock, he shouted, "I'm going to come!"

Miguel growled.

"Ahhh!" he screamed.

The first squirt shot down Miguel's throat. He dropped his shoulders, allowing his head to fall against the table. With a second charge, he swallowed at high speed as the third curled on his tongue.

Decorated in pearl liquid, Miguel held his tongue out for his attention. Crawling on top, he shoved his tongue into his mouth. He tasted his own cum in the back of his throat. He kissed him deep.

Miguel confirmed, "You enjoy your own cum's taste, don't you, pig boy."

"I'll taste anything you give me." Miguel's cock grew harder over him. He reached down and said, "Your turn."

"No, *bebé*, we have to go to the wedding. The limo is downstairs waiting for us. My load is for my ass later." He stood and pulled him up with his usual strong force, yanking his shorts back up with one swift tug. He adjusted his massive cock to shift back over to the right.

"What do you mean?" He didn't follow.

"You can use it as lube when you fuck me."

"Mig…you'll bottom for me?"

"*Sí*, of course."

"Have you ever?"

"No," Miguel said and caressed his cheek. "But for you, Blake, I'd do anything you asked of me. Just as I know you'll be moving in, and we'll be starting our lives together." He kissed him. "You're going to say yes."

Realizing they hadn't talked about monogamy yet, he forced a smile and headed to the hotel lobby with Miguel.

Blake held on to Miguel's arm as they walked through the crowd at St. Patrick's Cathedral on the corner of Fifth Avenue and Fifty-First Street. With all the many socialites, bodyguards, and photographers, he figured it would take them about an hour to get inside. The Gothic-revival church held twenty-four-hundred guests. At check-in, the paparazzi piled in, snapping photos. He spotted Taddy with Warner greeting people on the red carpet.

Leave it to the Tittoni Royal wedding to have a red carpet.

"Hi, Warner." He greeted Taddy's boyfriend as they came up to the queue for photos. "It's great to see you."

"Blake, nice haircut. Hello, Miguel. Taddy has been filling me on your week. Sounds like you guys have had quite the adventure. I'm happy for you both." Warner's warm, hazel gaze confirmed his sincerity.

"Maybe next time you won't be gone from me for so long, Big Daddy," Taddy teased, pointing her finger over his Roman nose as he wrapped his broad arms around her. "Then I won't have to give you a status report on our friends." Slightly lifting her off the floor, Warner kissed her.

"When will it be your turn to get married?" Miguel asked.

"Mig." Mortified, Blake noticed the fearful shake of Taddy's head. Maybe Miguel didn't know she didn't believe in matrimony.

"Soon. I'm working on it," Warner answered. "What about you two?"

"Blake is letting me know tonight if he's going to be moving in with me." Miguel's confidence dazzled.

They stepped up to the cameras. Blake put his hand on Miguel's chest to stop him from going any further and whispered in his ear, "You realize these photos—of us holding hands—will be on the cover of the tabloids tomorrow." The press was already having a field day with his personal life due to Diego's arrest.

"What a great way to tell the world who I am and who I'd like to be with." Miguel grabbed him by the jaw and demanded, "I hate this game you're playing. Tell me right now you're moving in with me. We can celebrate today." He kissed him as he cupped his hands over his ass.

"Later, I promise."

Miguel's parents' acceptance and their question about their relationship must've kicked his desire for them to live together into warp speed.

He fell forward into the public kiss. For as long as he remembered, Miguel embodied hush-hush. He'd never granted media interviews on his artwork, let alone his personal life. But there he stood frenching his friend for all the magazines, bloggers, and TV stations to see.

The flashbulbs went off. One photographer shouted, "Mr. Santana, does this mean you're out about your sexuality?"

"*Sí*, I'm gay." He smiled and kissed him on the cheek.

At the top of the stairs, Taddy and Warner waited for them both. "Jesus Mary. That kiss was flippin' genius. You two make quite the couple."

Waving the photographers off after the initial round of photos, he walked Miguel into the cathedral. The nave was decorated brilliantly in white roses. The sounds of instruments playing along with the sweet smell of the flowers transported all of the week's drama far away. Lex Easton, one of his best friends for life, was getting married.

Off to the right, Miguel took him by the hand over to the St. Anthony of Padua altar. "I better go check on the groom." He was standing up for Massimo. The guys were meeting in a different vestibule.

"I'll see you at the altar."

He kissed him one more time on the lips, and they said their goodbyes. With Taddy on his arm, they walked over to the private area reserved for Lex to wait with her bridal party.

"I'm proud of Miguel. Aren't you?" he asked Taddy as they walked past another layer of additional security, finding their way to Lex. She'd roped off a dressing area near the West Fiftieth Street entrance.

"Darling, of course I am. But I'm more proud of you. You're going to move in with him."

"I'm not so sure about that."

She pulled him into a confessional booth tucked in the corner behind the Sacred Heart statue. The smell of frankincense tickled his nose.

They stood shoulder to shoulder. "Why did you do that?'

"Once we walk into Lex's dressing room, the rest of the night belongs to her. No Vive, Warner, Miguel, or your fiascos. Got it?"

"Dah. You're such a drama queen, Taddy." He turned to leave, but she put her hands on the door.

"Why wouldn't you want to move in with Miguel?"

"I can't."

"You selfish little—"

"Yes, for once I'm going to think of myself. I am not ready for another relationship. Ever since Miguel came out to his parents, he's been up my ass, literally, to have some type of Lex and Massimo love affair. Well, I can't do it again."

"Darling, if you don't grow some balls and realize Miguel is the best thing you'll ever get and embrace him, I'll—"

"Shut up, Taddy. You won't do shit. You can give relationship advice when you and Warner are living as one. Or when you've taken your parents back into your life, but until then, mind your own business."

"Whoa. That was a low blow." She pouted as they stood in silence for a minute.

"Sorry. I'm on edge today. I don't want to be here. I hate weddings, and the more Miguel sees this bridal crap, the more he's going to be farting matrimony. God, I sound more jaded than Thor." He hated being cynical, but it was true.

She cupped his face with her hands as her nose touched his. "What Diego did was disgusting. He'll answer to God when it's his time. It's in the law's hands now. You have to move on. Let love into your life again. You're allowed to be scared, but don't you dare reject Miguel. He loves you. Don't you love him?"

"Very much so. But love is not enough."

"Darling, it's one hell of a start." She stood tall, almost hitting her head in the booth. "Now, tonight, Miguel wants an answer. So, do what I always do."

"What's that?"

"Dance, have fun. Get him excited and then exhausted. He'll forget."

"I'll try. I need more time." Blake found both their conversation and its setting claustrophobic.

"You wanna wait another decade to tell him?" She turned the knob.

"That could work."

"Come on." Taddy opened the door.

"I never thought this day would come." Birdie clapped her jeweled hands in Lex's direction.

"Don't start crying again, Mom." She turned away from the full-length mirror and faced her bridal party. Taddy and Blake leaned against the far wall, both brimming with smiles and glassy eyes. "Guys, not you, too."

"Sorry." Taddy blew her nose on a hanky as Jemma came in the room with Massimo's sister, Paloma.

"My darling, you look *magnifica*. Better than I did at my first and third wedding, *si*?" Europe's hottest supermodel, Jemma always knew just what to say. "Massimo is going to die at the altar when he sees you." She put her hand on Lex's baby bump. "The both of you."

There was a knock at the door. Birdie opened it to see Jemma's two bi-sexual lovers Rocco and Luigi walk in.

"*Ciao*. We have a gift for the bride from the groom. The prince asked that you open this before the wedding." Rocco, whose eyes should've stayed on his girlfriend Jemma, stared at Blake as if he'd seen his next meal of cock.

"Talk about waiting until the last minute." Lex recognized the velvet burgundy jewelry box from Massimo's sister's store, Gems of Distinction. She looked over at Paloma who encouraged her to read the attached card out loud. "*Principessa,* this gift of brilliance will never outshine or be as flawless as you are. Forever, my perfect bride. *Ti amo.* Your Masi Salami."

Everyone howled. "He'll never change." Birdie rolled her eyes then added, "Let's hope they're not more gold handcuffs."

"My Masi." Her heart skipped when she saw the necklace inside. White diamonds in all shapes and sizes cascaded down a short platinum chain. Each stone was accented by a pink and then a smaller, yellow diamond.

"Here, let me." Taddy came up behind her, "No Photoshop needed on these pictures today, baby cakes. You are the prettiest bride. I know Eddie is looking down on us, too. I can feel his presence."

Never had Lex heard her say that before about her dad.

Birdie nodded in agreement, giving her a kiss on the cheek. "Your father is here, in spirit. I've been talking to him all day. He's as proud of you as I am."

"Oh, mom…"

"Guys, come close. Group hug." Birdie grabbed onto their hands as the music outside changed songs. She recited a quick prayer. Then they filed in line with Miguel and Warner who waited out in the hall.

Alone, Lex stood with Blake. "Thank you for giving me away." He'd been so quiet the last half-hour she had no idea what had gotten into him. She straightened his bowtie. "Are you okay?"

"That Rocco guy creeps me out." Blake's handsome face flushed.

"Rocco, Luigi, and Jemma have been a throuple for a few years now. She loves them, so be nice. Tell Thor the same. I know you two get snotty around bisexual men."

He bit his lip as if holding back criticism. "Lex, before I give you away I'd like to ask you one question. I promise I'll keep it between us."

"Shoot." She entertained him.

"Why Massimo?"

"Ahhh. You mean why am I marrying him out of all the thousands of men who threw themselves at my feet?" Actually, she couldn't remember dating any men other than Massimo.

"Yes. How did you know Massimo was the one?" Blake extended his arm to hold on to as she adjusted her shoe. The Stuart Weitzman heels sparkled.

"Truth is I hated what I knew of Massimo before I ever officially made his acquaintance. He had a horrible womanizing reputation, his company was ripping me off, and he thought his shit didn't stink. Then I met him and loathed him all the more."

"Then how did you fall in love?"

"Hook-ups aren't reserved for just you gay boys. Girls get horny, too. A one-night stand with Masi and I'd be on my way, that's all I wanted. The night we had sex, I knew he wouldn't let me go."

"Lust. You were blinded by it."

"Maybe at first, but lust fades. What was left in our afterglow of crazy monkey sex was my friendship with a man who was smart, and who respected me as much as I did him. Plus, Masi always puts me first. Without any doubt, I know he always will."

"I see." Looking puzzled, Blake didn't appear to have gotten the answer he hoped for.

Lex continued. "I knew I wanted to marry him because I can trust him with my life, kids, and business. Trust is something my parents didn't have for one another in their marriage. Sure, they loved each other, but Mom never trusted Dad."

"Yes, Birdie has mentioned it a few times."

"Masi isn't perfect. He's cocky as hell, lives life large, must be the center of attention, is driven to make money, and has the biggest dick I've ever seen." She caught herself smiling at her own words. "But then again, so do I. Well… minus the penis." She reached for her bouquet. "Thor did an amazing job with these flowers."

"He certainly did." Blake smiled at her and held the door. "Ready to get married?"

"After merging two companies together, having his baby, and another one on the way, I can without a doubt say hell yes."

The sunlight coming in from the stained glass windows highlighted a kaleidoscope of colors on her gown. She went to take the first step down the aisle, but Blake stopped her.

"Before we go, there's something I'd like to say."

Hearing the seriousness in his voice, she tried to clear her mind and gave him her undivided attention.

"Thank you for always being my best friend. You helped me through my divorce, never told my secrets, got Vive into rehab, and keep Taddy in line. Most importantly, you keep us all together as a family."

"Blake." With a gasp, she put her hand on his chest.

"I may never have a husband or kids, but having you and the girls in my life is more than I could ask for. I love you, Lex."

"Dammit. Don't make me cry before I get down the aisle." She stomped her heel. "We'll always have one another Blake. I love you, too."

The music started and the attendees stood. One step at a time, Lex walked slowly to the front, smiling at Birdie's usual guest list of Gaga, Madonna, and Beyoncé. As if a lifetime passed, she found herself looking up at Prince Massimo Tittoni. She could hear Taddy's sniveling behind her when they stood at the altar. The priest asked if anyone should object to their marriage. Jokingly, Massimo looked out at the crowd, waiting for a reply.

There wasn't one.

The mass went on for over an hour. Lex kept one hand with Massimo and another on her bump, celebrating the baby growing inside her. She thought about her father, and like Taddy and her mom had moments earlier, felt Eddie's presence in the church, too.

During the blessing of their union, she knelt down next to Massimo, leaned on the gold rail and folded her hands into a prayer. For the first time since Eddie's suicide, she addressed him.

Dad, I know you're here today, watching us. Heck, if Taddy says you're here, then so be it. My world ended when you died, but slowly it's come alive again. Thank you for looking over me and Mom, for bringing Massimo into my life, and giving me my babies. I love you, Daddy...and I forgive you for leaving us. I may never understand why you killed yourself, but one day I'll see you again, and maybe I'll get my answer. Oh, and please check in on Vive.

"*Bella*, don't cry." Massimo reached over and wiped a tear. "You okay?"

"I am now, Masi."

The night at The Plaza ballroom flew by. The couple's first dance had come and gone. Blake waltzed with Lex during what was more commonly known as the father/daughter dance to one of Eddie's ballads. Toasts were spoken and the Sylvia Weinstock seventeen-tier cake cut, served, and eaten. Mango and chocolate were the two best flavors in the bunch.

Then it was party time.

Miguel grabbed Blake's hips, gyrating him closer. It made him happy to see his friend so free and expressive. But it also made him anxious and sick. He wouldn't return home with him later as anticipated. He wondered if his friend would ever talk to him again.

Please forgive me.

He put his arms around him and tried to focus on enjoying the next hour. His last sixty minutes with his best friend before he'd dropped the F-bomb. Swinging his hips with Miguel's, he felt their cocks growing hard against each other. It was their moment in the shower all over again. Their shoulders went in and out in unison with the music.

"When you're in love, you'll know it, you'll feel it, your body will tell you." Birdie sang her chorus on stage to an excited audience. Catchy, it was a remix to one of her earlier songs from the 'eighties.

Miguel slipped his hands over the back of his ass. The lights spun around the ballroom with a flash. Then everything went dark. Pushing his chest against Miguel's, he felt his heartbeat against his chest.

"Let your body tell you what your mind fails to realize." Birdie's song sped up.

His body vibrated to the music, but it remained impossible to keep up with Miguel's insatiable Latin pace. Everything on him danced. He stepped back, letting his friend get into his groove.

The music changed out as Birdie's song came to a close and Kiki's boyfriend, DJ Dejon, spun techno. It pulsated through his body as Thor stood over at the far door, passing out favors. Guests were starting to leave.

He felt a man come up behind him to dance with him. The guy's crotch rested right at his butt. Moving to the left, the guy began to fondle him.

Oh, brother.

Blake stepped away from the stranger. He put himself in Miguel's arms to avoid the groping from behind.

"Appears you may have found your man for the three-way you have on your *Seven Desires*." Miguel smiled, looking right in his eyes with dead seriousness.

"What did you say?" The room felt as if it was spinning.

When he'd made the *Seven Desires* with Thor, it was fictitious. There weren't supposed to be any sentiments. No love. No friends. Just S-E-X. He thought for sure he might've experienced a three-way with someone he didn't know or have feelings for. He didn't imagine Miguel as his man to finish the list. He'd assumed all along that it would be with an unknown or a stranger.

Diego and his failed marriage came back at him. An open relationship was the beginning of the end. It had been easy for his ex-husband to fuck a stranger in their bed. Diego expected him to watch or join in if he wanted his husband to touch him. Sometimes, he'd even make him wear a mask so he wouldn't have to look at him. The Madonna-whore complex had amplified. But he wasn't into it. *Ever.* He was never touched. He never watched. They never talked.

Miguel leaned in and said, "Looks as if the guy behind you is interested. He keeps staring at us."

"He may have us mixed up with someone else." He rested his head against Miguel's shoulder, hoping this would stop. *Please tell me this isn't happening.*

Miguel's smile faded. "I didn't want to do a three-way. I was against it."

He pulled his head back to face him. "What—" A sudden alarm caused any words he attempted to stay wedged in his throat. He felt as if he were being choked. He assumed Miguel might push for a group sex-a-thon. How did he misgauge that?

The rumor about Miguel for years had been that he was a fucking pig with men. Blake remained surprised he hadn't been outed ages before about his sexuality. He worried Miguel would force him to have multiple partners if he stayed any longer through the week. The seconds flying by in slow motion reminded him how Diego had begged him to have a three-way. He didn't want to. It wasn't who he was. But Diego argued it would help them get back on the lovemaking wagon again.

"I never wanted to share you. But you've helped me with my parents. I'd do *this* for you," Miguel said without any doubt on his face.

He struggled to remain dancing, hoping the guy would go away behind him. Hoping Miguel would shut the fuck up. Hoping the damn song would change. Hoping the lights would come up and reveal the guy featured a hideous face with no teeth and his friend wouldn't be attracted to him. *How is he into me and then into someone else?*

"Come here." Miguel motioned for the guy. He tempted him with his Mr. Santana dominating Latin looks.

Ménage à trois will start in five seconds...

No, no, no, Shocked, Blake turned around as he was sandwiched between the two tall, hot, and sweaty muscled men. *Fuck, it's Rocco. Gorgeous. Drop-dead hot.*

Rocco's hands went around his ass and pulled him closer. Miguel's hands came up over Blake's chest, teasing him.

Pressing into them, Rocco had that look in his eyes as if asking for permission to kiss him, to join in.

Ménage à trois will start in four seconds...

Without Miguel noticing, he begged, "Go away."

Ignoring him, Rocco inched closer to Miguel. Rocco placed his arms around his shoulders and brought them all together.

Fuck. Shit. Damn.

Ménage à trois will start in three seconds...

Blake couldn't breathe. Was this how gay life would be for him? Dancing to loud bass music and being groped by Rocco in the dark while his lover watched—was that it? He didn't want it. Thor was right at lunch the other day. Lycra and lemons aside, this wasn't him. Who the hell was he kidding?

Ménage à trois will start in one second...

"Excuse me." He elbowed Rocco's chest and broke Miguel's grip. "I have to use the restroom." He didn't wait for a response or look back.

Blake darted for the main hallway to leave.

"*Blake!*" Miguel shouted after him as his heart sank. He watched him take off for the exit, unable to figure out what had gotten into him. He'd been flattered and excited to introduce him to his parents who'd come to the wedding and he'd gotten along so well with Mr. and Mrs. Morgan who'd taken off back to Connecticut about an hour before.

He was proud to have Blake on his arm.

Blake wanted a three-way; it was one of his *Seven Desires*. He sure as hell didn't want an open relationship, but he'd make the sacrifice if it was important to him. Five years without any sex was unimaginable to him. He'd pretty much resigned himself to letting Blake do whatever he desired as long as it was healthy, safe, and *he* was with him when he did it.

Rocco stepped closer and put his hands on his biceps. He leaned in as if to kiss him, but he turned his head. "I'm taken." He gritted his teeth, trying to make his displeasure evident.

"So am I. Maybe my boyfriend and girlfriend will join us later." In an attempt to be sexy, the dude glared at his body up and down then licked his lips. He put his hand on his pectoral muscles. "Nice chest."

"Sorry to have called your attention. We're not interested." He grabbed the guy's wrist and yanked it to his side. "Have a good night."

The guy frowned. "Whatever, buddy." Rocco danced himself over to another couple.

Miguel picked up speed and followed Blake down a long hallway. He passed a roped-off area and headed into where they'd had cocktail hour earlier in the night. The smaller ballroom's walls were decorated in large-scale photos. Most were Taddy and Lex as young children. At the end of the room, an oversized sepia-tone picture hung with precedence on the wall—Taddy, Lex, Vive, Blake, and himself, all in smiles.

He'd never seen the photo. Maybe eighteen at the time, they hugged one another during their freshman year at Columbia University. The others had been a tight group but welcomed Miguel with open arms.

He stopped for a second and stared at their facial expressions in more detail. Taddy was in the middle, confident as ever and facing the camera as if saying she'd rule the world one day. Vive stood to the side with her fist in the air in full party mode. Lex held up a flower to her nose, her head resting against Taddy's shoulder. He witnessed his own eyes on the cameraman. Thor had taken the picture, if he remembered correctly. Blake gazed up at Miguel as if lost in his face and couldn't care less about the picture being taken. His attention at the time was captured by...Miguel. Blake's love for him had been just as obvious then as it was now, but Miguel hadn't been ready for gay love back then.

He'd barely been able to take in his own sexuality at the age of eighteen, let alone some confident guy from Avon Porter who had it all figured out.

You had all the answers, Mr. Morgan.

Blake's confidence intimidated him back then. But since his divorce, he didn't seem as self-assured as he used to. It was as if they'd flipped roles. Diego not showing him any love had, in a way, deteriorated him from who he once was.

The double doors down the hall slammed with a loud thud, snapping his mind back into focus. He remembered they led to a small powder room Lex had used to change into bridal gowns two and three.

He approached the vestibule and turned the doorknob. Locked. He knocked and said, "Blake, open the door." He put his ear up to the engraved wood in bewilderment. Blake's heavy breathing was audible from the other side.

"Are you alone?" Blake asked through the crack between the two adjoining doors.

"*Sí…*" He'd break the door down in *tres, dos, uno.*

The door opened, and Blake peeked out into the hall over his shoulder. "I thought you would've brought Rocco back with you."

"Cut the crap." He pushed his way through, closed the door, and relocked it.

"What in the hell is the matter with you?" He stepped forward.

Blake backed up onto the sofa. He pulled a throw pillow over his lap as if uncomfortable with being in his presence.

"You said you were going to the bathroom." He studied Blake's actions with confusion.

"I was. This is a bathroom." Blake wiped his eyes, not making eye contact with him.

He stepped closer to the sofa and stood near him. "Why are you crying?"

"I need to go home. I don't want to finish my list. It's not me. I don't want a relationship with you. I'm sorry, Mig. I can't do this. I'm a boring guy from Connecticut who's not exciting." He pulled the pillow in closer.

"*Boring?* Is this how you think of yourself?"

Blake was a complex man. One not easy to know on an intimate level, but he was pretty sure he'd just figured it out. Mad he hadn't come to the conclusion earlier, he would've never agreed to help him with his sexual fantasies knowing it would torment him. It occurred to him what Diego really did. He'd ruined Blake's self-confidence to be loved.

"My ex told me I bored him." A tear-smothered voice came from his shaking lips. He glanced up for the first time revealing the hurt in his eyes.

"Now we're getting somewhere." He cupped his face in his hands. His cheeks were damp and warm. He lowered himself to sit next to him, wiping his eyes as Blake kept his lids closed. "Open your eyes for me."

Bright flecks stared up at him. *Your eyes are bluer than ever when you cry, but don't cry, Blake.*

His nose was running and his jaw was shaking as he tried to free his face from his grip. He didn't intend to let Blake go. "We only have one thing on your list left to complete. You've never mentioned it, not once." He wiped Blake's upper lip with his hand.

"I wrote my *Seven Desires* over drinks with Thor and Vive." His cry twisted into a snorted laugh. "It was their influence, a fantasy with a stranger."

"I'm no stranger." He pulled him closer.

"You're my best friend. I could never share you with another man." He spoke in a low tone, but his eyes remained steady.

"*Bueno*, because I don't want to share you," he confessed, feeling glad they were having the conversation. In truth, he had pulled Rocco on the dance floor to test Blake.

"What?" Blake's tears dried.

"I told you what I wanted, yet you pushed me away." His intentions were relentless. He was going to get what was his and what he'd wanted.

"I'm scared you'll change your mind. You'll wake up one day and want something else...as Diego did."

His friend's mouth dipped into a deeper frown, one he didn't think was possible. Blake sat up to leave, giving off the vibe he found their conversation futile, not expecting it to go anywhere.

But he pulled Blake's face closer to his and looked deep into his eyes. "I've wanted you for the last ten years." Realizing that was when Blake usually walked off, he lifted his right leg up and over Blake's lower body, locking him in and keeping him from going anywhere.

Blake's back fell against the pillows.

He declared, "I'm confident I won't waiver on my dedication to you."

"Really?" Blake's eyebrows drew up as one.

"I am *not* MLD. I'm not going to use you for your money. I have my own. I promise you, I will never do the sick things that man has done."

White teeth flashed. He wasn't quite there yet, as he sensed Blake held back.

"I don't have intimacy issues, either."

"*Shush.*" Blake put his hand over Miguel's lips. "I haven't been honest about what I want from you. Remember when I said my ex invited strangers over to our house twenty-four-seven? He rubbed my face in it."

It pained him to hear this again. "*Sí.* But you're okay now. That's all that matters."

"I don't feel okay. I feel foolish for wanting something so traditional. I know I have to let that dream go."

"Why?"

"'Cause it's not part of our culture. Gay marriage is silly. Monogamy between two men is unrealistic."

Blake sounded like so many of the men he'd been with over the years. Jaded.

"You want conventional," he muttered under Blake's fingers. He kissed his pointer then his middle finger.

"Don't laugh. I know you're a playboy, Mig."

"Perhaps at one time I was." He didn't have any answers for why he'd gone with the flow. Why he hadn't stood up to Diego years before. Why he hadn't confessed his love for Blake earlier. His value system was the same as Blake's all along. He'd just taken the long road to get there.

"Having one partner your whole life seems insane. I know, what, maybe twenty gay couples? None are exclusive. But it's what *I've* always wanted. It's just not meant to be." Blake reeked of hopelessness.

He removed Blake's hand from his lips with a nipping bite. "I'm not laughing." He kissed his hand again and held on to it. "Do you remember at the Exhale Bliss Spa, I told you I didn't think you knew me very well?" He pushed his body up over his as they became horizontal. With forceful intention, he rested his weight down over him. His friend's face reddened as he squirmed.

Blake rolled his watery eyes. "I know you."

"No, *bebé*, you don't. You've never asked me what I want in a relationship. You based my future on my past."

"Meaning?" Blake locked his feet with his, accepting his captivity.

"There's no one I'd rather have more than you. I've wanted you my entire life. I'll *only* want *you*."

"Promise?" Blake sounded tentative-optimistic.

"*Us* was my whole goal this week. Not to break in your ass, though your virgin bottom was tempting. I wanted to show you my heart." He glided his thumb over Blake's right eyebrow. "Show you how much I've always wanted you and still do." A deep peace came over him, one he'd hoped for and struggled to secure for as long as he could remember. "You're very special to me, and I can't imagine my life without you."

"I love you, Mig. I always have." Blake leaned up and continued, "I don't want to get hurt."

"I love you, too." He wrapped Blake in his arms and sank his tongue into his mouth with a passionate kiss. He closed his eyes for a second, allowing himself to experience something new—love. He made love bites at his neck and then said, "I won't ever hurt you, unless you want me to." He laughed at his BDSM implication.

"So, we can be piggy with one another...but no one else."

"That's *my* dream."

He heard the door open and turned a frown toward whoever was intruding on their intimate moment.

"There you two are. Stop fucking and come outside!" Thor shouted, flicking the bathroom lights on and off.

"Why outside?" he asked.

"Massimo has a fireworks show across the street in Central Park. Let's go."

"Of course he does." He helped Blake to his feet and asked, "You okay?"

"Yes, I'm better than okay. Wanna know why?"

"Why?"

"Because I'm moving in with you."

His heart felt as it was a part of the fireworks, exploding with joy as he embraced Blake.

They ran out of The Plaza, crossed the street, and went into Central Park just as the first burst of firecrackers lit the sky. He held Blake's hand. Instead of looking up at the sky, he glanced out at his friends. Taddy and Warner kissed passionately as if they'd just met. Lex and Massimo danced to the cheers of onlookers and Birdie Easton stared at him for a second before extending a thumbs-up to say he'd done A-Okay.

Epilogue

Thank You, Paloma Tittoni

One Week Later in Sitges, Spain

On Miguel's thirtieth birthday, the first he'd celebrated since he was a kid, he held his boyfriend's hand and walked down the sandy beach. His Barcelona exhibit was a triumph. His parents, along with Inez, Cierra, and Ofielia, came to Spain. Mr. and Mrs. Morgan came and attempted to buy up the art which didn't sell within the first hour. To his fortune, the art gallery owner had pre-sold the pieces; about eighty percent of them. The New York tabloids hit with pictures of Blake on his arm after the royal wedding, tagging Miguel Santana as their generation's Salvador Dali. Diego's trial was set to begin in three months, and Vive had only tried to leave rehab once. But she went right back in and kept at it.

There was only one more thing he needed before he'd be at complete bliss.

He stopped and gripped Blake's hips, pulling his long legs close. He wouldn't let him run away. Barefoot, he pressed his toes over Blake's in the sand, keeping him captive.

"Mig," he said, wiggling. Blake's cheeks flushed, creating a contrast against his fair skin.

"I need to ask you something." He felt hot tears fall down his cheeks as a knot formed in stomach.

Wiping his face, Blake asked, "I've never seen you cry. Isn't that my job? We've celebrated your success every night this week here in Spain. Why the tears?"

His boyfriend was clueless as usual.

"You said you'd never get married again." As the words began to run together to form a sentence, he gathered his usual confidence, remembering the toast he'd made to his family at his coming-out dinner, to live life. "But I'm hoping this time it'll stick."

Blake's jaw hung open. "Miguel—"

"Mr. Morgan...I've loved you since the first day I met you." He dug into his pocket and pulled out a gold band. Holding it in his hand, the metal shimmered against the sunset as a promise for a good tomorrow. "Will you marry me?"

His boyfriend's brows arched up in surprise. After a few silent moments he said, "Under one condition."

"Anything..."

"I want a baby within our first year together," Blake pressed on.

He felt light on his feet.

"*Sí*, of course." He didn't imagine the Santana-Morgan family starting off any other way.

"Then *yes*, I'll marry you!"

Miguel kissed him and slipped the ring on his finger. It was a perfect fit.

"Is this from the Paloma Tittoni gem store?"

He laughed and hugged his fiancé.

The End

Acknowledgments

Muchas gracias, Señor Manuel for inspiring my beloved Mexican hero Miguel Santana in *Unsaid*. You are *mucho caliente*. I love you more than Tucson. Thank you, Dom Edward and Master Elliot for all of your fisting, electricity, and water sports advice because this novel wouldn't be the same without your BDSM insights. As always, huge hugs to my lifelong friend Julie, since my characters would be lost without you and so would I. Many kudos to my beta-readers, Nicole, Chrissy, Jackie, Jodie, Kateria, Jenifer, and everyone on Wattpad.

As well as to the book reviewers at S&M's Book Obsessions, I Love Lady Porn, Harlequin Junkies, Book Whores, Kricket's Chirps, Under the Covers, Midwest Book Reviews, The Book Enthusiast, We Love Kink, Romance Reviews Today, Ever After Romance, Swept Away by Romance, USA Today Happily Ever After, Reviews by Crystal, Storm Goddess, and Please Another Book for the wonderful media coverage on *The Manhattanites* series.

Great appreciation to Marisa Corvisiero, an amazing literary agent and lawyer who wears designer smarty pants and I adore you for it. Thank you J.B. for putting up with me while I write. Courtney Howell, I enjoyed the crack of your whip, and I thank you kindly. Big hugs to Chris Jacen who critiqued an earlier version of this manuscript, Stacy D. Holmes, and Kristin at Hot Tree Editing for your amazing editorial services. Your feedback changed Blake's life from drab to fab. And to my family and friends who championed this novel: George, Pauline, Adam, Julie, Bailee, Sara, Kelly, Shari, Pat, Hector, Lynn, Michele, Holly, Nackie and Shane…love you, always.

About Avery Aster

New York Times bestselling author Avery Aster pens *The Manhattanites*, a contemporary erotic romance series of full-length, stand-alone novels, and the naughty new adult prequel companion series *The Undergrad Years*.

As a resident of New York City and a graduate from New York University, Avery gives readers an inside look at the city's glitzy nightlife, socialite sexcapades and tall tales of the über-rich and ultra-famous.

Connect with Avery

Newsletter: http://eepurl.com/CQ665

Facebook: http://www.FaceBook.com/AveryAster

Twitter: http://www.Twitter.com/AveryAster

Goodreads: http://www.goodreads.com/AveryAster

Instagram: https://instagram.com/averyaster

Pinterest: http://www.Pinterest.com/AveryAster

Tumblr: http://www.averyaster.tumblr.com

Tsū: http://www.tsu.co/AveryAster

Website: http://www.AveryAster.com

Also by Avery Aster

A Smexy Excerpt

Craving more of *The Manhattanites*? Enjoy the first two chapters of *Unconventional*.

Unconventional

by Avery Aster

From the NYT Bestselling author of *The Manhattanites* series and for fans of such films as *Vicky Cristina Barcelona* and *Wild Things* comes a ménage romance posing the question; can two men share the same woman forever?

They are the best of friends and the greatest of lovers. Two men and one woman, searching for fortune and fame, bound together by an eroticism their money and power can't buy them. *Luigi*, the romantic alpha hunk. *Rocco,* the exotic bisexual. *Jemma*, the insatiable beauty who possesses them both.

From their first rendezvous in Milan, the three set out on a wicked course, jet-setting from the kinky underground sex clubs of Berlin, to the lavish palaces of Moscow, to New York's high society in pursuit of pleasure. They have only each other to care for. That is...until a baby comes along and changes their destiny.

But which of them is the father? And will they continue their poly relationship or give in to convention?

Special Gratitude To

Pamela, Susan, Lisa, Britany, and Risa!

Avery Aster

Cast of Characters

Major Players

Luigi Bova (39): Jemma and Rocco's rich and powerful lover who operates the Girasoli Garment Company. He'll do anything to have Jemma's hand in marriage and give her the stability she's always yearned for. But will it be at Rocco's expense or his own?

Rocco Cazzo (29): Hunk du jour and making no apologies about it, he's the House of Tittoni's estate manager. Enjoying being with his first and only girlfriend, Jemma, he desperately wants to have children and start a family.

Jemma Fereti (37): A former supermodel turned fashion designer at Girasoli Garments. As a breast cancer survivor, she lives life to the fullest, especially when it comes to loving two men at the same time.

Supporting Cast

Lex Easton (30): Owner of Easton Essentials, she's a fashionista who's married to Prince Massimo Tittoni and doing her best to keep the fashion empire she co-created relevant.

Prince Massimo (36): Husband to Lex, CEO of Girasoli Garments, royal heir to the House of Tittoni and ruler of Isola di Girasoli. He's Luigi, Rocco, and Jemma's boss.

Taddy Brill (30): A diva millionaire who dates billionaire Warner Truman. She is the owner of Brill, Inc., the PR firm which promotes Jemma Couture. Whatever Taddy says, goes!

Blake Morgan III (29): Engaged to his boyfriend, Miguel Santana, he graduated from Columbia University and works as Managing Partner at Brill, Inc. He's doing his best to keep Jemma calm.

Vive Farnworth (30): A former party girl and heiress to Farnworth Firewater liquors. She's the Editor-in-Chief of *Debauchery* Magazine who writes the nasty review which could ruin Jemma's career.

The Companies

Jemma Couture: Europe's most exclusive high-end fashion line for women. It retails to all the luxury boutiques in the world.

Girasoli Garment Company: A one-hundred-year-old textile manufacturer and owner of Jemma Couture. They also own Easton Essentials.

Brill, Inc.: A Fortune 500 company and New York's eminent fashion and beauty public relations and branding firm, which is retained by Girasoli Garments.

Debauchery **Magazine**: Read by four million people weekly, covering all things salacious in the fashion, beauty and celebrity arena.

The Locations

Isola di Girasoli: A Mediterranean island south of Sicily and east of Tunisia. Formerly the Republic of Girasoli, today it is united with Italy. It is one-hundred-twenty-five square miles accessible via boat or air. In the eighteenth century, it was founded as a sunflower plantation, and today it is a resort and casino vacation destination.

Milan: Home to such fashion super-brands as Prada, Armani and Dolce & Gabbana, Milan remains the world's fashion capital. Its elite fashion district is the "*quadrilatero della moda*" and the city's common area has a population of about 1.3 million. It is the headquarters for Girasoli Garment Company and the location for the House of Tittoni's estate.

Manhattan: Its population is about 1.5 million (excluding all areas off the island). It is the launch pad for such iconic fashion designers as Donna Karan, Calvin Klein, Betsey Johnson, Michael Kors, Marc Jacobs and countless others. It is the headquarters for Easton Essentials, Brill Inc, *Debauchery* Magazine and the US offices of Jemma Couture.

Avery Aster

Author's Note

Dear Readers,

Luigi, Rocco, and Jemma were introduced as part of the supporting cast in my novel, *Undressed* (Massimo & Lex). They're back with more drama, Italian style and getting their own story. This time, Jemma gets pregnant. Unsure which boyfriend is the father, will this be the end of their poly relationship or just the beginning? Find out in *Unconventional*.

Love,

Avery

LET'S

a love poem

I'LL…unease you, totally tease you

MEN…look at me, want to make love to me

WOMEN…want to be me, hate me

Let's not dance around the subject

YOU…may lust after me, maybe even marry me,
I'll carry your baby

HOW DID WE…veer this far left, get so fucked
up

WE…started the relationship out so right, ended
so wrong

Let's try again

MAKE.....your dreams come true, alleviate your
worst fears

PLEASE…warm my heart, try not to smash it,
too

Let's mend our broken hearts

FLASHBACKS…to our passionate nights, to
when you found me

AS LOVERS…we know no shame, we don't place blame, we have this secret place in time

NEVER…hesitate to be the one, take my soul apart

Let's set our secrets free

FEELS LIKE…something so right, total submission and satisfaction

THESE DREAMS…like perfume on my wrist, are closer than this

YOU SAY…I'm crazy, that I'm in the danger zone

Let's open the door

I KNOW…I'm loving like never before, we belong together

MANY TIMES…I feel alone without you at my side, I speak of aberrant behavior

ARE YOU…hot tonight, feeling naughty

I…want you, gotta have you

YOU ARE MY…devotion, lover

LET'S…be forever

Part One

A Girl Just Wants To Have Fun!

THE MANHATTANITES

love, friendship, scandal, and drama to the hilt

"Since Jemma's cancer diagnosis, we often compare her to silent screen goddess Jean Harlow or late heartthrob River Phoenix. She lives life in the fast lane, enjoying each day as it comes. I know she fears that one day it'll end. Maybe that's why getting tied down with two husbands and a baby wasn't on her short list of things to do. But as any fabulous Manhattanite will tell you, life is a challenge—meet it head-on. Life is a dream—own your desires. Life is a gift—keep giving to others. Life is love—open your heart."—Taddy Brill, CEO of Brill, Inc., girlfriend to Big Daddy, and overall bestie to Lex, Blake, and Vive.

Chapter One

Jemma, Will You Marry Us?

Luigi
Three Months Ago
Isola di Girasoli, Mediterranean Sea

On top of the cliff, overlooking the blue sea, I grabbed my boyfriend's hand, pulled him to my side and asked, "Ready, *bello*?"

Rocco's short nails grazed my skin. He'd been biting them all week. He always did when he was nervous.

"Jemma is going to say yes..." he whispered in my ear.

"*Sì*, of course she is."

A few days before, we'd selected the spot.

He'd suggested, "This is where we'll ask her to marry us,"

I'd agreed.

The view, the place... so magical and *perfetto*.

Inhaling deeply, I smelled the briny air filled with the faint sticky aroma of sunflowers. The ground was covered in them, and Isola di Girasoli had even been named after them. Growing on vivid green stalks, their bright yellow faces open, reaching up to the white sky for warmth and light. They were gleefully rooted about, almost as if cheering us on.

In a way, Rocco and I were similar to those flowers reaching for something—nourishment and love.

We got down on our knees, and the warm soil pressed under my legs. Glancing up at the woman we loved, we each took her hand.

Jemma Fereti. Tall. Striking. Ours. We called her *dolce* because she always tasted like tiramisu when we kissed.

As I studied her finger, the one I'd put the ring on, I thought about us…

For me, taking Jemma as my bride, and Rocco as my groom, meant forever. My life spent searching for intention would soon be complete. Together they made up my everything.

For Rocco, our union symbolized something he'd yearned for: a family.

Hopefully for Jemma it would mean peace after her year-long battle with breast cancer.

"*Amore*, go on. Ask her." Patience wasn't Rocco's virtue.

"Give me a minute—"

In private, we'd talked about the day for the past few months. We'd picked out the perfect engagement ring: a Tittoni Gems of Distinction twelve-carat pink diamond, a custom-made work of art from Manhattan for Jemma. And two simple gold bands for Rocco and myself. We'd planned the vacation: a week alone on the island, getting time away. Only the three of us. This was one of Jemma's favorite Mediterranean locals. She'd grown up there with her royal friend, Prince Massimo Tittoni, who ruled over the small country.

Having Jemma's hand in marriage was all Rocco and I ever desired. Over the past few years, we'd loved each other as a thruple. Our special togetherness had been all her doing.

Never in my wildest dreams had I imagined an open poly relationship with one woman and another man working out. Certain jealousy and games would poison the affair, but it hadn't tarnished our lovemaking in the least.

That is till now. Rocco yearned for more, and frankly, so did I. Especially when Prince Massimo granted the Poly Marriage Act, legalizing the rights for those who loved openly to wed.

"*Dolce*…we'd like to ask you something…" I got the words out. I wasn't one to talk much. Regardless, Rocco had insisted it come from me. After all, I'd been with Jemma for almost a year before we'd met him.

My boyfriend was the well-spoken one. The one in touch with his feelings. The man who'd glued the three of us together in ways which went beyond the boundaries of sex. He was the first and only man I'd ever had sex with, and I liked it. Oh, God, I fucking loved it! I loved *him*.

"My *amore*—" Uncertainty quivered in Jemma's voice.

My left hand reached deep inside my pocket. I pulled out the diamond and held it up to her, sparkling in the sunshine, and asked, "Will you marry us?"

With a smile, Rocco's face beamed.

Her mouth dropped open, asking, "Huh?" Deep grooves etched her high forehead. Her eyes, usually varying shades of amber, dilated to black. The lips I loved kissing—full and sensual—had evaporated into her mouth as she chewed on them, clearly unsure how to respond.

Hearing the quick intake of Rocco's breath, he bit on his nails for a second before blurting out, "Luigi and I love you. We want to spend the rest of our lives with you. Let's share every day together. Start a family. Grow old with each other. *Dolce*, what do you say?"

My girlfriend cupped his face in her hands, her darkly painted nails gliding over his olive skin. She stared at him as if searching for what to say before reaching down, pressing her lips against his, and replying with a kiss.

One could get lost in Rocco's face: a square jawline, thick eyebrows which framed his intense eyes, and a dimple on each cheek. He was the sexiest man I'd ever laid eyes on.

Kind and loving.

"My darling, you know since my chemo I cannot conceive a child."

"We can adopt. Get a surrogate," he defended, enthusiasm bubbling in his voice about all of the options we had before us. "We can afford to do whatever you want."

Money for us wasn't a problem. When it came to living the luxury lifestyle—private jets, fast cars, fierce clothes, gourmet food—we had it all. Working for Girasoli Garment Company and the House of Tittoni had afforded us that much.

"I love you both and would like nothing more than to share the rest of my life with you. We have a *buono* thing going."

"What better reason than for us to marry?" Determined, he got to his feet and then helped me up.

Putting my arms around them, the three of us brought our foreheads together as one. This felt good, us embracing and talking about our future.

Her long eyelashes fluttered. Avoiding eye contact, her attention cast on our feet.

Our toes were covered in sand crystals. We'd been at the beach all day drinking Bellinis, making love.

"Why do you two wanna screw this up with marriage?" Almost contemptuously, the "m" word came out of her mouth as she clenched her jaw.

Oh, boy...

Irritated, I shifted my weight from one foot to another as my mind spun with bewilderment. I knew she'd be resistant for how this would play out, but Rocco and I had the answers. All she had to do was try.

Just say yes.

In the past, Jemma had filled our ears with stories of how her parents had fought till her mother had dropped dead from a heart attack. Mr. and Mrs. Fereti's marriage wasn't anything to emulate. It'd caused Jemma to avoid confrontation and commitment over the years at all cost. As a result, she rarely got deep with us, instead focusing on her fashion designer career, hot sex, and her Manhattanite friends.

"You're cancer-free now. It's time for us to get on with our lives," I reminded, hoping she'd celebrate life and not fear it. For the past year, time had stood still for all three of us.

We'd been with Jemma through every phase of her breast cancer, from her first diagnosis to her mastectomy, radiation, and reconstructive surgery. Each step of the way we'd been at her side, taking care of her. How could she not see "forever" with us? Surely, we saw our future with her.

Baffled and starting to get nauseous over the fact she even questioned our proposal, a bitter taste came up in the back of my throat.

We weren't losing her. Were we?

"I'm living my life with you two. That's enough for me. We don't need *marriage* to make our relationship any more official, Luigi. Weddings ruin everything." Her mind seemed to whirl. She rubbed her temples for a minute before saying, "And we don't need to have babies either, Rocco."

I glanced over at him, his almond-shaped eyes glistening. He was the emotional one, so I comforted. "Don't...cry." Wiping my cheek with my thumb I then kissed him.

His body trembled, leaning into me. All muscle, Rocco appeared strong and firm on the outside, like pasta cooked *al dente*, but on the inside, he was sensorial. Unlike any man I'd ever met. *Don't get me wrong. He's not weak, just hypersensitive.*

"What's gotten into you two?" The tone in her voice set alarm bells ringing as she became increasingly uneasy.

Surprised by her reply, I didn't have an answer.

She continued. "I knew this vacation would bring us closer together, but we're here to relax and unwind. Not get stressed out about our future. A piece of paper saying we love one another means nothing about how we're to spend the rest of our lives."

"How can you say that?" he asked.

"What matters is how we treat each other while in this relationship." With a toss of her head, she tried to laugh the whole topic off, that famous supermodel smile on her face.

Regardless, I could see right through her. It was as if someone else stood before us.

Jemma was terrified of commitment.

I'd seen her behave as such before. Not often.

It was the same face she had the day she'd confessed to being in love with Rocco. Regardless, I accepted him. I'd not only grown to love him, but in time became madly in love with him, too. There would never be another man for me other than Rocco. I wasn't gay when I'd met him.

Merda, at times I don't think I'm even a bisexual, because I don't look at other guys. Rocco is the only man who turns me on. However, I guess that's why one calls me "bi" although I'm not fond of that term. I hate any sexual orientation labels, such as homo, hetero, bi, etc.

I'm a man who loves a woman.

I'm a man who also loves another man.

That's all that matters to me!

It was also the same face she had when the doctor had told her she had cancer.

We'd detected it early. Rocco had found the lump just under the lower part of her breast as we'd been giving her a massage that night. He was the one who'd demanded she go see a doctor. I didn't know where we'd be without him.

She'd beaten cancer. Her will to live, and the early diagnosis, had given her a good chance for survival. *Jemma Fereti is the strongest woman I know. An original. There's no one like her.*

Words... I didn't have any. I struggled for what to say next. Uncertainty aroused deep inside me, which was a first. Usually I was in control, knew what I want, and got it, too. But right then? Nothing appeared to be working in my favor.

"*Dolce*, Luigi and I are serious." Rocco's voice rose. Arching his back, he continued, "He's going to ask you one more time. Give us your answer, *per favore*."

A sense of hope made me focus as I repeated, "Will you marry us?"

In silence, we waited.

Over the cliff, the wind blew in from the ocean upon us. Jemma's black hair had been growing back since her therapy, and it covered her eyes. Rocco bit his nails faster the longer he couldn't see her face.

Her chin turned up a bit, causing the sun to cast a halo over her. Since the day we'd met, she'd been our angel, our white light for happiness.

Today, will all that change?

Every fiber of my body tensed, and I hated the feeling. Usually I was a confident man.

"No...I can't...I won't. There's no need or room for marriage in our lives." She placed the palm of her delicate hand on Rocco's broad chest. "If you want children so badly, you have my permission to have another woman carry your baby. Regardless, I don't think I have much left in me to give to a child, not after what I've been through. Being a mom takes a lot of energy. You'll need to raise that child on your own or with Luigi."

His tan skin illuminated with tears, flooding his face. He pushed his wavy, black hair behind his ears.

My heart broke. I hated to see him suffer.

"And Luigi, if you want to wed, take Rocco's hand in marriage. The two of you can sign the papers. Nevertheless, my darling, it's not going to change anything between us. I love what we have, but if matrimony is what you want—some lifetime guarantee—I won't stand in your way of happiness."

Taking in what she'd said, I dipped my chin in acknowledgment but gave no reply.

"I'm sorry, *amore*," she mouthed in my direction.

Breathe. Just breathe.

I couldn't.

Her refusal was as if I was hearing the doctor say she'd had breast cancer all over again.

Out of the corner of my eyes, I only saw black. A sense of grave hopelessness washed over my optimistic spirit. I didn't think it was possible to feel a chill in the warm sun, on that beautiful island, and surrounded by evergreen. Nevertheless, I did. As if we were in the Arctic, snow falling upon us.

"Our *happiness* is with you, Jemma." In a numb voice, I reminded her how important she was to us, and then kissed her on the lips.

When her mouth broke from mine, she whispered in my ear, "Can we go on…with what we have?"

I pulled back and asked, "What do you mean?"

"The three of us, loving each other. Even if that means you won't be calling me your wife or the mother of your children?"

Alarmingly, my pulse skittered. Clenching my jaw, I realized we were making compromises about our relationship. My eyes snapped shut, trying to block out the truth that I wanted marriage, to see Rocco be a *padre*. Lying through my teeth, I answered, "*Sì*, I'm sure."

I don't have the heart to call it quits. Not now. Probably not tomorrow, either.

"*Grazie*, I love you." Her slender hand slinked behind the back of my neck as relief graced her lips in the expression of a smile.

Chest rising, inhaling through my mouth, I attempted to return the gesture but couldn't.

Sad. Pissed off. This wasn't how love was supposed to go. Was it? However, I couldn't see my life without her.

Together, we faced Rocco.

His nose shiny, red.

"*Bello*, can't we just keep things the way they are?" she asked.

"Give me some time to process this—" He turned into himself. "I don't know what I want. But I *do* know I don't want to be without you two."

A yearning of wanting it to work, more than ever, rocketed through me. Rocco was so vulnerable. He needed us, and we needed him. Didn't Jemma see how we couldn't live without her?

As we watched Jemma head back to our private oasis on the beach, I slipped the diamond into my front pocket. The ring would never adorn *dolce's* finger.

The pain in my heart, as if I'd just been stabbed, made it hard to even look at Rocco. I should've stood my ground. But who gives their girlfriend an ultimatum when proposing marriage? I didn't expect it to turn out like this. Such a disaster.

The hand he'd been nervously biting started to bleed. I reached for it, giving him a squeeze.

"One day this isn't going to be enough for me. I want more for my life. I deserve it, too," he said and hugged me.

"I know you do, *bello*," I muttered. "I do, too."

We'd just said our piece to move on in our own life directions. Maybe not that day. Maybe not the next. However, someday, the notion of not getting married and having children with Jemma might destroy Rocco and me if we stayed in the relationship for too long.

Chapter Two

Damn Vive Farnworth! My career is O-V-E-R

Jemma
Present Day
The Girasoli Garment Company Corporate Office, Milan, Italy

Merda!

On a scale from one to ten. One being…craporama. Ten being…the effin' fudgesicle worst day of my cat-litter stinking life. That day, the day after my couture fashion collection had hit the European runways, I, Jemma Fereti, former runway supermodel turned fashion designer, was having an eleven.

Yup. That's way worse than smelling cat pee. Trust me.

Damn that Vive Farnworth at Debauchery *magazine and her nasty ass editorial.*

With my cell in my hand, I glared at the article on the screen so hard I thought my corneas would surely catch on fire. Or worse, my eyeballs might just pop out of their socket and soar across the room as two Ping-Pong balls, bouncing off Lex, Taddy, and Blake, who stood before me.

Vive's headline read, *"Jemma Couture's NEW Fashion Collection is Shit."*

That was exactly what it said. *Shit.* Clear as the Tuscan sun and to the point. I plus fashion equals…poop.

My fashion collection that season which I'd so fondly titled Death Star Galactica was a failure.

This was bad. So very bad.

Almost as horrific as the time I'd learned my career as Europe's highest paid runway model was over. Dead in the water. Overnight, I'd become…unbookable. Why? Cause I'd turned thirty-frickin'-five. The fashion industry was ruthless. Hence why that afternoon I was freaking the fudge out.

Almost as bad as the time my *madre* had passed away and I'd told my *padre* at the funeral that I was in a poly relationship with two of the most wonderful men on the planet.

I'd thought he'd be happy for me. Didn't he want to see my needs were being taken care of? That I was A-Okay.

Umm. No!

Giving an ultimatum, he'd argued, "I didn't spend over a million dollars, put you in Milano's best schools, and raise you to be a *signora* to have you turn into the laughingstock of Italy. You're not a whore. Either *they* go or *I* do."

Cool as gelato, I'd kept calm, but had eventually lost my patience and declared, "*Padre*, I didn't survive a double mastectomy and reconstructive surgery in my thirties to have you tell me how to live my friggin' life. *Arrivederci.*"

The Big C and little ta-ta was what I had. *But the Big C and little ta-ta isn't who I am. No fucking way, my darlings. I refuse to let it define me. I'm a fighter. I'm a survivor.*

Regardless, my heart broke that day my *padre* had protested my relationship. He'd never understand, so we hadn't talked since. Did I miss him? *Sì.* But I had to live my life by *my* rules, not his. Maybe I was selfish. After my diagnosis and treatment, I realized life goes by in a blink, and it's too short to not do as you please. *And I am doing exactly that.*

Which leads me to the third worst moment of my so-called fabulous life. I already told 'ya what it was…

That day was almost as scary as the time the doctor had said, "Jemma, you have breast cancer." Mentally, I'd never recovered from the mastectomy. Physically, Milan's top plastic surgeon had reconstructed my breasts after I'd kicked the Big C in the ass. To be honest, they looked better than they did before the diagnosis. Implants. Never thought I'd have two artificial silicone pillows put in me, but damn, they look fucking fabulous.

I have been cancer-free for the two years. *Knock on wood.* My breasts seem and sometimes feel real, but having mine removed wasn't just a shock to my system. Cancer had destroyed my sense of self. My boyfriends don't see the fear I have: that it'll come back, that one day I could get sick again. I wouldn't survive the next time around, I already knew it. *More about that later. Much later. I need to keep my mind on work.*

One would think after having their father disown them, experiencing the career highs and lows I have, and battling breast cancer I wouldn't get that stressed out—not anymore. After all, this is Death Star Galactica. Only fashion, not world peace. Regardless, I was indeed stressed.

Sì, it was the fourth worst day of my life. For sure.

I stood in front of my colleague's desk, Lex Easton. The day before, she'd flown in from Manhattan to help me with the fashion show.

"This is…horrible." Slouched over the keyboard, she glared at the local newspaper and shrieked for the umpteenth time, "Horrible!"

Oh, all right. I should be honest and state it wasn't only *Debauchery* magazine which had slammed my latest work. No, my darlings! How about the *Milano News, New York Times, London Herald,* and *Paris Tribune* to boot. Pretty much every blog, newspaper, magazine, and TV station from New York to Timbuktu had ripped my latest creations to pieces. *I'm ruined. Ruined, I tell you.*

"Say something!" I shouted around the room at everyone, resting my eyes upon Taddy Brill.

Strikingly gorgeous. Think Rita Hayworth. Unusually tall. The woman radiates beauty even during moments of high client drama, such as this one. Figures. That's why she works in public relations.

Taddy owns the PR firm the Girasoli Garment Company retains to promote our brands, Easton Essentials and Jemma Couture. In hopes of saving me from the catastrophe, she'd jetted in from New York after the Milan show tanked with her business partner, Blake Morgan. *Miracles do happen, so per favore, God, I for sure need one.*

"Give me a minute. I'm...thinking."

She wouldn't even make eye contact with me.

You know it's bad when your own publicist can't even stand the sight of you. I'd love to curl up into a ball right now, stuff my face with a fist full of Mint Milano cookies, and die. Just die, I tell you.

She hid behind her thick, wavy, gorgeous red hair, and picked at her long acrylic nails. I wanted to shake her like a piggybank but instead of coins falling out, I'd be loaded with ideas on how to fix my fashion line.

"Tsk. Tsk." Blake, Taddy's cohort, stood next to her. He kept making this annoying noise, shaming me with his beautiful lips as if I were a poodle who'd just taken a whiz on the carpeting. I was tempted to smack his cute face.

I couldn't take it anymore. The silence was choking me, so I had to ask.

"Are you going to fire me?"

Air caught in my throat the second that question left my mouth. In fear my legs would buckle, I leaned against the edge of Lex's desk and crossed my arms. I was either going to black out or vomit. Hopefully not pass out in my own vile. *God, that would suck.*

Girl, brace yourself.

While I waited for Lex's reply, the room started to spin and my peripheral vision blurred. I could already hear her saying, "Fuck yes, you stupid cow."

The woman has a major potty mouth, FYI.

Without notice, Lex inhaled so loudly, I thought her nostrils might snort up the ivory damask wallpaper decorating the office. Then she said, "If you weren't my hubbies life-long friend, a woman I respected, and cared for as family…then yes, Jemma, I'd have no choice but to terminate your role as the lead designer on Jemma Couture."

"On the very label I created?"

She nodded. "If Perry Ellis can fire Marc Jacobs for his grunge collection, we can definitely terminate you over Death Star Galactica."

"Jil Sander has left her own line three times already," Blake added.

"That's by her own accord," I clarified, wondering if she'd been pushed out of her own company. Sure, I'd heard of it happening in our industry. But to me? I mean really!

This was complete and utter malarkey. I called bullshit.

Jemma Couture had been a huge hit when it launched a few years back. It had all started on a scandal: a see-through, nude dress bedazzled in thousands of Swarovski crystals which Lex had worn the night she got caught screwing Prince Massimo by paparazzi. That dress and those images had launched her as a fashion icon and me as the designer who'd created it.

Gowns start at around ten thousand dollars. We've dressed the First Lady of the United States as well as Meryl, Julia, and many other starlets for the Academy Awards. Using only the best Italian fabrics was our trademark. That and sexy, revealing silhouettes. We were hot.

Were being the keyword there.

Frickin' A.

"The one my husband and I funded." Lex pulled her shiny blonde hair back behind her ear and cleared her throat. "You know in this fashion industry, one bad season may ruin a brand."

"Then I'll resign from the company—" Hot, wet tears streaked down my face. I couldn't believe this was happening.

"Let's not be drastic," Blake interrupted and made his way over to me. "I may not have a vagina, but I know why women buy this brand."

Spearheading many of the lifestyle accounts alongside Taddy, Blake was a branding guru. Aside from his wit and intelligence, he was rather famous amongst New York City's society.

"Why?" Taddy and Lex asked simultaneously.

"Because they want to feel feminine and beautiful when wearing Jemma Couture. Tell us what exactly you were thinking with those military jumper pants?"

Insulted, I tried to stay strong and answered, "Those are raspberry mocha space gowns. Not pants. There's a seam up the front."

"Yes, Miss Thing, a seam which splits the bottom of the dress into a pair of pants. Hello." His bright blue eyes rolled dramatically at my reply. He sassed on, reading me to fashion designer shame.

"Err...I guess I kind of went off on one of my creative tangents and lost track of the Jemma Couture consumer."

Usually when I veered off course, the ending would come out fabulous. The previous year's ostrich feathers with gold-plated caviar beading was a colossal hit, and *Harper's Bazaar* had hailed it the gown of the century. But the military trooper dress, not so much.

"What was your inspiration for this collection?" The head of Brill, Inc. dipped her head in my direction.

"Star Wars is coming back to the big screen this year and I got excited about the outer space fantasy, so I ran with it. I wanted us to be edgy. You know...different. Hence Death Star Galactica." I said the name of the season's collection proudly. Dammit, I still had a sense of pride.

"Ohhh. The collection is *different* all right. Try 'not wearable'. And having the models carry machine guns was over the top," Lex stated.

"Those were laser guns," I defended. "They shot confetti, adding a layer of surprise to the show."

Everyone stared at me as if I'd lost my mind.

"Hey now." I sighed. "It's not my fault when the guns went off the entire front row of attendees got scared and hit the floor, hiding under their seats."

"Bitch, please. I peed my pants," Blake added.

Lex covered her mouth, hiding what appeared to be a giggle. It so wasn't a good time to laugh.

"This season isn't you," Taddy declared, throwing her hands in the air as she stood from the high-back chair. "Jemma Couture is a formal evening gown line, not activewear. More importantly, I'm pissed at myself for not seeing the press samples and the collection before the show started. From here on out, Brill, Inc. will need to clear all garments before they hit the runway. You've lost the right for final approval."

"*Mi spiace*." Mortified, I apologized. "Truly, sorry."

In reality, I never let anyone see my work before show time. Those were my rules. But would I mind designing by committee? I wasn't so sure about that.

Taddy paced the room like a lion trapped in a cage. Swaying her hips, the heavily jeweled bangles on her arms jingled. The noise added with Blake's 'tsk-tsk' and Lex's sighs of 'horrific' was causing my attention-deficit disorder (ADD) to go wonky. The littlest sounds set me off.

Oh, God, I wish she'd just spill it. Otherwise, I might climb the walls.

"*Signorina* Brill, *per favore*, what should we do?" I begged her for an idea.

Brill, Inc. had built the media messages for Girasoli's two brands: Easton Essentials, which was a line Lex had started, and my brand Jemma Couture, from day one. I may have created a bad collection that week, but I wasn't stupid. We'd be nowhere if it wasn't for Taddy and Blake getting our dresses onto the bodies of every mover and shaker in the world.

"I have a strategy to save your gorgeous bum. Totally out of the box. It's going to require you to be a bit exposed and vulnerable."

"Ugh…" Two words which were so not me. I chewed my bottom lip for a second before saying, "*Sì*, all right. Let's hear it."

"It's clear you've lost your mojo. Your sexy, girly ways went out the window with those military space pants and laser guns."

"Perhaps," I agreed, unsure of where she was going with this.

"It's normal for designers to take sabbaticals, traveling abroad to get inspired for their next collection."

"My darlings, I can't leave Rocco and Luigi behind for that long. They can be…how do you say in English…possessive."

"When was the last time you had a romantic night of crazy monkey sex with them?" Blake asked, his manicured brow arched high.

Needing to stall to come up with an answer, I couldn't remember when, so I asked for clarification. "Toe-curling?"

"Pussy-eating, clit-shaking, butt-fucking, fantastical fun," Blake added.

"Hmmm…" *Oh, dear. These New Yorkers can be crass at times.* "I don't recall. Maybe three months ago when we were on the Isola di Girasoli. We celebrated my second year of being cancer-free."

When I'd first met Luigi and Rocco, we'd *fare l'amore* in the middle of the night, early morning, middle of the freaking day, and before bedtime. So, a few times a day.

Then lovemaking sorta went to twice a day, to once a day. A few times a week. Followed by once on Sundays. I couldn't tell you the last time I had my pussy eaten, clit shaken, butt fucked, or anything fantastically fun happen between us.

Dannazione.

"I dunno…"

"Exactly." Taddy turned to face me, her green eyes finally locked with mine. "No sex in your life equals bad fashion designs. This is easy to see how this happened."

"It is?" I wasn't following them.

"You have two lovers for a reason, honey. You used to be an insatiable woman."

"Really?" Suddenly feeling self-conscious, I ran a hand over the back of my neck.

"You oozed sex."

"I did?" With my hands, I rubbed a tense spot on my shoulder. I didn't need sex. Christ, I just needed a day at the spa.

"You radiated pheromones which drove all men, and some women, wild."

"Get the fudge outta here." I giggled. For the first time in twenty-four hours, I'd laughed, and it felt good. The week's fashion show nearly killed me. I folded my arms, realizing how lame I'd become, and tried to remember the old me. "I guess you're right. I used to be a sex goddess."

"Yes, Miss Thing. It sorta freaked me out." Blake laughed, too.

Taddy shushed him. "Listen, I spoke with Vive on the plane ride over here. The rehab facility let her come to Europe just for the show. Then she went right back in for treatment at that detox farm. She is an honest journalist and wrote what she saw."

Their bestie had been sobering up for a while. Personally, I cared for Vive more when she was tipsy. Her articles weren't as vicious then. So I reminded them, "*Signorina* Farnworth said my collection was s-h-i-t."

"I can't disagree with her," Lex grumbled.

"According to Vive, the press will give you a second chance. That is, of course, honey, if you ask for one. Ready for my idea?" Taddy's hands folded under her chin, her high cheekbones appearing more pronounced. Perhaps she was sucking them in. "I propose you take a leave of absence from Jemma Couture and Girasoli Garment Company. Come back when you're revived."

"And what the hell will I do to *revive* myself?"

"Play tennis," Blake suggested.

"Sports bore me."

"Have sex." Taddy placed her hands on my shoulders trying to reassure me. Giving me a tight squeeze, she continued, "Lots of *hawt* sex. Go on holiday with Luigi and that adorable Rocco. Get Massimo to give them the time off work. We'll publicize your trip."

"Genius. A sexual safari. I love this idea," Lex complimented as she wrote something down.

"Each destination will be an erotic adventure which the three of you will experience together." Taddy's hold on my shoulders tightened. From the flushed hue on her face, I could tell she was thinking about Luigi, Rocco, and I getting it on across the globe.

Oh, brother.

"Honey, we'll do a photo shoot of your men and you: having sugar kink play in the sex dungeons of Berlin, naked in the gardens of Moscow. Yes! This is your redemption with the press. Everyone knows you're in a poly thingy. Sweet Jesus dick-a-licious, it's in *Vogue*. Literally. Let's play this up and get you back on the sex bike."

Indeed, my ménage relationship was more than common knowledge. The ad slogan for Jemma Couture featured me in a grape-hued, silk organza gown with Rocco and Luigi on each arm dressed handsomely in tuxedos and stated, *"You can have it all."*

Other tag lines we'd used over the years were, *"Have your cake and eat it, too,"* and my personal favorite, *"Why stop at just one."* That could easily apply to the amount of men one keeps in their bed or the number of gowns one has in their closet.

What can I say, other than I'm a woman of excess? I adore stimulation. Blame it on my ADD.

"Peddle that sex bike, Miss Thing. Peddle fast. Peddle hard. Peddle as if there's no tomorrow. Let's go!" Blake cheered.

"Would Massimo agree to this?" I asked, glancing over at Lex. Her husband was a ruthless businessman. He wasn't cheap but he always expected a return on his investment, and I hated to disappoint him. We'd grown up together. He trusted me to bring the best for the collection and I'd failed. Realizing what a disappointment this had turned into for everyone, I noticed a knot building in my throat.

"Let me talk to Masi. He'll do anything to help you design a collection which sells. If that means giving Rocco and Luigi time off to go sex you up, then so be it."

"A *vacanza*. I haven't had one in ages."

Sitting back, I dried my eyes with the cashmere sleeve from my sweater, the fabric scratching against my skin. Then it hit me.

Oh, no. I can't.

I had a flashback to the last time Rocco, Luigi, and I were alone together for an extended weekend. Luigi had got down on one knee with Rocco at his side and asked for our hands in marriage.

I'm not the marrying kind. I don't believe in happily ever after.

My parents fought as cats and dogs 'til the day my *madre* dropped dead from the stress of it all. No, thank you.

And what if I got sick again? I couldn't put the boys through that. It wasn't right. I wanted no part in matrimony.

After I'd said no, Luigi had licked his wounds and dropped the topic. Regardless, it had sparked a sense of urgency in Rocco to start a family, as if babies were falling from the skies. He wouldn't let up.

Over the weeks he'd said, a million times, "We should at least talk about starting a family. You know adoption."

The whole idea of us on a holiday and them wanting to take our relationships to the next level—which I knew they'd do, because that was what they always did when we spent too much time together—sorta scared the bejesus out of me. Never mind the fact the boys had replaced my latest copies of *Elle* and *Town & Country* magazine at home with *Bambino* magazine and *Brides*.

Barf!

I honestly just wanted to have fun. Nothing serious. Nothing heavy. *Life is too short for drama. The Big C taught me that.*

"What if I say no?"

Let's get real here. A few months before, I'd learned I couldn't go through with that much alone time with them or I'd go out of my mind. Luigi was so intense, and Rocco could be rather emotional. Between the two of them, I didn't stand a chance when we hung out for an extended period of time.

"Why on Earth would you?"

"I don't wanna go on some sexscapade with my boys. They'll talk about marriage and babies."

"So what?" Lex sneered through her tight lips. The woman had already popped out one baby and had one more on the way.

"Let me work in the office. Fix my designs. Prepare for next season."

"Jemma, why are you afraid to be alone with them?"

"Things between Rocco, Luigi, and I are *bueno* right now. I want them to stay that way. For now. Forever."

"Is that even possible?" Blake asked.

Poor guy had already gone through one divorce, but he'd found a new love along the way and was engaged to try again. In a way, I admired that about him, because he had hope for his future. I wasn't hopeless, but I just didn't queef glitter and rainbows like he and Lex did when it came to matrimony.

They glared at me for a minute before Blake muttered, "Grow up." Or at least it sounded as though he'd said that. Maybe it was my paranoia talking.

True, I did need to be more mature when it came to my relationships. After the cancer, I'd just wanted to feel good again. I couldn't promise anyone a future. I could only give what I had each day. Not the next. Why couldn't more people just live in the present? Thinking ahead always overwhelmed me.

On that note, I shook my head.

They gaped at my refusal.

Speechless. The silence in the room hung above us as a gray cloud.

"Then, Jemma, you may either resign or be fired." Lex pushed her chair back and crossed her legs. "Personally, I suggest running with Taddy's brilliant publicity idea."

Hell to the no.

"Okay then. In the same vein as Jil Sander, I also quit from my own company. *Arrivederci*, my darlings." In a snit, I found my footing and stomped out of the room.

Fuck these Manhattanites. I'm done with Jemma Couture.

Get Unconventional

http://AveryAster.com/Unconventional